Sue saw the change in his manner.

THE FORTUNES OF
OLIVER HORN

THE FORTUNES OF OLIVER HORN

BY

F. HOPKINSON SMITH

ILLUSTRATED BY

WALTER APPLETON CLARK

CHARLES SCRIBNER'S SONS

NEW YORK ::::::::::::::::::::1911

I DEDICATE THIS BOOK TO THE MEMORY OF

"THE MAN OF ALL OTHERS ABOUT KENNEDY SQUARE MOST BELOVED, AND THE MAN OF ALL OTHERS LEAST UNDERSTOOD — RICHARD HORN, THE DISTINGUISHED INVENTOR."

F. H. S.

CONTENTS

vii

CONTENTS

ILLUSTRATIONS

THE FORTUNES OF
OLIVER HORN

CHAPTER I

THE OLD HOUSE IN KENNEDY SQUARE

Kennedy Square, in the late fifties, was a place of birds and trees and flowers; of rude stone benches, sagging arbors smothered in vines, and cool dirt-paths bordered by sweet-smelling box. Giant magnolias filled the air with their fragrance, and climbing roses played hide and seek among the railings of the rotting fence. Along the shaded walks laughing boys and girls romped all day, with hoop and ball, attended by old black mammies in white aprons and gayly colored bandannas; while in the more secluded corners, sheltered by protecting shrubs, happy lovers sat and talked, tired wayfarers rested with hats off, and staid old gentlemen read by the hour, their noses in their books.

Outside of all this color, perfume, and old-time charm, outside the grass-line and the rickety wooden

1

fence that framed them in, ran an uneven pavement splashed with cool shadows and stained with green mould. Here, in summer, the watermelon-man stopped his cart; and here, in winter, upon its broken bricks, old Moses unhooked his bucket of oysters and ceased for a moment his droning call.

On the shady side of the square, and half-hidden in ivy, was a Noah's Ark church, topped by a quaint belfry holding a bell that had not rung for years, and faced by a clock-dial all weather-stains and cracks, around which travelled a single rusty hand. In its shadow to the right lay the home of the Archdeacon, a stately mansion with Corinthian columns reaching to the roof and surrounded by a spacious garden filled with damask roses and bushes of sweet syringa. To the left crouched a row of dingy houses built of brick, their iron balconies hung in flowering vines, the windows glistening with panes of wavy glass purpled by age.

On the sunny side of the square, opposite the church, were more houses, high and low; one all garden, filled with broken-nosed statues hiding behind still more magnolias, and another all veranda and honeysuckle, big rocking-chairs and swinging hammocks; and still others with porticos curtained by white jasmine or Virginia creeper.

Half-way down this stretch of sunshine—and what a lovely stretch it was—there had stood for years

2

THE OLD HOUSE IN KENNEDY SQUARE

a venerable mansion with high chimneys, sloping roof, and quaint dormer-windows, shaded by a tall sycamore that spread its branches far across the street. Two white marble steps guarded by old-fashioned iron railings led up to the front door, which bore on its face a silver-plated knocker, inscribed in letters of black with the name of its owner—" Richard Horn." All three, the door, the white marble steps, and the silver-plated knocker—not to forget the round silver knobs ornamenting the newel posts of the railings— were kept as bright as the rest of the family plate by that most loyal of servants, old Malachi, who daily soused the steps with soap and water, and then brought to a phenomenal polish the knocker, bell-pull, and knobs by means of fuller's-earth, turpentine, hard breathing, and the vigorous use of a buckskin rag.

If this weazened-faced, bald-headed old darky, resplendent in white shirt-sleeves, green baize apron, and never-ceasing smile of welcome, happened to be engaged in this cleansing and polishing process—and it occurred every morning—and saw any friend of his master approaching, he would begin removing his pail and brushes and throwing wide the white door before the visitor reached the house, would there await his coming, bent double in profound salutation. Indeed, whenever Malachi had charge of the front steps he seldom stood upright, so constantly was he occupied— by reason of his master's large acquaintance—in either crooking his back in the beginning of a bow, or straightening it up in the ending of one.

To one and all inquiries for Mr. Horn his answer during the morning hours was invariably the same:

" Yes, sah, Marse Richard's in his li'l room wrastlin' wid his machine, I reckon. He's in dar now, sah—" this with another low bow, and then slowly recovering his perpendicular with eyes fixed on the retreating figure, so as to be sure there was no further need of his services, he would resume his work, drenching the steps again with soap-suds or rubbing away on the door-plate or door-pull, stopping every other moment to blow his breath on the polished surface.

When, however, someone asked for young Oliver, the inventor's only son, the reply was by no means so definite, although the smile was a trifle broader and the bow, if anything, a little more profound.

" Marse Oliver, did you say, sah? Dat's a difficult question, sah. Fo' Gawd I ain't seen him since breakfas'. You might look into Jedge Ellicott's office if you is gwine downtown, whar dey do say he's studyin' law, an' if he ain't dar—an' I reckon he ain't—den you might drap in on Mister Crocker, whar Marse Oliver's paintin' dem pictures; an' if he ain't dar, den fo-sho he's wid some o' de young ladies, but which one de Lawd only knows. Marse Oliver's like the rabbit, sah—he don't leab no tracks," and Malachi would hold his sides in a chuckle of so suffocating a

4

nature that it would have developed into apoplexy in a less wrinkled and emaciated person.

Inside of the front door of this venerable mansion ran a wide hall bare of everything but a solid mahogany hat-rack and table with glass mirror and heavy haircloth settee, over which, suspended from the ceiling, hung a curious eight-sided lantern, its wick replaced with a modern gas-burner. Above were the bedrooms, reached by a curved staircase guarded by spindling mahogany bannisters with slender hand-rail —a staircase so pure in style and of so distinguished an air that only maidens in gowns and slippers should have tripped down its steps, and only cavaliers in silk stockings and perukes have waited below for their hands.

Level with the bare hall, opened two highly polished mahogany doors, which led respectively into the drawing-room and library, their windows draped in red damask and their walls covered with family portraits. All about these rooms stood sofas studded with brass nails, big easy-chairs upholstered in damask, and small tables piled high with magazines and papers. Here and there, between the windows, towered a bookcase crammed with well-bound volumes reaching clear to the ceiling. In the centre of each room was a broad mantel sheltering an open fireplace, and on cold days —and there were some pretty cold days about Kennedy Square—two roaring wood-fires dispensed comfort, the welcoming blaze of each reflected in the shining brass fire-irons and fenders.

Adjoining the library was the dining-room with its well-rubbed mahogany table, straight-backed chairs, and old sideboard laden with family silver, besides a much-coveted mahogany cellaret containing some of that very rare Madeira for which the host was famous. Here were more easy-chairs and more portraits—one of Major Horn, who fell at Yorktown, in cocked hat and epaulets, and two others in mob-caps and ruffles —both ancient grandmothers of long ago.

The " li'l room ob Marse Richard," to which in the morning Malachi directed all his master's visitors, was in an old-fashioned one-story out-house, with a sloping roof, that nestled under the shade of a big tulip-tree in the back yard—a cool, damp, brick-paved old yard, shut in between high walls mantled with ivy and Virginia creeper and capped by rows of broken bottles sunk in mortar. This out-building had once served as servants' quarters, and it still had the open fireplace and broad hearth before which many a black mammy had toasted the toes of her pickaninnies, as well as the trap-door in the ceiling leading to the loft where they had slept. Two windows which peered out from under bushy eyebrows of tangled honeysuckle gave the only light; a green-painted wooden door, which swung level with the moist bricks, the only entrance.

THE OLD HOUSE IN KENNEDY SQUARE

It was at this green-painted wooden door that you would have had to knock to find the man of all others about Kennedy Square most beloved, and the man of all others least understood—Richard Horn, the distinguished inventor.

Perhaps at the first rap he would have been too absorbed to hear you. He would have been bending over his carpenter-bench—his deep, thoughtful eyes fixed on a drawing spread out before him, the shavings pushed back to give him room, a pair of compasses held between his fingers. Or he might have been raking the coals of his forge—set up in the same fireplace that had warmed the toes of the pickaninnies, his long red calico working-gown, which clung about his spare body, tucked between his knees to keep it from the blaze. Or he might have been stirring a pot of glue—a wooden model in his hand—or hammering away on some bit of hot iron, the brown paper cap that hid his sparse gray locks pushed down over his broad forehead to protect it from the heat.

When, however, his ear had caught the tap of your knuckles and he had thrown wide the green door, what a welcome would have awaited you! How warm the grasp of his fine old hand; how cordial his greeting.

"Disturb me, my dear sir," he would have said in answer to your apologies, "that's what I was put in the world for. I love to be disturbed. Please do it every day. Come in! Come in! It's delightful to get hold of your hand."

If you were his friend, and most men who knew him were, he would have slipped his arm through your own, and after a brief moment you would have found yourself poring over a detailed plan, his arm still in yours, while he showed you the outline of some pin, or lever, needed to perfect the most marvellous of all discoveries of modern times—his new galvanic motor.

If it were your first visit, and he had touched in you some sympathetic chord, he would have uncovered a nondescript combination of glass jars, horseshoe magnets, and copper wires which lay in a curious shaped box beneath one of the windows, and in a voice trembling with emotion as he spoke, he would have explained to you the value of this or that lever, and its necessary relation to this new invention of his which was so soon to revolutionize the motive power of the world. Or he would perhaps have talked to you as he did to me, of his theories and beliefs and of what he felt sure the future would bring forth.

"The days of steam-power are already numbered. I may not live to see it, but you will. This new force is almost within my grasp. I know people laugh, but so they have always done. All inventors who have benefited mankind have first been received with ridicule. I can expect no better treatment. But I have no fear of the result. The steady destruction of our forests and the eating up of our coal-fields must throw us back on chemistry for our working power. There is only one solution of this problem—it lies in the employment of a force which this machine will compel to our uses. I have not perfected the apparatus yet, as you see, but it is only a question of time. Tomorrow, perhaps, or next week, or next year—but it will surely come. See what Charles Bright and this Mr. Cyrus Field are accomplishing. If it astonishes you to realize that we will soon talk to each other across the ocean, why should the supplanting of steam by a new energy seem so extraordinary? The problems which they have worked out along the lines of electricity, I am trying to work out along the lines of galvanism. Both will ultimately benefit the human race."

And while he talked you would have listened with your eyes and ears wide open, and your heart too, and believed every word he said, no matter how practical you might have been or how unwilling at first to be convinced.

On another day perhaps you might have chanced to knock at his door when some serious complication had vexed him—a day when the cogs and pulleys upon which he had depended for certain demonstration had become so tangled up in his busy brain that he had thoughts for nothing else. Then, had he pushed back his green door to receive you, his greeting might have been as cordial and his welcome as hearty, but before long you would have found his eyes gazing into vacancy, or he would have stopped half-way in an answer to your question, his thoughts far away. Had you loved him you would then have closed the green door behind you and left him alone. Had you remained you would, perhaps, have seen him spring from his seat and pick up from his work-bench some unfinished fragment. This he would have plunged into the smouldering embers of his forge and, entirely forgetful of your presence, would have seized the handle of the bellows, his eyes intent on the blaze, his lips muttering broken sentences. At these moments, as he would peer into the curling smoke, one thin hand upraised, the long calico gown wrinkling about his spare body, the paper cap on his head, he would have looked like some alchemist of old, or weird necromancer weaving a mystic spell. Sometimes, as you watched his face, with the glow of the coals lighting up his earnest eyes, there would have flashed across his troubled features, as heat lightning illumines a cloud, some sudden brightness from within followed by a quick smile of triumph. The rebellious fragment had been mastered. For the hundredth time the great motor was a success!

And yet, had this very pin or crank or cog, on

10

which he had set such store, refused the next hour
or day or week to do its work, no trace of his disappointment would have been found in his face or
speech. His faith was always supreme; his belief
in his ideals unshaken. If the pin or crank would
not answer, the lever or pulley would. It was the
" adjustment " that was at fault, not the principle.
And so the dear old man would work on, week after
week, only to abandon his results again, and with
equal cheerfulness and enthusiasm to begin upon another appliance totally unlike any other he had tried
before. " It was only a mile-stone," he would say;
" every one that I pass brings me so much nearer the
end."

If you had been only a stranger—some *savant*,
for instance, who wanted a problem in mechanics
solved, or a professor, blinded by the dazzling light of
the almost daily discoveries of the time, in search of
mental ammunition to fire back at curious students
daily bombarding you with puzzling questions; or
had you been a thrifty capitalist, holding back a first
payment until an expert like Richard Horn had
passed upon the merits of some new labor-saving device of the day; had you been any one of these, and
you might very easily have been, for such persons
came almost daily to see him, the inventor would not
only have listened to your wants, no matter how absorbed he might have been in his own work, but he

11

would not have allowed you to leave him until he was sure that your mind was at rest.

Had you, however, been neither friend nor client, but some unbeliever fresh from the gossip of the Club, where many of the *habitués* not only laughed at the inventor's predictions for the future, but often lost their tempers in discussing his revolutionary ideas; or had you, in a spirit of temerity, entered his room armed with arguments for his overthrow, nothing that your good-breeding or the lack of it would have permitted you to have said could have ruffled his gentle spirit. With the tact of a man of wide experience among men, he would have turned the talk into another channel—music, perhaps, or some topic of the day—and all with such exquisite grace that you would have forgotten the subject you came to discuss until you found yourself outside the yard and halfway across Kennedy Square before realizing that the inventor had made no reply to your attacks.

But whoever you might have been, whether the friend of years, the anxious client, or the trifling unbeliever, and whatever the purpose of your visit, whether to shake his hand again for the very delight of touching it, to seek advice, or to combat his theories, you would have carried away the impression of a man whose like you had never met before—a man who spoke in a low, gentle voice, and yet with an authority that compelled attention; enthusiastic over the

12

things he loved, silent over those that pained him; a scholar of wide learning, yet skilled in the use of tools that obeyed him as readily as nimble fingers do a hand; a philosopher eminently sane on most of the accepted theories of the day and yet equally insistent in his support of many of the supposed sophistries and so-called "fanaticisms of the hour"; an old-time aristocrat holding fast to the class distinctions of his ancestors and yet glorying in the dignity of personal labor; a patriot loyal to the traditions of his State and yet so opposed to the bondage of men and women that he had freed his own slaves the day his father's will was read; a cavalier reverencing a woman as sweetheart, wife, and mother, and yet longing for the time to come when she, too, could make a career, then denied her, coequal in its dignity with that of the man beside her.

A composite personality of strange contradictions; of pronounced accomplishments and yet of equally pronounced failures. And yet, withal, a man so gracious in speech, so courtly in bearing, so helpful in counsel, so rational, human, and lovable, that agree with him or not, as you pleased, his vision would have lingered with you for days.

When night came the inventor would rake the coals from the forge, and laying aside his paper cap and calico gown, close the green door of his shop, cross the brick pavement of the back yard, and ascend the stairs with the spindling bannisters to his dressing-room. Here Malachi would have laid out the black swallow-tail coat with the high velvet collar, trousers to match, double-breasted waistcoat with gilt buttons, and fluffy cravat of white silk.

Then, while his master was dressing, the old servant would slip down-stairs and begin arranging the several rooms for the evening's guests—for there were always guests at night. The red damask curtains would be drawn close, the hearth swept clean, and fresh logs thrown on the andirons. The lamp in the library would be lighted, and his master's great easy-chair wheeled close to a low table piled high with papers and magazines, his big-eyed reading-glasses within reach of his hand. The paper would be unfolded, aired at the snapping blaze, and hung over the arm of the chair. These duties attended to, the old servant, with a last satisfied glance about the room, would betake himself to the foot of the staircase, there to await his master's coming, glancing overhead at every sound, and ready to conduct him to his chair by the fire.

When Richard, his toilet completed, appeared at the top of the stairs, Malachi would stand until his master had reached the bottom step, wheel about, and, with head up, gravely and noiselessly precede him into the drawing-room—the only time he ever dared to walk before him—and with a wave of the hand and the air of a prince presenting one of his palaces, would say—" Yo' char's all ready, Marse Richard; bright fire burnin'." Adding, with a low, sweeping bow, now that the ceremony was over—" Hope yo're feelin' fine dis evenin', sah."

He had said it hundreds of times in the course of the year, but always with a salutation that was a special tribute, and always with the same low bow, as he gravely pulled out the chair, puffing up the back cushion, his wrinkled hands resting on it until Richard had taken his seat. Then, with equal gravity, he would hand his master the evening paper and the big-bowed spectacles, and would stand gravely by until Richard had dismissed him with a gentle " Thank you, Malachi; that will do." And Malachi, with the serene, uplifted face as of one who had served in a temple, would tiptoe out to his pantry.

It had gone on for years—this waiting for Richard at the foot of the staircase. Malachi had never missed a night when his master was at home. It was not his duty—not a part of the established *régime* of the old house. No other family servant about Kennedy Square performed a like service for master or mistress. It was not even a custom of the times.

It was only one of " Malachi's ways," Richard would say, with a gentle smile quivering about his lips.

" I do dat 'cause it's Marse Richard—dat's all,"

15

Malachi would answer, drawing himself up with the dignity of a chamberlain serving a king, when some-one had the audacity to question him—a liberty he always resented.

They had been boys together—these two. They had fished and hunted and robbed birds' nests and gone swimming with each other. They had fought for each other, and been whipped for each other many and many a time in the old plantation-days. Night after night in the years that followed they had sat by each other when one or the other was ill.

And now that each was an old man the mutual ser-vice was still continued.

"How are you getting on now, Malachi—better? Ah, that's good—" and the master's thin white hand would be laid on the black wrinkled head with a soothing touch.

"Allus feels better, Marse Richard, when I kin git hold ob yo' han', sah—" Malachi would answer.

Not his slave, remember. Not so many pounds of human flesh and bone and brains condemned to his service for life; for Malachi was free to come and go and had been so privileged since the day the old Horn estate had been settled twenty years before, when Richard had given him his freedom with the other slaves that fell to his lot; not that kind of a servitor at all, but his comrade, his chum, his friend; the one man, black as he was, in all the world who in laying down his life for him would but have counted it as gain.

Just before tea Mrs. Horn, with a thin gossamer shawl about her shoulders, would come down from her bedroom above and join her husband. Then young Oliver himself would come bounding in, always a little late, but always with his face aglow and always bubbling over with laughter, until Malachi, now that the last member of the family was at home, would throw open the mahogany doors, and high tea would be served in the dining-room on the well-rubbed, unclothed mahogany table, the plates, forks, and saucers under Malachi's manipulations touching the polished wood as noiselessly as soap-bubbles.

Tea served and over, Malachi would light the candles in the big, cut-glass chandelier in the front parlor—the especial pride of the hostess, it having hung in her father's house in Virginia.

After this he would retire once more to his pantry, this time to make ready for some special function to follow; for every evening at the Horn mansion had its separate festivity. On Mondays small whist-tables that unfolded or let down or evolved from half-moons into circles, their tops covered with green cloth, were pulled out or moved around so as to form the centres of cosey groups. Some extra sticks of hickory would be brought in and piled on the andirons, and the huge library-table, always covered with the magazines of

17

the day—*Littell's, Westminster, Blackwood's,* and the *Scientific Review,* would be pushed back against the wall to make room.

On Wednesdays there would be a dinner at six o'clock, served without pretence or culinary assistance from the pastry-cook outside—even the ices were prepared at home. To these dinners any distinguished strangers who were passing through the city were sure to be invited. Malachi in his time had served many famous men—Charles Dickens, Ole Bull, Macready, and once the great Mr. Thackeray himself with a second glass of "that pale sherry, if you please," and at the great man's request, too. An appreciation which, in the case of Mr. Thackeray, had helped to mollify Malachi's righteous wrath over the immortal novelist's ignorance of Southern dishes:

"Dat fat gemman wid de gold specs dat dey do say is so mighty great, ain't eat nuffin yet but soup an' a li'l mite o' 'tater," he said to Aunt Hannah on one of his trips to the kitchen as dinner went on. "He let dat tar'pin an' dem ducks go by him same as dey was pizen. But I lay he knows 'bout dat ole yaller sherry," and Malachi chuckled. "He keeps a' retchin' fur dat decanter as if he was 'feared somebody'd git it fust."

On Fridays there would invariably be a musicale—generally a quartette, with a few connoisseurs to listen and to criticise. Then the piano would be

18

drawn out from its corner and the lid propped up, so that Max Unger of the " Harmonie " could find a place for his 'cello behind it, and there still be room for the inventor with his violin—a violin with a tradition, for Ole Bull had once played on it and in that same room, too, and had said it had the soul of a Cremona—which was quite true when Richard Horn touched its strings.

On all the other nights of the week Mrs. Horn was at home to all who came. Some gentle old lady from across the Square, perhaps, in lace caps and ribbons, with a work-basket filled with fancy crewels, and whose big son came at nine o'clock to take her home; or Oliver's young friends, boys and girls; or old Doctor Wallace, full of the day's gossip; or Miss Lavinia Clendenning, with news of the latest Assembly; or Nathan Gill with his flute.

But then it was Nathan always, whatever the occasion. From the time Malachi unlocked the front doors in the morning until he bolted them for the night, Nathan came and went. The brick pavements were worn smooth, the neighbors said, between the flute-player's humble lodgings in a side street and the Horn house, so many trips a day did the old man make. People smiled at him as he hurried along, his head bent forward, his long pen-wiper cloak reaching to his heels, a wide-brimmed Quaker hat crowning his head.

19

And always, whenever the night or whatever the function or whoever the guests, a particular side-table was sure to be moved in from Malachi's pantry and covered with a snow-white cloth which played an important part in the evening's entertainment. This cloth was never empty. Upon its damask surface were laid a pile of India-blue plates and a silver basket of cake, besides a collection of low glass tumblers with little handles, designed to hold various brews of Malachi's own concoctions, which he alone of all the denizens of Kennedy Square could compound, and the secret of which unhappily has perished with him.

And what wondrous aromas, too!

You may not believe it, but I assure you, on the honor of a Virginian, that for every one of these different nights in the old house on Kennedy Square there were special savory odors emanating from these brews, which settled at once and beyond question the precise function of the evening, and all before you could hand your hat to Malachi. If, for instance, as the front door was opened the aroma was one of hot coffee and the dry smell of fresh wafer-biscuit mingled with those of a certain brand of sherry, then it was always to be plain whist in the parlor, with perhaps only Colonel Clayton and Miss Clendenning or some one of the old ladies of the neighborhood, to hold hands in a rubber. If the fumes of apple-toddy mingled with the fragrance of toasted apples were wafted your way, you might be sure that Max Unger, and perhaps Bobbinette, second violin, and Nathan—whatever the function it was always Nathan, it must be remembered—and a few kindred spirits who loved good music were expected; and at the appointed hour Malachi, his hands encased in white cotton gloves, would enter with a flourish, and would graciously beg leave to pass, the huge bowl held high above his head filled to the brim with smoking apple-toddy, the little pippins browned to a turn floating on its top.

If the occasion was one of great distinction, one that fell on Christmas or on New Year's, or which celebrated some important family gathering, the pungent odor of eggnog would have greeted you even before you could have slipped off your gum-shoes in the hall, or hung your coat on the mahogany rack. This seductive concoction—the most potent of all Malachi's beverages—was always served from a green and gold Chinese bowl, and drunk not from the customary low tumblers, but from special Spode cups, and was, I must confess, productive of a head—for I myself was once tempted to drink a bumper of it at this most delightful of houses with young Oliver, many years ago, it is true, but I have never forgotten it—productive of an *aching* head, I think I said, that felt as big in the morning as the Canton bowl in which the mixture had been brewed.

Or, if none of these functions or festivals were

taking place, and only one or two old cronies had dropped in on their way from the Club, and had drawn up their chairs close to the dining-room table, and you had happened to be hanging up your hat in the hall at that moment, you would have been conscious of an aroma as delicate in flavor as that wafted across summer seas from far-off tropic isles; of pomegranates, if you will, ripening by crumbling walls; of purple grapes drinking in the sun; of pine and hemlock; of sweet spices and the scent of roses, or any other combination of delightful things which your excited imagination might suggest.

You would have known then just what had taken place; how, when the gentlemen were seated, Malachi in his undress blue coat and brass buttons had approached his master noiselessly from behind, and with a gravity that befitted the occasion had bent low his head, his hands behind his back, his head turned on one side, and in a hushed voice had asked this most portentous question:

"Which Madeira, Marse Richard?"

The only answer would have been a lifting of the eyebrow and an imperceptible nod of his master's head in the direction of the mahogany cellaret.

Malachi understood.

It was the Tiernan of '29.

And that worthy "Keeper of the Privy Seal and Key," pausing for an instant with his brown jug of

THE OLD HOUSE IN KENNEDY SQUARE

a head bent before the cellaret, as a Mohammedan
bends his head before a wall facing Mecca, had thereupon unlocked its secret chambers and had produced
a low, deeply cut decanter topped by a wondrous glass
stopper. This he had placed, with conscious importance, on a small table before the two or three devotees gathered together in its honor, and the host,
removing the stopper, had filled the slender glasses
with a vintage that had twice rounded the Cape—
a wine of such rare lineage and flavor that those who
had the honor of its acquaintance always spoke of it
as one of the most precious possessions of the town—
a wine, too, of so delicate an aroma that those within
the charmed circle invariably lifted the thin glasses
and dreamily inhaled its perfume before they granted
their palates a drop.

Ah, those marvellous, unforgettable aromas that
come to me out of the long ago with all the reminders
they bring of clink of glass and touch of elbow, of
happy boys and girls and sweet old faces. It is forty
years since they greeted my nostrils in the cool, bare,
uncurtained hall of the old house in Kennedy Square,
but they are still fresh in my memory. Sometimes
it is the fragrance of newly made gingerbread, or the
scent of creamy custard with just a suspicion of
peach-kernels; sometimes it is the scent of fresh
strawberries—strawberries that meant the spring, not
the hot-house or Bermuda—and sometimes it is the

smell of roasted oysters or succulent canvas-backs! Forty years ago—and yet even to-day the perfume of a roasted apple never greets me but I stand once more in the old-fashioned room listening to the sound of Nathan's flute; I see again the stately, silver-haired, high-bred mistress of the mansion with her kindly greeting, as she moves among her guests; I catch the figure of that old darkey with his brown, bald head and the little tufts of gray wool fringing its sides, as he shuffles along in his blue coat and baggy white waistcoat and much-too-big gloves, and I hear the very tones of his voice as he pushes his seductive tray before me and whispers, confidentially:

"Take a li'l ob de apple, sah; dat's whar de real 'spression ob de toddy is."

CHAPTER II

It was one of those Friday evenings, then, when
the smell of roast apples steeping in hot toddy came
wafting out the portals of Malachi's pantry—a smell
of such convincing pungency that even the most in-
frequent of frequenters having once inhaled it, would
have known at the first whiff that some musical function was in order. The night was to be one of unusual
interest.

Nathan Gill and Max Unger were expected, and
Miss Lavinia Clendenning, completing with Richard
a quartette for 'cello, flute, piano, and violin, for
which Unger had arranged Beethoven's Overture to
" Fidelio."

Nathan, of course, arrived first. On ordinary occasions another of those quaint ceremonies for which the
house was famous would always take place when the
old flute-player entered the drawing-room—a ceremony which brought a smile to the lips of those who
had watched it for years, and which to this day brings
one to those who recall it. Nathan, with a look of
quizzical anxiety on his pinched face, would tiptoe
cautiously into the room, peering about to make sure

of Richard's presence, his thin, almost transparent fingers outspread before him to show Richard that they were empty. Richard would step forward and, with a tone of assumed solicitude in his voice, would say:

"Don't tell me, Nathan, that you have forgotten your flute?" and Nathan, pausing for a moment, would suddenly break into a smile, and with a queer little note of surprise in his throat, and a twinkle in his eye, would make answer by slowly drawing from his coat-tail pocket the three unjointed pieces, holding them up with an air of triumph and slowly putting them together. Then these two old "Merry-Andrews" would lock arms and stroll into the library, laughing like school-boys.

To-night, however, as Nathan had been specially invited to play, this little ceremony was omitted. On entering the hall the musician gave his long, black, pen-wiper cloak and his hat to Malachi, and supporting himself by his delicate fingers laid flat on the hall-table, extended first one thin leg, and then the other, while that obsequious darky unbuttoned his gaiters. His feet free, he straightened himself up, pulled the precious flute from his coat-tail pocket and carefully joined the parts. This done, he gave a look into the hall-mirror, puffed out his scarf, combed his straight white hair forward over his ears with his fingers, and at Malachi's announcement glided through the open doorway to Mrs. Horn's chair, the flute in his hand held straight out as an orator would have held his roll.

The hostess, who had been sitting by the fire, her white gossamer shawl about her spare shoulders, rose from her high-backed chair and, laying aside her knitting-needles and wools, greeted the musician with as much cordiality—and it must be confessed with as much ceremony—as if she had not seen him a dozen times that week. One of the charms of the Horn mansion lay in these delightful blendings of affection and formality.

"Am I a little early?" he asked with as much surprise as if he were not as certain to be early when music was concerned as he was to be late in everything else. "Yes, my dear madam—I see that I am early, unless Miss Lavinia is late."

"You never could be too early, Nathan. Lavinia will be here in a moment," she answered, with a smile, resuming her seat.

"I'm glad that I'm ahead of her for once," he replied, laughing. Then, turning to the inventor, who had come forward from where he had been studying the new score, he laid his hand affectionately on Richard's shoulder, as a boy would have done, and added: "How do you like Unger's new arrangement?—I've been thinking of nothing else all day."

27

"Capital! Capital!" answered Richard, slipping his arm into Nathan's, and drawing him closer to the piano. "See how he has treated this adagio phrase," and he followed the line with his finger, humming the tune to Nathan. "The modulation, you see, is from E Major to A Major, and the flute sustains the melody, the effect is so peculiarly soft and the whole so bright with passages of sunshine all through it —oh, you will love it."

While these two white-haired enthusiasts with their heads together were studying the score, beating time with their hands, after the manner of experts to whom all the curious jumble of dots and lines that plague so many of us are as plain as print, Malachi was receiving Miss Clendenning in the hall. Indeed, he had answered her knock as Nathan was passing into the drawing-room.

The new arrival bent her neck until Malachi had relieved her of the long hooded cloak, gave a quick stamp with her little feet as she shook out her balloon skirts, and settled herself on the hall-settee while Malachi unwound the white worsted "nubia" from her aristocratic throat. This done, she, too, held a short consultation with the hall-mirror, carefully dusting, with her tiny handkerchief, the little pats of powder still left on her cheeks, and with her jewelled fingers smoothing the soft hair parted over her forehead, and tightening meanwhile the side-

28

combs that kept in place the clusters of short curls which framed her face. Then, with head erect and a gracious recognition of the old servant's ministrations, she floated past Malachi, bent double in her honor.

"Oh, I heard you, Nathan," she laughed, waving her fan toward him as she entered the room. "I'm not one minute late. Did you ever hear such impudence, Sallie, and all because he reached your door one minute before me," she added, stooping to kiss Mrs. Horn. Punctuality was one of the cardinal virtues of this most distinguished, prim, precise, and most lovable of old maids. "You are really getting to be dreadful, Mr. Nathan Gill, and so puffed up —isn't he, Richard?" As she spoke she turned abruptly and faced both gentlemen. Then, with one of her rippling laughs—a laugh that Richard always said reminded him of the notes of a bird—she caught her skirts in her fingers, made the most sweeping of courtesies and held out her hands to the two gentlemen who were crossing the room to meet her.

Richard, with the bow of a Cavalier, kissed the one offered him as gallantly as if she had been a duchess, telling her he had the rarest treat in store for her as soon as Unger came, and Nathan with mock devotion held the other between his two palms, and said that to be scolded by Miss Clendenning was infinitely better than being praised by anybody else. These pleasantries over, the two old gallants returned to the piano to wait for Max Unger and to study again the crumpled pages of the score which lay under the soft light of the candles.

The room relapsed once more into its wonted quiet, broken only by the whispered talk of well-bred people careful not to disturb each other. Mrs. Horn had begun to knit again. Miss Clendenning stood facing the fire, one foot resting on the fender.

This wee foot of the little lady was the delight and admiration of all the girls about Kennedy Square, and of many others across the seas, too—men and women for that matter. To-night it was encased in a black satin slipper and in a white spider-web stocking, about which were crossed two narrow black ribbons tied in a bow around the ankle—such a charming little slipper peeping out from petticoats all bescalloped and belaced! Everything in fact about this dainty old maid, with her trim figure filling out her soft white fichu, still had that subtlety of charm which had played havoc with more than one heart in her day. Only Sallie Horn, who had all the dear woman's secrets, knew where those little feet had stepped and what hopes they had crushed. Only Sallie Horn, too, knew why the delicate finger was still bare of a plain gold ring. The world never thought it had made any difference to Miss Lavinia, but then the world had never peeped under the lower lid of Miss Clendenning's heart.

Suddenly the hushed quiet of the room was broken by a loud knock at the front door, or rather by a series of knocks, so quick and sharp that Malachi started from his pantry on the run.

"That must be Max," said Richard. "Now, Lavinia, we will move the piano, so as to give you more room."

Mrs. Horn pushed back her chair, rose to her feet, and stood waiting to receive the noted 'cellist, without whom not a note could be sounded, and Miss Clendenning took her foot from the fender and dropped her skirts.

But it was not Max!

Not wheezy, perspiring old Max Unger after all, walking into the room mopping his face with one hand and with the other lugging his big 'cello, embalmed in a green baize bag—he would never let Malachi touch it—not Max at all, but a fresh, rosy-cheeked young fellow of twenty-two, who came bounding in with a laugh, tossing his hat to Malachi —a well-knit, muscular young fellow, with a mouth full of white teeth and a broad brow projecting over two steel-blue eyes that were snapping with fun.

With his coming the quiet of the place departed and a certain breezy atmosphere permeated the room as if a gust of cool wind had followed him. With him, too, came a hearty, whole-souled joyousness— a joyousness of so sparkling and so radiant a kind

31

that it seemed as if all the sunshine he had breathed for twenty years in Kennedy Square had somehow been stored away in his boyish veins.

"Oh, here you are, you dear Miss Lavinia," he cried out, his breath half gone from his dash across the Square. "How did you get here first?"

"On my two feet, you stupid Oliver," cried Miss Lavinia, shaking her curls at him. "Did you think somebody carried me?"

"No, I didn't; but that wouldn't be much to carry, Miss Midget." His pet name for her. "But which way did you come? I looked up and down every path and——"

"And went all the way round by Sue Clayton's to find me, didn't you? Oh, you can't throw dust in the Midget's eyes, you young rascal!" and she stretched up her two dainty hands, drew his face toward her, and kissed him on the lips.

"There—" and she patted his cheek— "now tell me all about it, you dear Ollie. What did you want to see me for?" she added with one of those quick divinations that made her so helpful a confidante. Then, in a lowered voice— "What has Sue done?"

"Nothing—not one thing. She isn't bothering her head about me. I only stopped there to leave a book, and——"

Mrs. Horn, with laughing, inquiring eyes, looked

up from her chair at Miss Clendenning, and made a little doubting sound with her lips. Black-eyed Sue Clayton, with her curls down her back, home from boarding-school for the Easter holidays, was Oliver's latest flame. His mother loved to tease him about his love-affairs; and always liked him to have a new one. She could see farther into his heart she thought when the face of some sweet girl lay mirrored in its depths.

Oliver heard the doubting sound his mother made, and, reaching over her chair, flung his arms about her neck and kissed her as if she had been a girl.

"Now, don't you laugh, you dear old motherkins," he cried, drawing her nearer to him until her face touched his. "Sue don't care a thing about me, and I *did* promise her the book, and I ran every step of the way to give it to her—didn't I, Uncle Nat?" he added, gayly, hoping to divert the topic. "You were behind the sun-dial when I passed—don't you remember?" He shrank a little from the badinage.

The old musician heard the question, but only waved his flute behind him in answer. He did not even lift his head from beside Richard's at the score.

Oliver waited an instant, and getting no further reply, released his hold about his mother's neck, now that he had kissed her into silence, and turned to Miss Clendenning again.

"Come, Miss Lavinia—come into the library. I've

something very important to talk to you about. Really, now; no nonsense about it! You've plenty of time—old Max won't be here for an hour, he's always late, isn't he, mother? "

Miss Clendenning turned quietly, lifted her eyes in a martyr-like way toward Mrs. Horn, who shook her head playfully in answer, and with Oliver's arm about her entered the library. She could never refuse any one of the young people when they came to her with their secrets—most important and never-to-be-postponed secrets, of course, that could hardly wait the telling. Her little tea-room across the Square, with its red damask curtains, its shiny brass andirons, easy-chairs and lounges, was really more of a confessional than a boudoir. Many a sorrow had been drowned in the cups of tea that she had served with her own hand in egg-shell Spode cups, and many a young girl and youth who had entered its cosey interior with heavy hearts had left it with the sunshine of a new hope breaking through their tears. But then everybody knew the bigness of Miss Clendenning's sympathies. It was one of the things for which they loved her.

She, of course, knew what the boy wanted now. If it were not to talk about Sue Clayton it was sure to be about some one of the other girls. The young people thought of nothing else but their love-affairs, and talked of nothing else, and the old people loved to live their youth over again in listening. It was one of the traditional customs of Kennedy Square.

Miss Clendenning settled herself in a corner of the carved haircloth sofa, touched her side-combs with her finger to see that they were in place, tucked a red cushion behind her back, crossed her two little feet on a low stool, the two toes peeping out like the heads of two mice, and taking Oliver's hand in hers said, in her sweet, coaxing voice:

" Now, you dear boy, it is Sue, isn't it? "

" No! "

" Not Sue? Who then? "

" Mr. Crocker. "

" What Mr. Crocker? " She arched her eyebrows and looked at him in surprise. The name came as a shock. She knew of Mr. Crocker, of course, but she wanted Oliver to describe him. Surely, she thought, with a sudden sense of alarm, the boy has not fallen in love with the daughter of that shabby old man.

" Why, the landscape-painter—the one father knows. I have been taking drawing lessons of him and he says I've got a lot of talent and that all I want is practice. He says that if I begin now and draw from the cast three or four hours a day that by the end of the year I can begin in color; and then I can go to New York and study, and then to Paris. "

The little lady scrutinized him from under her eyelids. The boy's enthusiasm always delighted her;

she would often forget what he was talking about, so interested was she in following his gestures as he spoke.

"And what then?"

"Why then I can be a painter, of course. Isn't that a great deal better than sitting every day in Judge Ellicott's dingy office reading law-books? I hate the law!"

"And you love Mr. Crocker?"

"Yes, don't you?"

"I don't know him, Ollie. Tell me what he is like."

"Well, he isn't young any more. He's about father's age, but he's a splendid old man, and he's so poor! Nobody buys his pictures, nor appreciates him, and, just think, he has to paint portraits and dogs and anything he can get to do. Don't you think that's a shame? Nobody goes to see him but father and Uncle Nat and one or two others. They don't seem to think him a gentleman." He was putting the case so as to enlist all her sympathies at once.

"He has a daughter, hasn't he?" She was probing him quietly and without haste. Time enough for her sympathies to work when she got at the facts.

"Yes, but I don't like her very much, for I don't think she's very good to him." Miss Clendenning smothered a little sigh of relief; there was no danger, thank Heaven, in that direction! What, then, could he want, she thought to herself.

"And he's so different from anybody I ever met," Oliver continued. "He doesn't talk about horses and duck-shooting and politics, or music or cards like everyone you meet, except Daddy, but he talks about pictures and artists and great men. Just think, he was a young student in Düsseldorf for two years, and then he shouldered a knapsack and tramped all through Switzerland, painting as he went, and often paying for his lodgings with his sketches. Then he was in Paris for ever so long, and now he is here, where——"

"Where you tell me he is painting dogs for a living," interrupted Miss Clendenning. "Do you think, you young scapegrace, that this would be better than being a lawyer like Judge Ellicott?" and she turned upon him with one of her quick outbursts of mock indignation.

"But I'm not going to paint dogs," he replied, with some impatience. "I am going to paint women, like the Sir Peter Lely that Uncle John Tilghman has. Oh, she's a beauty! I took Mr. Crocker to see her the other day. It had just been brought in from the country, you know. You should have heard him go on. He says there's nobody who can paint a portrait like it nowadays. He raved about her. You know it is Uncle John Tilghman's grandmother when she was a girl." His voice suddenly dropped to a more serious tone as he imparted this last bit of information.

Miss Clendenning knew whose grandmother it was, and knew and loved every tone in the canvas. It had hung in the Tilghman Manor-House for years and was one of its most precious treasures, but she did not intend to stop and discuss it now.

"Mr. Crocker wants me to copy it just as soon as I draw a little better. Uncle John will let me, I know."

Miss Clendenning tapped her foot in a noiseless tattoo upon the stool, and for a time looked off into space. She wanted to draw him out, to know from what depth this particular enthusiasm had sprung. She was accustomed to his exuberance of spirits, it was one of the many things she loved him for. If this new craze were but an idle fancy, and he had had many of them, it would wear itself out, and the longer they talked about it the better. If, however, it sprang from an inborn taste, and was the first indication of a hitherto undeveloped talent forcing itself to the surface, the situation was one demanding the greatest caution. Twigs like Oliver bent at the wrong time might never straighten out again.

"And why did you come to me about this, Ollie; why don't you talk to your father?"

"I have. He doesn't object. He says that Mr.

Crocker is one of the rare men of the time, and that only inexperience among the people here prevents him from being appreciated. That's what he goes to see him for. It isn't father that worries me, it's mother. I know just what she'll say. She's got her heart set on my studying law, and she won't listen to anything else. I wouldn't object to the law if I cared for it, but I don't. That's what makes it come so hard."

"And you want me to speak to your mother?"

"Yes, of course. That's just what I *do* want you to do. Nobody can help me but you," he cried with that coaxing manner which would have seemed effeminate until one looked at his well-built, muscular body and the firm lines about his mouth. "You tell her of all the painters you knew in London when you lived there, and of what they do and how they are looked up to, and that some of them are gentlemen and not idlers and loafers. Mother will listen to you, I know, and maybe then when I tell her it won't be such a shock to her. Do you know it is incomprehensible to me, all this contempt for people who don't do just the same things that their grandfathers did. And how do I know, too, that they are right about it all? It seems to me that when a man is *born* a gentleman and *is* a gentleman he can follow any occupation he pleases. Instead of his trade making him respectable he should make *it* so." He spoke

39

with a virility she had never suspected in him before, this boy whom she had held in her arms as a baby and who was still only the child to her.

"But, Ollie," she interrupted, in some surprise, "you must never forget that you are your father's son. No one is absolutely independent in this world; everyone has his family to consider." She was becoming not only interested now, but anxious. Mr. Crocker had evidently been teaching the boy something besides the way to use his pencil. Such democratic ideas were rare in Kennedy Square.

"Yes, I know what you mean." He had sprung from his seat now and was standing over her, she looking up into his face. "You mean that it is all right for me to go into old Mr. Wardell's counting-house because he sells coffee by the cargo, but that I can't take a situation in Griggson's grocery here on the corner because he sells coffee by the pound. You mean, too, that it is possible for a man to be a professor or president of a college and still be a gentleman, but if he teaches in the public school he is done for. You mean, too, that I could saw off a patient's leg and still be invited to Uncle Tilghman's house to dinner, but that if I pulled out one of his teeth I could only eat in his kitchen."

Miss Clendenning threw back her head and laughed until the combs in her side-curls needed refastening, but she did not interrupt him.

40

"I can't get this sort of thing into my head and I never will. And father doesn't believe in it any more than I do, and I don't think that mother would if it wasn't for a lot of old people who live around this square and who talk of nothing all day but their relations and think there's nobody worth knowing but themselves. Now, you've *got* to talk to mother; I won't take no for an answer," and he threw himself down beside her again. "Come, dear Midget, hold up your right hand and promise me now, before I let you go," he pleaded in his wheedling way that made him so lovable to his intimates, catching her two hands in his and holding them tight.

Of course she promised. Had she ever refused him anything? And Oliver, a boy again, now that his confessions were made, kissed her joyously on both cheeks and instantly forgetting his troubles as his habit was when prospects of relief had opened, he launched out into an account of a wonderful adventure Mr. Crocker once had in an old town in Italy, where he was locked up over-night in a convent by mistake; and how he had slept on his knapsack in the chapel, and what the magistrate had said to him the next day, and how he had to paint a portrait of that suspicious officer to prove he was a painter and a man of the best intentions. In his enthusiasm he not only acted the scene, but he imi-

41

tated the gesture and dialect of the several parties to the escapade so perfectly that the little lady, in her delight over the story, quite forgot her anxiety and even the musicale itself, and only remembered the quartette when Malachi, bowing obsequiously before her, said:

"Dey's a-waitin' for you, Miss Lavinia. Mister Unger done come and Marse Richard say he can't wait a minute."

When she and Oliver entered the drawing-room the 'cellist was the centre of the group. He was stripping off the green baize cover from his instrument and at the same time was apologizing, in his broken English, for being so late. Richard was interrupting him with enthusiastic outbursts over the new score which still lay under the wax candles lighting the piano, and which he and Nathan, while waiting for the musician, had been silently practising in sundry bobs of their heads and rhythmic beatings of their hands.

"My dear Max," Richard continued, with a hand on the musician's shoulder, patting him in appreciation as he spoke, "we will forgive you anything. You have so exactly suited to the 'cello the opening theme. And the flute passages!—they are exquisitely introduced. We will let Miss Clendenning decide when she hears it—" and he turned Unger's head in the direction of the advancing lady. "Here she

42

comes now; you, of course, know the fine quality of Miss Clendenning's ear."

Herr Unger placed his five fat fingers over his waist-band, bowed as low to Miss Lavinia as his great girth would permit, and said:

"Ah, yes, I know. Miss Clendenning not only haf de ear, she haf de life in de end of de finger. De piano make de sound like de bird when she touch it."

The little lady thanked him in her sweetest voice, made a courtesy, and extended her hand to Max, who kissed it with much solemnity, and Richard, putting his arm around the 'cellist's fat shoulders, conducted him across the room, whereupon Nathan, with the assumed air of an old beau, offered his crooked elbow to Miss Clendenning as an apology for having reached the house before her. Then, seating her at the piano with a great flourish, he waved his hand to Oliver, who had drawn up a chair beside his mother, and with a laugh, cried:

"Here, you young lover, come and turn the leaves for Miss Lavinia. It may keep you from running over other people in the dark, even if they are accused of hiding behind sun-dials."

With the beginning of the overture Mrs. Horn laid down her work, and drawing her white gossamer shawl about her shoulders gave herself up to the enjoyment of the music. The overture was one of her favorites—one she and Richard had often played together as a duet in their younger days.

Leaning back in her easy-chair with half-closed eyes, her clear-cut features in silhouette against the glow of the fire, her soft gray curls nestling in the filmy lace that fell about her temples, she expressed, in every line of her face and figure, that air of graceful repose which only comes to those highly favored women who have all their lives been nurtured in a home of loving hands, tender voices, and noiseless servants—lives of never-ending affection without care or sorrow.

And yet had you, even as she sat there, studied carefully this central figure of the Horn mansion—this practical, outspoken, gentle-voiced, tender wife and mother, tenacious of her opinions, yet big enough and courageous enough to acknowledge her mistakes; this woman, wise in counsel, sympathetic in sorrow, joyous with the young, restful with the old, you would have discovered certain lines about her white forehead which advancing years alone could not have accounted for.

These lines seemed all the deeper to-night. Only a few hours before, Richard had come to her, while Malachi was arranging his clothes, with the joyful news of a new device which he had developed during the day for his motor. He could hardly wait to tell her, he had said. The news was anything but

44

joyful to her. She knew what it meant—she knew what sums had been wasted on the other devices, involving losses which at this time they could so little afford. She was glad, therefore, to free her mind for the moment from these anxieties; glad to sit alone and drink in the melodies that the quartette set free.

As she sat listening, beating time noiselessly with her thin, upraised hand, her head resting quietly, a clear, silvery note—clear as a bird's—leaped from Nathan's flute, soared higher and higher, trembled like a lark poised in air, and died away in tones of such exquisite sweetness that she turned her head in delight toward the group about the piano, fixing her gaze on Nathan. The old man's eyes were riveted on the score, his figure bent forward in the intensity of his absorption, his whole face illumined with the ecstasy that possessed him. Then she looked at Richard, standing with his back to her, his violin tucked under his chin, his body swaying in rhythm with the music. Unger sat next to him, his instrument between his knees, his stolid, shiny face unruffled by the glorious harmonies of Beethoven.

Then her glance rested on Oliver. He was hanging over the piano whispering in Miss Clendenning's ear, his face breaking into smiles at her playful chidings. If the pathos of the melody had reached him he showed no sign of its effects.

45

Instantly there welled up in her heart a sudden gush of tenderness—one of those quick outbursts that often overwhelm a mother when her eyes rest on a son whose heart is her own—an outburst all the more intensified by the melody that thrilled her. Why should her heart have been troubled? Here was her strong hope! Here was her chief reliance! Here the hope of the future. How could she doubt or suffer when this promise of the coming day was before her in all the beauty and strength of his young manhood.

With the echoes of Nathan's flute still vibrating in her, and with her mind filled with the delight of these fresh hopes, she suddenly recalled the anxious look on her boy's face as he led Miss Clendenning into the library—a new look—one she had never seen before. Still under the quickening spell of the music she began to exaggerate its cause. What had troubled him? Why had he told Lavinia, and not her? Was there anything serious?—something he had kept from her to save her pain?

From this moment her mind became absorbed in her boy. With restless, impatient fingers she began thrumming on the arm of her chair. Oliver would tell her, she knew, before many hours, but she could not wait—she wanted to know at once.

With the ending of the first part of the overture, and before the two gentlemen had laid down their instruments to grasp Unger's hands, she called to Miss Clendenning, who sat at the piano alone, Oliver having slipped away unobserved.

"Lavinia——"

Miss Clendenning raised her eyes in answer. "Come over and sit by me, dear, while the gentlemen rest."

Miss Clendenning picked up her white silk mits and fan lying beside the candles, and moved toward the fireplace. Malachi saw her coming—he was always in the room during the interludes—and with an alacrity common to him when the distinguished little lady was present, drew up a low chair beside his mistress and stood behind it until she took her seat. Miss Clendenning smoothed out her skirt and settled herself with the movement of a pigeon filling her nest. Then she laid her mits in her lap and fanned herself softly.

"Well, Sallie, what is it? Did you ever hear Nathan play so well?" she asked, at last.

"What did Oliver want, my dear?" replied Mrs. Horn, ignoring her question. "Is there anything worrying him, or is Sue at the bottom of it?"

The little woman smiled quizzically. "No, Sallie —not Sue—not this time. That little rattle-brain's affections will only last the week out. Nothing very important—that is, nothing urgent. We were talking about the Tilghman portraits and the Lely that Cousin John has brought into town from Clay‑ more Manor, and what people should and should not do to earn their living, and what professions were respectable. I thought one thing and Ollie thought another. Now, what profession of all others would you choose for a young man starting out in life?"

"What has he been telling you, Lavinia? Does he want to leave Judge Ellicott's office?" Mrs. Horn asked, quietly. She always went straight to the root of any matter.

"Just answer my question, Sallie."

"I'd rather he'd be a lawyer, of course; why?"

"Suppose he won't, or can't?"

"Is that what he told you, Lavinia, on the sofa?" She was leaning forward, her cheek on her hand, her eyes fixed on the blazing logs.

"He told me a great many things, half of them boy's talk. Now answer my question; suppose he couldn't study law because his heart wasn't in it, what then?"

"I know, Lavinia, what you mean." There was an anxious tone now in the mother's voice. "And Oliver talked to you about this?" As she spoke she settled back in her chair and a slight sigh escaped her.

"Don't ask me, Sallie, for I'm not going to tell you. I want to know for myself what you think, so that I can help the boy."

48

STRAINS FROM NATHAN'S FLUTE

Mrs. Horn turned her head and looked toward Richard. She had suspected as much from some hints that Judge Ellicott had dropped when she had asked him about Oliver's progress. "He is still holding down his chair, Madam." She thought at the time that it was one of the Judge's witticisms, but she saw now that it had a deeper meaning. After some mo·ments she said, fixing her eyes on Miss Clendenning:

"Well, now, Lavinia, tell me what *you* think. I should like your opinion. What would you wish to do with him if he were your son?"

Miss Lavinia smiled and her eyes half-closed. For a brief moment there came to her the picture of what such a blessing would have been. Her son! No! It was always somebody else's son or daughter to whom her sympathy must go.

"Well, Sallie," she answered—she was leaning over now, her hands in her lap, apparently with lowered eyelids, but really watching Mrs. Horn's face from the corner of her eye—"I don't think we can make a clergyman out of him, do you?" Mrs. Horn frowned, but she did not interrupt. "No, we cannot make a parson out of him. I meant, my love, something in surplices, not in camp-meetings, of course. Think of those lovely pink cheeks in a high collar and Bishop's sleeves, wouldn't he be too sweet for anything?" and she laughed one of her little cooing laughs. "Nor a doctor," she continued, with a slight interrogation in her tone, "nor a shop-keeper, nor a painter"—and she shot a quick glance from under her arching eyebrows at her companion —but Mrs. Horn's face gave no sign—"nor a musician. Why not a musician, Sallie, he sings like an angel, you know?" She was planting her shafts all about the target, her eyes following the flight of each arrow.

Mrs. Horn raised her head and laid her hand firmly on Miss Clendenning's wrist.

"We won't have him a shopkeeper, Lavinia," she said with some positiveness, "nor a barber, nor a painter, nor a cook, nor a dentist. We'll try and keep him a gentleman, my dear, whatever happens. As for his being a musician, I think you will agree with me, that music is only possible as an accomplishment, never when it is a profession. Look at that dear old man over there"—and she pointed to Nathan, who was bending forward running over on his flute some passages from the score, his white hair covering his coat-collar behind—"so absolutely unfitted for this world as he is, so purposeless, so hopelessly inert. He breathes his whole soul into that flute and yet——"

"And a good deal comes out of it sometimes, my dear—to-night, for instance," laughed Miss Lavinia. "Did you catch those bird-like notes?"

"Yes, and they thrilled me through and through,

50

but sweet as they are they haven't helped him make a career."

At this moment Richard called to Unger, who had been sitting on the sofa in the library, "cooling off," he said, as he mopped his head with a red handkerchief, one of Malachi's cups in his hand.

Miss Lavinia caught sight of the 'cellist's advancing figure and rose from her seat. "I must go now," she said, "they want to play it again." She moved a step forward, gave a glance at her side-curls in the oval mirror over the mantel, stopped hesitatingly, and then bending over Mrs. Horn said, thoughtfully, her hand on her companion's shoulder, "Sallie, don't try to make water run uphill. If Ollie belonged to me I'd let him follow his tastes, whatever they were. You'll spoil the shape of his instep if you keep him wearing Chinese shoes," and she floated over to join the group of musicians.

Mrs. Horn again settled herself in her chair. She understood now the look on Oliver's face. She was right then; something was really worrying him. The talk with Miss Lavinia had greatly disturbed her— so much so that she could not listen to the music. Again her eyes rested on Oliver, who had come in and joined the group at the piano, all out of breath with his second run across the Square—this time to tell Sue of Miss Clendenning's promise. He was never happy unless he was sharing what was on his mind with another, and if there was a girl within reach he was sure to pour it into her willing ears.

Mrs. Horn looked at him with a pang about her heart. From which side of the house had come this fickleness, this instability and love of change in Oliver's character? she asked herself—a new interest every day—all the traditions of his forefathers violated. How could she overcome it in him? how make him more practical? Years before, when she had thought him proud, she had sent him to market and had made him carry home the basket on his arm, facing the boys who laughed at him. He had never forgotten the lesson; he was neither proud nor lazy any more. But what could she do in a situation like this?

Harassed by these doubts her eyes wandered over Oliver's slender, well-knit muscular figure as he stood whispering to Miss Clendenning. She noticed the fine, glossy hair brushed from the face and worn long in the neck, curling behind the ears. She noted every movement of his body: the graceful way in which he talked with his hands, using his fingers to accentuate his words, and the way in which he shrugged his shoulders—the shrug of a Frenchman, although not a drop of their blood could be found in his veins—and in the quick lifting of the hand and the sidelong glance of the eye, all so characteristic of Richard when some new thought or theory reached

his brain for the first time. Gradually and uncon‑
sciously she began to compare each feature of Oliver's
face with that of the father who stood beside him:
the alert blue eyes, overhanging brow and soft silki‑
ness of the hair—identically the same, even the way
it lay in the neck. And again she looked at Richard,
drawing the bow as if in a dream.

Instantly a thought entered her mind that drove
the blood from her cheeks. These vacillations of
her husband's! This turning from one thing to an‑
other—first the law, then these inventions that never
lead anywhere, and now Oliver beginning in the
same way, almost in the same steps! Could these
traits be handed down to the children? Would Oli‑
ver be like Richard in——

Instinctively she stopped short before the disloyal
thought could form itself in her brain, straightened
herself in her chair, and closed her lips tight.

The music ceased; Nathan laid his flute on the
piano; Unger rose from his seat, and Richard turned
to talk to Miss Clendenning. But she was unmindful
of it all—she still sat in her chair, her eyes searching
the blazing logs, her hands in her lap.

Only Malachi with his silver tray recalled her to
consciousness.

CHAPTER III

If in the long summer days Kennedy Square was haunted by the idle and the weary, in the cool summer nights its dimly lighted paths were alive with the tread of flying feet, and its shadowy benches gay with the music of laughter and merry greetings.

With the going down of the sun, the sidewalks were sprinkled, and the whole street about the Square watered from curb to curb, to cool its sun-baked cobbles. The doors and windows of all the houses were thrown wide to welcome the fresh night-air, laden with the perfume of magnolia, jasmine, and sweet-smelling box. Easy-chairs and cushions were brought out and placed on the clean steps of the porches, and the wide piazzas covered with squares of china-matting to make ready for the guests of the evening.

These guests would begin to gather as soon as the twilight settled; the young girls in their pretty muslin frocks and ribbons, the young men in white duck suits and straw hats. They thronged the cool, well-swept paths, chattered in bunches under the big trees, or settled like birds on the stone seats and

54

benches. Every few minutes some new group, fresh from their tea-tables, would emerge from one of the houses, poise like a flock of pigeons on the top step, listen to the guiding sound of the distant laughter, and then swoop down in mad frolic, settling in the midst of the main covey, under the big sycamores until roused at the signal of some male bird in a straw hat, or in answer to the call of some bare-headed songstress from across the Square, the whole covey would dash out one of the rickety gates, only to alight again on the stone steps of a neighbor's porch, where their chatter and pipings would last far into the night.

It was extraordinary how, from year to year, these young birds and even the old ones remembered the best perches about the Square. On Colonel Clayton's ample portico—big enough to shelter half a dozen covies behind its honeysuckles—both young and old would settle side by side; the younger bevy hovering about the Judge's blue-eyed daughter—a bird so blithe and of so free a wing, that the flock always followed wherever she alighted. On Judge Bowman's wide veranda only a few old cocks from the club could be found, and not infrequently, some rare birds from out of town perched about a table alive with the clink of glass and rattle of crushed ice, while next the church, on old Mrs. Pancoast's portico, with its tall Corinthian columns—Mr. Pancoast was the archdeacon of the Noah's ark church—one or two old grandmothers and a grave old owl of a family doctor were sure to fill the rocking-chairs. As for Richard Horn's marble steps they were never free from stray young couples who flew in to rest on Malachi's chairs and cushions. Sometimes only one bird and her mate would be tucked away in the shadow of the doorway; sometimes only an old pair, like Mrs. Horn and Richard, would occupy its corners.

These porticoes and stone door-steps were really the open-air drawing-rooms of Kennedy Square in the soft summer nights. Here ices were served and cool drinks—sherbets for the young and juleps and sherry cobblers for the old. At the Horn house, on great occasions, as when some big melon that had lain for days on the cool cellar floor was cut (it was worth a day's journey to see Malachi cut a melon), the guests would not only crowd the steps, but all the hall and half up the slender staircase, where they would sit with plates in their laps, the young men serving their respective sweethearts.

This open-air night-life had gone on since Kennedy Square began; each door-step had its *habitués* and each veranda its traditions. There was but one single porch, in fact, facing its stately trees whereon no flocks of birds, old or young, ever alighted, and that belonged to Peter Skimmerton—the meanest man in town—who in a fit of parsimony over candles, so the girls said, had bared his porch of every protecting vine and had placed opposite his door-step a glaring street gas-lamp—a monstrous and never-to-be-forgotten affront.

And yet, free and easy as the life was, no stranger sat himself down on any one of these porches until his pedigree had been thoroughly investigated, no matter how large might be his bank-account nor how ambitious his soarings. No premeditated discourtesy ever initialed this exclusiveness and none was ever intended. Kennedy Square did not know the blood of the stranger—that was all—and not knowing it they could not trust him. And it would have been altogether useless for him to try to disguise his antecedents—especially if he came from their own State— or any State south of it. His record could be as easily reached and could be as clearly read as a title-deed. Even the servants knew. Often they acted as Clerks of the Rolls.

"Dat Mister Jawlins, did you ask 'bout?" Malachi would say. "Why you know whar he comes f'om. He's one o' dem Anne Rundle Jawlinses. He do look mighty peart an' dey do say he's mighty rich, but he can't fool Malachi. I knowed his gran'pa," and that wise and politic darky, with the honor of the house before his eyes, would shake his head knowingly and with such an ominous look, that had you not known the only crime of the poor grandfather to

have been a marriage with his overseer's daughter—
a very worthy woman, by the way—instead of with
some lady of quality, you would have supposed he
had added the sin of murder to the crime of low
birth. On the other hand, had you asked Malachi
about some young aristocrat who had forgotten to
count his toddies the night before, that Defender of
the Faith would have replied:

"Lawd bress ye! Co'se dese young gemmens like
to frolic—an' dey do git dat way sometimes—tain't
nuthin'. Dem Dorseys was allers like dat—" the
very tones of his voice carrying such convictions of
the young man's respectability that you would have
felt safe in keeping a place at your table for the de-
linquent, despite your knowledge of his habits.

This general intimacy between the young people,
and this absolute faith of their elders in the quality
of family blood, was one of the reasons why every
man about Kennedy Square was to be trusted with
every other man's sister, and why every mother gave
the latch-key to every other mother's son, and why
it made no difference whether the young people came
home early or late, so that they all came home when
the others did. If there were love-making—and of
course there was love-making—it was of the old-
fashioned, boy-and-girl kind, with keepsakes and
pledges and long walks in the afternoons and whispered secrets at the merry-makings. Never anything

else. Woe betide the swain who forgot himself ever
so slightly—there was no night-key for him after
that, nor would any of the girls on any front steps
in town ever look his way again when he passed—
and to their credit be it said, few of the young
men either. From that day on the offender became a pariah. He had committed the unpardonable
sin.

As for these young men, this life with the girls
was all the life they knew. There were fishing parties, of course, at the "Falls" when the gudgeons
were biting, and picnics in the woods; and there were
oyster roasts in winter, and watermelon parties in
summer—but the girls must be present, too. For in
those simple days there were no special clubs with
easy-chairs and convenient little tables loaded with
drinkables and smokables—none for the young Oli-
vers, and certainly none for the women. There was,
to be sure, in every Southern city an old mausoleum
of a club—sometimes two—each more desolate than
the other—haunted by gouty old parties and *bon-
vivants;* but the young men never passed through
their doors except on some call of urgency. When
a man was old enough to be admitted to the club
there was no young damosel on Malachi's steps, or
any other steps, who would care a rap about him.
His day was done.

For these were the days in which the woman ruled

in court and home—championed by loyal retainers who strove hourly to do her bidding. Even the gray-haired men would tell you over their wine of some rare woman whom they had known in their youth, and who was still their standard of all that was gentle and gracious, and for whom they would claim a charm of manner and stately comeliness that—". my dear sir, not only illumined her drawing-room but conferred distinction on the commonwealth."

"Mrs. Tilghman's mother, were you talking about?" Colonel Clayton or Richard Horn, or some other old resident would ask. "I remember her perfectly. We have rarely had a more adorable woman, sir. She was a vision of beauty, and the pride of our State for years."

Should some shadow have settled upon any one of these homes—some shadow of drunkenness, or love of play, or shattered brain, or worse—the woman bore the sorrow in gentleness and patience and still loved on and suffered and loved and suffered again, hoping against hope. But no dry briefs were ever permitted to play a part, dividing heart and hearth. Kennedy Square would have looked askance had such things been suggested or even mentioned in its presence, and the dames would have lowered their voices in discussing them. Even the men would have passed with unlifted hats either party to such shame.

Because of this loyalty to womankind and this

reverence for the home—a reverence which began with the mother-love and radiated to every sister they knew—no woman of quality ever earned her own bread while there was an able-bodied man of her blood above ground to earn it for her. Nor could there be any disgrace so lasting, even to the third and fourth generation, as the stigma an outraged community would place upon the renegade who refused her aid and comfort. An unprogressive, quixotic life if you will—a life without growth and dominant personalities and lofty responsibilities and God-given rights—but oh! the sweet mothers that it gave us, and the wholesomeness, the cleanliness, the loyalty of it all.

With the coming of summer, then, each white marble step of the Horn mansion, under Malachi's care, shone like a china plate.

"Can't hab dese yere young ladies spile dere clean frocks on Malachi's steps—no, sah," he would say; "Marse Oliver'd r'ar an' pitch tur'ble."

There were especial reasons this year for these extra touches of rag and brush. Malachi knew "de signs" too well to be deceived. Pretty Sue Clayton, with her soft eyes and the mass of ringlets that framed her face, had now completely taken possession of Oliver's heart, and the old servant already had been appointed chief of the postal service—two letters a day sometimes with all the verbal messages in between.

This love-affair, which had begun in the winter, was not yet of so serious a nature as to cause distress or unhappiness to either one of their respective houses, nor had it reached a point where suicide or an elopement were all that was left. It was, in truth, but a few months old, and so far the banns had not been published. Within the last week Miss Sue had been persuaded " to wait for him—" that was all. She had not, it is true, burdened her gay young heart with the number of years of her patience. She and Oliver were sweethearts—that was enough for them both. As proof of it, was she not wearing about her neck at the very moment a chain which he had fashioned for her out of cherry-stones; and had she not given him in return one of those same ringlets, and had she not tied it with a blue ribbon herself? And above all—and what could be more conclusive— had she not taken her hair down to do it, and let him select the very tress that pleased him best?—and was not this curl, at that very moment, concealed in a pill-box and safely hidden in his unlocked bureau-drawer, where his mother saw it with a smile the last time she put away his linen? This love-affair—as were the love-affairs of all the other young people— was common gossip around Kennedy Square. Had there been any doubts about it, it would only have been necessary to ask any old Malachi, or Hannah, or Juno. They could have given every detail of the affair, descanting upon all its joys and its sorrows.

Sweet girls of the days gone by, what crimes some of you have to answer for! At least one of you must remember how my own thumb was cut into slits over these same cherry-stones, and why the ends of your ringlets were tucked away in a miniature box in my drawer, with the pressed flowers and signet-ring, and the rest of it. And you could—if you would—recall a waiting promise made to me years and years ago. And the wedding! Surely you have not forgotten that. I was there, you remember—but not as the groom.

On one particular evening in June—an evening that marked an important stage in the development of Oliver's fortunes—the front porch, owing to Malachi's attentions, was in spotless condition—steps, knocker, and round silver knobs.

Sue and Oliver sat on the top step; they had stolen across from the Clayton porch on some pretended errand. Sue's chin was in her hand, and Oliver sat beside her pouring out his heart as he had never done before. He had realized long ago that she could never understand his wanting to be a painter as Miss Clendenning had done, and so he had never referred to it since the night of the musicale, when he had raced across the Square to tell her of his talk with the little lady. Sue, as he remembered afterward, had listened abstractedly. She would have preferred at the time his running in to talk about herself rather than about his queer ambitions. She was no more interested now.

"Ollie, what does your father say about all this?" she finally asked in a perfunctory way. "Would he be willing for you to be a painter?" It bored her to listen to Oliver's enthusiastic talk about light and shade, and color and perspective, and what Mr. Crocker had said and what Mr. Crocker was doing, and what Mr. Crocker's last portrait was like. She was sure that nobody else around Kennedy Square talked of such things or had such curious ambitions. They shocked her as much as Oliver's wearing some outlandish clothes would have done—making him conspicuous and, perhaps, an object of ridicule.

"Father's all right, Sue. He's always right," Oliver answered. "He believes in Mr. Crocker, just as he believes in a lot of things that a good many people around here don't understand. He believes the time will come when they will value his pictures, and be proud to own them. But I don't care who owns mine. I just want the fun of painting them. Just think of what a man can do with a few tubes of color, a brush, and a bit of canvas. So I don't care if they never buy what I paint. I can get along

64

somehow, just as Mr. Crocker does. He's poor, but just see how happy he is. Why, when he does a good thing he's nothing but a boy, he's so glad about it. I always know how his work has gone when I see his face."

"But, Ollie, he's so shabby, and his daughter gives music-lessons. Nobody *thinks* of inviting her anywhere." Sue's eyes were shut tight, with an expression of assumed contempt, and her little nose was straight up.

"Yes—but that doesn't hurt his pictures, Sue." There was a slight trace of impatience in Oliver's tone.

"Well, perhaps it doesn't—but you don't want to be like him. I wouldn't like to see you, Ollie, going about with a picture under your arm that everybody knew you had painted yourself. And suppose that they would want to buy your pictures? How would you feel now to be taking other people's money for things you had painted?"

The boy caught his breath. It seemed useless to pursue the talk with Sue. She evidently had no sympathy with his aspirations.

"No—but I wish I could paint as he does," he answered, mechanically.

Sue saw the change in his manner. She realized, too, that she had hurt him in some way. She drew nearer and put her hand on his arm.

"Why, you can, Ollie. You can do anything you want to; Miss Lavinia told me so." The little witch was mistress of one art—that of holding her lover— but that was an art of which all the girls about Kennedy Square approved.

"No, I can't," he replied, forgetting in the caressing touch of her hand the tribute to his ability, and delighted that she was once more in sympathy with him. "Mother wouldn't think of my being an artist. She doesn't understand how I feel about it, and Miss Lavinia, somehow, doesn't seem to be favorable to it either. I've talked to her lots of times— she was more encouraging at first, but she doesn't seem to like the idea now. I've been hoping she'd fix it so I could speak to mother about it. Now she tells me I had better wait. I can't see why. Miss Lavinia knows what an artist's life can be, for she knew plenty of painters when she was in London with her father, and she loves pictures, too, and is a good judge—nobody here any better. She told me only a week ago how much one of these Englishmen was paid for a little thing as big as your hand, but I've forgotten the amount. I don't see why I can't paint as well as those fellows. Do you know, Sue, I'm beginning to think that about half the people in Kennedy Square are asleep? They really don't seem to think there is anything respectable but the law. If they are right, how about all the men who painted the great pictures and built all the cathedrals, or the men who wrote all the poems and histories? Mother, of course, wants me to be a lawyer. Because I'm fitted for it?—not a bit of it! Simply because father was one before me and his father before him, and Uncle John Tilghman another, and so on back to the deluge."

Sue drew away a little and turned her head toward the Square as if in search of someone. Oliver noticed the movement and his heart sank again. He saw but too clearly how little impression the story of his ambitions had made upon her. Then the thought flashed into his mind that he might have offended her in some way, clashing against her traditions and her prejudices as he had done. He bent toward her and laid his hand in hers.

"Little girl," he said, in a softened tone, "I can't make you unhappy, too. Mother is enough for me to worry about—I haven't talked it all out to you before, but don't you get a wrong idea of what I'm going to do—" and he looked up into her face and tightened his hold upon her fingers, his eyes never wavering from her own.

The girl allowed his hand to remain an instant, then quickly withdrew her own and started up. Coyness is sometimes fear in the timid heart that is stepping into the charmed circle for the first time.

"There goes Ella Dorsey and Jack—" she cried,

67

springing down the steps. " Ella! El—la! " and an answering halloo came back, and the two started from Malachi's steps and raced up the street to join their young friends.

CHAPTER IV

AN OLD-FASHIONED MORTGAGE

Pretty Sue Clayton with her ringlets and rosy cheeks had not been Oliver's only listener.

His mother had been sitting inside the drawing-room, just beside the open window. She had spoken to Sue and Oliver when they first mounted the steps, and had begged them both to come in, but they had forgotten her presence. Unintentionally, therefore, she had heard every word of the conversation. Her old fears rushed over her again with renewed force. She had never for a moment supposed that Oliver wanted to be a painter—like Mr. Crocker! Now at last she understood his real object in talking to Lavinia the night of the musical.

"Richard," she called softly to her husband sitting in the adjoining room, in the chair that Malachi, in accordance with the old custom, had with his sweeping bow made ready for him. The inventor had been there since tea was over, lying back in his seat, his head resting on his hand. He had had one of his thoughtful days, worrying over some detail of his machine, still incomplete. The new device of which he had told her with such glee had failed, as had the others. The motor was still incomplete.

"Richard," she repeated.

"Yes, my dear," he answered, in his gentle voice. He had not heard her at first.

"Bring your chair over here."

The inventor rose instantly and, crossing the room, took a seat beside her, his hand finding hers in the dark.

"What is this you have been saying to Oliver about artists being great men?" she asked. "He's got a new idea in his head now—he wants to be a painter. I've thought for some time that Mr. Crocker was not a proper person for him to be so much with. He has evidently worked on the boy's imagination until he has determined to give up the law and study art."

"How do you know?"

"I've just heard him tell Sue Clayton so. All he wants now is my consent—he says he has yours."

The inventor paused, and gently smoothed his wife's fingers with his own.

"And you would not give it?" he inquired.

"How could I? It would ruin him—don't you know it?" There was a slight tinge of annoyance in her voice—not one of fault-finding, but rather of anxiety.

"That depends, my dear, on how well he could succeed," he answered, gently.

"Why, Richard!" She withdrew her hand quickly from his caressing touch, and looked at him in undisguised astonishment. "What has his *succeeding* to do with it? Surely you cannot be in earnest? I am willing he should do anything to make his living, but not that. No one we know has ever been a painter. It is neither respectable nor profitable. You see what a dreadful existence Mr. Crocker leads —hardly an associate in town, and no acquaintances for his daughter, and he's been painting ever since he was a boy. Oliver could not earn a penny at such work."

"Money is not everything, my dear, nor social recognition. There are many things I would value more."

"What are they?" She was facing him now, her brows knit, a marked antagonism in her voice.

"Good manners and good taste, Sallie, and kindly consideration for another's feelings," he answered. He spoke calmly and kindly, as was his custom. He had lived almost all his life with this high-strung Sallie Horn, whose eyes flashed now and then as they had done in the old days when he won her hand. He knew every side of her temperament. "Good manners, and good taste"—he repeated, as if wishing to emphasize his thoughts—"Oliver has all of these, and he has, besides, loyalty to his friends. He never speaks of Mr. Crocker but with affection, and

I love to hear him. That man is an artist of great talent, and yet it seems to be the fashion in this town to ridicule him. If Ollie has any gifts which would fit him to be a painter, I should be delighted to see him a painter. It is a profession despised now, as are many others, but it is the profession of a gentleman, for all they say, and a noble one!" Then he stopped and said, thoughtfully, as if communing with himself—"I wish he could be a painter. Since Gilbert Stuart's time we have had so few men of whom we can boast. This country will one day be proud to honor her artists."

Mrs. Horn sank back in her chair. She felt the hopelessness of all further discussion with her husband. "He would not have talked this way ten years ago," she said to herself. "Everything has gone wrong since he left the law." But to her husband she said:

"You always measure everything by your hopes, Richard, and you never look at the practical side of anything. Ollie is old enough to begin to think how he will earn his bread. I see now how hopeless it is for us to try and make a lawyer of him—his heart is not in it. I have come little by little to the conclusion that what he wants most is hard work, and he wants it right away, just as soon as we can find something for him to do—something with his hands, if necessary, not something full of dreams and imaginings," and her voice rose in its earnestness. "I am getting more and more anxious about him every day," she added, suddenly controlling herself, "and when you encourage him in foolish vagaries you only make it harder for me, dear," and her voice softened and broke with emotion.

"He ought to have gone into the laboratory, Sallie," Richard added quickly, in a reflective tone—laying his hand on her shoulder as he noticed the change of voice—"just as I wanted him to do when he left school. There is a future for scientific men in this country which you do not see—a future which few around me seem to see. Great changes are coming, not only in science, but in the arts and in all useful knowledge. If Ollie can add to the brilliancy of this future by becoming a brilliant painter, able to help educate those about him, there could be no higher calling for him. Three things are coming, my dear —perhaps four." The inventor had risen from his seat and stood beside her, his eyes turned away into the dark as if he were addressing some unseen person. "The superseding of steam, aërial locomotion, and the education of the common people, black and white. One other may come—the freeing of the slaves—but the others are sure. Science, not money, nor family traditions, nor questions of birth, will shape the destinies of the country. We may not live to see it, but Oliver will, and I want him to be where he can help on the movement. You were opposed to his becoming a scientist, and I feel assured made a mistake. Don't stand in his way again, dear."

"Yes, Richard, I was opposed to it, because I did not want him to waste his time over all sorts of foolish experiments, which would certainly—" She did not finish the sentence. Her anxiety had not yet gone as far as that. With a quick gesture she rose from her chair, and drawing her white gossamer shawl about her shoulders—left the room and walked out onto the front steps, followed by Richard.

If the inventor heard the thrust he did not reply. He would not argue with his wife over it, nor did it check the flow of his courtesy. She had never seen the value of what he was striving for, but she would in time he knew.

"Yes, I think it is cooler out here," was all he said, as he placed a cushion to soften her seat on the threshold. When he had arranged another pillow behind her back and hunted round the dark parlor for a stool for her feet, he found a chair for himself and sat down beside her. She thanked him, but her thoughts were evidently far away. She was weighing in her mind what must be her next move if Oliver persisted in this new departure. Richard broke the silence.

"I haven't told you of the good offer I've had for the farm, Sallie."

"No, but we're not going to sell it, of course." She was leaning back against the jamb of the door as she spoke, the shawl hanging loose, her delicate white hands in her lap. It was an idle answer to an idle question, for her mind was still with Oliver.

"Well, I hadn't thought of doing so until to-day," he answered, slowly, "but I had a notice from the bank that they must call in the mortgage, and so I thought I might as well sell the whole place, pay off the debt, and use the balance for——"

"Sell the farm, Richard?" It was her hand now that sought his, and with a firm grasp as if she would restrain him then and there in his purpose.

"Yes, I can get several thousand dollars over and above the mortgage, and I need the money, Sallie. It will only be a temporary matter——" and he smoothed her arm tenderly, speaking as a lover of long standing might do who is less absorbed with the caress than with the subject under discussion. "The motor will be ready in a few weeks—as soon as the new batteries are finished. Then, my dear, you won't have to curtail your expenses as you have done." His voice was full of hope now, a smile lighting his face as he thought of all the pleasure and comfort his success would bring her.

"But you said that same thing when you were working on the steam-valve, for which you put that very mortgage on the farm, and now that's all gone and——"

"The failure of the steam-valve, as I have always told you, was due to my own carelessness, Sallie. I should have patented it sooner. They are making enormous sums on it, I hear, and are using my cut-off, and I think dishonestly. But the motor has been protected at every new step that I have taken. My first patent of August 13, 1856, supersedes all others, and cannot be shaken. Now, my dear, don't worry about it—you have never known me to fail, and I won't now. Besides, you forget my successes, Sallie—the turbine water-wheel and the others. It will all come right."

"It will never come right." She had risen from her seat and was standing over him, both hands on his shoulders, her eyes looking down into his, her voice trembling. "Oh, Richard, Richard! Give up this life of dreams you are living, and go back to your law-office. You always succeeded in the law. This new career of yours is ruining us. I can economize, dear, just as I have always done," she added, with another sudden change of tone, bending over him and slipping her hand caressingly into his. "I will do everything to help you. I did not mean to be cross a moment ago. I was worried about Oliver's talk. I have been silent so long—I must speak. Don't be angry, dear, but you must keep the farm.

I will go myself and see about the mortgage at the bank—we cannot—we must not; go on this way—we will have nothing left."

He patted her arm again in his gentle way—not to calm her fears, he knew so well that she was wrong, but to quiet the nerves that he thought unstrung.

"But I need this extra money for some improvements which I——"

"Yes, I know you *think* so, but you don't, Richard, you don't. For Heaven's sake, throw the motor out into the street, and be done with it. It will ruin us all if things go on as they have done."

The inventor raised his eyes quickly. He had never seen her so disturbed in all their married life. She had never spoken in this way before.

"Don't excite yourself, Sallie," he said, gravely, and with a certain air of authority in his manner. "You'll bring on one of your headaches—it will all come right. Come, my dear, let us go into the house. People are passing, and will wonder."

She followed him back into the drawing-room, his hand still held fast in hers.

"Promise me one thing," she said, stopping at the door and looking up into his eyes, "and I won't say another word. Please do nothing more about the farm unless you let me know. Let me think first how I can help. It will all come out right, as you say, but it will be because we will make it come

right, dear." She drew his face down toward her
with one hand and kissed him tenderly on his cheek.
Then she bade him good-night and resumed her seat
by the window, to watch for Oliver's return.

Try as she would, she could not banish her fears.
The news of Richard's intention to pay off the loan by
selling the farm had sent a shudder through her heart
such as she had never before experienced, for that
which she had dreaded had come to pass. Loyal as
she had always been to her husband, and proud as she
was of his genius and accomplishments, and sympathetic as they were in all else that their lives touched
upon, her keen, penetrating mind had long since di-
vined the principal fault that lay at the bottom of her
husband's genius. She saw that the weak point in his
make-up was not his inventive quality, but his inability to realize any practical results from his inventions when perfected. She saw, too, with equal
certainty how rapidly their already slender means
were being daily depleted in costly experiments—
many of which were abandoned as soon as tried, and
she knew full well that the end was but a question
of time. Even when he had abandoned the law, and
had exchanged his office near the Court-house for his
shop in the back yard, and had given his library to
his young students, she had not despaired; she still
had faith in his genius.

She had first become uneasy when the new steam

cut-off had failed to reimburse him. When this catastrophe was followed by his losing every dollar of his interest in the improved cotton-gin, because of his generosity to a brother inventor, her uneasiness had become the keenest anxiety. And now here was this new motor, in which he seemed more absorbed than in any other of his inventions. This was to plunge them into still greater difficulties and jeopardize even the farm.

Richard had not been disturbed by it all. Serene and hopeful always, the money question had counted for nothing with him. His compensation lay in the fact that his theories had been proved true. Moreover, there were, he knew, other inventions ahead, and more important discoveries to be made. If money were necessary, these new inventions would supply it. Such indifference to practical questions was an agony to one of her temperament, burdened as she was by the thought of their increasing daily expenses, the magnitude of which Richard never seemed to appreciate.

And yet until to-night, when Richard had made his announcement about the mortgage, she had made no protest, uttered no word of censure. Neither had any jar or discord ever disturbed the sweet harmony of their home-life. And she had only behaved as any other wife in Kennedy Square would have done in like circumstances. Remonstrances against a husband's business methods were never made in the best families. In his own house Richard was master. So she had suffered on and held her peace, while Richard walked with his head in the clouds, unconscious of her doubts. The situation must now be met, and she determined to face it with all her might. " The farm shall not be sacrificed, if I can help it," she kept repeating to herself; " any economy is better than that disaster."

When at last the shock of the news of the threat- ened disaster had passed, and she had regained her customary composure, she decided to act at once and at head-quarters, outside of Richard's help or knowl- edge. She would send for Colonel Clayton, one of the directors of the bank, in the morning, and see what could be done to postpone for a time the bank's action. This would give her time to think what next could best be done to save the property. This set- tled in her mind, she gave herself up to the more important and pressing need of the moment—the dissuading of Oliver from this new act of folly.

At the end of an hour she was still sitting by the drawing-room window, straining her eyes across the Square, noting every figure that passed into the radi- ance of the moonlight, her mind becoming clearer as her indomitable will, which had never failed her in domestic crises, began to assert itself.

When her eye fell at last upon her son, he was

walking with swinging gait up the long path across the Square, whistling as he came, his straw hat tilted on one side, his short coat flying free. He had taken Sue home, and the two had sat on her father's steps in the moonlight long after the other boys and girls had scattered to their homes. The Colonel had come in while they were talking, and had bade them good-night and gone up to bed.

Girl as she was, Sue already possessed that subtle power of unconscious coquetry which has distinguished all the other Sue Claytons of all the other Kennedy Squares the South over since the days of Pocahontas. She had kept Oliver's mind away from the subject that engrossed him, and on herself; and when, at last, standing between the big columns of the portico she had waved her hand, good-night, and had gained his promise to stop in the morning on his way to the office, for just another word, she felt sure that his every thought was of her. Then she had closed the big front door—she was the last person in the house awake—and tripped upstairs, not lighting her candle until she had peeped through her shutters, and had found him standing on the other side of the street looking toward the house. He made a handsome picture of a lover, as he stood in the moonlight, and Sue smiled complacently to herself at the delicate attention paid her, but Oliver's eyes, the scribe is ashamed to say, were not fixed on the particular pair of green blinds that concealed this adorable young lady, certainly not with any desire to break through their privacy. One of the unforgivable sins—nay, one of the impossible sins—about Kennedy Square would have been to have recognized a lady who looked, even during the daytime, out from a bedroom window: much less at night. That was why Sue did not open her blinds.

Nor, indeed, was Oliver occupied with the question of Sue's blinds at all. He had for the moment in fact completely forgotten the existence of his lady-love. He was, if the truth must be told, studying the wonderful effect of the white light of the moon flooding with its radiance the columns and roof of the Clayton house, the dark magnolias silhouetted against the flight of steps and the indigo-blue of the sky. He had already formulated in his mind the palette with which he would paint it, and had decided that the magnolias were blue-black and not green, and the steps greenish-white. He had, furthermore, determined to make an outline of it in the daylight, and talk to Mr. Crocker about it. Sue's eyes, which but a moment before had so charmed him, no longer lingered in his memory—nor even in any one of the far corners of his head and heart. It was only when her light flashed up that he awoke to the realization of what he was doing, and even this breach of good manners was forgotten by him in his delight over the effect which the red glow of the candle gave to the whole composition.

With the picture clearly stamped upon his brain, he turned and stepped quickly across the Square, and in another moment he had thrown his mother a kiss through the window, and rushing inside had caught her in his arms.

"Poor motherkins—and you all alone," he cried. "Why, I thought you and father had gone to bed long ago."

"No, son—I was waiting for you." He laid his fresh young face against hers, insisting that she must go to bed at once; helping her upstairs awkwardly, laughing as he went—telling her she was the sweetest girl he ever knew and his best sweetheart—kissing her pale cheeks as they climbed the steps together to his room.

She had determined, as she sat by the window, to talk to him of what she had overheard him say to Sue, and of her anxiety over Richard's revelations, but his joyous kiss had robbed her of the power. She would wait for another time—she said to herself—not to-night, when he was so happy.

"Anybody at Sue's, Ollie?" she asked, lighting his candle.

"Only the boys and girls—Tom Pitts, Charley Bowman, Nellie Talbot, and one or two others. The Colonel came in just before I left."

"But the Colonel will be home to-morrow, will he not?" she asked, quickly, as if something forgotten had been suddenly remembered.

"Yes—think so—" answered Oliver, taking off his coat and hanging it over the chair—"because he was just up from Pongateague. He and Major Pitts got thirty-seven woodcock in two days. Tom wants me to go down with him some day next week."

A shade of anxiety crossed the mother's face.

"What did you tell him, son?" She moved a chair nearer the bureau and sat down to watch him undress, as she had always done since the day she first tucked him into his crib.

"Oh, I said I would ask you." He was loosening his cravat, his chin thrown up, the light of the candle falling over his well-knit shoulders and chest outlined through his white shirt.

"Better not go, Ollie—you've been away so much lately."

"Oh, dearie," he protested, in a tone as a child would have done, "what does a day or two matter? Be a darling old mother and let me go. Tom has a gun for me, and Mr. Talbot is going to lend us his red setter. Tom's sister is going, too, and so are her cousins. Just think, now, I haven't had a day in the country for a coon's age." His arms were round her neck now. He seemed happier over the excuse to caress her than anxious about her possible refusal.

84

She loosened one of his hands and laid it on her cheek.

"No holidays, son? Why you had two last week, when you all went out to Stemmer's Run," she said, looking up into his face, his hand still in hers.

"Yes, but that was fishing!" he laughed as he waved an imaginary rod in his hands.

"And the week before, when you spent the day at Uncle Tilghman's?" she continued, smiling sadly at him, but with the light of an ill-concealed admiration on her face.

"Ah, but mother, I went to see the Lely! That's an education. Oh, that portrait in pink!" He was serious now, looking straight down into her eyes— talking with his hands, one thumb in air as if it were a bit of charcoal and he was outlining the Lely on an equally real canvas. "Such color, mother— such an exquisite poise of the head and sweep to the shoulder—" and the thumb described a curve in the air as if following every turn of Lely's brush.

Her eyes followed his gestures—she loved his enthusiasm, although she wished it had been about something else.

"And you don't get any education out of the Judge's law-books?"

"No, I wish I did." The joyous look on his face was gone now—his hand had fallen to his side. "It gets to be more of a muddle every day—" and then he added, with the illogical reasoning of youth—" all the lawyers that ever lived couldn't paint a picture like the Lely."

Mrs. Horn closed her eyes. It was on her tongue to tell him she knew what was in his heart, but she stopped; no, not to-night, she said firmly to herself, and shut her lips tight—a way she had of bracing her nerves in such emergencies.

Oliver in turn saw the expression of anxiety that crossed his mother's face and the thin drawn line of the lips. One word from her and he would have poured out his heart. Then some shadow that crossed her face silenced him. " No, not to-night—" he said to himself. " She has been sitting up for me and is tired—I'll tell her to-morrow."

" Don't go with Tom Pitts, my son," she said, calmly. " I'd rather you'd stay; I don't want you to go this time. Perhaps a little later—" and a slight shiver went through her as she rose from her chair and moved toward him.

He made no protest. Her final word was always law to him—not because she dominated him, but because his nature was always to be in harmony with the thing he loved. Because, too, underneath it all was that quality of tenderness to all women old and young, which forbade him to cause one of them pain. Almost unconsciously to himself he had gone through a process by which from having yielded her the obedience of a child, he now surrendered to her the pleasures of his youth when the old feeling of maternal dominance still controlled her in her attitude to him. She did not recognize the difference, and he had but half-perceived it, but the difference had already transformed him from a boy into a man, though with unrecognized powers of stability as yet. In obeying his mother, then at twenty-two, or even in meeting the whims and conceits of his sweethearts, this quality of tenderness to the woman was always uppermost in his heart. The surrender of a moment's pleasure seemed so little to him compared to the expression of pain he could see cross their faces. He had so much to make him happy—what mattered it if out of a life so full he should give up any one thing to please his mother.

Patting him on the cheek and kissing him on the neck, as she had so often done when some sudden wave of affection overwhelmed her, she bade him good-night at last.

Once outside in the old-fashioned hall, she stopped for a moment, her eyes fixed on the floor, the light from the hall-lamp shining on her silver hair and the shawl about her shoulders, and said slowly to herself, as if counting each word:

"What—can I do—to save this boy—from—himself?"

CHAPTER V

Richard, when he waked, made no allusion to the
mortgage nor to his promise the night before, to take
no steps in the matter without her consent, nor could
Mrs. Horn see that the inventor had given the subject further thought. He came in to breakfast with
his usual serenity of mien, kissed her gallantly
on the cheek—in all their married life this dear old
gentleman had never forgotten this breakfast kiss—
and taking his seat opposite her, he picked up the
new *Scientific Review*, just in by the morning mail,
and began cutting the leaves. She tried to draw him
into conversation by asking him when the note on
the mortgage was due, but his mind was doubtless
absorbed by some problem suggested by the *Review*
before him, for without answering—he, of course,
had not heard her—he rose from his chair, excused
himself for a moment, opened a book in his library,
studied it leisurely, and only resumed his seat when
Malachi gently touched his elbow and said:

" Coffee purty nigh done sp'ilt, Marse Richard."

Breakfast over, Richard picked up his letters,

and with that far-away look in his eyes which his wife knew so well, walked to the closet, took down his long red calico gown, slipped it over his coat, and with a loving pat on his wife's shoulder as he passed, and with the request that no one but Nathan should see him that morning, made his way through the damp brick-paved back yard to the green door of his " li'l " room.

Mrs. Horn watched his retreating figure from the window—his head bent, his soft hair stirred by the morning air, falling about his shoulders. His serenity; his air of abstraction; of being wrapped in the clouds as it were—borne aloft by the power of a thought altogether beyond her, baffled her as it always did. She could not follow his flights when he was in one of these uplifted moods. She could only watch and wait until he returned again to the common ground of their daily love and companionship.

Brushing a quick tear from her eyes with an impatient sigh, she directed Malachi to go to Oliver's room and tell him he must get up at once, as she wanted him to carry a message of importance. She had herself rapped at her son's door as she passed on her way downstairs, and Malachi had already paid two visits to the same portal—one with Oliver's shoes and one on his own account. He had seen his mistress's anxiety, and knowing that his young master

89

had come in late the night before, had mistaken the cause, charging Mrs. Horn's perturbation to Oliver's account. The only response Oliver had made to either of his warnings had been a smothered yawn and a protest at being called at daylight. On his third visit Malachi was more insistent, the hall-clock by that time having struck nine.

"Ain't you out'en dat bed yit, Marse Oliver? Dis yere's de third time I been yere. Better git up; yo' ma's gittin' onres'less."

"Coming, Mally. Tell mother I'll be down right away," called Oliver, springing out of bed. Malachi stepped softly downstairs again, bowed low to his mistress, and with a perfectly straight face said:

"He's mos' ready, mistis. Jes' a-breshin' ob his ha'r when I opened de do'. Spec' Marse Oliver over-slep' hisse'f, or maybe nobody ain't call him——"

He could not bear to hear the boy scolded. He had begun to shield his young master in the days when he carried him on his shoulder, and he would still shade the truth for him whenever he considered necessity required it.

When Oliver at last came downstairs it was by means of the hand-rail as a slide, a dash through the hall and a bound into the breakfast-room, followed by a joyous good-morning, meeting his mother's "How could you be so late, my boy," without any defence of his conduct, putting one hand under her

90

chin and the other around her neck, and kissing her where her white hair parted over her forehead.

Malachi waited an instant, breathing freer when he found that his statement regarding Oliver's toilet had passed muster, and then shuffled off to the kitchen for hot waffles and certain other comforting viands that Aunt Hannah, the cook, had kept hot for her young master, Malachi's several reports having confirmed her suspicions that Oliver, as usual, would be half an hour late.

"What a morning, motherkins," Oliver cried. "Such a sky, all china-blue and white. Oh, you just ought to see how fine the old church looms up behind the trees. I'm going to paint that some day, from my window. Dad had his breakfast?" and he glanced at the empty seat and plate. "Sausage, eh? Mally, got any for me?" and he dragged up his chair beside her, talking all the time as he spread his napkin and drew the dishes toward him.

He never once noticed her anxious face, he was so full of his own buoyant happiness. She did not check his enthusiasm. This breakfast-hour alone with her boy—he was almost always later than Richard—was the happiest of the day. But her heart was too heavy this morning to enjoy it. Instead of listening with her smile of quiet satisfaction, answering him now and then with a gayety of humor which matched his own, she was conscious only of the wait-

ing for an opportunity to break into his talk without jarring upon his mood. At last, with a hesitating emphasis that would have alarmed anyone less
wrapped in his own content than her son, she
said:

" Ollie, when you finish your breakfast I want you,
on your way to Judge Ellicott's office, to stop at
Colonel Clayton's and ask him to be good enough
to come and see me as soon as he can on a little
matter of business. Tell him I will keep him but a
minute. If you hurry, my son, you'll catch him before he leaves the house."

The die was cast now. She had taken her first
step without Richard's hand to guide her—the
first in all her life. It was pain to do it—the
more exquisite because she loved to turn to him
for guidance or relief, to feel the sense of his
protection. Heretofore he had helped her in every
domestic emergency, his soft, gentle hand soothing
and quieting her, when troubles arose. She had
wavered during the night between her duty to her
family in saving the farm, and her duty to her husband in preserving unbroken the tie of loyal dependence that had always bound them together. Many
emotions had shaken her as she lay awake, her eyes
fixed on the flutings in the canopy of the high-post
bedstead which the night-lamp faintly illumined,
Richard asleep beside her, dreaming doubtless of cogs

and pulleys and for the hundredth time of his finding the one connecting link needed to complete the
chain of his success.

But before the day had broken, her keen, penetrating mind had cut through the fog of her doubts.
Come what may, the farm should never be given up.
Richard, for all his urgent need of money to perfect his new motor, should not be allowed to sacrifice
this the only piece of landed property which they
possessed, except the roof that sheltered them all.
The farm saved, she would give her attention to
Oliver's future career. On one point her mind was
firmly made up—he should never, in spite of what his
father said, become a painter.

Oliver hurried through his breakfast, cut short
Malachi's second relay of waffles to the great disappointment of that excellent servitor, and with his
mother's message for the moment firmly fixed in his
mind, tilted his hat on one side of his head and started
across Kennedy Square, whistling as he went.

Mrs. Horn moved her seat to the window and
looked out upon the brick-paved yard. The door of
the shop was shut. Richard was already at work, for
a thin curl of blue smoke was rising from the chimney. As she sat looking out upon the tulip-tree and
the ivy-covered wall beyond, a strange, unaccountable
sense of loneliness new in her experience came over
her. The lines about her mouth settled more firmly,

93

and the anxious look that had filled her eyes changed to one of determination.

"Nobody can help," she said to herself with a sigh. "I must do it all myself;" and picking up her basket of keys she mounted slowly to her room.

Once outside the front door, with the fresh, clear air stirring to a silver-white the leaves of the maples, the birds singing in the branches and the sky glistening overhead, one of those sudden changes of mood to which our young hero was subject swept over him. The picture of the dear mother whom he loved and whose anxious face had at last filled his thoughts, by some shifting of the gray matter of this volatile young gentleman's brain had suddenly become replaced by another.

Pretty Sue Clayton, her black eyes snapping with fun, her hand so soon to be outstretched in welcome, was now the dominating figure in his mental horizon. Even Sir Peter Lely's girl in pink and the woodcock shooting with Tom Pitts, and all the other delights that had filled his brain had become things of the past as he thought of Sue's greeting. For the time being this black-eyed little witch with the ringlets about her face had complete possession of him.

He had not thought of her, it is true, for five consecutive minutes since he had bidden her good-night ten hours ago; and he would, I am quite sure, have forgotten even his promise to see her this morning had not his mother's message made his going to her house imperative. And yet, now that the prospect of having a glimpse of her face was assured, he could hardly wait until he reached her side.

Not that he had some new thing to tell her—something that had bubbled up fresh from the depths of his heart over-night. Indeed, had that portion of this young gentleman's anatomy been searched with a dark lantern, it can safely be said that not the slightest suggestion of this fair inamorata's form or lineaments would have been found lurking in any one of its recesses. Furthermore, I can state positively—and I knew this young gentleman quite well at the time—that it was not Sue at all that he longed for at this precise moment, even though he hurried to meet her. It was more the *woman in her*—the something that satisfied his inner nature when he was with her—her coy touches of confidence, her artless outbursts of admiration, looking up in his face as she spoke, the dimples playing about the corners of her mouth. He revelled in all those subtle flatteries and cajoleries, and in all the arts to please of which she was past mistress. He loved to believe her—she intended that he should—when she told him how different he was from anybody about Kennedy Square, and how nobody swam or rode or danced as he did; nor wore their hair so becomingly, nor their clothes—especially the gray jacket buttoned up close under the chin, nor carried themselves as they walked, nor——

Why go on? We all know exactly how she said it, and how sincere she seemed, and how we believed it all (and do now, some of us), and how blissful it was to sit beside her and hear her voice and know that this most adorable of women really believed that the very sun itself rose and set in our own adorable persons.

Because of all this and of many other things with which we have nothing to do, our young hero saw only Sue's eyes when that maiden, who had been watching for him at the library window, laid her hand on the lapel of his coat in her coaxing way. No wonder he had forgotten everything which his mother had asked him to do. I can forgive him under the circumstances—and so can you. Soft hands are very beguiling, sometimes—and half-closed lids—Well! It is a good many years ago, but there are some things that none of us ever forget.

Blinded by such fascinations it is not at all astonishing that long before Oliver regained his senses the Colonel had left the house for the day. That distinguished gentleman would, no doubt, have waited the young prince's pleasure in his library had he known of his errand. But since the Colonel had unfortunately taken himself off, there was nothing, of course, for our Oliver to do but to remain where he

was until noon—this was Sue's way out of the diffi•
culty—and then to catch the Colonel at the bank
where he could always be found between twelve and
one o'clock, or where Mr. Stiger, the cashier, could
lay his hands on him if he was anywhere in the neighborhood, a suggestion of Sue's which at once relieved
Oliver from further anxiety, Mr. Stiger being one
of his oldest and dearest friends.

By the time, however, that Oliver had reached the
bank the Colonel had left for the club, where he
would have been too happy, no doubt—being the
most courteous of colonels, etc., etc.—" if his dear
young friend had only sent him word," etc.

All this our breathless young Mercury—Oliver
never walked when he could run—learned some hours
later from old Mr. Stiger, the cashier, who punched
him in the ribs at the end of every sentence in which
he conveyed the disappointing information, calling
him " Creeps," at short intervals, and roaring with
laughter at the boy's account of the causes leading up
to his missing the Colonel.

" Gone to the club, Creeps, don't I tell you
(—punch in the ribs—); gone to get a little sip of
Madeira and a little bit of woodcock (—punch over
the heart—), and a little—oh, I tell you, you young
dog—" (this punch straight on the breast-bone)—
" you ought to be a bank director—you hear!—a big
fat bank director, and own a big house up in the

Square, if you want to enjoy yourself—and have a pretty daughter—Oh, you young rascal! " This last punch bent Oliver double, and was followed by an outburst of uncontrollable laughter from Stiger.

These same punchings and outbursts had gone on since the days that Oliver was in short trousers and Stiger was superintendent of the Sunday-school which the boy had attended in his early years—Stiger was still superintendent and of the same school: cashiers had to have certificates of character in those days. A smooth-shaven, round-headed old fellow was Stiger, with two little dabs of side-whiskers, a pair of eyes that twinkled behind a pair of gold spectacles, and a bald head kept polished by the constant mopping of a red silk handkerchief. His costume in the bank was a black alpaca coat and high black satin stock, which grabbed him tight around the neck, and held in place the two points of his white collar struggling to be free. Across his waist-line was a square of cloth. This, in summer, replaced his waistcoat, and, in winter, protected it from being rubbed into holes by constant contact with the edge of the counter.

His intimacy with Oliver dated from one hot Sunday morning years before, when Oliver had broken in upon the old gentleman's long prayers by sundry scrapings of his finger-nails down the whitewashed wall of the school-room, producing a blood-cooling and most irreverent sound, much to the discomfort of the worshippers.

"Who made that noise?" asked Mr. Stiger, when the amen was reached.

"Me, sir."

"What for?"

"To get cool. It makes creeps go down my back."

From that day the old cashier had never called Oliver anything but "Creeps."

Oliver, in a spirit of playful revenge, made caricatures of his prosecutor in these later years, enlarging his nose, puffing out his cheeks, and dressing him up in impossible clothes. These sketches he would mail to the cashier as anonymous communications, always stopping at the bank the next day to see how Stiger enjoyed them. He generally found them tacked up over the cashier's desk. Some of them were still there when Stiger died.

Carried away by the warm greetings of the old cashier, and the hearty, whole-souled spirit of companionship inherent in the man—a spirit always dear to Oliver—he not only stayed to make another caricature of the old fellow, over which the original laughed until the tears ran down his fat cheeks, but until all the old sketches were once more taken from the drawer or examined on the wall and laughed at over again, Stiger praising him for his cleverness and predicting all kinds of honors and distinctions for him when his talents became recognized. It was just the atmosphere of general approval in which our young hero loved to bask, and again the hours slipped away and three o'clock came and went and his mother's message was still undelivered. Nor had he been at Judge Ellicott's office. This fact was not impressed upon him by the moon-faced clock that hung over the cashier's desk—time made no difference to Oliver—but by the cashier himself, who began stuffing the big books into a great safe built into the wall, preparatory to locking it with a key that could have opened the gate of a walled town, and which the old gentleman took home with him every night and hung on a nail by his bed.

Thus it came to pass that another half hour had struck before Oliver mounted the steps of the Chesapeake Club in search of the elusive Colonel.

The fat, mahogany-colored porter, who sat all day in the doorway of the club, dozing in his lobster-shell bath-chair, answered his next inquiry. This ancient relic, who always boasted that no gentleman member of the club, dead or alive, could pass him without being recognized, listened to Oliver's request with a certain lifeless air—a manner always shown to strangers—and shuffled away to the reading-room to find the Colonel.

The occupant of this bath-chair was not only one of the characters of the club but one of the characters of the town. He was a squat, broken-kneed old darky, with white eyebrows arching over big brass spectacles, a flat nose, and two keen, restless monkey eyes. His hands, like those of many negroes of his age, were long and shrivelled, the palms wrinkled as the inside of a turkey's foot and of the same color and texture. His two feet, always in evidence, rested on their heels, and were generally encased in carpet slippers—shoes being out of the question owing to his life-long habit of storing inside his own person the drainings of the decanters, an idiosyncrasy which produced a form of gout that only carpet slippers could alleviate. In his earlier life he had carried General Washington around in his arms, had waited on Henry Clay, and had been body-servant to Lafayette, besides holding the horses of half the generals of the War of 1812—at least, he said so, and no man of his color dared contradict him.

The years of service of this guardian of the front door dated back to the time when the Chippendale furniture of Colonel Ralph Coston, together with many of the portraits covering the walls, and the silver chafing-dishes lining the sideboard, had come into the possession of the club through that gentleman's last will and testament. Coston was the most beloved of all the epicures of his time, and his famous terrapin-stew—one of the marvellous delicacies of the period —had been cooked in these same chafing-dishes. The

101

mahogany-colored Cerberus had been Coston's slave as well as butler, and still belonged to the estate. It was eminently proper, therefore, that he should still maintain his position at the club as long as his feet held out.

While he was gone in search of the Colonel, Oliver occupied himself for a moment in examining one of the old English sporting prints that ornamented the side-walls of the bare, uncarpeted, dismal hall. It was the second time that he had entered these sacred doors —few men of his own age had ever done as much. He had stopped there once before in search of his father, when his mother had been taken suddenly ill. He recalled again the curious spiral staircase at the end of the hall where his father had met him and which had impressed him so at the time. He could see, too, the open closet out of which Mr. Horn had taken his overcoat, and which was now half-filled with hats and coats.

From the desolate, uninviting hall, Oliver passed into the large meeting-room of the club fronting the street, now filled with members, many of whom had dropped in for half an hour on their way back to their offices. Of these some of the older and more sedate men, like Judge Bowman and Mr. Pancoast, were playing chess; others were seated about the small tables, reading, sipping toddies, or chatting together. A few of the younger bloods, men of forty or thereabouts, were standing by the uncurtained windows watching the belles of the town in their flounced dresses and wide leghorn hats, out for an afternoon visit or promenade. Among these men Oliver recognized Howard Thom, son of the Chief-Justice, poor as a church mouse and fifty years of age if a day. Oliver was not surprised to find Thom craning his neck at the window. He remembered the story they told of this perennial beau—of how he had been in love with every woman in and around Kennedy Square, from Miss Clendenning down to the latest débutante, and of how he would tell you over his first toddy that he had sown his wild oats and was about to settle down for life, and over his last—the sixth, or seventh, or eighth—that the most adorable woman in town, after a life devoted to her service, had thrown him over, and that henceforth all that was left to him was a load of buckshot and six feet of earth.

Oliver bowed to those of the members he knew, and wheeling one of the clumsy mahogany chairs into position, sat down to await the arrival of Colonel Clayton.

Meanwhile his eyes wandered over the desolate room with its leather-covered chairs and sofas and big marble mantel bare of every ornament but another moon-faced clock—a duplicate of the one at the bank—and two bronze candelabra flanking each end, and then on the portraits of the dead and gone members which relieved the sombre walls—one in a plum-colored coat with hair tied in a queue being no other than his own ancestor. He wondered to himself where lay the charm and power to attract in a place so colorless, and he thought, as was his habit with all interiors, how different he would want it to be if he ever became a member. His fresh young nature revolted at the dinginess and bareness of the surroundings. He couldn't understand why the men came here and what could be the fascination of sitting round these cold tables talking by the hour when there was so much happiness outside—so much of light and air and sunshine free to everybody.

He was, moreover, a little constrained and uncomfortable. There was none of the welcome of Mr. Crocker's studio about this place, nor any of the comforting companionship of the jolly old cashier, who made the minutes fly as if they had wings; and that, too, in a musty bank far more uninviting even than the club. He remembered his mother's message now—and he remembered her face and the anxious expression—as we always remember duties when we are uncomfortable. He meant to hurry home to her as soon as the Colonel dismissed him, and tell her how it had all happened, and how sorry he was, and what a stupid he had been, and she would forgive him as she had a hundred times before.

A MESSAGE OF IMPORTANCE

As he sat absorbed in these thoughts his attention was attracted by a conversation at the adjoining table between that dare-devil cross-country rider, Tom Gunning of Calvert County, old General McTavish of the Mexican War, and Billy Talbot the exquisite. Gunning was in his corduroys and hunting-boots. He always wore them when he came to town, even when dining with his friends. He had them on now, the boots being specially in evidence, one being hooked over the chair on which he sat and within a foot of Oliver's elbow. None of these peculiarities, however, made the slightest difference in Kennedy Square, so far as Gunning's social position was concerned—Tom's mother having been a Carroll and his grandfather once Governor of the State.

The distinguished cross-country rider was telling General McTavish, immaculate in black wig, blue coat, pepper-and-salt trousers and patent-leather shoes, and red-faced Billy Talbot, of an adventure that he, Gunning, had had the night before while driving home to his plantation. The exquisite's costume was in marked contrast to those of the other two—it was his second change that day. At this precise moment he was upholstered in peg-top, checker-board trousers, bob-tail Piccadilly coat, and a one-inch brim straw hat, all of the latest English pattern. Everything, in fact, that Billy possessed was English, from a rimless monocle decorating his left eye, down to the animated door-mat of a skye-terrier that followed at his heels.

Oliver saw from the way in which McTavish leaned over the table, protecting the tray with his two arms, that he was in command of the decanter, and that the duty of alleviating the thirst of his companions had devolved upon the General. Billy Talbot sat with his hat tipped back on his head, his chin resting on his abbreviated cane, his eyes fixed on Gunning. Both McTavish and Talbot were listening intently to the cross-country rider's story.

"And you say you were sober, Gunning?" Oliver heard the General ask, with a scrutinizing look at Tom. Not with any humorous intent—more with the manner of a presiding officer at a court-martial, determined to establish certain essential facts.

"As a clock, General. The first thing I knew the mare shied and I came pretty near landin' in the dirt." (The lower county men always dropped their g's.) "He was lyin', I tell you, right across the road. If it hadn't been for Kitty, I would have run him down. I got out and held on to the reins, and there he was, sir, stretched out as drunk as a lord, flat on his back and sound asleep. I saw right away that he was a gentleman, and I tied the mare to a tree, picked him up with the greatest care, laid him on the side of the road, put his hat under his head, and made him as comfortable as I could, when, by George, sir! I

106

hadn't any more than got back to my buggy, when bang! went a ball within a foot of my head!"

The General, who, as he listened, had been re-pointing the waxed ends of his dyed mustache with his lemon-colored kid gloves, now leaned back in his chair.

"Fired at you, sir?" The General had served both at Chapultepec and Buena Vista, and was an authority where gunpowder was concerned.

"That's just what he did. Came near takin' the top of my head off! Hadn't been so dark he would have done it."

"Good God! you don't tell me so!" exclaimed the General, mopping his lips with his perfumed handkerchief. "Were you armed, Gunning?"

"No, sir, I was entirely at his mercy and absolutely defenceless. Well, I grabbed the reins to quiet the mare and then I hollered out—'What the devil do you mean, sir, by tryin' to blow the top of my head off?' I could see now that he had raised himself up on his elbow and was lookin' at me in a way I did not like.

"'What do you mean by disturbin' my rest, sir,' he called back.

"'Well, but my dear sir, you were lyin' in the middle of the road and might have been run over.'

"'It's none of your business where I lie,' he hol-

lered back. 'I go to sleep where I damn please, sir.
I consider it a very great liberty.'

"'I beg your pardon, sir,' I said. 'I did not intend any trespass—' I was walkin' toward him now.
I did not want him to shoot again.

"'That's sufficient, sir,' he said. 'No gentleman
can do more. There's my hand, sir. Allow me, sir,
to offer you a drink. If you will roll me over, you
will find my flask in my coat-tail pocket.'

"Well, I rolled him over, took a drink, and then
I brought the mare alongside, helped him in and
drove him home to my house. He was a most delightful gentleman. Didn't leave my place until four
o'clock in the mornin'. He lives about fifteen miles
below me. He told me his name was Toffington. Do
you happen to know him, Talbot?" said Gunning,
turning to Billy.

"Toffington, Toffington," said Billy, dropping his
eye-glasses with a movement of his eyebrows. He
had listened to the story without the slightest comment. "No, Tom, unless he is one of those upper
county men. There was a fellow I met in London
last year—" (Billy pronounced it "larst yarh," to
Oliver's infinite amusement) "with some such name
as that. He and I went over to Kew Gardens with
the Duke of ——."

Gunning instantly turned around with an impatient gesture—nobody ever listened to one of Billy's

A MESSAGE OF IMPORTANCE

London stories, they being the never-ending jokes around Kennedy Square—faced the General again, much to Oliver's regret, who would have loved above all things to hear Billy descant on his English experiences.

"Do you, General, know anybody named Toffington?" asked Tom.

"No, Gunning—but here comes Clayton, he knows everybody in the State that is worth knowing. What you have told me is most extraordinary—most extraordinary, Gunning. It only goes to show how necessary it is for every man to be prepared for emergencies of this kind. You should never go unarmed, sir. You had a very narrow escape—a *very* narrow escape, Gunning. Here, Clayton—come over here."

Oliver pulled his face into long lines. The picture of Gunning taking a drink with a man who a moment before had tried to blow the top of his head off, and the serious way in which the coterie about the table regarded the incident, so excited the boy's risibles that he would have laughed outright had not his eye rested on the Colonel walking toward him.

The Colonel, evidently, did not hear McTavish's call. His mind was occupied with something much more important. He had been finishing a game of whist upstairs, and the mahogany-colored Cerberus had not dared to disturb him until the hand was played out. The fact that young Oliver Horn had

109

called to see him at such an hour and in such a place had greatly disturbed him. He felt sure that something out of the ordinary had happened.

"My dear boy," he cried, as Oliver rose to meet him, "I have this instant heard you were here, or I never should have kept you waiting a moment. Nothing serious—nothing at home?"

"Oh, no, Colonel. Only a word from mother, sir. I missed you at the bank and Mr. Stiger thought that I might better come here," and he delivered his mother's message in a low voice and resumed his seat again.

The Colonel, now that his mind was at rest, dropped into a chair, stroked his goatee with his thumb and forefinger, and ran over in his mind the sum of his engagements.

"Tell your dear mother," he said, "that I will do myself the honor of calling upon her on my way home late this afternoon. Nothing will give me greater pleasure. Now stay awhile with me and let me order something for you, my boy," and he beckoned to one of the brown-coated servants who had entered the room with a fresh tray for the Gunning table.

"No, thank you, Colonel; I ought not to stop," Oliver replied, in an apologetic way, as he rose from his seat. "I really ought to go back and tell mother," and with a grasp of Clayton's hand and a bow to one

or two men in the room who were watching his movements—the Colonel following him to the outer door
—Oliver took himself off, as was the duty of one so
young and so entirely out of place among a collection of men all so knowing and distinguished.

CHAPTER VI

In full justice to the Chesapeake Club the scribe must admit that such light-weights as Billy Talbot, Tom Gunning, and Carter Thom did not fairly represent the standing of the organization. Many of the most cultivated and enlightened men about Kennedy Square and the neighboring country enjoyed its privileges; among them not only such men as Richard Horn, Nathan Gill, the Chief-Justice of the State, and those members of the State Legislature whose birth was above reproach, but most of the sporting gentry of the county, as well as many of the more wealthy planters who lived on the Bay and whose houses were opened to their fellow-members when the ducks were flying.

Each man's lineage, occupation, and opinions on the leading topics of the time were as well known to the club as to the man himself. Any new-comer presenting himself for membership was always subjected to the severest scrutiny, and had to be favorably passed upon by a large majority of the committee before a sufficient number of votes could be secured for his election.

112

AMOS COBB'S ADVICE

The only outsider elected for years had been Amos Cobb, of Vermont, the abolitionist, as he was generally called, who invariably wore black broadcloth, and whose clean-shaven face—a marked contrast to the others—with its restless black eyes, strong nose, and firm mouth, was as sharp and hard as the rocks of his native State. His election to full membership of the Chesapeake Club was not due to his wealth and commercial standing—neither of these would have availed him—but to the fact that he had married a daughter of Judge Wharton of Wharton Hall, and had thus, by reason of his alliance with one of the first families of the State, been admitted to all the social privileges of Kennedy Square. This exception in his favor, however, had never crippled Cobb's independence nor stifled his fearlessness in expressing his views on any one of the leading topics of the day. The Vermonter had worked with his hands when a boy on his father's farm, and believed in the dignity of labor and the blessings of self-support. He believed, too, in the freedom of all men, black and white, and looked upon slavery as a crime. He expressed these sentiments openly and unreservedly, and declared that no matter how long he might live South he would never cease to raise his voice against a system which allowed a man—as he put it—" to sit down in the shade and fan himself to sleep while a lot of niggers whose bodies he owned were sweating in a corn-field to help feed and clothe him."

These sentiments, it must be said, did not add to his popularity, although the time had not yet arrived when he would have been thrown into the street for uttering them.

Nathan Gill was a daily visitor. He was just mounting the club steps, his long pen-wiper cloak about his shoulders, as Oliver, after his interview with Colonel Clayton, passed down the street on his way back to his mother. Nathan shook hands with the Colonel, and the two entered the main room, and seated themselves at one of the tables.

Billy Talbot, who had moved to the window, and who had been watching Oliver until he disappeared around the corner, dropped his eye-glass with that peculiar twitch of the upper lip which no one could have imitated, and crossed the room to where Nathan and Colonel Clayton had taken their seats. Waggles, the scrap of a Skye terrier, who was never three feet from Billy's heels, instantly crossed with him. After Billy had anchored himself and had assumed his customary position, with his feet slightly apart, Waggles, as was his habit, slid in and sat down on his haunches between his master's gaiters. There he lifted his fluffy head and gazed about him. The skill with which Mr. Talbot managed his dog was only equalled by the dexterity with which he managed his eye-glass; he never inadvertently stepped on the one nor unconsciously let slip the other. This caused Mr. Talbot considerable mental strain, but as it was all to which he ever subjected himself he stood the test bravely.

"Who is that young man, Colonel?" Billy began, as he bent his head to be sure that Waggles was in position. He had been abroad while Oliver was growing up, and so did not recognize him.

"That's Richard Horn's son," the Colonel said, without raising his eyes from the paper. The Colonel never took Billy seriously.

"And a fine young fellow he is," broke in Nathan, straightening himself proudly.

"Hope he don't take after his father, Gill. By the way, what's that old wisionary doing now?" drawled Billy, throwing back the lapels of his coat, and slapping his checked trousers with his cane. "Larst time you talked to me about him he had some machine with w'eels and horse-shoe magnets, didn't he? He hasn't been in here for some time, so I know he's at work on some tomfoolery or other. Amazing, isn't it, that a man of his blood, with a cellar of the best Madeiwa in the State, should waste his time on such things. Egad! I cawn't understand it." Some of Billy's expressions, as well as his accent, came in with his clothes. "Now, if I had that Madeiwa, do you know what I'd do with it? I'd——"

"Perfectly, Billy," cried a man at the next table, who was bending over a game of chess. "You'd drink it up in a week." Talbot had never been known by any other name than Billy, and never would be as long as he lived.

When the laugh had subsided, Nathan, whose cheeks were still burning at the slighting way in which Billy Talbot had spoken of Richard, and who had sat hunched up in his chair combing the white hair farther over his ears with his long, spare fingers, a habit with him when he was in deep thought, lifted his head and remarked, quietly, addressing the room rather than Talbot:

"Richard's mind is not on his cellar; he's got something to think of besides Madeira and cards and dogs." And he looked toward Waggles. "You will all, one day, be proud to say that he lived in our town. Richard is a genius, one of the most remarkable men of the day, and everybody outside of this place knows it; you will be compelled to admit it yet. I left him only half an hour ago, and he is just perfecting a motor, gentlemen, which will——"

"Does it go yet, Nathan?" interrupted Cobb, who was filling a glass from a decanter which a brown-coated darky had brought him. Cobb's wife was Nathan's cousin, and, therefore, he had a right to be familiar. "I went to see his machine the other day, but I couldn't make anything out of it. Horn

116

is a little touched here, isn't he?" and he tapped his forehead and smiled knowingly.

"No, Amos, the motor was not running when I left the shop," answered Nathan, dryly and with some dignity, "but it will be, he assured me, perhaps by to-morrow." He could fight Billy Talbot, but he never crossed swords with Cobb, never in late years. Cobb was the one man in all the world, he once told Richard, with whom he had nothing in common.

"Oh, to-morrow?" And Cobb whistled as he put down the decanter and picked up the day's paper. It was one of Cobb's jokes—this "to-morrow" of his neighbors. "What was a Northern man's to-day was always a Southern man's to-morrow," he would say. "I hope this young man of whom you speak so highly is not walking in the footsteps of this genius of a father? He looks to me like a young fellow that had some stuff in him if anybody would bring it out."

The half-concealed sneer in Cobb's voice grated also on old Judge Bowman, who threw down his book and looked up over his bowed spectacles. He was a testy old fellow, with a Burgundy face and shaggy white hair, a chin and nose that met together like a parrot's, and an eye like a hawk. It was one of his principles to permit none of his intimates to speak ill of his friends in his hearing. Criticisms, therefore, by

117

an outsider like Cobb were especially obnoxious to him.

"Richard Horn's head is all right, Mr. Cobb, and so is his heart," he exclaimed in an indignant tone. "As for his genius, sir—Gill is within the mark. He *is* one of the remarkable men of our day. You are quite right, too, about his young son, who has just left here. He has all the qualities that go to make a gentleman, and many of those which will make a jurist. He is now studying law with my associate, Judge Ellicott—a profession ennobled by his ancestors, sir, and one for which what you call his ' stuff,' but which we, sir, call his ' blood,' especially fits him. You Northern men, I know, don't believe in blood. We do down here. This young man comes of a line of ancestors that have reflected great credit on our State for more than a hundred years, and he is bound to make his mark. His grandfather on his mother's side was our Chief Justice in 1810, and his great-grandfather was——"

"That's just what's the matter with most of you Southerners, Judge," interrupted Cobb, his black eyes snapping. " You think more of blood than you do of brains. We rate a man on Northern soil by what he does himself, not what a bundle of bones in some family burying-ground did for him before he was born. Don't you agree with me, Clayton?"

"I can't say I do, Cobb," replied the Colonel,

slowly, stirring his toddy. "I never set foot on your soil but once, and so am unfamiliar with your ways." He never liked Cobb. "He's so cursedly practical, and so proud of it, too," he would often say; "and if you will pardon me, sir—a trifle underbred."

"When was that?" asked Cobb, looking over the top of his paper.

"That was some years ago, when I chased a wounded canvas-back across the Susquehanna River, and had to go ashore to get him; and I want to tell you, sir, that what you call 'your soil' was damned disagreeable muck. I had to change my boots when I got back to my home, and I've never worn them since." And the Colonel crushed the sugar in his glass with his spoon as savagely as if each lump were the head of an enemy, and raised the mixture to his mouth.

Amos's thin lips curled. The high and lofty air of these patricians always exasperated him. The shout of laughter that followed the Colonel's reply brought the color to his cheeks.

"Chased him like a runaway nigger, I suppose, Clayton, didn't you? and wrung his neck when you got him—" retorted Amos, biting his lips.

"Of course, like I would any other piece of my property that tried to get away, or as I would wring the neck of any man who would help him—" And the Colonel looked meaningly at the Vermonter and

119

drained his glass with a gulp. Then smothering his anger, he moved away to the window, where he watched Mr. Talbot, who had just left the club and who at the moment was standing on the corner making his daily afternoon inspection of the two connecting streets; an occupation which Billy varied by saluting each new-comer with a slap of his cane on his checker-board trousers and a stentorian " Bah Jove! " Waggles meanwhile squatting pensively between his gaiters.

When an hour later the Colonel presented himself at the Horn mansion, no trace of this encounter with Cobb was in his face nor in his manner. Men did not air their grievances in their own nor anyone's else home around Kennedy Square.

Mrs. Horn met him with her hand extended. She had been watching for Oliver's return with a degree of impatience rarely seen in her. She had hoped that the Colonel would have called upon her before he went to his office, and could not understand his delay until Oliver had given his account of the morning mishaps. She was too anxious now to chide him. It was but another indication of his temperament, she thought—a fault to be corrected with the others that threatened his success in life.

Holding fast to the Colonel's hand she drew him to one of the old haircloth sofas and told him the whole story.

"Do not give the mortgage a thought, my dear
Sallie," the Colonel said, in his kindest manner,
when she had finished speaking, laying his hand on
her wrist. "My only regret is that it should have
caused you a moment's uneasiness. I know that our
bank has lately been in need of a large sum of
money, and this loan, no doubt, was called in by
the board. But it will be all right—if not I will
provide for it myself."

"No—I do not want that, and Richard, if he
knew, would not be willing either. Tell me, please,
how this money is loaned," and she turned and looked
earnestly into his face. "What papers are passed,
and who signs them? I have never had anything to
do with such matters, and you must explain it all
clearly."

"A note signed by Richard and made payable on
a certain date was given to the bank, and the mortgage was deposited as security."

"And if the note is not paid?"

"Then the property covered by the mortgage is
sold, and the bank deducts its loan—any balance,
of course, is paid over to Richard."

"And when the sale is put off—what is done
then?"

"A new note is given," and here the Colonel
stopped as if in doubt, "and sometimes a second name
is placed on the note increasing the security. But,

Sallie, dear, do not let this part of it ever again cross your mind. I will attend to it should it become necessary. It is not often," and the Colonel waved his hand gallantly, " that a Clayton can do a Horn a service."

" Thank you, dear friend, and it is just like you to wish to do it, but this I cannot agree to. I have thought of another way since you have been talking to me. Would it—" and she stopped and looked down on the floor, " would it be of any use if I signed a note myself? This house we live in is my own, as you know, and would be an additional security to the bank if anything should happen."

The offer was so unusual that the Colonel caught his breath. He looked at her in astonishment, but her eyes never wavered. He felt instantly that, however lightly he might view the subject, the matter was intensely serious with her. The Colonel half rose to his feet, and with a bow that in Kennedy Square had earned for him the title of " the Chesterfield of his time, sir," placed his hand on his heart.

" My dear Sallie," he said, " not a member of the board could refuse. It would at once remove any obstacle the directors might have."

" Thank you, then we will leave it so, and I will have the papers prepared at once."

" And is this Richard's advice? " the Colonel ventured to ask, slowly regaining his seat. There were some misgivings still lingering in his Chesterfieldian mind as to whether the proudest man he knew, gentle as he was, would not forbid the whole transaction.

" No. He does not know of my purpose, and you will please not tell him. He only knows that I am opposed to allowing the property to be sold, and he has promised me that he will take no steps in the matter without my consent. All I want you to do now is to tell him that the bank has decided to let the matter stand. This obligation hereafter will be between me and the board, and I will pledge myself to carry it out. And now, one thing more before you go, and I ask this because you have seen him grow up and I know you love him. What shall I do with Oliver? "

The Colonel again caught his breath. Gallant gentleman of the old school, as he was, with a profound respect for the other sex, the question startled him. According to his experience and traditions, the fathers generally looked after the welfare of the sons and found them places in life—not the mothers.

" What do you want to do with him? " he asked, quietly.

" I want him to go to work. I am afraid this life here will ruin him."

" Why, I thought he was studying law with Ellicott." The announcement could not have been very

123

surprising to the Colonel. He doubtless knew how much time Oliver spent at Judge Ellicott's office.

"He no doubt *thinks* he's studying, dear friend, but he really spends half his time in old Mr. Crocker's studio, who puts the worst possible notions into his head, and the balance of his time he is with your Sue," and she smiled faintly.

"For which you can hardly blame him, dear lady," and the Colonel bent his head graciously.

"No, for she is as sweet as she can be, and you know I love her dearly, but they are both children, and will be for some years. You don't want to support them, do you? and you know Richard can't," and there flashed out from her eyes one of those quizzical glances which the Colonel remembered so well in her girlhood.

The Colonel nodded his head, but he did not commit himself. He had never for a moment imagined that Oliver's love-affair would go as far as that, and, then again, he knew Sue.

"What do you suggest doing with him? I will help, of course, in any way I can," he said, after a pause, during which Mrs. Horn sat watching every expression that crossed his face.

"I don't know. I have not fully made up my mind. I have been greatly disturbed over Oliver. He seems to be passing through one of those dangerous crises which often come to a boy. What do you think of my sending him to New York?"

"*The North*, Sallie! Why, you wouldn't send Oliver up North, would you?"

The announcement this time gave the Colonel so genuine a shock that it sent the blood tingling to his cheeks. Really, the idiosyncrasies of the Horn family were beyond his comprehension! Evidently Richard's vagaries had permeated his household.

"I do not like the influence of the North on our young men, my dear Madam." The Colonel spoke now with great seriousness and with some formality, and without any of the Chesterfieldian accompaniments of tone or gesture. "If he were my boy, I should keep him here. He is young and light-hearted, I know, and loves pleasure, but that will all come out of him. Let him stay with Ellicott; he will bring him out all right. There is a brusqueness and a want of refinement among most Northern men that have always grated on me. You can see it any day in Amos Cobb."

As he spoke a slight flush overspread his listener's face. The positiveness of his tone, she thought, carried with it a certain uncomplimentary criticism of her suggestion. The Colonel saw it, and, as if in apology and to prove his case, added, in a gentler tone: "Only this afternoon at the club I heard

125

Cobb speaking in the most outrageous manner about our most treasured institutions. It is not his fault perhaps. It is the fault of his breeding, but it is unbearable all the same. Keep Oliver here. He has a most engaging and lovable nature, is as clean and sweet as a girl, and I haven't a doubt but what he will honor both you and his blood. Take my word for it, and keep him at home. He is young yet, barely twenty-two—there is plenty of time for him." And the Colonel rose from the sofa, lifted Mrs. Horn's fingers to his lips and bowed himself out.

The Colonel only told the truth, as he saw it. In his day and generation men of twenty-two were but boys, and only gray-beards ruled the State and counting-house. The Senators were indeed grave and reverend seigniors, and the merchants, in their old-fashioned dress-coats, looked more like distinguished diplomats than buyers and sellers of produce. In those days, too, the young man with a mustache was thought presuming and dangerous, and the bank who would have selected a cashier under forty would have caused a run on its funds in a week after the youth had been appointed to his position.

After the Colonel's departure Mrs. Horn sat in deep thought. The critical tones of his voice still lingered in her memory. But her judgment had not been shaken nor was her mind satisfied. Oliver still

126

troubled her. The Colonel's advice might be **right,** but she dared not rely upon it.

The next day she sent for Amos Cobb: Malachi took the message this time, not Oliver. Cobb came on the minute. He was greatly surprised at Mrs. Horn's note, for although his wife was an intimate friend of Mrs. Horn's, and he himself would have been welcome, he was seldom present at any of the functions of the house and could not be considered one of its intimate guests. He did not like music, he said to his wife, when urged to go, and, as he did not play chess or drink Madeira, he preferred to stay at home.

Malachi relieved Amos of his hat, and conducted him into Mrs. Horn's presence with rather a formal bow—quite different from the low salaam with which he had greeted Colonel Clayton. " Dat bobobalish'-nest, Mister Cobb, jes' gone in de parlor," he said to Aunt Hannah when he regained the kitchen. " Looks like he lived on parsimmons, he dat sour."

Mrs. Horn received her visitor cordially, but with a reserve which she had not maintained toward the Colonel, for Cobb had never represented to her anything but a money standard pure and simple. It was only when the Colonel had mentioned his name, and then only because of her urgent need of just such sound practical advice as she knew he could give that she had determined to seek his services—quite

127

as she would have consulted an architect or an attorney.

The Vermonter took his seat on the extreme edge of the sofa, squared his shoulders, pulled up the points of his high collar, touched together the tips of all his fingers, and looked straight at his hostess.

" I am greatly obliged to you for coming," she began, " for I know how busy you are, but I have a question to ask of you which I feel sure you can answer better than anyone I know. It is about my son Oliver. I am going to be perfectly frank with you, and I want you to be equally frank with me." And she summed up Oliver's aims, temptations, and failings with a skill that gained the Vermonter's closest attention. " With all this," she continued, " he is affectionate, loves me dearly, and has never disobeyed me in his life. It is his love of change that worries me—his instability—one thing one moment, and another the next. It seems to me the only way to break this up is to throw him completely on his own resources so that he may realize for once what life really means. Now tell me—" and she looked searchingly into Cobb's face, as if eager to note the effect of her question—" if he were your only son, would you, in view of all I have told you, send him to New York to make his start in life, or would you keep him here? "

The Vermonter's face had begun to lighten as she

progressed, and had entirely cleared when he learned why he had been sent for. He had been afraid, when he received her note, that it had been about the mortgage. Cobb was chairman of the Loan Committee at the bank, had personally called attention to Richard's note being overdue, and had himself ordered its payment.

"My two boys are at school in Vermont, Madam," he answered, slowly.

"But Oliver must earn his own living," she said, earnestly. "His father will have nothing to give him."

Cobb made no reply. He was not surprised. Most all of these aristocratic Southerners were on their last legs. He was right about the note, he said to himself—it was just as well to have it paid—and he made a mental memorandum to inquire about it as soon as he reached his office, and have it pressed for settlement at once. Business matters must be kept intact.

"What do you want him to do, Madam?" he asked, looking at her keenly from under his bushy eyebrows.

"Anything to earn his bread," she replied, in a decided tone.

Cobb passed his hand over his face, pinched his chin with his thumb and forefinger, and looked out of the window. The answer pleased him. It pleased him, too, to be consulted by the Horns on a matter of this kind. It pleased him most of all to realize that when these aristocrats who differed with him politically got into a financial hole they had to send for him to help pull them out.

For a moment the Vermonter remained in deep thought. "Here is a Southern woman," he said to himself, "with some common-sense and with a head on her shoulders. If her husband had half her brains I'd let the mortgage stand." Then he turned and faced her squarely, his eyes boring into hers.

"Send him to New York, by all means, Madam, or anywhere else out of here," he said, firmly, but with a kindly tone in his voice. "When you decide, let me know—I will give him a letter to a business friend of mine who lives on the Hudson, a short distance above the city, who may help him. But let me advise you to send him at once. I saw your son yesterday at the club, and he exactly fits your measure, except in one respect. He's got more grit in him than you give him credit for. I looked him over pretty carefully, and if he gets in a tight place you needn't worry about him. He'll pull out, or my name isn't Cobb. And now one thing more—" and he rose stiffly from the sofa and buttoned up his coat— "don't give him any pocket-money. Chuck him out neck and heels into the world and let him shift for himself. That's the way I was treated, and that's the way I got on. Good-day."

CHAPTER VII

A SEAT IN UNION SQUARE

Within a day's journey of Kennedy Square lay another wide breathing-space, its winding paths worn smooth by countless hurrying feet.

Over its flat monotony straggled a line of gnarled willows, marking the wanderings of some guileless brook long since swallowed up and lost in the mazes of the great city like many another young life fresh from green fields and sunny hill-sides. This desert of weeds and sun-dried, yellow grass, this kraal for scraggly trees and broken benches, breasted the rush of the great city as a stone breasts a stream, dividing its current—one part swirling around and up Broadway to the hills and the other flowing eastward toward Harlem and the Sound. Around its four sides, fronting the four streets that hemmed it in, ran a massive iron railing, socketed in stone and made man-proof and dog-proof by four great iron gates. These gates were opened at dawn to let the restless in, and closed at night to keep the weary out.

Above these barriers of stone and iron no joyous magnolias lifted their creamy blossoms; no shy

131

climbing roses played hide-and-seek, blushing scarlet when caught. Along its foot-worn paths no drowsy Moses ceased his droning call; no lovers walked forgetful of the world; no staid old gentlemen wandered idly, their noses in their books.

All day long on its rude straight-backed benches and over its thread-bare turf sprawled unkempt women with sick babies from the shanties; squalid, noisy children from the rookeries; beggars in rags, and now and then some hopeless wayfarer—who for the moment had given up his search for work or bread and who rested or slept until the tap of a constable's club brought him to consciousness and his feet.

At night, before the gates were closed—ten o'clock was the hour—there could always be found, under its dim lamps, some tired girl, sitting in the light for better protection while she rested, or some weary laborer on the way home from his long day's work, and always passing to and fro, swinging his staff, bullying the street-rats who were playing tag among the trees, and inspiring a wholesome awe among those hiding in the shadows, lounged some guardian of the peace awaiting the hour when he could drive the inmates to the sidewalk, and shut the gates behind them with a bang.

Here on one of these same straight-backed wooden seats one September night—a night when the air was heavy with a blurred haze, through which the lamps peered as in a fog, and the dust lay thick upon the leaves—sat our Oliver.

Outside the square—all about the iron fence, and surging past the big equestrian statue, could be heard the roar and din of the great city—that maelstrom which now seemed ready to engulf him. No sound of merry laughter reached him, only rumbling of countless wheels, the slow thud of never-ending, crowded stages lumbering over the cobbles, the cries of the hucksters selling hot corn, and the ceaseless scrapings of a thousand feet.

He had sat here since the sun had gone down watching the crowds, wondering how they lived and how they had earned their freedom from such cares as were now oppressing him. His heart was heavy. A long-coveted berth, meaning self-support and independence and consequent relief to his mother's heart, had been almost within his grasp. It was not the place he had expected when he left home. It was much more menial and unremunerative. But he had outlived all his bright hopes. He was ready now to take anything he could get to save him from returning to Kennedy Square, or what would be still worse —from asking his mother for a penny more than she had given him. Rather than do this he would sweep the streets.

As he leaned forward on the bench, his face in his hands, his elbows on his knees, his thoughts went back to his father's house. He knew what they were all doing at this hour; he could see the porches crowded with the boys and girls he loved, their bright voices filling the night-air, Sue in the midst of them, her curls about her face. He could see his father in the big chair reading by the lamp, that dear old father who had held his hands so tenderly and spoken with such earnestness the day before he had left Kennedy Square.

"Your mother is right," Richard had said. "I am glad you are going, my son; the men at the North are broader-minded than we are here, and you will soon find your place among them. Great things are ahead of us, my boy. I shall not live to see them, but you will."

He could see his mother, too, sitting by the window, looking out upon the trees. He knew where her thoughts lay. As his mind rested on her pale face his eyes filled with tears. "Dear old mother," he said to himself—"I am not forgetting, dearie. I am holding on. But oh, if I had only got the place to-day, how happy you would be to-morrow."

A bitter feeling had risen in his heart, when he had opened the letter which had brought him the news of the loss of this hoped-for situation. "This is making one's way in the world, is it?" he had said to himself with a heavy sigh. Then the calm eyes of his mother had looked into his again, and he had felt the pressure of the soft hand and heard the tones of her voice:

"You may have many discouragements, my son, and will often be ready to faint by the way, but stick to it and you will win."

His bitterness had been but momentary, and he had soon pulled himself together, but his every resource seemed exhausted now. He had counted so on the situation—that of a shipping-clerk in a dry-goods store—promised him because of a letter that he carried from Amos Cobb's friend. But at the last moment the former clerk, who had been laid off because of sickness, had been taken back, and so the weary search for work must begin again.

And yet with everything against him Oliver had no thought of giving up the struggle. Even Amos Cobb would have been proud of him could he have seen the dogged tenacity with which he clung to his purpose—a tenacity due to his buoyant, happy temperament, or to his devotion to his mother's wishes; or (and this is more than probable) to some drops of blood, perhaps, that had reached his own through his mother's veins—the blood of that Major with the blue and buff coat, whose portrait hung in the dining-room at home, and who in the early days had braved the flood at Trenton side by side with the Hero of the Bronze Horse now overlooking the bench on which Oliver sat; or it may be of that other

135

ancestor in the queue whose portrait hung over the mantel of the club and who had served his State with distinction in his day.

Whatever the causes of these several effects, the one dominating power which now controlled him was his veneration for his mother's name and honor. For on the night succeeding Amos Cobb's visit after she had dropped upon her knees and poured out her heart in prayer she had gone into Oliver's bedroom, and shutting the door had told him of the mortgage; of his father's embarrassment, and the danger they suffered of losing the farm — their only hope for their old age — unless success crowned Richard's inventions. With his hand fast in hers she had given him in exact detail all that she had done to ward off this calamity; recounting, word by word, what she had said to the Colonel, lowering her voice almost to a whisper as she spoke of the solemn promise she had made him—involving her own and her husband's honor—and the lengths to which she was prepared to go to keep her obligations to the bank.

Then, her hand still clasping his, the two sitting side by side on his bed, his wondering, startled eyes looking into hers—for this world of anxiety was an unknown world to him—she had by slow stages made him realize how necessary it was that he, their only son, and their sole dependence, should begin at once

136

to earn his daily bread; not only on his own account but on hers and his father's. In her tenderness she had not told him that the real reason was his instability of purpose; fearing to wound his pride, she had put it solely on the ground of his settling down to some work.

"It is the law of nature, my son," she had added. "Everything that lives must *work* to live. You have only to watch the birds out here in the Square to convince you of that. Notice them to-morrow, when you go out. See how busy they are; see how long it takes for any one of them to get a meal. You are old enough now to begin to earn your own bread, and you must begin at once, Ollie. Your father can no longer help you. I had hoped your profession would do this for you, but that is not to be thought of now."

Oliver, at first, had been stunned by it all. He had never before given the practical side of life a single thought. Everything had gone along smoothly from his earliest remembrance. His father's house had been his home and his protection; his room with its little bed and pretty hangings and all its comforts —a room cared for like a girl's—had always been open to him. He had never once asked himself how these things came about, nor why they continued. These revelations of his mother's therefore were like the sudden opening of a door covering a vault over which he had walked unconsciously and which now, for the first time, he saw yawning beneath him.

"Poor daddy," were his first words. "I never knew a thing about his troubles; he seems always so happy and so gentle. I am so sorry—dear daddy— dear dad—" he kept repeating.

And then as she spoke there flashed into his mind the thought of his own hopes. They were shattered now. He knew that the art career was dead for him, and that all his dreams in that direction were over.

He was about to tell her this, but he stopped before the words were formed. He would not add his own burden to her sorrow. No, he would bear it alone. He would tell Sue, but he would not tell his mother. Next there welled up in his heart a desire to help this mother whom he idolized, and this father who represented to him all that was kind and true.

"What can I do? Where can I go, dearie?" he cried with sudden resolve. "Even if I am to work with my hands I am ready to do it, but it must be away from here. I could not do it here at home with everybody looking on; no, not here! not here!"

This victory gained, the mother with infinite tact, little by little, unfolded to the son the things she had planned. Finally with her arms about his neck, smoothing his cheek with her hands she told him of Amos Cobb's advice and of his offer, adding:

138

" He will give you a letter to his friend who lives at Haverstraw near New York, my boy, with whom you can stay until you get the situation you want."

The very impracticability of this scheme did not weigh with her. She did not see how almost hopeless would be the task of finding employment in an unknown city. Nor did the length of time her son might be a burden on a total stranger make any difference in her plans. Her own home had always been open to the friends of her friends, and for any length of time, and her inborn sense of hospitality made it impossible for her to understand any other conditions. Then again she said to herself: " Mr. Cobb is a thoroughly practical man, and a very kind one. His friend will welcome Oliver, or he would not have allowed my son to go." She had repeated, however, no word of the Vermonter's advice " to chuck the boy out neck and heels into the world and let him shift for himself," although the very Spartan quality of the suggestion, in spite of its brusqueness, had greatly pleased her. She could not but recognize that Amos understood. She would have faced the situation herself if she had been in her son's place; she said so to herself. And she hoped, too, that Oliver would face it as bravely when the time came.

As for the temptations that might assail her boy

in the great city, she never gave them a thought. Neither the love of drink nor the love of play ran in her own or Richard's veins—not for generations back. " One test of a gentleman, my son," Richard always said, " lies in the way in which he controls his appetites—in the way he regards his meat and drink. Both are foods for the mind as well as for the body, and must be used as such. Gluttons and drunkards should be classed together." No, her boy's heart might lead him astray, but not his appetites, and never his passions. She was as sure of that as she was of his love.

As she talked on, Oliver's mind, yielding to her stronger will as clay does to a sculptor's hand, began to take shape. What at first had looked like a hardship now began to have an attractive side. Perhaps the art career need not be wholly given up. Perhaps, too, there was a better field for him in New York than here—old Mr. Crocker had always told him this. Then, too, there was something of fascination after all, in going out alone like a knight-errant to conquer the world. And in that great Northern city, too, with its rush and whirl and all that it held for him of mystery! How many times had Mr. Crocker talked to him by the hour of its delights. And Ellicott's chair! Yes, he could get rid of that. And Sue? Sue would wait—she had promised him she would; no, there was no doubt about Sue! She

140

would love him all the better if he fought his battle alone. Only the day before she had told him of the wonderful feats of the White Knight, that the new English poet had just written about and that everybody in Kennedy Square was now reading.

Above all there was the delight of another sensation—the sensation of a new move. This really pleased him best. He was apparently listening to his mother when these thoughts took possession of him, for his eyes were still fixed on hers, but he heard only a word now and then. It was his imagination that swayed him now, not his will nor his judgment. He would have his own adventures in the great city and see the world as Mr. Crocker had done, he said to himself.

"Yes, dearie, I'll go," he answered quickly. "Don't talk any more about it. I'll do just as you want me to, and I'll go anywhere you say. But about the money for my expenses? Can father give it to me?" he asked suddenly, a shade of anxiety crossing his face.

"We won't ask your father, Ollie," she said, drawing him closer to her. She knew he would yield to her wishes, and she loved him the better for it, if that were possible. "I have a little money saved which I will give you. You won't be long finding a good place."

"And how often can I come back to you?" he

cried, starting up. Until now this phase of the situation had not entered his mind.

"Not often, my boy—certainly not until you can afford it. It is costly travelling. Maybe once or twice a year."

"Oh, then there's no use talking, I can't go. I can't—can't, be away from you that long. That's going to be the hardest part." He had started from his seat and stood over her, a look of determination on his face.

"Oh, yes, you can, my son, and you will," she replied, as she too rose and stood beside him, stopping the outburst of his weakness with her calm voice, and quieting and soothing him with the soft touch of her hand, caressing his cheek with her fingers as she had so often done when he, a baby, had lain upon her breast.

Then with a smile on her face, she had kissed him good-night, closed the door, and staggering along the corridor steadying herself as she walked, her hand on the walls, had thrown herself upon her bed in an agony of tears, crying out:

"Oh, my boy—my boy! How can I give you up? And I know it is forever!"

And now here he is foot-sore and heart-sore, sitting in Union Square, New York, the roar of the great city in his ears, and here he must sit until the cattle-barge which takes him every night to the house of Amos Cobb's friend is ready to start on her voyage up the river.

He sat with his head in his hands, his elbows on his knees, not stirring until a jar on the other end of the bench roused him. A negro hod-carrier, splashed with plaster, and wearing a ragged shirt and a crownless straw hat, had taken a seat beside him. The familiarity of the act startled Oliver. No negro wayfarer would have dared so much in his own Square at home.

The man reached forward and drew closer to his own end of the bench a bundle of sawed ends and bits of wood which he had carried across the park on his shoulder.

Oliver watched him for a moment, with a feeling amounting almost to indignation. "Were the poverty and the struggle of a great city to force such familiarities upon him," he wondered. Then something in the negro's face, as he wiped the perspiration from his forehead with the back of his hand, produced a sudden change of feeling. "Was this man, too, without work?" Oliver asked himself, as he felt the negro's weariness, and realized for the first time, the common heritage of all men.

"Are you tired, Uncle?" he asked.

"Yes, a little mite. I been a-totin' dis kindlin' from way up yander in Twenty-third Street where the circus useter be. Dey's buildin' a big hotel dere uow—de Fifth Avenue dey calls it. I'm a-carryin' mortar for de brick-layers an' somehow dese sticks is monst'ous heavy after workin' all day."

"Where do you live?" asked Oliver, his eyes on the kindling-wood.

"Not far from here, sah; little way dis side de Bow'ry. Whar's yo'r home?" And the old man rose to his feet and picked up his bundle.

The question staggered Oliver. He had no home, really none that he could call his own—not now.

"Oh, a long way from here," he answered, thoughtfully, without raising his head, his voice choking.

The old negro gazed at him for a moment, touched his hat respectfully, and walked toward the gate. At the entrance he wheeled about, balanced the bundle of wood on his shoulder and looked back at Oliver, who had resumed his old position, his eyes on the ground. Then he walked away, muttering:

"'Pears like he's one o' my own people calling me uncle. Spec' he ain't been long from his mammy."

Two street-rats now sneaked up toward Oliver, watched him for a moment, and whispered to each other. One threw a stone which grazed Oliver's head, the other put his hand to his mouth and yelled: "Spad, spad," at the top of his voice. Oliver understood the epithet, it meant that he wore clean linen, polished shoes, and perhaps, now and then, a pair of gloves. He had heard the same outcry in his own city, for the slang of the street-rat is Volapük the world over. But he did not resent the assault. He was too tired to chase any boys, and too despondent to answer their taunts.

A constable, attracted by the cries of the boys, now passed in front of him swinging his long staff. He was about to tap Oliver's knees with one end of it, as a gentle reminder that he had better move on, when something in the young man's face or appearance made him change his mind.

" Hi, sonny," he cried, turning quickly and facing Oliver, " yer can't bum round here after ten, ye know. Keep yer eyes peeled for them gates, d'ye hear? "

If Oliver heard he made no reply. He was in no mood to dispute the officer's right to order him about. The gates were not the only openings shut in his face, he thought to himself; everything seemed closed against him in this great city. It was not so at home on Kennedy Square. Its fence, was a shackly, moss-covered, sagging old fence, intertwined with honeysuckles, full of holes and minus many a paling; where he could have found a dozen places to crawl through. He had done so only a few weeks before with Sue in a mad frolic across the Square. Besides, why should the constable speak to him at all? He knew all about the hour of closing the

145

New York gates without the policeman reminding
him of it. Had he not sat here every night waiting
for that cattle-boat? He hated the place cordially,
yet it was the only spot in that great city to which
he could come and not be molested while he waited
for the barges. He always selected this particular
bench because it was nearest the gate that led to the
bronze horse. He loved to look at its noble con-
tour silhouetted against the sky or illumined by the
street-lamps, and was seldom too tired to be inspired
by it. He had never seen any work in sculpture to
be compared to it, and for the first few days after
his arrival, he was never content to end the day's
tramping until he stood beneath it, following its outlines, his heart swelling with pride at the thought
that one of his own nationality and not a Euro-
pean had created it. He wished that his father, who
believed so in the talent of his countrymen, could
see it.

Suddenly, while he was still resenting the familiarity of the constable, his ears were assailed by the
cry of a dog in pain; some street-rat had kicked him.

Instantly Oliver was on his feet. A small spaniel
was running toward him, followed by half a dozen
boys who were pelting him with stones.

Oliver sprang forward as the dog crouched at his
feet; caught him up in his arms and started for the
rats, who dodged behind the tree-trunks, calling

"Spad, spad," as they ran. Then came the voice of the same constable.

"Hi, yer can't bring that dog in here."

"He's not my dog, somebody has hurt him," said Oliver in an indifferent tone, examining carefully the dog's legs to see if any bones were broken.

"If that ain't your dog what yer doin' with him? See here, I been a-watchin' ye. Yer got ter move on or I'll run ye in. D'ye moind?"

Oliver's eyes flashed. In all his life no man had ever doubted his word, nor had anyone ever spoken to him in such terms.

"You can do as you please, but I will take care of this dog, no matter what happens. You ought to be ashamed of yourself to see him hurt, and not want to protect him. You're a pretty kind of an officer."

A crowd began to gather.

Oliver was standing with the dog under one arm, holding the little fellow close to his breast, the other bent with fist tight shut as if to defend himself.

"I am, am I? yer moon-faced spad! I'll show ye," and he sprang toward Oliver.

"Here now, Tim Murphy," came a sharp voice, "kape yer hands off the young gintleman. He ain't a-doin' nothin', and he ain't done nothin'. Thim divils hit the dog, I seen 'em myself."

The officer turned quickly and faced a big, broad-shouldered Irish woman, bare-headed, her sleeves

147

rolled up to her elbows, every line in her kindly face
replete with indignation.

"Don't put yer hands on him, or I'll go to the
lock-up an' tell McManus."

"Oh, it's you, is it, Mrs. Mulligan?" said the
officer, in a conciliatory tone.

"Yes, it's me. The young gintleman's right. It's
the b'ys ye oughter club into shape, not be foolin'
yer time over the dog."

"Well, ye know it's agin the rules to let dogs inside the gates," he retorted as he continued his stroll
along the walk, swinging his club as he went, puffing
out his chest and cheeks with his old air as he moved
toward the gate.

"Yes, an' so it's agin the rules," she called after
him, "to have them rapscallions yellin' like mad an'
howlin' bloody murder when a body comes up here
to git a breath o' air."

"Is the dog hurt, sir?" and she stepped close to
Oliver and laid her big hand on the dog's head, as
it lay nestling close to Oliver's side.

"No, I don't think so—he would have been if I
had not got him."

The dog, under the caress, raised his head, and a
slight movement of his tail expressed his pleasure.
Then his ears shot forward. A young man about
Oliver's own age was rapidly walking up the path,
with a quick, springy step, whistling as he came. The

dog, with a sudden movement, squirmed himself from under Oliver's arm and sprang toward him.

"Oh, it's you, Mr. Fred, is it?" broke out the woman, "and it's Miss Margaret's dog, too. Of course it's her dog, an' I was that dumb I didn't know it. But it's not me ye can thank for savin' its skin —it's the young gintleman here. Them divils would have killed it but for him."

"Is the dog yours, sir?" asked Oliver, raising his hat with that peculiar manner of his which always won him friends at first sight.

"No, I wish it were. It's Miss Margaret Grant's dog—one of our students. I am taking care of it while she is away. The little rascal ran out and got into the Square before I knew it. I live right across the street—you can see my house from here. Miss Grant will be ever so much obliged to you for protecting him."

"Oh, don't mention it. I got hold of him just in time, or these ruffians would have hurt him. I think the old lady here, however, is most to be thanked. We might both have been locked up," he added, smiling, "if she had not interfered. You know her, it seems."

"Yes, she's Mother Mulligan, as we call her. She's janitress of the Academy of Design, where I draw at night. My name's Fred Stone. Come over to where I live—it's only a step," and he looked straight into Oliver's face, his big blue eyes never wavering.

"Well, I will if you don't think it's too late," and the two young fellows, with a wave of their hands to the old woman, left the Square, the dog bounding before them.

Within the hour—in less time indeed, for the friendly light in the eyes of his new-found friend had shone straight into our boy's soul, warming and cheering him to his finger-tips, opening his heart, and bringing out all his secrets—Oliver had told Fred the story of his fruitless tramps for work; of his mother's hopes and fears; of his own ambitions and his aims. And Fred, his own heart wide open, had told Oliver with equal frankness the story of his own struggles; of his leaving his father's farm in the western part of the State, and of his giving up everything to come to New York to study art.

It was the old, old story of two chance acquaintances made friends by reason of the common ground of struggle and privation on which they stood; comrades fighting side by side in the same trenches for the same end, and both dreaming of the morrow which would always bring victory and never death. A story told without reserve, for the disappointments of life had not yet dulled their enthusiasm, nor had the caution acquired by its many bitter experiences yet checked the free flow of their confidences.

A SEAT IN UNION SQUARE

To Oliver, in his present despondent mood, the hand held out to him was more than the hand of a comrade. It was the hand of a strong swimmer thrust into the sea to save a drowning man. There were others then besides himself, he thought, as he grasped it, who were making this fight for bread and glory; there was something else in the great city besides cruelty and misery, money-getting and money-spending—something of unselfishness, sympathy and love.

The two sat on the steps of Fred's boarding-house —that house where Oliver was to spend so many happy days of his after-life—until there was only time enough to catch the barge. Reluctantly he bade his new-found comrade good-by and, waving his hand, turned the corner in the direction of the dock.

The edge of Oliver's cloud had at last caught the light!

CHAPTER VIII

Not only had the sunshine of a new friendship illumined the edge of Oliver's clouds, but before the week was out a big breeze laden with success had swept them so far out to sea, that none but the clearest of skies radiant with hope now arched above his happy face.

A paste-board sign had wrought this miracle.

One day he had been tramping the lower parts of the city, down among the docks, near Coenties Slip, looking up the people who on former visits had said: " Some other time, perhaps," or " If we should have room for another man we will be glad to remember you," or " We know Mr. Cobb, and shall be pleased," etc., etc., when he chanced to espy a strange sign tacked outside a warehouse door, a sign which bore the unheard-of-announcement—unheard of to Oliver, especially the last word, " SHIPPING CLERK WANTED."

No one, for weeks, had *wanted* anything that Oliver could furnish. Strangely enough too, as he afterward discovered, the bullet-headed Dutch porter had

152

driven the last tack into the clean, white, welcome face of the sign only five minutes before Oliver stopped in front of it. Still more out of the common, and still more incomprehensible, was the reply made to him by the head salesman, whom he found just inside the door—a wiry, restless little man with two keen black eyes, and a perfectly bald head.

" Yes, if you can mark boxes decently; can show any references; don't want too much pay, and can come *now*. We're short of a boy, and it's our busy season."

Oh! blessed be Mr. Crocker, thought Oliver, as he picked up a marking-brush, stirred it round and round in the tin pot filled with lamp-black and turpentine, and to his own and the clerk's delight, painted, on a clean board, rapidly and clearly, and in new letters too—new to the clerk—the full address of the bald-headed man's employers:

MORTON, SLADE & CO.,
121 Pearl Street, New York.

More amazing still were the announcements made by the same bald-headed man after Oliver had shown him Amos Cobb's recommendations: Oliver was to come to work in the morning, the situation to be permanent provided Cobb confirmed by letter the good wishes he had previously expressed, and provided

153

Mr. Morton, the senior partner, approved of the bald-head's action; of which the animated billiard-ball said there was not the slightest doubt as he, the ball, had charge of the shipping department, and was re-sponsible for its efficiency.

All of these astounding, incomprehensible and amazing occurrences Oliver had written to his mother, ending his letter by declaring in his enthusi-asm that it was his art, after all, which had pulled him through, and that but for his readiness with the brush, he would still be a tramp, instead of " rolling in luxury on the huge sum of eight dollars a week, with every probability of becoming a partner in the house, and later on a millionnaire." To which the dear lady had replied, that she was delighted to know he had pleased his employers, but that what had pleased her most was his never having lost heart while trying to win his first fight, adding: " The second victory will come more easily, my darling boy, and so will each one hereafter." Poor lady, she never knew how sore that boy's feet had been, nor how many times he had gone with half a meal or none at all, for fear of depleting too much the small store she had given him when he left home.

With his success still upon him, he had sallied forth to call upon young Fred Stone who had grasped his hand so warmly the night he had rescued the dog from the street-boys, and whose sympathy had gone

154

out to him so freely. He had written him of his good fortune, and Fred had replied, begging him to call upon him, and had appointed this same Friday night as the night of all others when he could entertain him best.

But Oliver is not the same boy who said good-by to Fred that moonlight night the week before. His eyes are brighter; his face is a-glow with ill-concealed pleasure. Even his step shows the old-time spring and lightness of the days at home—on his toes part of the time, as if restraining an almost uncontrollable impulse to stop and throw one or two handsprings just to relieve the pressure on his nerves.

When he reached the bench in the Square where he had sat so many nights with his head in his hands, one of those quick outbursts of enthusiasm took possession of him, the kind that sets young hearts singing with joy when some sudden shift of hope's kaleidoscope opens a wide horizon brilliant with the light of future success. With an exclamation of boyish glee he plumped himself down upon the hard planks of the bench, and jumped up again, pirouetting on his toe and slanting his hat over one eye as if in a spirit of sheer bravado against fate. Then he sauntered out of the iron gate to Fred's house.

Even as he waited on the stone steps of Miss Teetum's boarding-house for the dowdy servant-girl's return—such dirty, unkempt steps as they were, and such a dingy door-plate, spotted with rain and dust, not like Malachi's, he thought—he could hardly restrain himself from beating Juba with his foot, a plantation trick Malachi had taught him, keeping time the while with the palms of his hands on his shapely legs.

Meanwhile another young enthusiast is coming downstairs three steps at a time, this one bareheaded, all out of breath, and without a coat, who pours out his heart to the first Juba-beating enthusiast as the two climb the stairs together to the second enthusiast's room on the very top floor. He tells him of his delight at seeing him again and of the lot of fellows waiting to welcome him under the skylight; and of what a jolly lot the " Skylarkers " really are; and of Mr. Slade, Oliver's employer, whom Fred knows and who comes from Fred's own town; and of how much Mr. Slade likes a certain new clerk, one Oliver Horn, of Kennedy Square, he having said so the night before, this same Horn being the precise individual whose arm at that very moment was locked in Fred's own and which was now getting an extra squeeze merely for the purposes of identification.

All of this Fred poured into Oliver's willing ear without stopping to take breath, as they mounted the four long flights of stairs that led to the top floor, where, under the roof, there lived a group of

Bohemians as unique in their personalities as could be found the great city over.

When the two pairs of feet had at last reached the last flight of steps under the flat roof of the house, the "Skylarkers" were singing "Old Dog Tray" at the top of their voices, to the accompaniment of a piano, and of some other instruments, the character of which our young hero failed to recognize, although the strains had grown louder and louder as the young men mounted the stairs.

As Oliver stood in the open doorway and looked in through the haze of tobacco-smoke upon the group, he instantly became conscious that a new world had opened before him; a world, as he had always pictured it, full of mystery and charm, peopled by a race as fascinating to him as any Mr. Crocker had ever described, and as new and strange as if its members had been the denizens of another planet.

The interior was not a room, but a square low-ceiled hall into which opened some six or more small bedrooms, slept in, whenever sleep was possible, by an equal number of Miss Teetum's boarders. The construction and appointments of this open garret, with two exceptions, were similar to those of all other garrets of its class: it had walls and ceiling, once whitewashed, and now discolored by roof-leaks from a weather-beaten skylight; its floor was bare of carpet, and its well-worn woodwork was stained with time and use. Chairs, however, were scarce, most of the boarders and their guests being seated on the floor.

The two exceptions, already noted, were some crisp, telling sketches, big and little, in color and black-and-white, the work of the artist members of this coterie, which covered every square inch of the leak-stained surface of ceiling and wall, and the yellow-keyed, battered piano which occupied the centre of the open space and which stood immediately under two flaring gas-jets. At the moment of Fred's and Oliver's arrival the top of this instrument was ornamented by two musically inclined gentlemen, one seated cross-legged like a Turk, voicing the misfortunes of Dog Tray, the other, with his legs resting on a chair, beating time to the melody with a cane. This cane, at short intervals, he brought down upon the shoulders of any ambitious member who attempted to usurp his place. The chief object of the gathering, so far as Oliver's hasty glance could determine, was undoubtedly the making of as much noise as possible.

While the young men stood looking into the room waiting for the song to cease prior to Oliver's entry and introduction, Fred whispered hurriedly into his guest's ear some of the names, occupations, and characteristics of the group before him.

The cross-legged man with the long neck, drooping mustache, and ropy black hair, was none other

158

than Bowdoin, the artist—the only American who had taken a medal at Munich for landscape, but who was now painting portraits and starving slowly in consequence. He mounted to this eyry every Friday night, so as to be reminded of the good old days at Schwartz's. The short, big-mustached, bald-headed man swinging the cane, was Bianchi—Julius Bianchi—known to the Skylarkers as " The Pole," and to the world at large as an accomplished lithographer and maker of mezzotints. Bianchi was a piece of the early artistic driftwood cast upon our shores—an artist every inch of him—drawing from life, and handling the crayon like a master.

The pale-faced young fellow at the piano, with bulging watch-crystal eye-glasses and hair tucked behind his ears, was the well-known, all-round musician, Wenby Simmons—otherwise known as " Pussy Meow "—a name associated in some way with the strings of his violin. This virtuoso played in the orchestra at the Winter Garden, and occupied the bedroom next to Fred's.

The clean-shaven, well-groomed young Englishman standing behind Simmons and holding a coal-scuttle half full of coal which he shook with deafening jangle to help swell the chorus, was " My Lord Cockburn " so called—an exchange clerk in a banking-house. He occupied the room opposite Fred's.

With the ending of the chorus Fred Stone stepped

159

into the open space with his arm through that of his guest, and the noise was hushed long enough for the entire party to welcome the young Southerner—a welcome which kindled into a glow of enthusiasm when they caught the look of frank undisguised pleasure which lighted his face, and noticed the unaffected bow with which he entered the room, shaking hands with each one as Fred introduced him—and all with that warm, hearty, simple, courteous manner peculiar to his people.

The slight ceremony over—almost every Friday night some new guest was welcomed—Fred seated himself on the floor with his back to the whitewashed wall, although two chairs were at once offered them, and made room for Oliver, who settled down beside him.

As they sat leaning back, Oliver's eyes wandering over the room drinking in the strange, fascinating scene before him, as bewildering as it was unexpected, Fred—now that they were closer to the scene of action, again whispered or shouted, as the suddenly revived noise permitted, into Oliver's alert and delighted ears, such additional facts concerning the other members present as he thought would interest his guest.

The fat man behind the piano astride of a chair, a pipe in his mouth and a black velvet skull-cap on his head, was Tom Waller, the sheep-painter—Thomas

Brandon Waller, he signed it—known as the Walrus. He, too, was a boarder and a delightful fellow, although an habitual grumbler. His highest ambition was to affix an N. A. at the end of his name, but he had failed of election by thirty votes out of forty cast. That exasperating event he had duly celebrated at Pfaff's in various continued libations covering a week, and had accordingly, on many proper and improper occasions, renewed and recelebrated the event, breathing out meanwhile, between his pewter mugs, scathing anathemas against the "idiots" who had defeated him out of his just rights, and who were stupid enough to believe in the school of Verboeckhoeven. Slick and shiny Verboeckhoeven, "the mechanic," he would call him, with his fists closed tight, who painted the hair on every one of his sheep as if it were curled by a pair of barber's tongs—not dirty and woolly and full of suggestions as, of course, he—the great Waller, alone of all living animal-painters—depicted it. All of which, to Waller's credit, it must be parenthetically stated, these same "idiots" learned to recognize in after years as true, when that distinguished animal-painter took a medal at the Salon for the same picture which the Jury of N. A.'s had rejected at their Spring Exhibition.

The irreproachable, immaculate young person, with eyes half-closed, lying back in the arm-chair—one which he had brought from his own room—was

" Ruffle-shirt " Tomlins. He was the only member who dressed every day for dinner, whether he was going out afterward or not—spike-tailed coat, white tie and all. Tomlins not only knew intimately a lady of high degree who owned a box at the Academy of Music, in Fourteenth Street, and who invited him to sit in it at least once a season, but he had besides a large visiting acquaintance among the people of quality living on Irving Place. A very agreeable and kindly little man was " Ruffle-shirt " Tomlins— so Fred said—the sort of a little man whose philosophy of life was based on the possibility of catching more innocent, unwary flies with honey than he could with vinegar, and who, in consequence, always said nice things about everybody—sometimes in a loud tone enough for everybody to hear. This last statement of Fred's Tomlins confirmed ten minutes later by remarking, in a stage whisper to Waller:

" Did you see how that young Mr. Horn entered the room? Nobody like these high-bred Southerners, my boy. Quite the air of a man of the world— hasn't he? " To all of which the distinguished sheep-painter made no other reply than a slight nod of the head, as he blew a cloud of smoke toward the ceiling —Tomlins's immaculate appearance being a constant offence to the untidy painter.

The member with the stentorian voice, who was roaring out his opinions to Cockburn, Fred continued, was "Fog-horn" Cranch, the auctioneer. His room was next to Waller's. His weaknesses were gay-colored waistcoats and astounding cravats. He varied these portions of his dress according to wind, weather, and sales of the day—selecting blue for sunshiny mornings, black for rainy ones, green for pictures, red for household furniture, white for real estate, etc. Into these color-schemes he stuck a variety of scarf-pins—none very valuable or rare, but each one distinct—a miniature ivory skull, for instance, with little garnets for eyes, or tiny onyx dice with sixes on all sides.

The one man of all the others most beloved by Fred and every other boarder, guest, and *habitué* that gathered around the piano in this garret-room, and now conspicuous by his absence, he having gone to the circus opposite the Academy of Music, and not likely to return until late—a fact greatly regretted by Fred who made this announcement with lowered voice to Oliver—was a young Irishman by the name of McFudd—Cornelius McFudd, the life of the house, and whom Waller, in accordance with the general custom, had christened "Continuous McFuddle," by reason of the nature of the Hibernian's habits. His room was across the open space opposite Fred's, with windows overlooking the yard.

This condensation of good-nature, wit, and good-humor, Fred went on to say, had been shipped to

THE FORTUNES OF OLIVER HORN

"The States" by his father, a rich manufacturer of Irish whiskies in Dublin, that he might learn something of the ways of the New World. And there was not the slightest doubt in the minds of his comrades, so Fred assured Oliver, that he had not only won his diploma, but that the sum of his knowledge along several other lines far exceeded that of any one of his contemporaries. His allowances came regularly every month, through the hands of Cockburn, who had known him in London, and whose bank cashed McFudd's remittances—a fact which enabled my lord to a greater extent than the others to keep an eye on the Irishman's movements and expenditures.

Whatever deviltry was inaugurated on this top floor during the day as well as the night, and it was pretty constant, could be traced without much difficulty to this irrepressible young Irishman. If Tomlins found his dress-suit put to bed, with a pillow for a body and his crush-hat for a head; or Cranch found Waller's lay-figure (Waller often used his bedroom as a studio) sitting bolt upright in his easy-chair, with its back to him reading a newspaper—the servant having been told to announce to Cranch, the moment she opened the door, that "a gentleman was waiting for him in his room"; or Cockburn was sent off on some wild-goose chase uptown—it was safe to say that Mac was at the bottom of it all.

164

If, Fred added impressively, this rollicking, devil-may-care, perfectly sound and hearty young Hibernian had ever been absolutely, entirely, and completely sober since his sojourn in the land of the free, no one of his fellow-boarders had ever discovered it.

Of this motley gathering " Ruffle-shirt " Tomlins, the swell; " Fog-horn " Cranch, the auctioneer; " Walrus " Waller, the sheep-painter; " My Lord " Cockburn, the Englishman; Fred Stone and Cornelius McFudd, not only occupied the bedrooms, but had seats at Miss Teetum's table, four flights below. Bianchi and the others were the guests of the evening.

All this, and more, Fred poured into Oliver's willing ear in loud or soft tones, dependent upon the particular kind of bedlam that was loose in the room at the moment, as they sat side by side on the floor, Oliver's back supported by a pillow which Tomlins had brought from his own bed and tucked behind his shoulders with his own hand.

This courtesy had been followed by another, quite as comforting and as thoughtful. Cockburn, the moment Oliver's back touched the wall, had handed him a tooth-brush mug without a handle, filled to the brim with a decoction of Cockburn's own brewing, compounded hot according to McFudd's receipt, and poured from an earthen pitcher kept within reach of Cockburn's hand, and to which Oliver, in accordance

165

with his habitual custom, had merely touched his lips, he being the most temperate of young gentlemen.

While they talked on, stopping now and then to listen to some outburst of Cranch, whose voice drowned all others—or to snatches of song from Wenby Simmons, the musician, or from Julius Bianchi, Waller's voice managed to make itself felt above the din with an earnestness that gained the attention and calmed all the others.

" You don't know what you're all talking about," he was heard to say. He was still astride his chair, his pipe in his hand. " Inness's picture was the best thing we had in the Exhibition, except Eastman Johnson's ' Negro Life at the South.' Kensett's ' Lake George ' was——"

" What—that Inness smear? " retorted " My Lord " Cockburn, who still stood with the coal-scuttle in his hand ready for another chorus. " Positively, Waller, you Americans amuse me. Do you really think that you've got anybody about you who can paint anything worth having——"

" Oh! oh! Hear the high-cockalorum! Oh! oh! "

The sheep-painter raised his hand to command silence.

" Do I think we've got anybody about here who can paint?—you fog-headed noodle from Piccadilly? We've got a dozen young fellows in this very town that put more real stuff into their canvases than all your men put together. They don't tickle their things to death with detail. They get air and vitality and out-of-doors into their work, and———"

"Names! Names!" shouted "My Lord" Cockburn, rattling the scuttle to drown the answers to his questions.

"George Inness for one, and young McEntee and Sanford Gifford, and Eastman Johnson, Page, Casilear—a lot of them," shouted "The Walrus." "Go to the Exhibition and see for yourself, and you———"

The rest of the discussion was lost to Oliver's ears owing to the roar of Cranch's fog-horn, accompanied by another vigorous shaking of the scuttle, which the auctioneer caught away from "My Lord" Cockburn's grasp, and the pounding of Simmons's fingers on the yellow keys of the wheezy piano.

The tribute to Inness had not been missed by Oliver, despite the deafening noise accompanying its utterance. He remembered another green smear, that hung in Mr. Crocker's studio, to which that old enthusiast always pointed as the work of a man who would yet be heard from if he lived. He had never appreciated it himself at the time, but now he saw that Mr. Crocker must be right.

Someone now started the chorus—

Down among the dead men, down.

Instantly every man was on his feet crowding about the piano, Oliver catching the inspiration of the moment and joining in with the others. The quality of his voice must have caught the ear of some of the singers, for they gradually lowered their tones, leaving Oliver's voice almost alone.

Fred's eye glowed with pleasure. His new-found friend was making a favorable impression. He at once urged Oliver to sing one of his own Southern songs as the darkies sung them at home, and not as they were caricatured by the end men in the minstrel shows.

Oliver, at first abashed, and then anxious to contribute something of his own in return for all the pleasure they had given him, hummed the tune for Simmons, and in the hush that followed began one of the old plantation songs that Malachi had taught him, beginning with

> De old black dog he bay at de moon,
>   Away down yan ribber.
> Miss Bull-frog say she git dar soon,
>   Away down yan ribber.

As the melody rang through the room, now full and strong, now plaintive as the cooing of a dove or the moan of a whippoorwill, the men stood stock-still, their wondering eyes fixed on the singer, and it was not until the timely arrival of the Bull-frog and the escape of her lover had been fully told that the listening crowd allowed themselves to do much more than breathe. Then there came a shout that nearly raised the roof. The peculiar sweetness of Oliver's voice, the quaintness of the melody, the grotesqueness of his gestures—for it was pantomime as well as music —and the quiet simplicity and earnestness with which it had all been done, had captivated every man in the room. It was Oliver's first triumph—the first in all his life.

And the second was not far off, for in the midst of all the uproar that followed, as he resumed his place on the floor, Cockburn sprang to his feet and proposed Mr. Oliver Horn as a full member of the Skylarkers' Club. This was carried unanimously, and a committee of two, consisting of " Ruffle-shirt " Tomlins and Waller, were forthwith appointed to acquaint the said member, who stood three feet away, of his election, and to escort him to Tomlins's chair— the largest and most imposing-looking one in the room. This action was indorsed by the shouts and cat-calls of all present, accompanied by earthquake shakings of the coal-scuttle and the rattling of chair-legs and canes on the floor.

Oliver rose to his feet and stood blushing like a girl, thanking those about him in halting sentences for the honor conferred upon him. Then he stammered something about his not deserving their praise, for he could really sing very few songs—only those he had sung at home to help out an occasional chorus, and that he would be delighted to join in another

169

song if any one of the gentlemen present would start the tune.

These last suggestions being eminently distasteful to the group, were immediately drowned in a series of protests, the noise only ceasing when " Fog-horn " Cranch mounted a chair and in his best real estate voice commanded silence.

" Ladies and Gentlemen," thundered the auctioneer, " I have the honor to announce that the great barytone, Mr. Oliver Horn, known to the universe as the ' Musical Cornucopia,' late of the sunny South, and now a resident of this metropolis, will delight this company by singing one of those soul-moving plantation melodies which have made his name famous over two hemispheres. Mr. ' Pussy Me-ow ' Simmons, the distinguished fiddling pianist, late of the Bowery, very late, I may remark, and now on the waiting list at Wallack's Theatre—every other month, I am told—will accompany him."

" Hear! Hear! " " Horn! Horn! " " Don't let him get away, Fred." " Song! Song! " was heard all over the room.

Oliver again tried to protest, but he was again shouted down by cries of—

" None of that! " " Can't fool us." " You know a barrel of 'em." " Song! Song! "

Cranch broke in again—" Mr. Horn's modesty, gentlemen, greatly endears him to his fellow-members, and we love him the better for it, but all the same—" and he raised his hand with the same gesture he would have used had it held an auctioneer's hammer— "All in favor of his singing again say 'Aye!' Going! Going! Gone! The ayes have it." In the midst of the cheering Cranch jumped from the chair and taking Oliver by the hand as if he had been a young prima donna at her first appearance, led him to the piano with all the airs and graces common to such an occasion.

Our young hero hesitated a moment, looked about in a pleased but helpless way, and nerving himself tried to collect his thoughts sufficiently to recall some one of the songs that were so familiar to him at home. Then Sue's black eyes looked into his—there must always be a woman helping Oliver—and the strains of the last song he had sung with her the night before he left home floated through his brain. (These same eyes were gazing into another's at the moment, but our young Oliver was unconscious of that lamentable fact.)

"Did you ever happen to hear 'The Old Kentucky Home'?" Oliver asked Simmons. "No? Well, it goes this way," and he struck the chords.

"You play it," said Simmons, rising from the stool.

"Oh, I can only play the chords, and not all of them right—" and he took Simmons's seat.

"Perhaps I can get through—I'll try it," he added, simply, and squared himself before the instrument and began the melody.

> The sun shines bright in the old Kentucky home,
>   'Tis summer, the darkies are gay.
> The corn-top's ripe and the meadow is in bloom,
>   While the birds make music all the day.
>
> Weep no more, my lady—oh, weep no more to-day !
> We'll sing one song for the old Kentucky home,
>   For the old Kentucky home far away.

As the words rolled from his lips Oliver seemed to forget the scene before him. Somehow he could see the light in Sue's eyes, as she listened, and hear her last words. He could hear the voice of his mother, and feel her hand on his head; and then, as the soft vowels and cadences of the quaint melody breathed themselves out, he could catch again the expression of delight on the face of Malachi—who had taught him the song—as he listened, his black cheek in his wrinkled palm. It was a supreme moment with Oliver. The thrill of happiness that had quivered through him for days, intensified by this new heaven of Bohemia, vibrated in every note he uttered.

The effect was equally startling on those about him. Cranch craned his head, and for once lowered his voice to a whisper in speaking to the man next him. Bowdoin, the painter, and one of the guests, left his seat and tip-toed to the piano, his eyes riveted on Oliver's face, his whole being absorbed in the melody. Bianchi and Waller so far lost themselves that their pipes went out, while Simmons was so entranced that he forgot to applaud when Oliver finished.

The effect produced was not so much due to the quality in Oliver's voice—sweet and sympathetic as it was—nor to his manner of singing, nor to the sentiment of the song itself, but to the fact of its being, with its clear, sweet notes, a positive contrast to all of noise and clamor that had gone before. This fact, more than any other, made his listeners hold their breath in wonder and delight. It came like the song of a bird bursting out after a storm and charming everyone with the beauty of its melody, while the thunder of the tempest still reverberated through the air.

In the hush of the death-like stillness that followed, the steady tramp of feet was heard on the staircase, and the next instant the head of a young man, with a rosy face and side-chop coachman whiskers, close-cut black hair and shoe-button eyes, glistening with fun, was craned around the jamb of the door.

It was the property of Mr. Cornelius McFudd!

He was in full evening dress, and as immaculate as if he had stepped out of a bandbox.

Whatever stimulants had permeated his system and fired his imagination had evidently escaped his legs, for they were as steady as those of a tripod. His entrance, in a measure, restored the assemblage to its normal condition. Mr. McFudd raised his hand impressively, checking the customary outbreak that always greeted his appearance on occasions like this, struck a deprecatory attitude and said, solemnly, in a rich, North-of-Ireland accent:

"Gentlemen, it is with the greatest surprise that I find ye contint to waste your time over such riotous proceedings as I know have taken place here to-night, when within a block of yez is a perfarmance that would delight yer souls. Think of a man throwing a hand-spring over——"

At this instant a wet sponge was fired point blank from an open bedroom door, missed McFudd's head by an inch and bounded down the staircase.

"Thank ye, Admiral Lord Cockburn, for yer civility," cried McFudd, bowing low to the open bedroom door, "and for yer good intintions, but ye missed it as yer did yer mither's blessing—and as ye do most of the things ye try to hit." This was said without raising his voice or changing a muscle of his face, his eyes fixed on the door inside of which stood Cockburn.

McFudd continued, "The perfarmance of this acrobat is one of the——"

174

Cries of " Don't you see you disturb the music? " " Go to bed! " " Somebody sit on McFudd! " etc., filled the room.

" Go on, gentlemen. Continue your insults; defame the name of an honest man who is attimpting to convey to yer dull comprehinsions some idea of the wonders of the acrobatic ring. I'll turn a handspring for yez meself that will illustrate what I mane," and Mr. McFudd carefully removed his coat and began sliding up his shirt-cuffs.

At this juncture " My Lord " Cockburn, who had come from behind the door, winked significantly at Waller, and creeping on all fours behind McFudd, just as that gentleman was about lifting his legs aloft, swept him off his feet by a twist of his arm, and deposited him on the small of his back next to Oliver, his head resting against the wall. There Waller stood over him with a chair, which he threatened to turn over him upside down and sit on if the prostrate Irishman moved an inch.

McFudd waved his hand sadly as if in acquiescence to the inscrutable laws of fate, begged the gentlemen present to give no further thought to his existence, and after a moment of silence continued his remarks on the acrobatic ring to Oliver in the same monotonous tone of voice which he had addressed to the room before Cockburn's flank movement had made him bite the dust.

175

"It may seem to you, Mr.— Mr.—, I haven't your name, sir," and he bent his head toward Oliver.

"Horn, sir," Oliver suggested. "Oliver Horn."

"Thanks, it may seem to you that I'm exaggerating, Mr. Oliver Horn, the wonder of this perfarmance, but——"

The rest of the sentence, despite the Hibernian's well-intentioned efforts, was not addressed to Oliver, but to the room at large, or rather to its furniture, or to be still more exact, to the legs of the piano, and such chairs and tables as the Irishman's prostrate body bumped into on the way to his room. For at that instant Waller, to save Oliver, as he pretended, from further annoyance, had caught the distinguished Hibernian by both feet, and in that position dragged him along the floor, as if he had been a wheelbarrow, McFudd's voice never changing its tone as he continued his remarks on physical culture, and the benefits which would accrue to the human race if they would practice the acrobat's hand-spring.

When Fred and Oliver had closed their bedroom door for the night, the guests having departed and all the regular boarders being supposedly secure in their beds (Fred without much difficulty had persuaded Oliver to share his own bed over night), there came a knock at Fred's door, and the irrepressible Irishman stalked in.

He had removed his vest, high collar, and shoes, and had the air and look of an athlete. The marvellous skill of the acrobat still occupied his mind.

"Don't disturb yourself, my dear Stone, but me deloightful conversation with yer friend, Mr. Horn, was interrupted by that wild beast of a Waller, and I wanted to finish it. I am quite sure I can do it—the trick I was telling ye of. I've been practizing in me room. It's as easy as rolling off a jaunting car."

"No, Mac, old man. Go to bed again," pleaded Fred.

"Not till I show ye, me boy, one of the most beautiful feats of agility——"

"Come off, Mac, I say," cried Fred, catching the Irishman around the waist.

"I'll come nothing! Unhand me, gentlemen, or by the—" and tearing himself free McFudd threw a hand-spring with the ease of a professional, toppled, for a moment, his feet in the air, scraped along the whitewashed wall with his heels, and sweeping the basins and pitchers filled with water from the washstand measured his length on the floor. Then came the crash of broken china, a deluge of water, and Fred and Oliver began catching up sponges and towels to stay the flood.

A minute later a man in a long gray beard and longer night-robe—one of the regular boarders—

177

bounded up the stairs two steps at a time and dashed through Fred's open door.

"By thunder, boys!" he cried, "I don't mind how much noise you make, rather like it; but what the devil are you trying to drown us out for? Wife is soaking—it's puddling down on our bed."

By this time every door had been flung open, and the room was filled with half-dressed men.

"It's that lunatic, McFudd. He's been to the circus and thinks he's Martello," cried Fred, pointing to the prostrate Irishman with the sponge which he had been squeezing out in the coal-scuttle.

"Or the clown," remarked Waller, stooping over McFudd, who was now holding his sides and roaring with laughter.

Long after Fred had fallen asleep, Oliver lay awake thinking of the night's pleasure. He had been very, very happy—happier than he had been for many months. The shouts of approval on his election to membership, the rounds of applause that had followed his rendering of the simple negro melodies, resounded in his ears, and the joy of it all still tingled through his veins. This first triumph of his life had brought with it a certain confidence in himself—a new feeling of self-reliance—of being able to hold his own among men, something he had never experienced before. This made it all the more exhilarating.

AN OLD SONG

And the company!

Real live painters who sold their pictures and who had studied in Munich, and who knew Paris and Dresden and all the wonderful cities of which Mr. Crocker had talked. And real musicians, too!—who played at theatres; and Englishmen from London, and Irishmen from Dublin, and all so jolly and unconventional and companionable. It was just as Mr. Crocker had described it, and just what he had about despaired of ever finding. Surely his cup of happiness was full to the brim.

We can forgive him; we who still remember those glimpses behind the scenes—our first and never-to-be-forgotten! How real everything seemed, even the grease-paint, the wigs, and the clothes. And the walking gentleman and the leading old man and low comedian! What splendid fellows they were and how we sympathized with them in their enforced exiles from a beloved land. How they suffered from scheming brothers who had robbed them of their titles and estates, or flint-hearted fathers who had turned them out of doors because of their infatuation for their " art " or because of their love for some dame of noble birth or simple lass, whose name—" Me boy, will be forever sacred! " How proud we were of knowing them, and how delighted they were at knowing us—and they so much older too! And how tired we got of it all—and of

179

them—and of all their kind when our eyes became accustomed to the glare and we saw how cheap and commonplace it all was and how much of its glamour and charm had come from our own inexperience and enthusiasm—and youth.

As Oliver lay with wide-open eyes, going over every incident of the evening, he remembered, with a certain touch of exultant pride, a story his father had told him of the great Poe, and he fell to wondering whether the sweetness of his own song, falling on ears stunned by the jangle of the night, had not produced a similar effect. Poe, his father had said, on being pressed for a story in the midst of a night of revelry in a famous house on Kennedy Square, had risen from his seat and repeated the Lord's Prayer with such power and solemnity that the guests, one and all, stunned and sobered, had pushed their chairs from the table and had left the house. He remembered just where his father sat when he told the story and the impression it had made upon him at the time. He wished Kennedy Square had been present to-night to have heard him and to have seen the impression his song had made upon those gathered about him.

Kennedy Square! What would dear old Richard Horn, with his violin tucked lovingly under his chin, and gentle, white-haired Nathan, with his lips caressing his flute, have thought of it all, as they listened to the uproar of Cockburn's coal-scuttle? And, that latter-day Chesterfield, Colonel John Howard Clayton, of Pongateague, whose pipe-stemmed Madeira glasses were kept submerged in iced finger-bowls until the moment of their use, and whose rare Burgundies were drunk out of ruby-colored soap-bubbles warmed to an exact temperature. What would this old aristocrat have thought of McFudd's mixture and the way it was served?

No! It was just as well that Kennedy Square, at the moment of Oliver's triumph, was fast asleep.

CHAPTER IX

The prying sun peeped through the dingy curtains of Fred's bedroom on the morning after Oliver's revels, stencilling a long slant of yellow light down its grimy walls, and awaking our young hero with a start. Except for the shattered remnants of the basins and pitchers that he saw as he looked around him, and the stringy towels, still wet, hanging over the backs of the chairs, he would not have recognized it as the same room in which he had met such brilliant company the night before—so kindly a glamour does the night throw over our follies.

With the vision of the room and its tokens of their frolic came an uneasy sense of an unpleasant remembrance. The thrill of his own triumph no longer filled his heart; only the memory of the uproar remained. As he caught sight of the broken pieces of china still littering the carpet, and recalled McFudd's sprawling figure, a slight color suffused his cheek.

The room itself, in the light of day, was not only cold and uninviting, but so bare of even the common-

182

est comforts that Oliver shivered. The bottoms were half out of the chairs; the painted wash-stand stood on a square of chilly oil-cloth; the rusty grate and broken hearth were unswept of their ashes; the carpet patched and threadbare. He wondered, as he studied each detail, how Miss Teetum could expect her boarders to be contented in such quarters.

He saw at a glance how much more cosey and restful the room might be made with the addition of a few touches here and there; a colored print or two— a plaster cast—a bit of cheap stuff or some gay-colored cushions. It surprised him, above all, to discover that Fred, who was studying art and should, therefore, be sensitive to such influences, was willing to live amid such desolate surroundings.

When he stepped out into the square hall, the scene of the night's revelry, and glanced about him, the crude bareness and reckless disorder that the merciful glow of the gas-light and its attendant shadows had kindly concealed, stood out in bold relief under the white light of the day now streaming through an oval skylight immediately above the piano. The floor was strewn with the various properties of the night's performance—overturned stools, china mugs, bits of lemon-peel, stumps of cigars, and stray pipes; while scattered about under the piano and between the legs of the chairs, and even upon the steps of the staircase, were the pieces of coal which Fog-horn

Cranch and Waller, who held the scuttle, had pounded into bits when they produced that wild jangle which had added so much of dignity and power to the bass notes of the Dead Man's Chorus.

These cold facts aroused in Oliver a sense of repugnance which he could not shake off. It was as if the head of some jolly clown of the night before had been suddenly thrust through the canvas of the tent in broad daylight, showing the paint, the wrinkles beneath, the yellow teeth, and the coarse mouth.

Oliver was about to turn back to Fred's room, this feeling of revolt strong upon him, when his attention was arrested by a collection of drawings that covered almost every square inch of the ceiling. To his astonishment he discovered that what in the smoke of the night before he had supposed to be only hasty sketches scrawled over the white plaster, were in reality, now that he saw them in a clearer atmosphere, effective pictures in pastel, oil, and charcoal. That the basis of these cartoons was but the grimy stain made by the water which had beaten through the rickety sash during the drive and thrash of winter storms, flooding the whitewashed ceiling and trickling down the side-walls in smears of brown rust, did not lessen their value in his eyes.

Closer inspection showed him that these discolorations—some round or curved, others straight or

angular—had been altered and amended as the signatures indicated by the deft pencils of Waller, Fred,
Bowdoin, and the others, into flying Cupids, Dianas,
Neptunes, and mermaids fit to grace the ceiling of
a salon if properly enlarged; while the up-and-down
smears had suggested the opportunity for caricatur-
ing half the boarders of the house. Every fresh leak
and its accompanying stains evidently presented a
new problem to the painters, and were made the subject of prolonged study and much consultation before
a brush was permitted to touch them, the point apparently being to help the discolorations express themselves with the fewest possible touches.

In addition to these decorations overhead, Oliver
found, framed in on the cleaner plaster of the side-
walls, between broad bands of black paint, several
taking bits of landscape in color and black and white;
stretches of coast with quaint boats and dots of figures; winter wood interiors with white plaster for
snow and scrapings of charcoal for tree-trunks, each
one marked with that sure crispness of touch which
denotes the master-hand. Moreover, the panels of all
the doors, as well as their jambs and frames, were
ornamented with sketches in all mediums, illustrat-
ing incidents in the lives of the various boarders
who occupied the rooms below, and who—so Fred
told him afterward—stole into this sacred spot on the
sly, to gloat over the night's work whenever a new

185

picture was reported and the rightful denizens were known to be absent.

As he stood absorbed before these marvels of brush and pencil, scrutinizing each one in turn, his sense of repulsion for the débris on the floor gave way to a feeling of enthusiasm. Not only were the sketches far superior to any he had ever seen, but the way in which they were done and the uses of the several mediums were a revelation to him. It was only when Fog-horn Cranch's big voice roused him to consciousness that he realized where he was. The auctioneer was coming out of his room, resplendent in a striped suit, gaiters, and white necktie—this being his real-estate day.

"My dear fellow," Cranch shouted, bringing his hand down on Oliver's shoulder, "do you know you've got a voice like an angel's?"

Before Oliver could reply, My Lord Cockburn joined them, his first word one of pleasure at meeting him, and his second a hope that he would know him better; then Fred ran out, flinging on his coat and laughing as he came. Under these combined influences of praise and good-cheer Oliver's spirits rose and his blood began once more to surge through his veins. With his old-time buoyancy he put his arm through Fred's, while the two tramped gayly down the four flights of stairs to be ushered into the long, narrow, stuffy dining-room on the basement floor, there to be presented to the two Misses Teetum, who as the young men entered bent low over their plates in unison. This perfunctory salute our young gen· tleman acknowledged by bowing grandly in return, after which he dropped into a seat next to Fred's— his back to a tin box filled with plates, placed over the hot-air register--drew out a damp napkin from a bone ring, and took a bird's-eye view of the table and its occupants.

The two Misses Teetum sat one at either end— Miss Ann, thin, severe, precise; Miss Sarah, stout, coy, and a trifle kittenish, as doubtless became a young woman of forty-seven, and her sister's junior by eight years. Miss Ann had evidently passed the dead-line of middle age, and had given up the fight, and was fast becoming a very prim and very proper old lady, but Miss Sarah, being out of range, could still smile, and nod her head, and shake her curls, and laugh little, hollow, girlish laughs, and other- wise disport herself in a light and kittenish way, after the manner of her day and age. All of which be- trayed not only her earnest desire to please, but her increasing anxiety to get in under matrimonial cover before one of Father Time's sharpshooters picked her off, and thus ended her youthful career.

The guests seated on either side of these two pre- siding goddesses, Oliver was convinced, as he studied the double row of faces, would have stretched the

187

wondering eyelids of Kennedy Square to their utmost limits.

Old Mr. Lang, who with his invalid wife occupied the room immediately below Fred's, and who had been so nearly drowned out the night before because of McFudd's acrobatic tendencies, sat on Fred's left. Properly clothed and in his right mind, he proved to be a most delightful old gentleman, with gold spectacles and snow-white side-whiskers, and a welcoming smile for everyone who entered. Fred said that the smile never wavered even when the old gentleman had been up all night with his wife.

Across the table, with her eye-glasses trained on Oliver, half concealed by a huge china " compoteer " (to quote the waitress), and at present filled with last week's fruit, caulked with almonds, sat Mrs. Southwark Boggs—sole surviving relic of S. B., Esq. This misfortune she celebrated by wearing his daguerreotype, set in plain gold, as a brooch with which she fastened her crocheted collar. She was a thin, faded, funereal-looking person, her body encased in a black silk dress, which looked as if it had been pressed and ironed over night, and her hands in black silk mitts which reached to her knuckles.

On Mrs. Boggs's right sat Bates—a rising young lawyer with political tendencies—one of the first men to cut his hair so " Zou-Zou " that it stood straight up from his forehead; and next to him Morgan, the editor, who pored over manuscript while his coffee got cold; and then Nelson, and Webster, and Cummings all graded in Miss Ann's mind as being eight, or ten, or twelve-dollar-a-week men, depending on the rooms that they occupied, and farther along, toward Miss Sarah, Cranch and Cockburn—five-dollar boys these (Fred was another), with the privilege of lighting their own coke fires, and of trimming the wicks and filling the bulbs of their own burning-fluid lamps. And away down in the far corner, crumpled up in his chair, crouched the cheery little hunchback, Mr. Crumbs, who kept a book-stall on Astor Place, where Bayard Taylor, Irving, Halleck, Bryant, and many another member of the Century Club used to spend their late afternoons delving among the old volumes on his shelves.

All these regular boarders, including Fog-horn Cranch and Fred, breakfasted at eight o'clock. Waller, the painter, and Tomlins, the swell, breakfasted at nine. As to that descendant of the Irish kings, Mr. Cornelius McFudd, he rose at ten, or twelve, or two, just as the spirit (and its dilutions of the night before) moved or retarded him, and breakfasted whenever Miss Ann or Miss Sarah, who had presided continuously at the coffee-urn from eight to ten, could spare one of her two servants to carry a tray to his room.

Last and by no means least, with her eyes devouring every expression that flitted across the new arrival's face, there beamed out beside Miss Ann, a tall, willowy young person, whom Fred, in answer to an inquiring lifting of Oliver's eyebrows, designated as the belle of the house. This engaging young woman really lived with her mother, in the next street, but flitted in and out, dining, or breakfasting, or spending a week at a time with her aunts, the Misses Teetum, whenever an opportunity offered—the opportunity being a vacant and non-paying room, one of which she was at the time enjoying.

This fair damsel, who was known to the boarders on the top floor as " our Phemy," and to the world at large as Miss Euphemia Teetum—the real jewel in her name was Phœbe, but she had reset it—had been especially beloved, so Fred informed Oliver, by every member of the club except Waller, who, having lived in boarding-houses all his life, understood her thoroughly. Her last flame—the fire was still smouldering—had been the immaculate Tomlins, who had won her heart by going into raptures, in one of his stage whispers, over the classic outlines of her face. This outburst resulted in Miss Euphemia appearing the following week in a silk gown, a Greek fillet and no hoops—a costume which Waller faithfully portrayed on the side-wall of the attic the night of her appearance—the fillet being reproduced by a strip of brass which the artist had torn from his easel and nailed to the plaster, and the classic curves of her hair by a ripple of brown paint.

This caricature nearly provoked a riot before the night was over, the whole club, including even the fun-loving McFudd, denouncing Waller's act as an outrage. In fact, the Hibernian himself had once been so completely taken off his feet—it was the first week of his stay—by the winning ways of the young lady, that Miss Ann had begun to have high hopes of Euphemia's being finally installed mistress in one of those shadowy estates which the distinguished Hibernian described with such eloquence. That these hopes did not materialize was entirely due to Cockburn, who took pains to enlighten the good woman upon the intangible character of the Hibernian's possessions, thus saving the innocent maiden from the clutches of the bold, bad adventurer. At least, that had been Cockburn's account of it when he came upstairs.

But it was at dinner that same night—for Oliver at Fred's pressing invitation had come back to dinner —that the full galaxy of guests and regulars burst upon our hero. Then came not only Miss Euphemia Teetum in a costume especially selected for Oliver's capture, but a person still more startling and imposing—so imposing, in fact, that when she entered the room one-half of the gentlemen present made little

191

backward movements with the legs of their chairs, as if intending to rise to their feet in honor of her presence.

This prominent figure in fashionable life, who had now settled herself on the right of Miss Ann—the post of honor at the table—and who was smiling in so gracious and condescending a manner as her eye lighted on the several recipients of her favor, was none other than the distinguished Mrs. Schuyler Van Tassell, of Tarrytown, another bird of passage, who had left her country-seat on the Hudson to spend the winter months in what she called the delights of " upper-tandem." She belonged to an ancient family—or, at least, her husband did—he was under the sod, poor soul, and therefore at peace—and, having inherited his estate—a considerable one—was to be treated with every distinction.

These several personages of low and high degree interested our young gentleman quite as much as our young gentleman interested them. He made friends with them all—especially with the ladies, who all agreed that he was a most charming and accomplished youth. This good opinion became permanent when Oliver had paid each in turn the compliment of rising from his seat when any one of them entered the room, as much a habit with the young fellow as the taking off of his hat when he came into a house, but which was so rare a courtesy at Miss Teetum's that each recipient appropriated the compliment as personal to herself.

These sentiments of admiration were shared, and to an alarming degree, by Miss Euphemia herself, who, on learning later that Oliver had decided to occupy half of Fred's room through the winter, had at once determined to remain during the week, the better to lay siege to his heart. This resolution, it is fair to Oliver to say, she abandoned before dinner was over, when her experienced eye detected a certain amused if not derisive smile playing around the corners of Oliver's mouth; a discovery which so impressed the young woman that she left him severely alone ever after.

And so it was that Oliver unpacked his trunk—the same old hair trunk, studded with brass nails, that had held his father's wardrobe at college—spread out and tacked up the various knick-knacks which his mother and Sue and Miss Clendenning had given him when he had left the old home, and began to make himself comfortable on the top floor of Miss Teetum's boarding-house on Union Square.

CHAPTER X

Our hero had been installed at Miss Teetum's for a month or more, when one night at dinner a tiny envelope about the size of a visiting-card was brought in by the middle-aged waitress and laid beside Simmons's plate. The envelope contained six orchestra seats at the Winter Garden and was accompanied by a note which read as follows: " Bring some of the boys; the piece drags."

The musician studied the note carefully and a broad smile broke over his face. As one of the first violins at the Winter Garden, with a wide acquaintance among desirable patrons of the theatre, he had peculiar facilities for obtaining free private boxes and orchestra chairs not only at his own theatre, but often at Wallack's in Broome Street and the old Bowery. Simmons was almost always sure to have tickets when the new piece needed booming, or when an old play failed to amuse and the audiences had begun to shrink. Indeed, the mystery of Mrs. Schuyler Van Tassell's frequent appearance in the left-hand proscenium box at the Winter Garden on

194

Friday nights—a mystery unexplained among the immediate friends in Tarrytown, who knew how she husbanded her resources despite her accredited wealth—was no mystery at all to the guests at Miss Teetum's table, who were in the habit of seeing just such tiny envelopes handed to Simmons during soup, and duly passed by him to that distinguished leader of society. Should more than two tickets be enclosed, Mrs. Van T. would, perhaps, invite Mr. Ruffle-shirt Tomlins, or some other properly attired person, to accompany her—never Miss Ann or the little hunchback, who dearly loved the play, but who could seldom afford to go—never anybody, in fact, who wore plain clothes or looked a compromising acquaintance.

On this night, however, Pussy Me-ow Simmons, ignoring Mrs. Van Tassell, turned to Oliver.

"Ollie," he whispered—the formalities had ceased between the members of the Skylarks—"got anything to do to-night?"

"No; why?"

And then, Simmons, with various imaginary poundings of imaginary canes on the threadbare carpet beneath his chair, and with sundry half-smothered bursts of real laughter in which Fred and Oliver joined, unfolded his programme for the evening—a programme which was agreed to so rapturously that the trio before dinner was over excused themselves

195

to their immediate neighbors and bounded upstairs, three steps at a time. There they pulled the Walrus out of his bed and woke up McFudd, who had gone to sleep before dinner, and whom nobody had called. Then having sent my Lord Cockburn to find Ruffle-shirt Tomlins, who by this time was paying court to Miss Euphemia in the front parlor, and having pinned a ticket to Mr. Fog-horn Cranch's door, with instructions to meet them in the lobby the moment he returned, they all slipped on their overcoats, picked up their canes, and started for the theatre.

Six young fellows, all with red blood in their veins, steel springs under their toes and laughter in their hearts! Six comrades, pals, good-fellows, skipping down the avenue as gay as colts and happy as boys—no thought for to-day and no care for to-morrow! Each man with a free ticket in his pocket and a show ahead of him. No wonder the bluecoats looked after them and smiled; no wonder the old fellow with the shaky legs, waiting at the corner for one of the squad to help him over, gave a sigh as he watched McFudd, with cane in air, drilling his recruits, all five abreast. No wonder the tired shop-girls glanced at them enviously as they swung into Broadway chanting the "Dead Man's Chorus," with Oliver's voice sounding clear as a bell above the din of the streets.

The play was a melodrama of the old, old school. There was a young heroine in white, and a handsome lover in top-boots and white trousers, and a cruel uncle who wanted her property. And there was a particularly brutal villain with leery eyes, ugly mouth, with one tooth gone, and an iron jaw like a bull-dog's. He was attired in a fur cap, brown corduroy jacket, with a blood-red handkerchief twisted about his throat, and he carried a bludgeon. When the double-dyed villain proceeded in the third act to pound the head of the lovely maiden to a jelly at the instigation of the base uncle, concealed behind a painted tree-trunk, and the lover rushed in and tried to save her, every pair of hands except Oliver's came together in raptures of applause, assisted by a vigorous hammering of canes on the floor.

"Pound away, Ollie," whispered Simmons; "that's what we came for; you are spoiling all our fun. The manager is watching us. Pound away, I tell you. There he is inside that box."

"I won't," said Oliver, in a tone of voice strangely in contrast with the joyousness of an hour before.

"Then you won't get any more free tickets," muttered Simmons in surprise.

"I don't want them. I don't believe in murdering people on the stage, or anywhere else. That man's face is horrible; I'm sorry I came."

Simmons laughed, and, shielding his mouth with his hand, repeated Oliver's outburst to Waller, who, having first sent news of it down the line, reached

197

over and shook Oliver's hand gravely, while he wiped
a theatrical tear from his eye; while my Lord Cockburn, with feet and hands still busy, returned word
to Oliver by Tomlins, " not to make a colossal ass of
himself." Oliver bore their ridicule good-naturedly,
but without receding from his opinion in any way,
a fact which ultimately raised him in the estimation
of the group. Only when the villain was thrown over
the pasteboard cliff into a canvas sea by the gentleman in top-boots, to be devoured by sharks or cut
up by pirates, or otherwise disposed of as befitted
so blood-thirsty and cruel a monster, did Oliver join
in the applause.

The play over, and Simmons having duly reported
to the manager—who was delighted with the activity
of the feet, but who advised that next time the sticks
be left at home—the happy party sailed up Broadway, this time by threes and twos, swinging their
canes as before, and threading their way in and out
of the throngs that filled the street.

The first stop was made at the corner of Thirteenth
Street by McFudd, who turned his troop abruptly to
the right and marched them down a flight of steps
into a cellar, where they immediately attacked a huge
wash-tub filled with steamed clams, and covered with
a white cloth to keep them hot. This was the bar's
free lunch. The clams devoured—six each—and the
necessary beers paid for, the whole party started to

retrace their steps, when Simmons stopped to welcome a new-comer who had entered the cellar un-
perceived by the barkeeper, and who was bending
over the wash-tub of clams, engaged in picking out
the smallest of the bivalves with the end of an iron
fork. He had such a benevolent, kindly face, and
was so courtly in his bearing, and spoke with so soft
and gentle a voice, that Oliver, who stood next to
Simmons, lingered to listen.

" Oh, my dear Simmons," cried the old gentleman,
" we missed you to-night. When are you coming
back to us? The orchestra is really getting to be de-
plorable. Miss Gannon quite broke down in her
song. We must protest, my boy; we must protest.
I saw you in front, but you should be wielding the
baton. And is this young gentleman one of your
friends? "

" Yes—Mr. Horn. Ollie, let me introduce you to
Mr. Gilbert, the actor "—and he laid his hand on
Oliver's shoulder—" dear John Gilbert, as we always
call him."

Oliver looked up into the kindly, sweet face of the
man, and a curious sensation passed over him. Could
this courtly, perfectly well-bred old gentleman, with
his silver-white hair, beaming smile and gentle voice,
the equal of any of his father's guests, be an actor?
Could he possibly belong to the profession which,
of all others, Oliver had been taught to despise? The

199

astonishment of our young hero was so great that for a moment he could not speak.

Simmons thought he read Oliver's mind, and came to his rescue.

"My friend, Mr. Horn, did not like the play to-night, Mr. Gilbert," he said. "He thinks the death-scene was horrible"—and Simmons glanced smiling at the others who stood at a little distance watching the interview with great interest.

"Dear me, dear me, you don't say so. What was it you objected to, may I ask?" There was a trace of anxiety in his voice.

"Why, the murder-scene, sir. It seemed to me too dreadful to kill a woman in that way. I haven't forgotten it yet," and a distressed look passed over Oliver's face. "But then I have seen but very few plays," he added—"none like that."

The old actor looked at him with a relieved expression.

"Ah, yes, I see. Yes, you're indeed right. As you say, it is quite a dreadful scene."

"Oh, then you've seen it yourself, sir," said Oliver, in a relieved tone.

The old actor's eyes twinkled. He, too, had read the young man's mind—not a difficult task when one looked down into Oliver's eyes.

"Oh, many, many times," he answered with a smile. "I have known it for years. In the old days, when they would smash the poor lady's head, they used to have a pan of gravel which they would crunch with a stick to imitate the breaking of the bones. It was quite realistic from the front, but that was given up long ago. How did *you* like the business to-night, Mr. Simmons?" and he turned to the musician.

"Oh, admirable, sir. We all thought it had never been better played or better put on," and he glanced again toward his companions, who stood apart, listening breathlessly to every word that fell from the actor's lips.

"Ah, I am glad of it. Brougham will be so pleased —and yet it shocked you, Mr. Horn—and you really think the poor lady minded it? Dear me! How pleased she will be when I tell her the impression it all made upon you. She's worked so hard over the part and has been so nervous about it. I left her only a moment ago—she and her husband wanted me to take supper with them at Riley's—the new restaurant on University Place, you know, famous for its devilled crabs. But I always like to come here for my clams. Allow me a moment—" and he bent over the steaming tub, and skewering the contents of a pair of shells with his iron fork held it out toward Oliver.

"Let me beg of you, Mr. Horn, to taste this clam. I am quite sure it is a particularly savory one. After this, my dear young friend, I hope you'll have a better opinion of me." And his eye twinkled. "I am really better than I look—indeed I am—and so, my dear boy, is this clam. Come, come, it is getting cold."

"What do you mean by ' a better opinion ' of you, Mr. Gilbert?" stammered Oliver. He had been completely captivated by the charm of the actor's manner. "Why shouldn't I think well of you?—I don't understand."

"Why—because I strangled the poor lady to-night. You know, of course—that it was *I* who played the villain."

"You!" exclaimed Oliver. "No, I did not, sir. Why, Mr. Gilbert, I can't realize—oh, I hope you'll forgive me for what I've said. I've only been in New York a short time, and——"

The old gentleman cut short Oliver's explanation with a wave of his fork, and looking down into the boy's face, said in a serious tone:

"My son, you're quite right. Quite right—and I like you all the better for it. All such plays are dreadful. I feel just as you do about them, but what can we actors do? The public will have it that way."

Another little prejudice toppled from its pedestal, another household tradition of Oliver's smashed into a thousand pieces at his feet! This rubbing and grinding process of man against man; this seeing with

one's own eyes and not another's was fast rounding
out and perfecting the impressionable clay of our
young gentleman's mind. It was a lesson, too, the
scribe is delighted to say, which our hero never forgot; nor did he ever forget the man who taught it.
One of his greatest delights in after-years was to raise
his hat to this incomparable embodiment of the dignity and courtliness of the old school. The old gentleman had long since forgotten the young fellow,
but that made no difference to Oliver—he would
cross the street any time to lift his hat to dear John
Gilbert.

The introduction of the other members of the club
to the villain being over—they had stood the whole
time, they were listening to the actor, each head uncovered—McFudd again marshalled his troop and
proceeded up Broadway, where, at Oliver's request,
they were halted at the pedestal of the big Bronze
Horse and within sight of their own quarters.

Here McFudd insisted that the club should sing
" God Save the Queen " to the Father of his Country,
where he sat astride of his horse, which was accordingly done, much to the delight of a couple of night-
watchmen, who watched the entire performance and
who, upon McFudd's subsequent inspection, proved
to be fellow-countrymen of the distinguished Hibernian.

Had the buoyant and irrepressible Irishman been

content with this patriotic outburst as the final wind-ing-up of the night's outing, and had he then and there betaken himself and his fellows off to bed, the calamity which followed, and which so nearly wrecked the Skylarks, might have been avoided.

It is difficult at any time to account for the work-ings of Fate or to follow the course of its agents. The track of an earth-worm destroys a dam; the parting of a wire wrecks a bridge; the breaking of a root starts an avalanche; the flaw in an axle dooms a train; the sting of a microbe depopulates a city. But none of these unseen, mysterious agencies was at work—nothing so trivial wrecked the Skylarks.

It was a German street-band!

A band whose several members had watched McFudd and his party from across the street, and who had begun limbering their instruments before the sextet had ceased singing; regarding the situa-tion, no doubt, as pregnant with tips.

McFudd did not give the cornet time to draw his instrument from its woollen bag before he had him by the arm.

"Don't put a mouthful of wind into that horn of yours until I spake to ye," he cried in vociferous tones.

The leader stopped and looked at him in a dazed way.

"I have an idea, gentlemen," added McFudd,

turning to his companions, and tapping his forehead. " I am of the opinion that this music would be wasted on the noight air, and so with your parmission I propose to transfer this orchestra to the top flure, where we can listen to their chunes at our leisure. Right about, face! Forward! March!" and McFudd advanced upon the band, wheeled the drum around, and, locking arms with the cornet, started across the street for the stone steps.

"Not a word out of any o' ye till I get 'em in," McFudd continued in a low voice, fumbling in his pocket for his night-key.

The musicians obeyed mechanically and tiptoed one by one inside the dimly lighted hall, followed by Oliver and the others.

"Now take off your shoes; you've four flights of stairs to crawl up, and if ye make a noise until I'm ready for ye, off goes a dollar of your pay."

The bass-drum carefully backed his instrument against the wall, sat down on the floor, and began pulling off his boots; the cornet and bassoon followed; the clarionet wore only his gum shoes, and so was permitted to keep them on.

"Now, Walley, me boy, do you go ahead and turn up the gas and open the piano, and Cockburn, old man, will ye kindly get the blower and tongs out of Freddie's room and the scuttle out of Tomlins's closet and the Chinese gong that hangs over me bed? And

205

all you fellers go ahead treading on whispers, d'ye moind?" said McFudd under his breath. "I'll bring up this gang with me. Not a breath out of any o' yez remimber, till I get there. The drum's unhandy and we got to go slow wid it," and he slipped the strap over his head and started upstairs, followed by the band.

The ascent was made without a sound until old Mr. Lang's door was reached, when McFudd's foot slipped, and, but for the bassoonist's head, both the Irishman and the drum would have rolled down-stairs. Lang heard the sound, and recognizing the character of the attendant imprecation, did not get up. "It's only McFudd," he said quietly to his suddenly awakened wife.

Once safe upon the attic floor the band who were entering with great gusto into the spirit of the occasion, arranged themselves in a half-circle about the piano, replaced their shoes, stripped their instruments of their coverings—the cornetist breathing noiseless-ly into the mouth-pieces to thaw out the frost—and stood at attention for McFudd's orders.

By this time Simmons had taken his seat at the piano; Cockburn held the blower and tongs; Cranch, who on coming in had ignored the card tacked to his door, and who was found fast asleep in his chair, was given the coal-scuttle; and little Tomlins grasped his own wash-basin in one hand and Fred's poker in the other. Oliver was to sing the air, and Fred was to beat a tattoo on Waller's door with the butt end of a cane. The gas had been turned up and every kerosene lamp had been lighted and ranged about the hall. McFudd threw off his coat and vest, cocked a Scotch smoking-cap over one eye, and seizing the Chinese gong in one hand and the wooden mallet in the other, climbed upon the piano and faced his motley orchestra.

"Attintion, gentlemen," whispered McFudd.

"The first chune will be 'Old Dog Tray,' because it begins wid a lovely howl. Remimber now, when I hit this gong that's the signal for yez to begin, and ye'll all come together wid wan smash. Then the band will play a bar or two, and then every man Jack o' ye will go strong on the chorus. Are yez ready?"

McFudd swung his mallet over his head; poised it for an instant; ran his eye around the circle with the air of an impresario; saw that the drum was in position, the horns and clarionet ready, the blower, scuttle, tongs, and other instruments of torture in place, and hit the gong with all his might.

The crash that followed woke every boarder in the house and tumbled half of them out of their beds.

Long before the chorus had been reached all the doors had been thrown open, and the halls and passageways filled with the startled boarders. Then certain mysterious-looking figures in bed-gowns, waterproofs, and bath-robes began bounding up the stairs, and a collection of dishevelled heads were thrust through the door of the attic. Some of the suddenly awakened boarders tried to stop the din by protest; others threatened violence; one or two grinned with delight. Among these last was the little hunchback, swathed in a blanket like an Indian chief, and barefooted. He had rushed upstairs at the first sound as fast as his little legs could carry him, and was peering under the arms of the others, rubbing his sides with glee and laughing like a boy. Mrs. Schuyler Van Tassell, whose head and complexion were not ready for general inspection, had kept her door partly closed, opening it only wide enough when the other boarders rushed by to let her voice through—always an unpleasant organ when that lady had lost her temper.

As the face of each new arrival appeared in the doorway, McFudd would bow gracefully in recognition of the honor of its presence, and redouble his attack on the gong. The noise he produced was only equalled by that of the drum, which never ceased for an instant—McFudd's orders being to keep that instrument going irrespective of time or tune.

In the midst of this uproar of brass, strings, sheep skin, wash-bowls, broken coal, pokers and tongs, a lean figure in curl-papers and slippers, bright red calico wrapper reaching to the floor, and a lighted

" Gentlemen, this is outrageous!"

candle in one hand, forced its way through the crowd at the door and stood out in the glare of the gaslights facing McFudd.

It was Miss Ann Teetum!

Instantly a silence fell upon the room.

"Gentlemen, this is outrageous!" she cried in a voice that ripped through the air like a saw. "I have put up with these disgraceful performances as long as I am going to. Not one of you shall stay in my house another night. Out you go in the morning, every one of you, bag and baggage!"

McFudd attempted to make an apology. Oliver stepped forward, the color mounting to his cheeks, and Waller began a protest at the unwarrantable intrusion, but the infuriated little woman waved them all aside and turning abruptly marched back through the door and down the staircase, preceded by the other female boarders. The little hunchback alone remained. He was doubled up in a knot, wiping the tears from his eyes, his breath gone from excessive laughter.

The Skylarkers looked at each other in blank astonishment. One of the long-cherished traditions of the house was the inviolability of this attic. Its rooms were let with an especial privilege guaranteeing its privacy, with free license to make all the noise possible, provided the racket was confined to that one floor. So careful had been its occupants to observe this rule, that noisy as they all were when once on the top floor, every man unlocked the front door at night with the touch of a burglar and crept upstairs as noiselessly as a footpad.

"I'm sorry, men," said McFudd, looking into the astounded faces about him. "I'm the last man, as ye know, to hurt anybody's feelings. But what the divil's got into the old lady? Who'd 'a' thought she would have heard a word of it down where she sleeps in the basement?"

"'Tis the Van Tassell," grunted the Walrus. "She's so mesmerized the old woman lately that she don't know her own mind."

"What makes you think she put her up to it, Waller?" asked Cranch.

"I don't think—but it's just like her," answered Waller, with illogical prejudice.

"My eye! wasn't she a beauty!" laughed Fred, and he picked up a bit of charcoal and began an outline of the wrapper and slippers on the side-wall.

Tomlins, Cranch, and the others had no suggestions to offer. Their minds were too much occupied in wondering what was going to become of them in the morning.

The German band by this time had regained their usual solidity. The leader seemed immensely relieved. He had evidently expected the next apparition to be a bluecoat with a pair of handcuffs.

"Put their green jackets on 'em," McFudd said to the leader quietly, pointing to the instruments. "We're much obliged to you and your men for coming up," and he slipped some notes into the leader's hand. "Now get downstairs, every man o' ye, as aisy as if ye were walking on eggs. Cranch, old man, will ye see 'em out, to kape that infernal drum from butting into the Van Tassell's door, or we'll have another hornet's nest. Begorra, there's wan thing very sure—it's little baggage *I'll* have to move out."

The next morning a row of six vacant seats stared Miss Ann out of countenance. The outcasts had risen early and had gone to Riley's for their breakfast. Miss Ann sat at the coffee-urn as stiff and erect as an avenging judge. Lofty purpose and grim determination were written in every line of her face. Mrs. Van Tassell was not in evidence. Her nerves had been so shattered by the "night's orgy," she had said to Miss Ann, that she should breakfast in her room. She further notified Miss Teetum that she should at once withdraw her protecting presence from the establishment, and leave it without a distinguished social head, if the dwellers on the top floor remained another day under the same roof with herself.

An ominous silence and depressing gloom seemed to hang over everybody. Several of the older men pushed back their plates and began drumming on the table-cloth with their fingers, a far-away look in their eyes. One or two talked in whispers, their coffee untasted. Old Mr. Lang looked down the line of empty seats and took his place with a dejected air. He was the oldest man in the house and the oldest boarder; this gave him certain privileges, one being to speak his mind.

"I understand," he said, unfolding his napkin and facing Miss Ann, "that you have ordered the boys out of the house?"

"Yes, I have," snapped out Miss Teetum.

Everybody looked up. No one recognized the tone of her voice, it was so sharp and bitter.

"Why, may I ask?"

"I will not have my house turned into a bear-garden, that's why!"

"That's better than a graveyard," retorted Mr. Lang. "That's what the house would be without them. I can't understand why you object. You sleep in the basement and shouldn't hear a sound; my wife and I sleep under them every night. If we can stand it, you can. You send the boys away, Miss Teetum, and we'll move out."

Miss Ann winced under the shot, but she did not answer.

"Do you mean that you're going to turn the young gentlemen into the street, Miss Ann?" whined Mrs.

Southwark Boggs in an injured tone, from her end of the table. " Are we going to have no young life in the house at all? I won't stay a day after they're gone."

Miss Teetum changed color, but she looked straight ahead of her. She evidently did not want her private affairs discussed at the table.

" I shall want my bill at the end of the week, now that the boys are to leave," remarked the little hunchback to Miss Ann as he bent over her chair. " Life is dreary enough as it is."

And so the boys stayed on.

Only one room became vacant at the end of the month. That was Mrs. Schuyler Van Tassell's.

CHAPTER XI

A CHANGE OF WIND

The affair of the brass band, with its dramatic and most unlooked-for ending, left an unpleasant memory in the minds of the members of the club, especially in Oliver's. His training had been somewhat different from that of the others present, and his over-sensitive nature had been more shocked than pleased by it all. While most of the other participants regretted the ill-feeling which had been aroused in Miss Teetum's mind, they felt sure—in fact, they knew—that this heretofore kind and gentle hostess could never have fanned her wrath to so white a heat had not some other hand besides her own worked the bellows.

Suspicion first fell upon a new boarder unaccustomed to the ways of the house, who, it was reported, had double-locked herself in at the first crash of the drum, and who had admitted, on being cross-examined by McFudd, that she had nearly broken her back in trying to barricade her bedroom door with a Saratoga trunk and a wash-stand. This theory was

214

abandoned when subsequent inquiries brought to light the fact that Mrs. Van Tassell, when the echoes of one of McFudd's songs had reached her ears, had stated a week before that no respectable boarding-house would tolerate uproars like those which took place almost nightly on the top floor, and that she would withdraw her protection from Miss Euphemia and leave the house at once and forever if the noise did not cease. This dire threat being duly reported to the two Misses Teetum had—it was afterward learned—so affected them both that Miss Ann had gone to bed with a chill and Miss Sarah had warded off another with a bowl of hot camomile tea.

This story, true as it undoubtedly was, did not entirely clear up the situation. One part of it sorely puzzled McFudd. Why did Miss Euphemia need Mrs. Van Tassell's protection, and why should the loss of it stir Miss Ann to so violent an outburst? This question no member of the Skylarks could answer.

The solution came that very night, and in the most unexpected way, Waller bearing the glad tidings.

Miss Euphemia, ignoring them all, was to be married at St. Mark's at 6 P.M. on the following Monday, and Mrs. Van Tassell was to take charge of the wedding reception in the front parlor! The groom was the strange young man who had sat for some days beside Miss Euphemia, passing as Miss Ann's

215

nephew, and who really was a well-to-do druggist with a shop on Astor Place. All of the regular boarders of the house were to be invited.

The explosion of this matrimonial bomb so cleared the air of all doubt as to the guilt of Mrs. Van Tassell, that a secret meeting, attended by every member of the Skylarks, was at once held in Waller's room with the result that Miss Ann's invitations to the wedding were unanimously accepted. Not only would the resident members go—so the original resolution ran—but the non-resident and outside members would also be on hand to do honor to Miss Euphemia and her distinguished chaperone. This amendment being accepted, McFudd announced in a sepulchral tone that, owing to the severity of the calamity and to the peculiarly painful circumstances which surrounded their esteemed fellow-skylarker, the Honorable Sylvester Ruffle-shirt Tomlins, his fellow-members would wear crape on their left arms for thirty days. This also was carried unanimously, every man except Ruffle-shirt Tomlins breaking out into the "Dead Man's Chorus"—a song, McFudd explained, admirably fitted to the occasion.

When the auspicious night arrived, the several dress-suits of the members were duly laid out on the piano and hung over the chairs, and each gentleman proceeded to array himself in costume befitting the occasion. Waller, who weighed 200 pounds, squeezed

216

himself into McFudd's coat and trousers (McFudd weighed 150), the trousers reaching a little below the painter's knees. McFudd wrapped Waller's coat about his thin girth and turned up the bagging legs of the unmentionables six inches above his shoes. The assorted costumes of the other members were equally grotesque. The habiliments themselves were of proper cut and make, according to the standards of the time—spike-tailed coats, white ties, patent-leather pumps, and the customary trimmings, but the effects produced were as ludicrous as they were incongruous, though the studied bearing of the gentlemen was meant to prove their unconsciousness of the fact.

The astonishment that rested on Mrs. Van Tassell's face when this motley group filed into the parlor and with marked and punctilious deference paid their respects to the bride, and the wrath that flashed in Miss Euphemia's eyes, became ever after part of the traditions of the club. Despite Mrs. Van Tassell's protest against the uproar on the top floor, she had invariably spoken in high terms to her friends and intimates of these very boarders—their acquaintance was really part of her social capital—commenting at the same time upon their exalted social and artistic positions. In fact, many of her own special guests had attended the wedding solely in the hope of being brought into more intimate relations with this distinguished group of painters, editors, and musicians, some of whom were already being talked about.

When, however, McFudd stood in the corner of Miss Teetum's parlor like a half-scared boy, pulling out the fingers of Waller's kid gloves, an inch too long for him, and Waller, Fred, and my Lord Cockburn stumbled over the hearth-rug one after the other, and Oliver, feeling like a guilty man and a boor, bowed and scraped like a dancing-master; and Bowdoin the painter, and Simmons and Fog-horn Cranch, talked platitudes with faces as grave as undertakers, the expectant special guests invited by Mrs. Van Tassell began to look upon her encomiums as part of an advertising scheme to fill Miss Teetum's rooms.

The impression made upon the Teetum contingent by the appearance and manners of the several members—even Oliver's reputation was ruined—was equally disastrous. It was, perhaps, best voiced by the druggist groom, when he informed Mrs. Van T. from behind his lemon-colored glove—that " if that was the gang he had heard so much of, he didn't want no more of 'em."

But these and other jollifications were not long to continue. Causes infinitely more serious were at work undermining the foundations of the Skylarks. The Lodge of Poverty, to which they all belonged, gay as it had often been, was slowly closing its door;

218

the unexpected, which always hangs over life, was about to happen; the tie which bound these men together was slowly loosening. Its members might give the grip of fellowship to other members in other lodges over the globe, but no longer in this one on the top floor of the house on Union Square.

One morning McFudd broke the seal of an important-looking letter bearing a Dublin post-mark on the upper right-hand corner of the envelope, and the family crest on its flap. For some moments he sat still, looking straight before him. Then two tears stole out and glistened on his lashes.

"Boys," he said, slowly, "the governor says I must come home," and he held up a steamer ticket and a draft that barely equalled his dues for a month's board and washing.

That night he pawned his new white overcoat with the bone buttons and velvet collar—the one his father had sent him, and which had been the envy of every man in the club, and invested every penny of the proceeds in a supper to be given to the Skylarks. The invitation ran as follows:

Mr. Cornelius McFudd respectively requests the pleasure of your presence at an informal wake to be held in honor of a double-breasted overcoat, London cut. The body and tail will be the ducks, and the two sleeves and velvet collar the Burgundy.

Riley's: 8 P.M. Third floor back.

The following week he packed his two tin boxes, boarded the Scotia, and sailed for home.

The keystone having dropped out, it was not long before the balance of the structure came down about the ears of the members. My Lord Cockburn the following week was ordered South by the bank to look after some securities locked up in a vault in a Georgia trust company, and which required a special messenger to recover them—the growing uneasiness in mercantile circles over the political outlook of the country having assumed a serious aspect. Cockburn had to swim rivers, he wrote Oliver in his first letter, and cross mountains on horseback, and sleep in a negro hut, besides having a variety of other experiences, to say nothing of several hair-breadth escapes, none of which availed him, as he returned home after all, without the bonds.

These financial straws, indicating the direction and force of the coming political winds, began to accumulate. The lull before the hurricane—the stagnation in commercial circles—became so ominous that soon the outside members and guests of the club ceased coming, being diligently occupied in earning their bread, and then Simmons sent the piano home —it had been loaned to him by reason of his profession and position—and only Fog-horn Cranch, Waller, Fred, Oliver, and Ruffle-shirt Tomlins were left.

A CHANGE OF WIND

After a while, Waller gave up his room and slept in his studio and got his meals at the St. Clair, or went without them, so light, by reason of the hard times, was the demand for sheep pictures of Waller's particular make. And later on Tomlins went abroad, and Cranch moved West. And so the ruin of the club was complete; and so, too, this merry band of roysterers, with one or two exceptions, passes out of these pages.

Dear boys of the long ago, what has become of you all since those old days in that garret-room on Union Square? Tomlins, I know, turned up in Australia, where he married a very rich and very lovely woman, because he distinctly stated both of those facts in an exuberant letter to Oliver when he invited him to the wedding. " Not a bad journey—only a step, my dear Ollie, and we shall be *so* delighted to see you." I know this to be true, for Oliver showed me the letter. Bowdoin went to Paris, where, as we all remember, he had a swell studio opening on to a garden, somewhere near the Arc de Triomphe, and had carriages stop at his door, and a butler to open it, and two maids in white caps to help the ladies off with their wraps. Poor Cranch died in Montana while hunting for gold, and my Lord Cockburn went back to London.

But does anybody know what has become of McFudd—irresistible, irresponsible, altogether delightful McFudd? that condensation of all that was joyous, rollicking, and spontaneous; that devotee of the tub and pink of neatness, immaculate, clean-shaven and well-groomed; that soul of good-nature, which no number of flowing bowls could disturb nor succeeding headaches dull; that most generous of souls, whose first impulse was to cut squarely in half everything he owned and give you your choice of the pieces, and who never lost his temper until you refused them both. If you, my dear boy, are still wandering about this earth, and your eye should happen to fall on these pages, remember, I send you my greeting. If you have been sent for, **and** have gone aloft to cheer those others who have gone before, and who could spare you no longer, speak a good word for me, please, and then, perhaps, I may shake your hand again.

With the dissolution of the happy coterie there came to Oliver many a lonely night under the cheap lamp, the desolate hall outside looking all the more desolate and uninviting with the piano gone and the lights extinguished.

Yet these nights were not altogether distasteful to Oliver. Fred had noticed for months that his room-mate no longer entered into the frolics of the club with the zest and vim that characterized the earlier days of the young Southerner's sojourn

among them. Our hero had said nothing while
the men had held together, and to all outward ap-
pearances had done his share not only with his singing, but in any other way in which he could help
on the merriment. He had covered the space al-
lotted to him on the walls with caricatures of the
several boarders below. He had mixed the salad at
Riley's the night of McFudd's farewell supper, with
his sleeves rolled up to the elbows and the cook's cap
on his head. He had lined up with the others at
Brown's on the Bowery; drank his " crystal cock-
tails "—the mildest of beverages—and had solemnly
marched out again with his comrades in a lock-step
like a gang of convicts. He had indulged in forty-
cent opera, leaning over the iron railing of the top
row of the Academy of Music, and had finished the
evening at Pfaff's, drinking beer and munching hard-
tack and pickles, and had laughed and sung in a dozen
other equally absurd escapades. And yet it was as
plain as daylight to Fred that Oliver's heart was no
longer centred in the life about him.

The fact is, the scribe is compelled to admit, the
life indulged in by these merry bohemians had begun
to pall upon this most sensitive of young gentlemen.
It really had not satisfied him at all. This was not
the sort of life that Mr. Crocker meant, he had said
to himself after a night at Riley's when Cranch had
sounded his horn so loud that the proprietor had

223

threatened to turn the whole party into the street. Mr. Crocker's temperament was too restful to be interested in such performances. As for himself, he was tired of it.

Nothing of all this did he keep from his mother. The record of his likes and dislikes which formed the subject-matter of his daily letters was an absorbing study with her, and she let no variation of the weather-vane of his tastes escape her. Nor did she keep their contents from her intimate friends. She had read to Colonel Clayton one of his earlier ones, in which he had told her of the concerts and of the way Cockburn had served the brew that McFudd had concocted, and had shown him an illustration Oliver had drawn on the margin of the sheet—an outline of the china mug that held the mixture—to which that Chesterfield of a Clayton had replied:

"What did I tell you, madame—just what I expected of those Yankees—punch from mugs! Bah!"

She had, too, talked their contents over with Amos Cobb, who, since the confidence reposed in him by the Horn family, had become a frequent visitor at the house.

"There's no harm come to him yet, madame, or he wouldn't write you of what he does. Boys will be boys. Let him have his fling," the Vermonter had replied with a gleam of pleasure in his eye. "If he has the stuff in him that I think he has, he will swim out and get to higher ground; if he hasn't, better let him drown early. It will give everybody less trouble."

The dear lady had lost no sleep over these escapades. She, too, realized that as long as Oliver poured out his heart unreservedly to her there was little to fear. In her efforts to cheer him she had sought, in her almost daily letters sent him in return, to lead his thoughts into other channels. She knew how fond he had always been of the society of women, and how necessary they were to his happiness, and she begged him to go out more. " Surely there must be some young girls in so great a city who can help to make your life happier," she wrote.

In accordance with her suggestions, he had at last put on his best clothes and had accompanied Tomlins and Fred to some very delightful houses away up in Thirty-third Street, and another on Washington Square, and still another near St. Mark's Place, where his personality and his sweet, sympathetic voice had gained him friends and most pressing invitations to call again. Some he had accepted, and some he had not—it depended very largely on his mood and upon the people whom he met. If they reminded him in any way, either in manners or appointments, of his life at home, he went again—if not, he generally stayed away.

Among these was the house of his employer, Mr.

Slade, who had treated him with marked kindness, not only inviting him to his own house, but introducing him to many of his friends—an unusual civility Oliver discovered afterward—not many of the clerks being given a seat at Mr. Slade's table. " I like his brusque, hearty manner," Oliver wrote to his mother after the first visit. " His wife is a charming woman, and so are the two daughters, quite independent and fearless, and entirely different from the girls at home, but most interesting and so well bred."

Another incident, too, had greatly pleased not only Oliver and his mother, but Richard as well. It happened that a consignment of goods belonging to Morton, Slade & Co. was stored in a warehouse in Charleston, and it became necessary to send one of the clerks South to reship or sell them, the ordinary business methods being unsafe, owing to the continued rumblings of the now rapidly approaching political storm—a storm that promised to be infinitely more serious than the financial stringency. The choice had fallen on Oliver, he being a Southerner, and knowing the ways of the people. He had advised with his mother and stood ready to leave at an hour's notice, when Mr. Slade's heart failed him.

" It's too dangerous, my lad," he said to Oliver. " I could trust you, I know, and I believe you would return safely and bring the goods or the money with you, but I should never forgive myself if anything

226

should happen to you. I will send an older man."
And he did.

It was at this time that Oliver had received Cockburn's letter telling him of his own experiences, and
he, therefore, knew something of the risks a man
would run, and could appreciate Mr. Slade's action
all the more. Richard, as soon as he heard of it, had
put down his tools, left his work-bench, and had gone
into his library, where he had written the firm a
letter of thanks, couched in terms so quaint and
courtly, and so full of generous appreciation of their
interest in Oliver, that Mr. Slade, equally appreciative, had worn it into ribbons in showing it to his
friends as a model of style and chirography.

Remembering his mother's wishes, and in appreciation of his employer's courtesy, he had kept up this
intimacy with the Slade family until an unfortunate
catastrophe had occurred, which while it did not affect his welcome at their house, ruined his pleasure
while there.

Mr. Slade had invited Oliver to dinner one rainy
night, and, being too poor to pay for a cab, Oliver,
in attempting to cross Broadway, had stepped into a
mud-puddle a foot deep. He must either walk back
and change his shoes and be late for dinner—an unpardonable offence—or he must keep on and run his
chances of cleaning them in the dressing-room. There
was no dressing-room available, as it turned out, and

the fat English butler had to bring a wet cloth out into the hall (oh! how he wished for Malachi!) and get down on his stiff knees and wipe away vigorously before Oliver could present himself before his hostess, the dinner in the meantime getting cold and the guests being kept waiting. Oliver could never look at those shoes after that without shivering.

This incident had kept him at home for a time and had made him chary of exposing himself to similar mortifications. His stock of clothes at best was limited—especially his shoes—and as the weather continued bad and the streets impassable, he preferred waiting for clearer skies and safer walking. So he spent his nights in his room, crooning over the coke fire with Fred, or all alone if Fred were at the Academy, drawing from the cast.

On these nights he would begin to long for Kennedy Square. He had said nothing yet about returning, even for a day's visit. He knew how his mother felt about it, and he knew how he had seen her struggle to keep the interest paid up on the mortgage and to meet the daily necessities of the house. The motor was still incomplete, she wrote him, and success was as far off as ever. The mortgage had again been extended and the note renewed—this time for a longer term, owing to some friend's interest in the matter whose name she could not learn. She, therefore, felt no uneasiness on that score, although there were still no pennies which could be spared for Oliver's travelling expenses, even if he could get leave of absence from his employers.

At these times, as he sat alone in his garret-room, Malachi's chuckle, without cause or reminder, would suddenly ring in his ears, or some low strain from his father's violin or a soft note from Nathan's flute would float through his brain. " Dear Uncle Nat," he would break out, speaking aloud and springing from his chair—" I wish I could hear you to-night."

His only relief while in these moods was to again seize his pen and pour out his heart to his mother or to his father, or to Miss Clendenning or old Mr. Crocker. Occasionally he would write to Sue—not often—for that volatile young lady had so far forgotten Oliver as to leave his letters unanswered for weeks at a time. She was singing " Dixie," she told him in her last *billet-doux*, now a month old, and wondering whether Oliver was getting to be a Yankee, and whether he would be coming home with a high collar and his hair cut short and parted in the middle.

His father's letters in return did not lessen his gloom. " These agitators will destroy the country, my son, if they keep on," Richard had written in his last letter. " It is a sin against civilization to hold your fellow-men in bondage, and that is why years

229

ago I gave Malachi and Hannah and the others their freedom, but Virginia has unquestionably the right to govern her internal affairs without consulting Massachusetts, and that is what many of these Northern leaders do not or will not understand. I am greatly disturbed over the situation, and I sincerely hope your own career will not be affected by these troubles. As to my own affairs, all I can say is that I work early and late, and am out of debt." Poor fellow! He thought he was.

Oliver was sitting thus one night, his head in his hands, elbows on his knees, gazing into the smouldering coals of his grate, his favorite attitude when his mind was troubled, when Fred, his face aglow, his big blue eyes dancing, threw wide the door and bounded in, bringing in his clothes the fresh, cool air of the night. He had been at work in the School of the Academy of Design, and had a drawing in chalk under his arm—a head of the young Augustus.

"What's the matter, Ollie, got the blues?"

"No, Freddie, only thinking."

"What's her name? I'll go and see her and make it up. Out with it—do I know her?"

Oliver smiled faintly, examined the drawing for a moment, and handing it back to Fred, said, sadly, "It's not a girl, Freddie, but I don't seem to get anywhere."

Fred threw the drawing on the bed and squeezed

230

himself into the chair beside his chum, his arm around
his neck.

"Where do you want to get, old man? What's
the matter—any trouble at the store?"

"No—none that I know of. But the life is so
monotonous, Fred. You do what you love to do. I
mark boxes all day till lunch-time, then I roll them
out on the sidewalk and make out dray tickets till
I come home. I've been doing that all winter; I
expect to be doing it for years. That don't get me
anywhere, does it? I hate the life more and more
every day."

(Was our hero's old love of change again asserting itself, or was it only the pinching of that Chinese
shoe which his mother in her anxiety had slipped on
his unresisting foot, and which he was still wearing to
please her? Or was it the upper pressure of some
inherent talent—some gift of his ancestors that would
not down at his own bidding or that of his mother
or anybody else's?)

"Somebody's got to do it, Ollie, and you are the
last man hired," remarked Fred, quietly. "What
would you like to do?"

Oliver shifted himself in the crowded chair until
he could look into his room-mate's eyes.

"Fred, old man," he answered, his voice choking,
"I haven't said a word to you about it all the time
I've been here, for I don't like to talk about a thing

231

that hurts me, and so I've kept it to myself. Now I'll tell you the truth just as it is. I don't want Mr. Slade's work nor anybody else's work. I don't like business and never will. I want to paint, and I'll never be happy until I do. That's it, fair and square."

"Well, quit Slade, then, and come with me."

"I would if it wasn't for mother. I promised her I would see this through, and I will." As he spoke the overdue mortgage and his mother's efforts to keep the interest paid passed in review before him.

Fred caught his breath. It astonished him, independent young Northerner as he was, to hear a full-grown man confess that his mother's apron-strings still held him up, but he made no comment.

"Why not try both?" he cried. "There's a place in the school alongside of me—we'll work together nights. It won't interfere with what you do downtown. You'll get a good start, and when you have a day off in the summer you can do some out-door work. Waller has told me a dozen times that you draw better than he did when he commenced. Come along with me."

This conversation, with the other incidents of the day, or rather that part of it which had reference to the Academy, was duly set forth in his next letter to his mother—not as an argument to gain her consent to his studying with Fred, for he knew it was the last thing she would agree to—but because it was

232

his habit to tell her everything. It would show her, too, how good a fellow Fred was and what an interest he took in his welfare. Her answer, three days later, sent him bounding upstairs and into their room like a whirlwind.

"Read, Fred, read!" he cried. "I can go. Mother says she thinks it would be the best thing in the world for me. Here, clap your eyes on that—" and Oliver held the letter out to Fred, his finger pointing to this passage: "I wish you would join Fred at the Academy. Now that you have a regular business that occupies your mind, and are earning your living, I have no objection to your studying drawing or learning any other accomplishment. You work hard all day, and this will rest you."

The cramped foot was beginning to spread! The Chinese shoe had lost its top button.

CHAPTER XII

Still another new and far more bewildering world was opened to Oliver the night that he entered the cast-room of the School of the National Academy of Design and took his seat among the students.

The title of the institution, high-sounding as it was, not only truthfully expressed the objects and purposes of its founders, but was wofully exact in the sense of its being national; for outside the bare walls of these rooms there was hardly a student's easel to be found the country over.

And such forlorn, desolate rooms; up two flights of dusty stairs, in a rickety, dingy loft off Broadway, within a short walk of Union Square—an auction-room on the ground floor and a bar-room in the rear. The largest of these rooms was used for the annual exhibition of the Academicians and their associates, and the smaller ones were given over to the students; one, a better lighted apartment, being filled with the usual collection of casts—the Milo, the Fighting Gladiator, Apollo Belvidere, Venus de

234

Medici, etc., etc.; the other being devoted to the uses of the life-class and its models. Not the nude. Whatever may have been done in the studios, in the class-room it was always the draped model that posed —the old woman who washed for a living on the top floor, or one of her chubby children or buxom daughters, or perhaps the peddler who strayed in to sell his wares and left his head behind him on ten different canvases and in as many different positions.

The casts themselves were backed up against the walls; some facing the windows for lights and darks, and others pushed toward the middle of the room, where the glow of the gas-jets could accentuate their better points. The Milo, by right of divinity, held the centre position—she being beautiful from any point of sight and available from any side. The Theseus and the Gladiator stood in the corners, affording space for the stools of two or three students and their necessary easels. Scattered about on the coarse, whitewashed walls were hung the smaller life-casts; fragments of the body—an arm, leg, or hand, or sections of a head—and tucked in between could be found cheap lithographic productions of the work of the students and professors of the Paris and Düsseldorf schools. The gas-lights under which the students worked at night were hooded by cheap paper shades of the students' own fashioning, and the lower sashes of the windows were smeared with whitewash or covered with newspapers to concentrate the light. During working hours the drawing-boards were propped upon rude easels or slanted on overturned chairs, the students sitting on three-legged stools.

A gentle-voiced, earnest, whole-souled old man— the one only instructor—presided over this temple of art. He had devoted his whole life to the sowing of figs and the reaping of thistles, and in his old age was just beginning to see the shoots of a new art forcing their way through the quickening clay of American civilization. Once in awhile, as assistants in this almost hopeless task, there would stray into his class-room some of the painters who, unconsciously, were founding a national art and in honor of whom a grateful nation will one day search the world over for marble white enough on which to perpetuate their memories: men as distinct in their aims, methods, and results as was that other group of unknown and despised immortals starving together at that very time in a French village across the sea—and men, too, equally deserving of the esteem and gratitude of their countrymen.

Oliver knew the names of these distinguished visitors to the Academy, as did all the other members of the Skylarks, and he knew their work. The pictures of George Inness, Sanford Gifford, Kensett, McEntee, Hart, Eastman Johnson, Hubbard, Church, Casilaer, Whittredge, and the others had

236

been frequently discussed around the piano on the top floor at Miss Teetum's, and their merits and supposed demerits often hotly contested. He had met Kensett once at the house of Mr. Slade, and McEntee had been pointed out to him as he left the theatre one night, but few of the others had ever crossed his path.

Of the group Gifford appealed to him most. One golden " Venice " of the painter, which hung in a picture-store, always delighted him—a stretch of the Lagoon with a cluster of butterfly sails and a far-away line of palaces, towers, and domes lying like a string of pearls on the horizon. There was another of Kensett's, a point of rocks thrust out like a mailed hand into a blue sea; and a McEntee of October woods, all brown and gold; but the Gifford he had never forgotten; nor will anyone else who has seen it.

No wonder then that all his life he remembered that particular night, when a slender, dark-haired man in loose gray clothes sauntered into the class-room and moved around among the easels, giving a suggestion here and a word of praise there, for that was the night on which Professor Cummings touched our young hero's shoulder and said: " Mr. Gifford likes your drawing very much, Mr. Horn "—a word of praise which, as he wrote to Crocker, steadied his uncertain fingers " as nothing else had ever done."

The students in his school were from all stations in life: young and old; all of them poor, and most of

237

them struggling along in kindred professions and occupations — engravers, house-painters, lithographers, and wood-carvers. Two or three were sign-painters. One of these—a big-boned, blue-eyed young fellow, who drew in charcoal from the cast at night, and who sketched the ships in the harbor during the day—came from Kennedy Square, or rather from one of the side streets leading out of it. There can still be found over the door of what was once his shop a weather-beaten example of his skill in gold letters, the product of his own hand. Above the signature is, or was some ten years since, a small decorative panel showing a strip of yellow sand, a black dot of a boat, and a line of blue sky, so true in tone and sure in composition that when Mr. Crocker first passed that way and stood astounded before it—as did Robinson Crusoe over Friday's footprint—he was so overjoyed to find another artist besides himself in the town, that he turned into the shop, and finding only a young mechanic at work, said:

"Go to New York, young man, and study, you have a career before you."

The old landscape-painter was a sure prophet; little pen-and-ink sketches bearing the initials of this same sign-painter now sell for more than their weight in gold, while his larger canvases on the walls of our museums and galleries hold their place beside the

238

work of the marine-painters of our own and other times and will for many a day to come.

This exile from Kennedy Square had been the first man to shake Oliver's hand the night he entered the cast-room. Social distinctions had no place in this atmosphere; it was the fellow who in his work came closest to the curve of the shoulder or to the poise of the head who proved, in the eyes of his fellow-students, his possession of an ancestry: but the ancestry was one that skipped over the Mayflower and went straight back to the great Michael and Rembrandt.

"I'm Jack Bedford, the sign-painter," he said, heartily. "You and I come from the same town," and as they grasped each other's hands a new friendship was added to Oliver's rapidly increasing list.

Oliver's seat was next to Fred, with Jack Bedford on his right. He had asked to join this group not only because he wanted to be near his two friends but because he wanted still more to be near the Milo. He had himself selected a certain angle of the head because he had worked from that same point of sight with Mr. Crocker, and it had delighted him beyond measure when the professor allowed him to place his stool so that he could almost duplicate his earlier drawing. His ambition was to get into the life-class, and the quickest road, he knew, lay through a good cast drawing. Every night for a week, therefore,

239

he had followed the wonderful lines of the Milo's beautiful body, which seemed to grow with warmth under the flare of the overhanging gas-jets.

These favored life students occupied the room next to the casts. Mother Mulligan, in full regalia of apron and broom, often sat there as a model. Oliver had recognized her portrait at once; so can anyone else who looks over the earlier studies of half the painters of the time.

" Oh, it's you, is it—" Mrs. Mulligan herself had cried when she met Oliver in the hall, " the young gentleman that saved Miss Margaret's dog? She'll be here next week herself—she's gone home for awhile up into the mountains, where her old father and mother live. I told her many times about. ye, and she'll be that pleased to meet ye, now that you're *wan* of us."

It was delightful to hear her accent the " wan." Mother Mulligan always thought the institution rested on her broad shoulders, and that the students were part of her family.

The old woman could also have told Oliver of Margaret's arrival at the school, and of the impression which she, the first and only girl student, made on the night she took her place before an easel. But of the reason of her coming Mrs. Mulligan could have told nothing, nor why Margaret had been willing to exchange the comforts of a home among the

240

New Hampshire hills for the narrow confines of a third-story back room, with Mrs. Mulligan as housekeeper and chaperon.

Fred knew all the details, of course, and how it had all come about. How a cousin of Margaret's who lived on a farm near her father's had one day, years before, left his plough standing in the furrow and apprenticed himself to a granite-cutter in the next town. How later on he had graduated in gravestones, and then in bas-reliefs, and finally had won a medal in Rome for a figure of " Hope," which was to mark the grave of a millionnaire at home. How when the statue was finished, ready to be set up, this cousin had come to Brookfield, wearing a square-cut beard, straight-out mustaches with needle-points, and funny shoes with square toes. How the girl had been disposed to laugh at him until he had told her stories of the wonderful cities beyond the sea and of his life among the painters and sculptors; then she showed him her own drawings, searching his face anxiously with her big eyes. How he had been so astounded and charmed by their delicacy and truth, that he had pleaded with her father—an obstinate old Puritan—to send her to New York to study, which the old man refused point-blank to do, only giving his consent at the last when her brother John, who had been graduated from Dartmouth and knew something of the outside world, had

241

joined his voice to that of her mother and her own. How when she at last entered the class-room of the Academy the students had looked askance at her; the usual talk had ceased, and for a time there had been an uncomfortable restraint everywhere, until the men found her laughing quietly at their whispered jokes about her. After that the " red-headed girl in blue gingham," as she was called, had become, by virtue of that spirit of *camaraderie* which a common pursuit develops, " one of us " in spirit as well as in occupation.

Fred had described it all to Oliver, and every night when Oliver came in from the hall, his eyes had wandered over the group of students in the hope of seeing the strange person. A girl studying art, or anything else for that matter, seemed to him to be as incongruous as for a boy to learn dress-making or for a woman to open a barber-shop. He knew her type, he said to himself: she would be thin and awkward, with an aggressive voice that would jar on the stillness of the room. And she would believe in the doctrines of Elizabeth Cady Stanton—a name never mentioned by his mother except apologetically and in a low voice—and when she became older she would address meetings and become conspicuous in church and have her name printed in the daily papers.

Our hero's mind was intent upon these phases of character always to be found, of course, in a girl who

242

would unsex herself to the extent that Miss Grant had done, when one night a rich, full, well-modulated voice sounding over his shoulder said:

"Excuse me, but Mother Mulligan tells me that you are Mr. Horn, Fred Stone's friend. I want to thank you for taking care of my poor Juno. It was very good of you. I am Margaret Grant."

She had approached him without his seeing her. He turned quickly to accost her and immediately lost so much of his breath that he could only stammer his thanks, and the hope that Juno still enjoyed the best of health. But the deep-brown eyes did not waver after acknowledging his reply, nor did the smile about the mouth relax.

"And I'm so glad you've come at last," she went on. "Fred has told me how you wanted to draw and couldn't. I know something myself of what it is to hunger after a thing and not get it."

He was on his feet now, the bit of charcoal still between his fingers, his shirt-cuff rolled back to give his hand more freedom. His senses were coming back, too, and there was buoyancy as well as youth in his face.

"Yes, I do love it," said Oliver, and his eyes wandered over her wonderful hair that looked like brown gold illumined by slants of sunshine, and then rested for an instant on her eyes. "I drew with old Mr. Crocker at home, but we only had one

243

cast, just the head of the Milo, and I was the only pupil. Here everything helps me. What are you at work on, Miss Grant?"

"I'm doing the Milo, too; my seat is right in front of yours. Oh! what a good beginning," and she bent over his drawing-board. "Why, this can't be your first week," and she scanned it closely. "One minute—a little too full under the chin, isn't it?" She picked up a piece of chalk, and pointed to the shaded lines, looking first with half-closed eyes at the full-sized cast before them, and then at the drawing.

"Yes, I think you're right," said Oliver, studying the cast also with half-closed eyes. "How will that do?" and he smudged the shadow with his finger-tip.

"Just right," she answered. "How well you have the character of the face. Isn't she lovely!—I know of nothing so beautiful. There is such a queenly, womanly, self-poised simplicity about her."

Oliver thought so too, and said so with his eyes, only it was of a face framed in brown-gold that he was thinking and not of one of white plaster. He was touched too by the delicate way in which she had commended his drawings. It was the "woman" in her that pleased him, just as it had been in Sue—that subtle, dominating influence which our fine gentleman could never resist.

He shifted his stool a little to one side so that he

244

could see her the better unobserved while she was arranging her seat and propping up her board. He
noticed that, although her face was tanned by the
weather, her head was set on a neck of singular white-
ness. Underneath, where the back hair was tucked
up, his eye caught some delicate filmy curls which
softened the line between her throat and head and
shone in the light like threads of gold. The shoulders sloped and the whole fulness of her figure ta-
pered to a waist firmly held by a leather belt. A
wholesome girl, he thought to himself, and good to
look at, and with a certain rhythmic grace about her
movements.

Her crowning glory, though, was her hair, which
was parted over her forehead and caught in a simple
twist behind. As the light fell upon it he observed
again how full it was of varying tones like those
found in the crinklings of a satin gown—yellow-gold
one minute and dark brown the next. Oliver wondered how long this marvellous hair might be, and
whether it would reach to the floor if it should burst
its fastenings and whether Sir Peter Lely would have
loved it too could he have seen this flood of gold bath-
ing her brow and shoulders.

He found it delightful to work within a few feet
of her, silent as they had to be, for much talking
was discountenanced by the professor: often hours
passed without any sound being heard in the room

but that of the scraping of the chairs on the bare floor
or the shifting of an easel.

Two or three times during the evening the old professor emerged from his room and overlooked his
drawing, patiently pointing out the defects and
as patiently correcting them. He was evidently
impressed with Oliver's progress, for he remarked
to Miss Grant, in a low voice:

" The new student draws well—he is doing first-
rate," and passed on. Oliver caught the expression
of satisfaction on the professor's face and inter-
preted it as in some way applying to his work, although he did not catch the words.

The old man rarely had to criticise Margaret's
work. The suggestions made to her came oftener
from the students than from the professor himself
or any one of the visiting critics. In these criticisms,
not only of her own work but of the others, everyone took part, each leaving his stool and helping in
the discussion, when the work of the night was over.
Fred's more correct eye, for instance, would be in-
valuable to Jack Bedford, the ex-sign-painter, who
was struggling with the profile of the Gladiator; or
Margaret, who could detect at a glance the faintest
departure from the lines of the original, would
shorten a curve on Oliver's drawing, or he in turn
would advise her about the depth of a shadow or the
spot for a high light.

As the nights went by and Oliver studied her the closer, the New England girl became all the more inexplicable to him. She was, he could not but admit, like no other woman he had ever met; certainly not in his present surroundings. She really seemed to belong to some fabled race—one of the Amazons, or Rhine maidens, or Norse queens for whom knights couched their lances. It was useless to compare her to any one of the girls about Kennedy Square, for she had nothing in common with any one of them. Was it because she was unhappy among her own people that she had thus exiled herself from her home, or had some love-affair blighted her life? Or could it be, as Fred had suggested, that she was willing to undergo all these discomforts and privations simply for love of her art? As this possible solution of the vexing problem became established in his mind, with the vision of Margaret herself before him, the blood mounted to his cheeks and an uncontrollable thrill of enthusiasm swept over him. He could forgive her anything if this last motive had really controlled and shaped her life.

Had he seen the more closely and with prophetic vision, he would have discerned, in this Norse queen with the golden hair, the mother of a long line of daughters, who, in the days to follow, would hang their triumphant shields beside those of their brothers, winning equal recognition in salon and gallery and conferring equal honor on their country. But Oliver's vision was no keener than that of any-one else about him. It was only the turn of Margaret's head that caught the young student's eye and the wealth of her brown-gold hair. With the future he had no concern.

What attracted him most of all in this woman who had violated all the known traditions of Kennedy Square, was a certain fearlessness of manner—an independence, a perfect ingenuousness, and a freedom from any desire to interest the students in herself. When she looked at any one of them, it was never from under drooping eyelids, as Sue would have done, nor with that coquettish, alluring glance to which he had always been accustomed. She looked straight at them with unflinching eyes that said, "I can trust you, and *will*." He had never seen exactly that look except in the portrait of his uncle's grandmother by Sir Peter Lely—the picture he had always loved. Strange to say, too, the eyes of the portrait were Margaret's eyes, and so was the color of the hair.

No vexed problems entered Margaret's head regarding the very engaging young gentleman who sat behind *her* stool. He merely represented to her another student—that was all; the little band was small enough, and she was glad to see the new ones come. She noticed, it is true, certain unmistakable differences—a peculiar, soft cadence in his voice as the words slipped from his lips without their final g's; a certain deference to herself—standing until she regained her seat, an attention which she attributed at first to embarrassment over his new surroundings and to his desire to please. She noticed, too, a certain grace in his movements—a grace that attracted her, especially in the way with which he used his hands, and in the way in which he threw his head up when he laughed; but even these differences ceased to interest her after the first night of their meeting.

But it did not occur to her that he came from any different stock than the others about her, or that his blood might or might not be a shade bluer than her own. What had really impressed her more than anything else—and this only flashed into her mind while she was looking in the glass one night at her own— were his big white teeth, white as grains of corn, and the cleanliness of his hands and nails. She liked these things about him. Some of the fingers that rested on her drawing-board were often more like clothes-pins than fingers, and shocked her not a little; some, too, were stained with acids, and one or more with printer's ink that no soap could remove.

Before the evening was over Oliver became one of the class-room appointments—a young man who sat one stool behind her and was doing fairly well with his first attempt, and who would some day be

249

able to make a creditable drawing if he had patience and application.

At the beginning of the second week a new student appeared—or rather an old one, who had been laid up at home with a cold. When Oliver arrived he found him in Margaret's seat, his easel standing where hers had been. He had a full-length drawing of the Milo—evidently the work of days—nearly finished on his board. Oliver was himself a little ahead of time—ahead of either Margaret or Fred, and had noticed the new-comer when he entered, the room being nearly empty. Jack Bedford was already at work.

"Horn," Jack cried, and beckoned to Oliver—"see the beggar in Miss Grant's seat. Won't there be a jolly row when she comes in?"

Margaret entered a moment later, her portfolio under her arm, and stood taking in the situation. Then she walked straight to her former seat, and said, in a firm but kindly tone:

"This is my place, sir. I've been at work here for a week. You see my drawing is nearly done."

The young man looked up. He toiled all day in a lithographer's shop, and these precious nights in the loft were his only glimpses of happiness. He sat without his coat, his shirt-sleeves liberally smeared with the color-stains of his trade.

"Well, it's my place, too. I sat here a week before I was taken sick," he said, in a slightly indig-nant tone, looking into Margaret's face in astonish-ment.

"But if you did," continued Margaret, "you see I am nearly through. I can't take another seat, for I'll lose the angle. I can finish in an hour if you will please give me this place to-night. You can work just as well by sitting a few feet farther along."

The lithographer, without replying, turned from her impatiently, bent over his easel, picked up a fresh bit of charcoal and corrected a line on the Milo's shoulder. So far as he was concerned the argument was closed.

Margaret stood patiently. She thought at first he was merely adding a last touch to his drawing before granting her request.

"Will you let me have the seat?" she asked.

"No," he blurted out. He was still bending over his drawing, his eyes fixed on the work. He did not even look up. "I'm going to stay here until I finish. You know the rules as well as I do. I wouldn't take your seat—what do you want to take mine for?" There was no animosity in his voice. He spoke as if announcing a fact.

The words had hardly left his lips when there came the sound of a chair being quickly pushed back, and Oliver stood beside Margaret. His eyes were flashing; his right shirt-cuff was rolled back, the bit of charcoal still between his fingers. Every muscle of his body was tense with anger. Margaret's quick instinct took in the situation at a glance. She saw Oliver's wrath and she knew its cause.

"Don't, Mr. Horn, please—please!" she cried, putting up her hand. "I'll begin another drawing. I see now that I took his seat when he was away, although I didn't know it."

Oliver stepped past her. "Get up, sir," he said, "and give Miss Grant her seat. What do you mean by speaking so to a lady?"

The apprentice—his name was Judson—raised his eyes quickly, took in Oliver's tense, muscular figure standing over him, and said, with a contemptuous wave of the hand:

"Young feller—you go and cool off somewhere, or I'll tell the professor. It's none of your business. I know the rules and—— "

He never finished the sentence—not that anybody heard. He was floundering on the floor, an overturned easel and drawing-board lying across his body; Oliver standing over him with his fists tightly clenched.

"I'll teach you how to behave to a lady." The words sounded as if they came from between closed teeth. "Here's your chair, Miss Grant," and with a slight bow he placed the chair before her and resumed his seat with as much composure as if he

252

had been in his mother's drawing-room in Kennedy Square.

Margaret was so astounded that for a moment she could not speak. Then her voice came back to her. " I don't want it," she cried, in a half-frightened way, the tears starting in her eyes. " It was never mine—I told you so. Oh, what have you done?"

Never since the founding of the school had there been such a scene. The students jumped from their chairs and crowded about the group. The life class, which were at work in another room, startled by the uproar, swarmed out eager to know what had happened and why—and who—and what for. Old Mother Mulligan, who had been posing for the class, with a cloak about her fat shoulders and a red handkerchief binding up her head, rushed over to Margaret, thinking she had been hurt in some way, until she saw the student on the floor, still panting and half-dazed from the effect of Oliver's blow. Then she fell on her knees beside him.

At this instant Professor Cummings entered, and a sudden hush fell upon the room. Judson, with the help of Mother Mulligan's arm, had picked himself up, and would have made a rush at Oliver had not big Jack Bedford stopped him.

" Who's to blame for this?" asked the professor, looking from one to the other.

Oliver rose from his seat.

"This man insulted Miss Grant and I threw him out of her chair," he answered quietly.

"Insulted you!" cried the professor, in surprise, and he turned to Margaret. "What did he say?"

"I never said a word to her," whined Judson, straightening his collar. "I told her the seat was mine, and so it is. That wasn't insulting her."

"It's all a mistake, professor—Mr. Horn did not understand," protested Margaret. "It *was* his seat, not mine. He began his drawing first. I didn't know it when I commenced mine. I told Mr. Horn so."

"Why did you strike him?" asked the professor, and he turned and faced Oliver.

"Because he had no business to speak to her as he did. She is the only lady we have among us and every man in the class ought to remember it, and every man has since I've been here except this one."

There was a slight murmur of applause. Judson's early training had been neglected as far as his manners went, and he was not popular.

The professor looked searchingly into Oliver's eyes and a flush of pride in the boy's pluck tinged his pale cheeks. He had once thrown a fellow-student out of a window in Munich himself for a similar offence, and old as he was he had never forgotten it.

"You come from the South, Mr. Horn, I hear," he said in a gentler voice, "and you are all a hot-tempered race, and often do foolish things. Judson meant no harm—he says so, and Miss Grant says so. Now you two shake hands and make up. We are trying to learn to draw here, not to batter each other's heads."

Oliver's eyes roved from one to the other; he was too astonished to make further reply. He had only done what he knew every other man around Kennedy Square would have done under similar circumstances, and what any other woman would have thanked him for. Why was everybody here against him—even the girl herself! What sort of people were these who would stand by and see a woman insulted and make no defence or outcry? He could not have looked his father in the face again, nor Sue, nor anyone else in Kennedy Square, if he had failed to protect her.

For a moment he hesitated, his eyes searching each face. He had hoped that someone who had witnessed the outrage would come forward and uphold his act. When no voice broke the stillness he crossed the room and taking the lithographer's hand, extended rather sullenly, answered, quietly: "If Miss Grant is satisfied, I am," and peace was once more restored.

Margaret sharpened her charcoals and bent over her drawing. She was so agitated she could not trust herself to touch its surface. "If I am *satisfied,*" she kept repeating to herself. The words, somehow,

255

seemed to carry a reproach with them. "Why shouldn't I be satisfied? I have no more rights in the room than the other students about me; that is, I thought I hadn't until I heard what he said. How foolish for him to cause all this fuss about nothing, and make me so conspicuous."

But even as she said the words to herself she remembered Oliver's tense figure and the look of indignation on his face. She had never been accustomed to seeing men take up the cudgels for women. There had been no opportunity, perhaps, nor cause, but even if there had been, she could think of no one whom she had ever met who would have done as much for her just because she was a woman.

A little sob, which she could not have explained to herself, welled up to her throat. Much as she gloried in her own self-reliance, she suddenly and unexpectedly found herself exulting in a quality heretofore unknown to her—that quality which had compelled an almost total stranger to take her part. Then the man himself! How straight and strong and handsome he was as he stood looking at Judson, and then the uplifted arm, the quick spring, and, best of all, the calm, graceful way in which he had handed her the chair! She could not get the picture out of her mind. Last, she remembered with a keen sense of pleasure the chivalrous look in his face when he held out his hand to the man who a moment before had received its full weight about his throat.

She had not regained mastery of herself even when she leaned across her drawing-board, pretending to be absorbed in her work. The curves of the Milo seemed in some strange way to have melted into the semblance of the outlines of other visions sunk deep in her soul since the days of her childhood—visions which for years past had been covered over by the ice of a cold, hard puritanical training, that had prevented any bubbles of sentiment from ever rising to the surface of her heart. As remembrances of these visions rushed through her mind the half-draped woman, with the face of the Madonna and the soul of the Universal Mother shining through every line of her beautiful body, no longer stood before her. It was a knight in glittering armor now, with drawn sword and visor up, beneath which looked out the face of a beautiful youth aflame with the fire of a holy zeal. She caught the flash of the sun on his breastplate of silver, and the sweep of his blade, and heard his clarion voice sing out. And then again, as she closed her eyes, this calm, lifeless cast became a gallant, blue-eyed prince, who knelt beside her and kissed her finger-tips, his doffed plumes trailing at her feet.

When the band of students were leaving the rooms that night, Margaret called Oliver to her side, and extending her hand, said, with a direct simplicity that carried conviction in every tone of her voice and in which no trace of her former emotions were visible:

"I hope you'll forgive me, Mr. Horn. I'm all alone here in this city and I have grown so accustomed to depending on myself that, perhaps, I failed to understand how you felt about it. I am very grateful to you. Good-night."

She had turned away before he could do more than express his regret over the occurrence. He wanted to follow her; to render her some assistance; to comfort her in some way. It hurt him to see her go out alone into the night. He wished he might offer his arm, escort her home, make some atonement for the pain he had caused her. But there was a certain proud poise of the head and swift glance of the eye which held him back.

While he stood undecided whether to break through her reserve and join her, he saw Mrs. Mulligan come out of the basement, stop a passing stage, and, helping Margaret in, take the seat beside her.

"I am glad she does not go out alone," he said to himself and turned away.

CHAPTER XIII

It was not long before the bare rooms of the
Academy School—owing to the political situation,
which necessitated the exercise of economies in
every direction—began to suffer.

One night the students found the gas turned out
and a small card tacked on the door of the outer hall.
It read—

> SCHOOL CLOSED FOR WANT OF
> FUNDS. WILL PERHAPS BE
> OPENED IN THE AUTUMN.

Signs of like character were not unusual in the history of the school. The wonder was, considering the
vicissitudes through which the Academy had passed,
that it was opened at all. From the institution's earlier beginnings in the old house on Bond Street, to
its flight from the loft close to Grace Church and
then to the abandoned building opposite the old hotel
near Washington Square, where Amos Cobb always

stayed when he came to New York, and so on down to its own home on Broadway, its history had been one long struggle for recognition and support.

This announcement, bitter enough as it was to Oliver, was followed by another even more startling, when he reached the office next day, and Mr. Slade called him into his private room.

"Mr. Horn," said his employer, motioning Oliver to a seat and drawing his chair close beside him so that he could lay his hand upon the young man's knee, "I am very sorry to tell you that after the first of June we shall be obliged to lay you off. It is not because we are dissatisfied with your services, for you have been a faithful clerk, and we all like you and wish you could stay, but the fact is if this repudiation goes on we will all be ruined. I am not going to discharge you; I'm only going to give you a holiday for a few months. Then, if the war-scare blows over we want you back again. I appreciate that this has come as suddenly upon you as it has upon us, and I hope you will not feel offended when, in addition to your salary, I hand you the firm's check for an extra amount. You must not look upon it as a gift, for you have earned every cent of it."

These two calamities were duly reported in a ten-page letter to his mother by our young hero, sitting alone, as he wrote, up in his sky-parlor, crooning over his dismal coke fire. "Was he, then, to begin over again the weary tramping of the streets?" he said to himself. "And the future! What did that hold in store for him? Would the time ever come when he could follow the bent of his tastes? He was getting on so well—even Miss Grant had said so—and it had not interfered with his work at the store, either. The check in his pocket proved that."

His mother's answer made his heart bound with joy.

"Take Mr. Slade at his word. He is your friend and means what he says. Find a place for the summer where you can live cheaply and where the little money which you now have will pay your way. In the fall you can return to your work. Don't think of coming home, much as I should like to put my arms around you. I cannot spare the money to bring you here now, as I have just paid the interest on the mortgage. Moreover, the whole of Kennedy Square is upset and our house seems to be the centre of disturbance. Your father's views on slavery are well known, and he is already being looked upon with disfavor by some of our neighbors. At the club the other night he and Judge Bowman had some words which were very distressing to me. Mr. Cobb was present, and was the only one who took your father's part. Your father, as you may imagine, is very anxious over the political situation, but I cannot think our people are going to fight and kill each other, as

Colonel Clayton predicts they will before another year has passed."

Oliver's heart bounded like a loosened balloon as he laid down his mother's letter and began pacing the room. Neither the political outlook, nor club discussions, nor even his mother's hopes and fears, concerned him. It was the sudden loosening of all his bonds that thrilled him. Four months to do as he pleased in; the dreadful mortgage out of the way for six months; his mother willing, and he with money enough in his pocket to pay his way without calling upon her for a penny! Was there ever such luck! All care rolled from his shoulders—even the desire to see his mother and Sue and those whom he loved at home was forgotten in the rosy prospect before him.

The next day he told Mr. Slade of his plans, and read him part of his mother's letter.

"Very sensible woman, your mother," his employer answered, with his bluff heartiness. "Just the thing for you to do; and I've got the very spot. Go to Ezra Pollard's. He lives up in the mountains at a little place called East Branch, on the edge of a wilderness. I fish there every spring, and I'll give you a letter to him."

Long before his day of departure came he had dusted out his old hair trunk—there were other and more modern trunks to be had, but Oliver loved this one because it had been his father's—gathered his painting materials together — his easel, brushes, leather case, and old slouch hat that he wore to fish in at home—and spent his time counting the days and hours when he could leave the world behind him and, as he wrote Fred, " begin to live."

He was not alone in this planning for a summer exodus. The other students had indeed all cut their tether-strings and disappeared long before his own freedom came. Jack Bedford had gone to the coast to live with a fisherman and paint the surf, and Fred was with his people away up near the lakes. As for the lithographers, sign-painters, and beginners, they were spending their evenings somewhere else than in the old room under the shaded gas-jets. Even Margaret, so Mother Mulligan told him, was up " wid her folks, somewheres."

" And she was that broken-hearted," she added, " whin they shut up the school—bad cess to 'em! Oh, ye would a-nigh kilt yerself wid grief to a-seen her, poor darlint."

" Where is her home? " asked Oliver, ignoring the tribute to his sympathetic tendencies. He had no reason for asking, except that she had been the only woman among them, and he accordingly felt that a certain courtesy was due her even in her absence.

" I've bothered me head loose tryin' to remimber, but for the soul o' me, I can't. It's cold enough up there, I know, to freeze ye solid, for Miss Margaret had wan o' her ears nipped last time she was home."

And so one fine morning in June, with Oliver bursting with happiness, the hair trunk and the leather case and sketching umbrella were thrown out at a New England way-station in the gray dawn from a train in which Oliver had spent the night curled up on one of the seats.

Just as he had expected, the old coach that was to carry him was waiting beside the platform. There was a rush for top seats, and Oliver got the one beside the driver, and the trunk and traps were stored in the boot under the driver's seat—it was a very small trunk and took up but little room—and Marvin cracked his whip and away everybody went, the dogs barking behind and the women waving their aprons from the porches of the low houses facing the road.

And it was a happy young fellow who filled his lungs with the fresh air of the morning and held on to the iron rail of the top seat as they bumped over the " Thank ye marms," and who asked the driver innumerable questions which it was part of the noted whip's duty and always his pleasure to answer. The squirrels darted across the road as if to get a look at the enthusiast and then ran for their lives to escape the wheels; and the crows heard the rumble and rose in a body from the sparse cornfields for a closer view;

and the big trees arched over his head, cooling the air and casting big shadows, and even the sun kept peeping over the edge of the hills from behind some jutting rock or clump of pines or hemlock as if bent on lighting up his face so that everybody could see how happy he was.

As the day wore on and the coach rattled over the big open bridge that spanned the rushing mountain-stream, Oliver's eye caught, far up the vista, the little dent in the line of blue that stood low against the sky. The driver said this was the Notch and that the big hump to the right was Moose Hillock, and that Ezra's cabin nestled at its feet and was watered by the rushing stream, only it was a tiny little brook away up there that anybody could step over.

" 'Tain't bigger'n yer body where it starts out fresh up in them mountings," the driver said, touching his leaders behind their ears with the lash of his whip. " Runs clean round Ezra's, and's jest as chuckfull o' trout, be gosh, as a hive is o' bees."

And the swing and the freedom of it all! No office-hours to keep; no boxes to nail up and roll out—nothing but sweetness and cool draughts of fresh mountain-air, and big trees that he wanted to get down and hug; and jolly laughing brooks that ran out to meet him and called to him as he trotted along, or as the horses did, which was the same thing, he being part of the team.

And the day! Had there ever been such another?
And the sky, too, filled with soft white clouds that
sailed away over his head—the little ones far in
advance and already crowding up the Notch, which
was getting nearer every hour.

And Marvin the driver—what a character he was
and how quaint his speech. And the cabins by the
road, with their trim fences and winter's wood piled
up so neatly under the sheds—all so different from
any which he had seen at the South and all so charming and exhilarating.

Never had he been so happy!

And why not? Twenty-three and in perfect
health, without a care, and for the first time in all
his life doing what he wanted most to do, with opportunities opening every hour for doing what he believed he could do best.

Oh, for some planet where such young saplings can
grow without hinderance from the ignorant and the
unsympathetic; where they can reach out for the sun
on all sides and stretch their long arms skyward; ·
where each vine can grow as it would in all the lux-
uriance of its nature, free from the pruning-knife
of criticism and the straitlaced trellis of convention-
ality—a planet on which the Puritan with his creeds,
customs, fads, issues, and dogmas, and the Cavalier
with his traditions and time-honored notions never
sat foot. Where every round peg fits a round hole,

and men toil with a will and with unclouded brows because their hearts find work for their hands and each day's task is a joy.

If the road and the country on each side of it, and the giant trees, now that they neared the mountains, and the deep ravines and busy, hurrying brooks had each inspired some exclamation of joy from Oliver, the first view of Ezra's cabin filled him so full of uncontrollable delight that he could hardly keep his seat long enough for Marvin to rein in his horses and get down and swing back the gate that opened into the pasture surrounding the house.

"Got a boarder for ye, Ezra," Marvin called to Oliver's prospective host, who had come down to meet the stage and get his empty butter-pails. Then, in a lower tone: "Sezs he's a painter chap, and that Mr. Slade sent him up. He's goin' to bunk in with ye all summer, he sezs. Seems like a knowin', happy kind er young feller."

They were pulling the pails from the rear boot, each one tied up in a wheat-sack, with a card marked "Ezra Pollard" sewed on the outside to distinguish it from the property of other East Branch settlers up and down the road.

Oliver had slipped from his seat and was tugging at his hair trunk. He did not know that the long, thin, slab-sided old fellow in a slouch hat, hickory shirt crossed by one suspender, and heavy cowhide boots was his prospective landlord. He supposed him to be the hired man, and that he would find Mr. Pollard waiting for him in the little sitting-room with the windows full of geraniums that looked so inviting and picturesque.

"Marve sez you're lookin' fur me. Come along. Glad ter see ye."

"Are you Mr. Pollard?" His surprise not only marked the tones of his voice but the expression of his face.

"No, jes' Ezry Pollard, that's all. Hope Mr. Slade's up and hearty?"

Mr. Slade was never so "up and hearty" as was Oliver that next morning.

Up with the sun he was, and hearty as a young buck out of a bed of mountain-moss.

"Time to be movin', ain't it?" came Ezra Pollard's voice, shouting up the unpainted staircase, "Hank's drawed a bucket out here at the well for ye to wash in. Needn't worry about no towel. Samanthy's got one fur ye, but ye kin bring yer comb."

At the sound of Ezra's voice Oliver sprang from the coarse straw mattress—it had been as eider-down to his stage-jolted body—pushed open the wooden blind and peered out. The sun was peeping over the edge of the Notch and looking with wide eyes into the saucer-shaped valley in which the cabin stood. The

fogs which at twilight had stolen down to the mead-
ows and had made a night of it, now startled into life
by the warm rays of the sun, were gathering up their
skirts of shredded mist and tiptoeing back up the
hill-side, looking over their shoulders as they fled.
The fresh smell of the new corn watered by the
night dew and the scent of pine and balsam from the
woods about him, filled the morning air. Songs of
birds were all about, a robin on a fence-post and two
larks high in air, singing as they flew.

Below him, bounding from rock to rock, ran the
brook, laughing in the sunlight and tossing the spray
high in the air in a mad frolic. Across this swirling
line of silver lay a sparse meadow strewn with rock,
plotted with squares of last year's crops—potatoes,
string-beans, and cabbages, and now combed into
straight green lines of early buckwheat and turnips.
Beyond this a ragged pasture, fenced with blackened
stumps, from which came the tinkle of cow-bells, and
farther on the grim, silent forest—miles and miles of
forest seamed by a single road leading to Moose Hillock and the great Stone Face.

Oliver slipped into his clothes; ran down the stairs
and out into the fresh morning air. As he walked
toward the well his eyes caught sight of Hank's
bucket tilted on one edge of the well-curb, over which
hung the big sweep, its lower end loaded with stone.
On the platform stood a wooden bench sloppy

with the drippings of the water-soaked pail. This bench held a tin basin and half a bar of rosin soap. Beside it was a single post sprouting hickory prongs, on which were hung as many cleanly scoured milk-pails glittering in the sun. On this post Hank had nailed a three-cornered piece of looking-glass—Hank had a sweetheart in the village below—a necessity and useful luxury, he told Oliver afterward, " in slickin' yerself up fer meals."

Once out in the sunshine Oliver, with the instinct of the painter suddenly roused, looked about him. He found that the cabin which had delighted him so in the glow of the afternoon, was even more enchanting in the light of the morning. To the plain, every-day, practical man it was but a long box with a door in the middle of each side, front and back—one opening into a sitting-room, which again opened into a bed-room in which Ezra and his wife slept, with the win-dows choked with geraniums, their red cheeks pressed against the small panes, and the other opening into a kitchen, connecting with a pantry and a long, rambling woodshed. To our young Raphael the simple cabin, from its homely sagging door to its broken-backed roof, covered with rotting shingles, was nothing less than an enchanted palace.

He remembered the shingles. He had reached up in the night and touched them with his hands. He remembered, too, the fragrance they gave out—a hot, dry, spicy smell. He remembered also the dried apples spread out on a board beside his bed, and the broken spinning-wheel, and the wasp's nest. He was sure, too, there were many other fascinating relics stored away in this old attic. But for the sputtering tallow-candle, which the night before was nearly burnt out, he would have examined everything else about him before he went to sleep.

Then his eye fell on the woodshed and the huge pile of chips that Hank's axe had made in supplying Samanthy's stove, and the rickety, clay-plastered buggy and buckboard that had never known water since the day of their birth. And the two muskrat skins nailed to the outside planking—spoils of the mill-dam, a mile below.

Yes; he could paint here!

With a thrill of delight surging through him he rolled up his sleeves, tilted the bucket, filled the basin with ice-cold water which Hank had drawn for him, a courtesy only shown a stranger guest, and plunging in his hands and face, dashed the water over his head. Samanthy, meanwhile, in sunbonnet and straight-up-and-down calico dress, had come out with the towel—half a salt-sack, washed and rewashed to phenomenal softness (an ideal towel is a salt-sack to those who know). Then came the rubbing until his flesh was aglow, and the parting of the wet hair with the help of Hank's glass, and with a toss of a stray

lock back from his forehead Oliver went in to breakfast.

It fills me with envy when I think of that first toilet
of Oliver's! I too have had just such morning dips
—one in Como, with the great cypresses standing
black against the glow of an Italian dawn; another
in the Lido at sunrise, my gondolier circling about me
as I swam; still a third in Stamboul, with the long
slants of light piercing the gloom of the stone dome
above me—but oh, the smell of the pines and the
great sweep of openness, with the mountains looking down and the sun laughing, and the sparkle and
joyousness of it all! Ah, what a lucky dog was this
Oliver!

And the days that followed! Each one a delight—
each one happier than the one before. The sun
seemed to soak into his blood; the strength of the
great hemlocks with their giant uplifted arms seemed
to have found its way to his muscles. He grew
stronger, more supple. He could follow Hank all
day now, tramping the brook or scaling the sides of
Bald Face, its cheeks scarred with thunderbolts.
And with this joyous life there came a light into his
eyes, a tone in his voice, a spring and buoyancy in
his step that brought him back to the days when he
ran across Kennedy Square and had no care for the
day nor thought for the morrow. Before the week
was out he had covered half a dozen canvases with

pictures of the house as he saw it that first morning, bathed in the sunshine; of the brook; the sweep of the Notch, and two or three individual trees that he had fallen in love with—a ragged birch in particular —a tramp of a birch with its toes out of its shoes and its bark coat in tatters.

Before the second week had arrived he had sought the main stage-road and had begun work on a big hemlock that stood sentinel over a turn in the highway. There was a school-house in the distance and a log-bridge under which the brook plunged. Here he settled himself for serious work.

He was so engrossed that he had not noticed the school-children who had come up noiselessly from behind and were looking in wonder at his drawings. Presently a child, who in her eagerness had touched his shoulder, broke the stillness in apology.

"Say, Mister, there's a lady comes to school every day. She's a painter too, and drawed Sissy Mathers."

Oliver glanced at the speaker and the group about her; wished them all good-morning and squeezed a fresh tube on his palette. He was too much absorbed in his work for prolonged talk. The child, emboldened by his cheery greeting, began again, the others crowding closer. "She drawed the bridge too, and me and Jennie Waters was sitting on the rail—she's awful nice."

Oliver looked up, smiling.

" What's her name? "

" I don't know. Teacher calls her Miss Margaret, but there's more to it. She comes every year."

Oliver bent over his easel, drew out a fine brush from the sheaf in his hand, caught up a bit of yellow ochre from his palette and touched up the shadow of the birch. " All the women painters must be Margarets," he said to himself. Then he fell to wondering what had become of her since the school closed. He had always felt uncomfortable over the night when he had defended " the red-headed girl in blue gingham," as she was called by the students. She had placed him in the wrong by misunderstanding his reasons for serving her. The students had always looked upon him after that as a quarrelsome person, when he was only trying to protect a woman from insult. He could not find it in his heart to blame her, but he wished that it had not happened. As these thoughts filled his mind he became so absorbed that the children's good-by failed to reach his ear.

That day Hank had brought him his luncheon—two ears of hot corn in a tin bucket, four doughnuts and an apple—the corn in the bottom of the bucket and the doughnuts and apple on top. He could have walked home for his midday meal, for he was within sound of Samanthy's dinner-horn, but he liked it better this way.

Leaving his easel standing in the road, he had waved his hand in good-by to Hank, picked up the bucket and had crept under the shadow of the bridge to eat his luncheon. He had finished the corn, thrown the cobs to the fish, and was beginning on the doughnuts, when a step on the planking above him caused him to look up. A girl in a tam-o'-shanter cap was leaning over the rail. The sun was behind her, throwing her face into shadow—so blinding a light that Oliver only caught the nimbus of fluffy hair that framed the dark spot of her head. Then came a voice that sent a thrill of surprise through him.

" Why, Mr. Horn! Who would have thought of meeting you here? "

Oliver was on his feet in an instant—a half-eaten doughnut in one hand, his slouch hat in the other. With this he was shading his eyes against the glare of the sun. He was still ignorant of who had spoken to him.

" I beg your pardon, I—*why*, Miss Grant! " The words burst from his lips as if they had been fired from a gun. " You here! "

" Yes, I live only twenty miles away, and I come here every year. Where are you staying? "

" At Pollard's. "

" Why, that's the next clearing from mine. I'm

at old Mrs. Taft's. Oh, please don't leave your luncheon."

Oliver had bounded up the bank to a place beside her.

"How good it is to find you here. I am so glad." He *was* glad; he meant every word of it. "Mrs. Mulligan said you lived up in the woods, but I had no idea it was in these mountains. Have you had your luncheon?"

"No, not yet," and Margaret held up a basket. "Look!" and she raised the lid. "Elderberry pie, two pieces of cake——"

"Good! and I have three doughnuts and an apple. I swallowed every grain of my hot corn like a greedy Jack Horner, or you should have half of it. Come down under the bridge, it's so cool there," and he caught her hand to help her down the bank.

She followed him willingly. She had seen him greet Fred, and Jack Bedford, and even the gentle Professor with just such outbursts of affection, and she knew there was nothing especially personal to her in it all. It was only his way of saying he was glad to see her.

Oliver laid the basket and tin can on a flat stone that the spring freshets had scoured clean; spread his brown corduroy jacket on the pebbly beach beside it, and with a laugh and the mock gesture of a courtier, conducted her to the head of his improvised table.

BELOW MOOSE HILLOCK

Margaret laughed and returned the bow, stepping backward with the sweep of a great lady, and settled herself beside him. In a moment she was on her knees bending over the brook, her hands in the water, the tam-o'-shanter beside her. She must wash her hands, she said—"there was a whole lot of chrome yellow on her fingers"—and she held them up with a laugh for Oliver's inspection. Oliver watched her while she dried and bathed her shapely hands, smoothed the hair from her temples and tightened the coil at the back of her head which held all this flood of gold in check, then he threw himself down beside her, waiting until she should serve the feast.

As he told her of his trip up the valley and the effect it made upon him, and how he had never dreamed of anything so beautiful, and how good the Pollards were; and what he had painted and what he expected to paint; talking all the time with his thumb circling about as if it was a bit of charcoal and the air it swept through but a sheet of Whatman's best, her critical eye roamed over his figure and costume. She had caught in her first swift, comprehensive glance from over the bridge-rail, the loose jacket and broad-brimmed planter's hat, around which, with his love of color, Oliver had twisted a spray of nasturtium blossoms and leaves culled from the garden-patch that morning; but now that he was closer, she

277

saw the color in his cheeks and noticed, with a suppressed smile, the slight mustache curling at the ends, a new feature since the school had closed. She followed too the curves of the broad chest and the muscles outlined through his shirt. She had never thought him so strong and graceful, nor so handsome. (The smile came to the surface now—an approving, admiring smile.) It was the mountain-climbing, no doubt, she said to herself, and the open-air life that had wrought the change.

With a laugh and toss of her head she unpacked her own basket and laid her contribution to the feast on the flat rock—the pie on a green dock-leaf, which she reached over and pulled from the water's edge, and the cake on the pink napkin—the only sign of city luxury in her outlay. Oliver's eye meanwhile wandered over her figure and costume—a costume he had never seen before on any living woman, certainly not any woman around Kennedy Square. The cloth skirt came to her ankles, which were covered with yarn stockings, and her feet were encased in shoes that gave him the shivers, the soles being as thick as his own and the leather as tough. (Sue Clayton would have died with laughter had she seen those shoes.) Her blouse was of gray flannel, belted to the waist by a cotton saddle-girth—white and red —and as broad as her hand. The tam-o'-shanter was coarse and rough, evidently home-made, and not at all like McFudd's, which was as soft as the back of a kitten and without a seam.

Then his eyes sought her face. He noticed how brown she was—and how ruddy and healthy. How red the lips—red as mountain-berries, and back of them big white teeth—white as peeled almonds. He caught the line of the shoulders and the round of the full arm and tapering wrist, and the small, well-shaped hand. "Queer clothes," he said to himself —"but the girl inside is all right."

Sitting under the shadow of the old bridge on the main highway, each weighed and balanced the other, even as they talked aloud of the Academy School, and the pupils, and the dear old Professor whom they both loved. They discussed the prospect of its doors being opened the next winter. They talked of Mrs. Mulligan, and the old Italian who sold peanuts, and whose head Margaret had painted; and of Jack Bedford and Fred Stone—the dearest fellow in the world—and last year's pictures—especially Church's "Niagara," the sensation of the year, and Whittredge's "Mountain Brook," and every other subject their two busy brains could rake and scrape up except —and this subject, strange to say, was the only one really engrossing their two minds—the overturning of Mr. Judson's body on the art-school floor, and the upsetting of Miss Grant's mind for days thereafter. Once Oliver had unintentionally neared the danger-line by mentioning the lithographer's name, but Margaret had suddenly become interested in the movements of a chipmunk that had crept down for the crumbs of their luncheon, and with a woman's wit had raised her finger to her lips to command silence lest he should be frightened off.

They painted no more that afternoon. When the shadows began to fall in the valley they started up the road, picking up Oliver's easel and trap—both had stood unmolested and would have done so all summer with perfect safety—and Oliver walked with Margaret as far as the bars that led into Taft's pasture. There they bade each other good-night, Margaret promising to be ready in the morning with her big easel and a fresh canvas, which Oliver was to carry, when they would both go sketching together and make a long blessed summer day of it.

That night Oliver's upraised, restless hands felt the shingles over his head more than once before he could get to sleep. He had not thought he could be any happier—but he was. Margaret's unexpected appearance had restored to him that something which the old life at home had always yielded. He was never really happy without the companionship of a woman, and this he had not had since leaving Kennedy Square. Those he had met on rare occasions in New York were either too conventional or self-conscious, or they seemed to be offended at his familiar Southern ways. This one was so sensible and companionable, and so appreciative and sympathetic. He felt he could say anything to her and she would know what he meant. Perhaps, too, by and by she would understand just why he had upset a man who had been rude to her.

Margaret lay awake, too—not long—not more than five minutes, perhaps. Long enough, however, to wish she was not so sunburnt, and that she had brought her other dress and a pair of gloves and a hat instead of this rough mountain-suit. Long enough, too, to recall Oliver's standing beside her on the bridge with his big hat sweeping the ground, the color mounting to his cheeks, and that joyous look in his eyes.

" Was he really glad to see me," she said to herself, as she dropped off into dreamland, " or is it his way with all the women he meets? I wonder, too, if he protects them all?"

And so ended a day that always rang out in Oliver's memory with a note of its own.

These dreams under the shingles! What would life be without them?

CHAPTER XIV

The weeks that followed were rare ones for Margaret and Oliver.

They painted all day and every day.

The little school-children posed for them, and so did the prim school-mistress, a girl of eighteen in spectacles with hair cut short in the neck. And old Jonathan Gordon, the fisherman, posed, too, with a string of trout in one hand and a long pole cut from a sapling in the other. And once our two young comrades painted the mill-dam and the mill—Oliver doing the first and Margaret the last; and Baker, the miller, caught them at it, and insisted in all sincerity that some of the money which the pictures brought must come to him, if the report were true that painters did get money for pictures. " It's my mill, ain't it?—and I ain't give no permission to take no part of it away. Hev I? "

They climbed the ravines, Margaret carrying the luncheon and Oliver the sketch-traps; they built fires of birch-bark and roasted potatoes, or made tea in the little earthen pot that Mrs. Taft loaned her. Or

282

they waited for the stage in the early morning, and went half a dozen miles down the valley to paint some waterfall Oliver had seen the day he drove up with Marvin, or a particular glimpse of Moose Hillock from the covered bridge, or various shady nooks and sunlit vistas that remained fastened in Oliver's mind, and the memory of which made him unhappy until Margaret could enjoy them, too.

The fact that he and a woman whom he had known but a little while were roaming the woods together, quite as a brother and sister might have done, never occurred to him. If it had it would have made no difference, nor could he have understood why any barrier should have been put up between them. He had been taking care of girls in that same way all his life. Every woman was a sister to him so far as his reverent protection over her went. The traditions of Kennedy Square had taught him this.

As the joyous weeks flew by, even the slight reserve which had marked their earlier intercourse began to wear off. It was " Oliver " and " Margaret " now, and even " Ollie " and " Madge " when they forgot themselves and each other in their work.

To Margaret this free and happy life together seemed natural enough. She had decided on the day of their first meeting that Oliver's interest in her was due wholly to his love of companionship, and not because of any special liking he might feel for her. Had she not seen him quite as cordial and as friendly to the men he knew? Satisfied on this point, Oliver began to take the place of a brother, or cousin, or some friend of her youth who loved another woman, perhaps, and was, therefore, safe against all contingencies, while she gave herself up to the enjoyment of that rare luxury—the rarest that comes to a woman—daily association with a man who could be big and strong and sympathetic, and yet ask nothing in return for what she gave him but her companionship and confidence.

In the joy of this new intercourse, and with his habit of trusting implicitly everyone whom he loved —man, woman, or child—Oliver, long before the first month was over, had emptied his heart to Margaret as completely as he had ever done to Miss Clendenning. He had told her of Sue and of Miss Lavinia's boudoir, and of Mr. Crocker and his pictures; and of his poor father's struggles and his dear mother's determination to send him from home—not about the mortgage, that was his mother's secret, not his own—and of the great receptions given by his Uncle Tilghman, and of all the other wonderful doings in Kennedy Square.

She had listened at first in astonishment, and then with impatience. Many of the things that seemed so important to him were valueless in her more practical eyes. Instead of a régime which ennobled those who enjoyed its privileges, she saw only a slavish devotion to worn-out traditions, and a clannish provincialism which proved to her all the more clearly the narrow-mindedness of the people who sustained and defended them. So far as she could judge, the qualities that she deemed necessary in the make-up of a robust life, instinct with purpose and accomplishment, seemed to be entirely lacking in Kennedy Square formulas. She saw, too, with a certain undefined pain, that Oliver's mind had been greatly warped by these influences. Mrs. Horn's domination over him, strange to say, greatly disturbed her; why, she could not tell. "She must be a proud, aristocratic woman," she had said to herself after one of Oliver's outbursts of enthusiasm over his mother; "wedded to patrician customs and with no consideration for anyone outside of her class."

And yet none of these doubts and criticisms made the summer days less enjoyable.

One bright, beautiful morning when the sky was a turquoise, the air a breath of heaven, and the brooks could be heard laughing clear out on the main road, Oliver and Margaret, who had been separated for some days while she paid a visit to her family at home, started to find a camp that Hank had built the winter before as a refuge while he was hunting deer. They had reached a point in the forest where two paths met, when Margaret's quick ear caught the sound of a human voice, and she stopped to listen.

"Quick—" she cried—"get behind these spruces, or he will see us and stop singing. It's old Mr. Burton. He is such a dear! He spends his summers here. I often meet him and he always bows to me so politely, although he doesn't know me."

A man of sixty—bare-headed, dressed in a gray suit, with his collar and coat over his arm and hands filled with wild-flowers, was passing leisurely along, singing at the top of his voice. Once he stopped, and, bending over, picked a bunch of mountain-berries which he tucked into a buttonhole of his flannel shirt, just before disappearing in a turn of the path.

Oliver looked after him for a moment. He had caught the look of sweet serenity on the idler's face, and the air of joyousness that seemed to linger behind him like a perfume, and it filled him with delight.

"There, Margaret! that's what I call a happy man. I'll wager you he has never done anything all his life but that which he loved to do—just lives out here and throws his heart wide open for every beautiful thing that can crowd into it. That's the kind of a man I want to be. Oh! I'm so glad I saw him."

Margaret was silent. She was walking ahead, her staff in her hand; the fallen trunks and heavy underbrush making it difficult for them to walk abreast.

"Do you think that he never had to work, to be

286

able to enjoy himself as he does?" she asked over her shoulder, with a toss of her head.

"Perhaps—but he loved what he was doing."

"No, he didn't—he hated it—hated it all his life." The tone carried a touch of defiance that was new to Oliver. He stepped quickly after her, with a sudden desire to look into her face. Ten minutes, at least, had passed during which he had seen only the back of her head.

Margaret heard his step behind her and quickened her own. Something was disturbing the joyousness of our young Diana this lovely summer morning.

"What did the old fellow do for a living, Margaret?" Oliver called, still trying to keep up with Margaret's springing step.

"Sold lard and provisions, and over the counter, too," she answered, with a note almost of exultation in her voice (she was thinking of Mrs. Horn and Kennedy Square). "Mrs. Taft knows him and used to send him her bacon. He retired rich some years ago, and now he can sing all day if he wants to."

It was Oliver's turn to be silent. The tones of Margaret's voice had hurt him. For some minutes he made no reply. Then wheeling suddenly he sprang over a moss-covered trunk that blocked her path, stepped in front of her, and laid his hand on her shoulder.

"Not offended, Margaret, are you?" he asked, looking earnestly into her eyes.

"No—what nonsense! Of course not. Why do you ask?"

"Well, somehow you spoke as if you were."

"No, I didn't; I only said how dear Mr. Burton was, and he *is*. How silly you are! Come—we will be late for the camp."

They both walked on in silence, now, he ahead this time, brushing aside the thick undergrowth that blocked the path.

The exultant tones in her voice which had hurt her companion, and which had escaped her unconsciously, still rang in her own ears. She felt ashamed of the outburst now as she watched him cutting the branches ahead of her, and thought how gentle and tender he had always been to her and how watchful over her comfort. She wondered at the cause of her frequent discontent. Then, like an evil spirit that would not down, there arose in her mind, as she walked on, the picture she had formed of Kennedy Square. She thought of his mother's imperious nature absorbing all the love of his heart and inspiring and guiding his every action and emotion; of the unpractical father—a dreamer and an enthusiast, the worst possible example he could have; of the false standards and class distinctions which had warped his early life and which were still dominating him. With

288

an abrupt gesture of impatience she stood still in the path and looked down upon the ground. An angry flush suffused her face.

"What a stupid fool you are, Margaret Grant," she burst out impatiently. "What are Kennedy Square and the whole Horn family to you?"

Oliver's halloo brought her to consciousness.

"Here's that slant, Margaret—oh, such a lovely spot! Hurry up."

"The slant" had been built between two great trees and stood on a little mound of earth surrounded by beds of velvety green moss—huge green winding sheets, under which lay the bodies of many giant pines and hemlocks. The shelter was made of bark and bedded down with boughs of sweet-balsam. Outside, on a birch sapling, supported by two forked sticks, hung a rusty kettle. Beneath the rude spit, half-hidden by the growth of the summer, lay the embers of the abandoned camp-fires that had warmed and comforted Hank and his companions the preceding winter.

Oliver raked the charred embers from under the tangled vines that hid them, while Margaret peeled the bark from a silver-birch for kindling. Soon a curl of blue smoke mounted heavenward, hung suspended over the tree-tops, and then drifted away in scarfs of silver haze dimming the forms of the giant trunks.

THE FORTUNES OF OLIVER HORN

Our young enthusiast watched the Diaz of a wood interior turn slowly into a Corot, and with a cry of delight was about to unstrap his own and Margaret's sketching-kits, when the sun was suddenly blotted out by a heavy cloud, and the quick gloom of a mountain-storm chilling the sunlit vista to a dull slate gray settled over the forest. Oliver walked over to the brook for a better view of the sky, and came back bounding over the moss-covered logs as he ran. There was not a moment to lose if they would escape being drenched to the skin.

The outlook was really serious. Old Bald Face had not only lost his smile—a marvellously happy one with the early sun upon his wrinkled countenance—but he had put on his judgment-cap of gray clouds and had begun to thunder out his disapproval of everything about him. Moose Hillock evidently heard the challenge, for he was answering back in the murky darkness. Soon a cold, raw wind, which had been asleep in the hills for weeks, awoke with a snarl and started down the gorge. Then the little leaves began to quiver, the big trees to groan, in their anxiety not knowing what the will of the wind would be, and the merry little waves that had chased each other all the morning over the sunny shallows of the brook, grew ashy pale as they looked up into the angry face of the Storm-God, and fled shivering to the shore.

UNDER A BARK SLANT

Oliver whipped out his knife, stripped the heavy outer bark from a white birch, and before the dashing rain could catch up with the wind, had repaired the slant so as to make it water-tight—Hank had taught him this—then he started another great fire in front of the slant and threw fresh balsam boughs on the bed that had rested Hank's tired limbs, and he and Margaret crept in and were secure.

The equanimity of Margaret's temper, temporarily disturbed by her vivid misconception of Kennedy Square, was restored. The dry shelter, the warm fire, the sense of escape from the elements, all filled her heart with gladness. Never since the day she met him on the bridge had she been so happy. Again, as when Oliver championed her in the old Academy school-room, there stole over her a vague sense of pleasure in being protected.

"Isn't it jolly!" she said as she sat hunched up beside him. "I'm as dry as a bone, not a drop on me."

Oliver was even more buoyant. There was something irresistibly cosey and comfortable in the shelter which he had provided for her—something of warmth and companionship and rest. But more intensely enjoyable than all was the thought that he was taking care of a woman for the first time in his life, as it seemed to him. And in a house of his own making, and in a place, too, of his own choosing, surrounded by the big trees that he loved. He had even outwitted the elements—the wind and the rain and the chill—in her defence. Old Moose Hillock could bellow now and White Face roar, and the wind and rain vent their wrath, but Margaret, close beside him, would still be warm and dry and safe.

By this time she had hung her tam-o'-shanter and jacket on a nail that she had found in the bark over her head, and was arranging her hair.

"It's just like life, Oliver, isn't it?" she said, as she tightened the coil in her neck. "All we want, after all, is a place to get into out of the storm and wet, not a big place, either."

"What kind of a place?" He was on his knees digging a little trench with his knife, piling up the moist earth in miniature embankments, so that the dripping from the roof would not spatter this Princess of his whom he had saved from the tempest outside.

"Oh, any kind of a place if you have people you're fond of. I'd love a real studio somewhere, and a few things hung about—some old Delft and one or two bits of stuff—and somebody to take care of me."

Oliver shifted his pipe in his mouth and looked up. Would she, with all her independence, really like to have someone take care of her? He had seen no evidence of it.

"Who?" he asked. He had never heard her

mention anybody's name—but then she had not told him everything.

He had dropped his eyes again, finishing the drain and flattening the boughs under her, to make the seat the easier.

"Oh, some old woman, perhaps, like dear old Mrs. Mulligan." There was no coquetry in her tone. She was speaking truthfully out of her heart.

"Anything more?" Oliver's voice had lost its buoyancy now. The pipe was upside down, the ashes falling on his shirt.

"Yes—lots of portraits to paint."

"And a medal at the Salon?" asked Oliver, brushing off the waste of his pipe from his coat-sleeve.

"Yes, I don't mind, if my pictures deserve it," and she looked at him quizzically, while a sudden flash of humor lightened up her face. "What would *you* want, Mr. Happy-go-lucky, if you had your wish?"

"I, Madge, dear?" he exclaimed, with a sudden outburst of tenderness, raising his body erect and looking earnestly into her eyes, which were now within a hand's breadth of his own. She winced a little, but it did not offend her, nor did she move an inch. "Oh, I don't know what I want. What I want, I suppose, is what I shall never have, little girl."

She wasn't his little girl, or anybody else's, she thought to herself—she was firmly convinced of that fact. It was only one of his terms of endearment. He had them for everybody—even for Hank and for Mrs. Taft—whom he called "Taffy," and who loved to hear him say it, and she old enough to be his grandmother! She stole a look into his face. There was a cloud over it, a slight knitting of the brows, and a pained expression about the mouth that were new to her.

"I'd like to be a painter," he continued, "but mother would never consent." As he spoke, he sank back from her slowly, his knees still bent under him. Then he added, with a sigh, "She wouldn't think it respectable. Anything but a painter, she says."

Margaret looked out through the forest and watched a woodpecker at work on the dry side of a hollow trunk, the side protected from the driving rain.

"And you would give up your career because she wants it? How do you know she's right about it? And who's to suffer if she's wrong? Be a painter, Oliver, if you want to! Your mother can't coddle you up forever! No mother should. Do what you can do best, and to please yourself, not somebody else," and then she laughed lightly as if to break the force of her words.

Oliver looked at her in indignation that anyone— even Margaret—should speak so of his mother.

It was the first time in all his life that he had heard
her name mentioned without the profound reverence
it deserved. Then a sense of the injustice of her
words took possession of him, as the solemn compact he had made with his mother not to be a burden on her while the mortgage was unpaid, rose in
his mind. This thought and Margaret's laugh softened any hurt her words had given him, although
the lesson that they were intended to teach lingered
in his memory for many days thereafter.

"You would not talk that way, Madge, if you
knew my dear mother," he said, quietly. "There is
nothing in her life she loves better than me. She
doesn't want me to be a painter because—" He
stopped, fearing she might not understand his
answer.

"Go on—why not?" The laugh had faded out
of her voice now, and a tone almost of defiance had
taken its place.

"She says it is not the profession of a gentleman," he answered, sadly. "I do not agree with
her, but she thinks so, and nothing can shake her."

"If those are her opinions, I wonder what she
would think of *me?*" There was a slight irritation in
her voice—somehow she always became irritable
when Oliver spoke of his mother. She was ashamed
of it, but it was true.

All his anger was gone now. Whatever opinion
295

the world might have on any number of things there could be but one opinion of Madge. "She would *love* you, little girl," he burst out as he laid his hand on her arm—the first time he had ever touched her with any show of affection. "You'd make her love you. She never saw anybody like you before, and she never will. That you are an artist wouldn't make any difference. It's not the same with you. You're a woman."

The girl's eyes again sought the woodpecker. It was stabbing away with all its might, driving its beak far into the yielding bark. It seemed in some way to represent her own mood. After a moment's thought she said thoughtfully as she rested her head on the edge of the slant:

"Ollie, what is a gentleman?" She knew, she thought, but she wanted him to define it.

"My father is one," he said, positively, "—and so is yours," and he looked inquiringly into her face.

"That depends on your standard. I don't know your father, but I do mine, and from what you have told me about yours I think they are about as different as two men can be. Answer my question—what is a gentleman?" She was leaning over a little, and tucking a chip under her toes to keep the water away from her shoes. Her eyes sought his again.

"A gentleman, Madge—why, you know what a gentleman is. He is a man well born, well educated, and well bred. That's the standard at home —at least, that's my mother's. Father's standard is the same, only he puts it in a different way. He says a gentleman is a man who tolerates other people's mistakes and who sympathizes with other people's troubles."

"Anything else?" She was searching his face now. There were some things she wanted to settle in her own mind.

"I don't think of anything else, Madge, dear—do you?" He was really dismissing the question. His thoughts were on something else—the way her hair curled from under her worsted cap and the way her pink ears nestled close to her head, especially the little indents at each corner of her mouth. He liked their modelling.

"And so according to your mother's and father's ideas, and those of all your aristocratic people at home, Hank here could not be a gentleman if he tried?"

The idea was new to Oliver. He had become conscious now. What had gotten into Margaret to-day?

"Hank?—no, certainly not. How could he?"

"By *being* a gentleman, Mr. Aristocrat. Not in clothes, mind you—nor money, nor furniture, nor wines, nor carriages, but in *heart*. Think a moment, Ollie," and her eyes snapped. "Hank finds a robin that has tumbled out of its nest, and spends half a day putting it back. Hank follows you up the brook and sees you try to throw a fly into a pool, and he knows just how awkwardly you do it, for he's the best fisherman in the woods—and yet you never see a smile cross his face, nor does he ever speak of it behind your back—not even to me. Hank walks across Moose Hillock to find old Jonathan Gordon to tell him he has some big trout in Loon Pond, so that the old man can have the fun of catching them and selling them afterward to the new hotel in the Notch. He has walked twenty-four miles when he gets back. Do these things make Hank a gentleman, or not?"

"Then you don't believe in Sir Walter Raleigh, Miss Democrat, simply because he was a lord?"

"Yes—but I always thought he wore his old cloak that day on purpose, so he could be made an earl." And a ripple of laughter escaped her lips.

Oliver laughed too, sprang to his feet, and held out his hands so as to lift her up. None of these fine-drawn distinctions really interested him—certainly not on this day, when he was so happy. Why, he wondered, should she want to discuss theories and beliefs and creeds, with the beautiful forest all about and the sky breaking overhead?

"Well, you've walked over mine many a time, Miss Queen Elizabeth, and you haven't decorated me yet, nor made me an earl nor anything else for it, and I'm not going to forgive you either," and he rose to his feet. "Look! Madge, look!" he cried, and sprang out into the path, pointing to the sunshine bursting through the trees—the storm had passed as suddenly as it had come. "Isn't it glorious! Come here quick! Don't wait a minute. I should try to get that with Naples yellow and a little chrome—what do you think?" he asked when she stood beside him, half closing his eyes, to get the effect the better.

Margaret looked at him curiously for a moment. She did not answer. "I cannot fasten his mind on anything in which I am interested," she said to herself, with a sigh, "nor shall I ever overcome these prejudices which seem to be part of his very life."

She paused a moment and an expression of pain passed over her face.

"Pale cadmium would be better," she said, quietly, with a touch of indifference in her tone, and led the way out of the forest to the main road.

CHAPTER XV

The autumn fires were being kindled on the mountains—fires of maple, oak, and birch. Along the leaf-strewn roads the sumach blazed scarlet, and over the rude stone fences blood-red lines of fire followed the trend of leaf and vine. Golden pumpkins lay in the furrows of the corn; showers of apples carpeted the grass of the orchards; the crows flew in straight lines, and the busy squirrels worked from dawn till dark.

Over all settled the requiem haze of the dead summer, blurring the Notch and softening Moose Hillock to a film of gray against the pale sky.

It had been a summer of very great sweetness and charm—the happiest of Oliver's life. He had found that he could do fairly well the things that he liked to do best; that the technical difficulties that had confronted him when he began to paint were being surmounted as the weeks went by, and that the thing that had always been a pain to him had now become a pleasure—pain, because, try as he might, the quality of the result was always below his hopes; a pleas-

300

ure, because some bit of bark, perhaps, or glint of light on moss-covered rock, or tender vista had at last stood out on his canvas with every tone of color true.

Only a painter can understand what all this meant to Oliver; only an out-of-door painter, really. The "studio-man" who reproduces an old study which years before has inspired him, or who evolves a composition from his inner consciousness, has no such thrills over his work. He may, perhaps, have other sensations, but they will lack the spontaneous outburst of enthusiasm over the old sketch.

And how glorious are the memories!

The victorious painter has been weeks over these same trees that have baffled him; he has painted them on gray days and sunny days; in the morning, at noon, and in the gloaming. He has loved their texture and the thousand little lights and darks; the sparkle of the black, green, or gray moss, and the delicate tones that played up and down their stalwart trunks. He has toiled in the heat of the day, his nerves on edge, and sometimes great drops of sweat on his troubled forehead. Now and then he has sprung from his seat for a farther-away look at his sketch. With a sigh and a heart bowed down (oh, how desolate are these hours!) he has noted how wooden and commonplace and mean and despicable his work was—what an insult he has cast upon the beautiful yellow birch, this outdoor, motionless, old model that has stood so patiently before him, posing all day without moving; its big arms above its head; its leaves and branches stock-still to make it all the easier for him.

Suddenly in all this depression, an inspiration has entered his dull brain—he will use burnt umber instead of Vandyke brown for the bark! or light chrome and indigo instead of yellow ochre and black for the green!

Presto! Ah, that's like it! Another pat, and another, and still one more!

How quickly now the canvas loses its pasty mediocrity. How soon the paint and the brush-marks and the niggly little touches fade away and the *thing itself* comes out and says "How do you do?" and that it is so glad to see him, and that it has been lurking behind these colors all day, trying to make his acquaintance, and he would have none of it. What good friends he and the sketch have become now; how proud he is of it, and of possessing it and of *creating* it! Then little quivery-quavers go creeping up and down his spine and away out to his finger-tips; and he *knows* that he has something really *good*.

He carries it home in his hand, oh, so carefully (he strapped its predecessor on his back yesterday without caring), and a dozen times he stops to look at its dear face, propping it against a stump for a better light, just to see if he had not been mistaken after all. He can hardly wait until it is dark enough to see how it looks by gas-light, or candle-light, or kerosene, or whatever else he may have in his quarters. Years after, the dear old thing is still hanging on his studio wall. He has never sold it nor given it away. He could not—it was too valuable, too constantly giving him good advice and showing him what the thing *was*. Not what he thought it was, or hoped it was, or would like it to be, but what it *was*.

Yes, there may be triumphs that come to men digging away on the dull highway of life—triumphs in business; in politics; in discovery; in law; medicine, and science. To each and every profession and pursuit there must come, and does come, a time when a rush of uncontrollable feeling surges through the victor's soul, crowning long hours of work, but they are as dry ashes to a thirsty man compared to the boundless ecstasy a painter feels when, with a becaked palette, some half-dried tubes of color, and a few worn-out, ragged brushes, he compels a six-by-nine canvas to glow with life and truth.

All this Oliver knew and felt. The work of the summer, attended at first with a certain sense of disappointment, had, during the last few weeks of sojourn, as his touch grew surer, not only become a positive pleasure to him, but had produced an exaltation that had kept our young gentleman walking

303

on clouds most of the time, his head in the blue ether.

Margaret's nice sense of color and correct eye had hastened this result. She could grasp at the first glance the masses of light and shade, giving each its proper value in the composition. She and Oliver really studied out their compositions together before either one set a palette, a most desirable practice, by the way, not only for tyros, but for Academicians.

This relying upon Margaret's judgment had become a habit with Oliver. He not only consulted her about his canvases, but about everything else that concerned him. He had never formulated in his mind what this kind of companionship meant to him (we never do when we are in the midst of it), nor had he ever considered what would become of him when the summer was over, and the dream would end, and they each would return to the customary dulness of life; a life where there would be no blue ether nor clouds, nor vanishing points, nor values, nor tones, nor anything else that had made their heaven of a summer so happy.

They had both lived in this paradise for weeks without once bringing themselves to believe it could ever end (why do not such episodes last forever?) when Oliver awoke one morning to the fact that the fatal day of their separation would be upon him in a week's time or less. Margaret, with her more

304

practical mind, had seen farther ahead than Oliver, and her laugh, in consequence, had been less spontaneous of late, and her interest in her work and in Oliver's less intense. She was overpowered by another sensation; she had been thinking of the day, now so near, when the old stage would drive up to Mrs. Taft's pasture-gate, and her small trunk and trap would be carried down on Hank's back and tumbled in, and she would go back alone to duty and the prosaic life of a New England village.

Neither of them supposed that it was anything else but the grief of parting that afflicted them, until there came a memorable autumn night—a night that sometimes comes to the blessed!—when the moon swam in the wide sky, breasting the soft white clouds, and when Oliver and Margaret sat together on the porch of Mrs. Taft's cottage—he on the steps at her feet, she leaning against the railing, the moonlight full upon her face.

They had been there since sunset. They had known all day what was in each other's mind, but they had avoided discussing it. Now they must face it.

"You go to-morrow, Madge?" Oliver asked. He knew she did. He spoke as if announcing a fact.

"Yes."

The shrill cry of a loon, like the cry of a child in pain, sifted down the ravine from the lake above and died away among the pines soughing in the night-wind. Oliver paused for a moment to listen, and went on:

"I don't want you to go. I don't know what I am going to do without you, Madge," he said with a long indrawn sigh.

"You are coming to us at Brookfield, you know, on your way back to New York. That is something." She glanced at him with a slightly anxious look in her eyes, as if waiting for his answer to reassure her.

He rose from his seat and began pacing the gravel. Now and then he would stop, flick a pebble from its bed with his foot, and walk on. She heard the sound of his steps, but she did not look at him, even when he stopped abruptly in front of her.

"Yes, I know, but—that will only make it worse." He was leaning over her now, one foot on the steps. "It tears me all to pieces when I think this is our last night. We've had such a good time all summer. You don't want to go home, do you?"

"No—I'd rather stay." The words came slowly, as if it gave her pain to utter them.

"Well—stay, then," he answered with some animation. "What difference does a few days make? Let us have another week. We haven't been over to Bog Eddy yet; please stay, Madge."

"No, I must go, Ollie."

"But we'll be so happy, little girl."

"Life is not only being happy, Ollie. It's very real sometimes. It is to me—" and a faint sigh escaped her.

"Well, but why make it real to-morrow? Let us make it real next week, not now."

"It would be just as hard for you next week. Why postpone it?" She was looking at him now, watching his face closely.

Her answer seemed to hurt him. With an impatient gesture he straightened himself, turned as if to resume his walk, and then, pushing away the end of her skirt, sat down beside her.

"I don't understand your theories, Madge, and I'm not going to discuss them. I don't want to talk of any such things; I'm too unhappy to-night. When I look ahead and think that if the Academy should not open, you wouldn't come back at all, and that I might not see you for months, I'm all broken up. What am I going to do without you, Madge?" His voice was quivering, and a note of pain ran through it.

"Oh, you will have your work—you'll do just what you did before I came up." She was holding herself in by main strength; why, she could not tell —fighting an almost irresistible impulse to hide her face on his breast and cry.

"What good will that do me when you are gone?"

307

he burst out, with a quick toss of his head and a certain bitterness in his tone.

"Well, but you were very happy before you saw me."

Again the cry of the loon came down the ravine. He turned and with one of his quick, impatient gestures that she knew so well, put his hand on her shoulder.

"Stop, Madge, stop! Don't talk that way. I can't stand it. Look at me!" The pain had become unbearable now. "You've got to listen. I can't keep it back, and I won't. I never met anybody that I loved as I do you. I didn't think so at first. I never thought I could think so, but it's true. You are not my sweetheart nor my friend, nor my companion, nor anything else that ever came into my life. You are my very breath, my soul, my being. I never want you to leave me. I should never have another happy day if I thought this was to end our life. I laid awake half the night trying to straighten it out, and I can't, and there's no straightening it out and never will be unless you love me. Oh, Madge! Madge! Don't turn away from me. Let me be part of you—part of everything you do—and are—and will be."

He caught her hand in his warm palm and laid his cheek upon it. Still holding it fast he raised his head, laid his other hand upon her hair, smoothing

308

it softly, and looked long and earnestly into her eyes as if searching for something hidden in their depths. Then, in a voice of infinite tenderness, he said:

"Madge, darling! Tell me true—could you ever love me?"

She sat still, her eyes fixed on his, her hand nestling in his grasp. Then slowly and carefully, one at a time, she loosened with her other hand the fingers that lay upon her hair, held them for an instant in her own, bent her head and touched them with her lips.

CHAPTER XVI

Brookfield village lay in a great wide meadow through which strayed one of Moose Hillock's lost brooks—a brook tired out with leaping from bowlder to bowlder and taking headers into deep pools, and plunging down between narrow walls of rock. Here in the meadow it caught its breath and rested, idling along, stopping to bathe a clump of willows; whispering to the shallows; laughing gently with another brook that had locked arms with it, the two gossiping together under their breath as they floated on through the tall grasses fringing the banks, or circled about the lily-pads growing in the eddies. In the middle of the meadow, just where two white ribbons of roads crossed, was a clump of trees pierced by a church-spire. Outside of this bower of green—a darker green than the velvet meadow-grass about it—glistened the roofs and windows of the village houses.

All this Oliver saw, at a distance, from the top of the stage.

As he drew nearer and entered the main street,

310

the clump of trees became giant elms, their interlaced branches making shaded cloisters of the village streets. The buildings now became more distinct; first a tavern with a swinging sign, and across the open common a quaint church with a white tower.

At the end of the avenue of trees, under the biggest of the elms, stood an old-fashioned farmhouse, its garden-gate opening on the highway, and its broad acres—one hundred or more—reaching to the line of the vagabond brook.

This was Margaret's home.

The stage stopped; the hair-trunk and sketch-trap were hauled out of the dust-begrimed boot and deposited on the sidewalk at the foot of the giant elm. Oliver swung back the gate and walked up the path in the direction of the low-roofed porch, upon which lay a dog, which raised its head and at the first click of the latch came bounding toward him, barking with every leap.

"Needn't be afraid, she won't hurt you!" shouted a gray-haired man in his shirt-sleeves, who had risen from his seat on the porch and who was now walking down the garden-path. "Get out, Juno! I guess you're the young man that's been painting with our Margaret up in the Gorge. She's been expecting you all morning. Little dusty, warn't it?"

Oliver's face brightened up. This must be Margaret's father!

311

"Mr. Grant, I suppose?"

"Yes, that's what they call me—Silas Grant. Let me take your bag. My son John will be here in a minute, and will help you in with your trunk. Needn't worry, it's all right where it is. Folks are middling honest about here," he added, with a dry laugh, and his hand closed on his guest's—a cold, limp, dead-fish sort of a hand, Oliver thought.

Oliver said he was sure of it, and that he hoped Miss Margaret was well, and the old man said she was, "Thank you," and Oliver surrendered the bag —it was his sketch-trap—and the two walked toward the house. During the mutual greetings the dog sniffed at Oliver's knees and looked up into his face.

"And I suppose this is Juno," our hero said, stopping to pat her head. "Good dog—you don't remember me?" It seemed easier somehow to converse with Juno than with her master. The dog wagged her tail, but gave no indications of uncontrollable joy at meeting her rescuer again.

"Oh, you've seen her? She's Margaret's dog, you know."

"Yes, I know, but she's forgotten me. I saw her before I ever knew—your daughter." It was a narrow escape, but he saved himself in time. "Blessed old dog," he said to himself, and patted her again.

By the time he had reached the porch-steps he had made, unconsciously to himself, a mental inventory of his host's special features: tall, sparsely built, with stooping shoulders and long arms, the big hands full of cold knuckles with rough finger-tips (Oliver found that out when his own warm fingers closed over them); thin face, with high cheek-bones showing above his closely-cropped beard and whiskers; gray eyes—steady, steel-gray eyes, hooded by white eyebrows stuck on like two tufts of cotton-wool; nose big and strong; square jaw hanging on a hinge that opened and shut with each sentence, the upper part of the face remaining motionless as a mask. Oliver remembered having once seen a toy ogre with a jaw and face that worked in the same way. He had caught, too, the bend of his thin legs, the hump of the high shoulders, and saw the brown skin of the neck showing through the close-cut white hair. Suddenly a feeling of repugnance amounting almost to a shrinking dislike of the man took possession of him —it is just such trifles that turn the scales of likes and dislikes for all of us. " Could this really be Margaret's father? " he said to himself. Through whose veins, then, had all her charm and loveliness come? Certainly not from this cold man without grace of speech or polish of manner.

This feeling of repugnance had come with a flash, and in a flash it was gone. On the top step of the low piazza stood a young girl in white, a rose in her hair, her arm around a silver-haired old lady in gray silk, with a broad white handkerchief crossed over her bosom.

Oliver's hat was off in an instant.

Margaret came down one step to greet him and held out both her hands. " Oh, we are so glad to welcome you! " Then turning to her companion she said: " Mother, this is Mr. Horn, who has been so good to me all summer."

The old lady—she was very deaf—cupped one hand behind her ear, and with a gracious smile extended the other to Oliver.

" I am so pleased you came, sir, and I want to thank you for being so kind to our daughter. Her brother John could not go with her, and husband and I are most too old to leave home now." The voice was as sweet and musical as a child's, not the high-keyed, strained tone of most deaf people. When they all stood on the porch level Margaret touched Oliver's arm.

" Speak slowly and distinctly, Ollie," she whispered, " then mother can hear you."

Oliver smiled in assent, took the old lady's thin fingers, and with a cordiality the more pronounced because of a certain guilty sense he had for his feeling of repugnance to her father, said:

" Oh, but think what a delight it was for me to be with her. Every day we painted together, and you can't imagine how much she taught me; you know

314

there is nobody in the Academy class who draws as well as your daughter." A light broke in Margaret's eyes at this, but she let him go on. " She has told you, of course, of all the good times we have had while we were at work " (Margaret had, but not all of them). " It is I who should thank *you*, not only for letting Miss Margaret stay so long, but for wanting me to come to you here in your beautiful home. It is my first visit to this—but you are standing, I beg your pardon," and he looked about for a chair.

There was only one chair on the porch—it was under Silas Grant.

" No, don't disturb yourself, Mr. Horn; I prefer standing," Mrs. Grant answered, with a deprecatory gesture as if to detain Oliver. No one in Brookfield ever intruded on Silas Grant's rights to his chair, not even his wife.

Silas heard, but he did not move; he had performed his duty as host; it was the women-folk's turn now to be pleasant. What he wanted was to be let alone. All this was in his face, as he sat hunched up between the arms of the splint rocker.

Despite the old lady's protest, Oliver made a step toward the seated man. His impulse was to suggest to his host that the lady whom he had honored by making his wife was at the moment standing on her two little feet while the lord of the manor was quietly reposing upon the only chair on the piazza,

315

a fact doubtless forgotten by his Imperial High-ness.

Mr. Grant had read at a glance the workings of the young man's mind, and knew exactly what Oliver wanted, but he did not move. Something in the bend of Oliver's back as he bowed to his wife had irritated him. He had rarely met Southerners of Oliver's class—never one so young—and was un-familiar with their ways. This one, he thought, had evidently copied the airs of a dancing-master; the wave of Oliver's hand—it was Richard's in reality, as were all the boy's gestures—and the fine speech he had just made to his wife, proved it. Instantly the instinctive doubt of the Puritan questioning the sincerity of whatever is gracious or spontaneous, was roused in Silas's mind. From that moment he be-came suspicious of the boy's genuineness.

The old lady, however, was still gazing into the boy's face, unconscious of what either her husband or her guest was thinking.

"I am so glad you like our mountains, Mr. Horn," she continued. "Mr. Lowell wrote his beautiful lines, ' What is so Rare as a Day in June,' in our vil-lage, and Mr. Longfellow never lets a summer pass without spending a week with us. And you had a comfortable ride down the mountains, and were the views enjoyable?"

"Oh, too beautiful for words!" It was Marga-

316

ret this time, not the scenery; he could not take his
eyes from her, as he caught the beauty of her throat
against the soft white of her dress, and the exquisite
tint of the October rose in contrast with the autumnal
browns of her hair. Never had he dreamed she
could be so lovely. He could not believe for one
moment that she was the Margaret he had known;
any one of the Margarets, in fact. Certainly not
that one of the Academy school in blue gingham
with her drawing-board in her lap, alone, self-poised,
and unapproachable, among a group of art-students;
or that other one in a rough mountain-skirt, stout-
shoes, and a tam-o'-shanter, the gay and fearless companion, the comrade, the co-worker. This Margaret was a vision in white, with arms bare to the elbow
—oh, such beautiful arms! and the grace and poise of
a duchess—a Margaret to be reverenced as well as
loved—a woman to bend low to.

During this episode, in which Silas sat studying
the various expressions that flitted across Oliver's
face, Mr. Grant shifted uneasily in his chair. At
last his jaws closed with a snap, while the two tufts
of cotton-wool, drawn together by a frown, deeper
than any which had yet crossed his face, made a
straight line of white. Oliver's enthusiastic outburst
and the gesture which accompanied it had removed
Silas Grant's last doubt. His mind was now made up.

The young fellow, however, rattled on, oblivious

now of everything about him but the joy of Margaret's presence.

"The view from the bend of the road was especially fine—" he burst forth again, his eyes still on hers. "You remember, Miss Margaret, your telling me to look out for it?" (he couldn't stand another minute of this unless she joined in the talk). "In my own part of the State we have no great mountains nor any lovely brooks full of trout. And the quantity of deer that are killed every winter about here quite astonishes me. Why, Mr. Pollard's son Hank, so he told me, shot fourteen last winter, and there were over one hundred killed around Moose Hillock. You see, our coast is flat, and many of the farms in my section run down to the water. We have, it is true, a good deal of game, but nothing like what you have here," and he shrugged his shoulders, and laughed lightly as if in apology for referring to such things in view of all the wealth of the mountains about him.

"What kind of game have you got?" asked Mr. Grant, twisting his head and looking at Oliver from under the straight line of cotton-wool.

Oliver turned his head toward the speaker. "Oh, wild geese, and canvas-back ducks and——"

"And negroes?" There was a harsh note in Silas's voice which sounded like a saw when it clogs in a knot, but Oliver did not notice it. He was too happy to notice anything but the girl beside him.

"Oh, yes, plenty of them," and he threw back his head, laughing this time until every tooth flashed white.

"You hunt them, too, don't you? With dogs, most of the time, I hear." There was no mistaking the bitterness in his voice now.

The boy's face sobered in an instant. He felt as if someone had shot at him from behind a tree.

"Not that I ever saw, sir," he answered, quickly straightening himself, a peculiar light in his eyes. "We love ours."

"Love 'em? Well, you don't treat 'em as if you loved 'em."

Margaret saw the cloud on Oliver's face and made a step toward her father.

"Mr. Horn lives in the city, father, and never sees such things."

"Well, if he does he knows all about it. You own negroes, don't you?" The voice was louder; the manner a trifle more insistent. Oliver could hardly keep his temper. Only Margaret's anxious face held him in check.

"No, not now, sir—my father freed all of his." The tones were thin and cold. Margaret had never heard any such sound before from those laughing lips.

319

Silas Grant was leaning forward out of his chair. The iron jaw was doing the talking now.

"Where are these negroes?" he persisted.

"Two of them are living with us, sir. They are in my father's house now."

"Rather shiftless kind of help, I guess. You've got to watch 'em all the time, I hear. Steal everything they get their hands on, don't they?" This was said with a dry, hard laugh that was meant to be conciliatory—as if he expected Oliver to agree with him now that he had had his say.

Oliver turned quickly toward his host's chair. For a moment he was so stunned and hurt that he could hardly trust himself to speak. He looked up and saw the expression of pain on Margaret's face, and instantly remembered where he was and who was offending him.

"Our house-servants, Mr. Grant, are part of our home," he said, in a low, determined voice, without a trace of anger. "Old Malachi, who was my father's body-servant, and who is now our butler, is as much beloved by everyone as if he were one of the family. For myself, I can never remember the time when I did not love Malachi."

Before her father could answer, Margaret had her hand on Oliver's shoulder.

"Don't tell all your good stories to father now," she said, with a grateful smile. "Wait until after dinner, when we can all hear them. Come, Mr. Horn, I know you want to get the dust out of your eyes." Then in an aside, " Don't mind him, Ollie. It's only father's way, and he's the dearest father in the world when you understand him," and she pressed his arm meaningly as they walked to the door.

Before they reached the threshold the gate swung to with a click, and a young man with a scythe slung over his shoulder strode up the path. He was in the garb of a farm-hand; trousers tucked into his boots, shirt open at the throat, and head covered by a coarse straw hat. This shaded a good-natured, sun-burnt face, lighted by two bright blue eyes.

" Oh, here comes my brother John," Margaret cried. " Hurry up, John—here's Mr. Horn."

The young man quickened his pace, stopped long enough to hang the scythe on the porch-rail, lifted his hat from his head, and, running up the short flight of steps, held out his hand cordially to Oliver, who advanced to meet him.

" Glad to see you, Mr. Horn. Madge has told us all about you. Excuse my rig—we are short of men on the farm, and I took hold. I'm glad of the chance, for I get precious little exercise since I left college. You came from East Branch by morning stage, I suppose? Oh, is that your trunk dumped out in the road? What a duffer I was not to know.

Wait a minute—I'll bring it in," and he sprang down the steps.

"No, let me," cried Oliver, running after him. He had not thought of his trunk since he had helped stow it in the boot outside Ezra Pollard's gate—but then he had been on his way to Margaret's!

"No, you won't. Stay where you are—don't let him come, Madge."

The two young men raced down the path, Juno scampering after them. John, who could outrun any man at Dartmouth, vaulted over the fence and had hold of the brass handle before Oliver could open the gate.

"Fair-play!" cried Oliver, and they each grasped a handle—either one could have held it out at arm's length with one hand—and brought it up the garden-path, puffing away in pantomime as if it weighed a ton, and into the house. There they deposited it in the bedroom that was to be Oliver's during the two days of his visit at Brookfield Farm, Margaret clapping her hands in high glee, and her mother holding back the door for them to pass in.

Silas Grant watched the young fellows until they disappeared inside the door, lifted himself slowly from his seat by his long arms, stretched himself, with a yawn, to his full height, and said aloud to himself as he pushed his chair back against the wall:

"His father's got a negro for body-servant, has

he, and a negro for butler—just like 'em. They all want somebody to wait on 'em."

At dinner Oliver sat on Mrs. Grant's right—her best ear, she said—Margaret next, and John opposite. The father was at the foot, in charge of the carving-knife.

During the pauses in the talk Oliver's eyes wandered around the room, falling on the queer paper lining the walls—hunting-scenes, with red-coated fox-hunters leaping five-barred gates; on the sideboard covered with silver, but bare of a decanter—only a pitcher filled with cider which Hopeful Prime, the servant, a woman of forty in spectacles, and who took part in the conversation, brought from the cellar; and finally on a family portrait that hung above the fireplace. A portrait was always a loadstone to Oliver.

Mrs. Grant had been watching his glance.

"That's Mr. Grant's great-uncle—old Governor Shaw," she said, with a pleased smile; "and the next one to it is Margaret's great-grandmother. This one—" and she turned partly in her chair and pointed to a face Oliver thought he had seen before, where, he couldn't remember—"is John Quincy Adams. He was my father's most intimate friend," and a triumphant expression overspread her face.

Oliver smiled, too, inwardly, to himself. The talk, to his great surprise, reminded him of Ken-

nedy Square. Family portraits were an inexhaust
ible topic of conversation in most of its homes. He
had never thought before that people at the North
had any ancestors—none they were very proud of.

John looked up and winked. "Great scheme
naming me after his Royal Highness," he said, in an
undertone. "Sure road to the White House; they
thought I'd make a good third."

Mrs. Grant went on, not having heard a word of
John's aside: "This table you're eating from, once
belonged to Mr. Adams. He gave it to my father,
who often spent a week at a time with him in the
White House."

"And I wish he was there now," interrupted Silas
from the foot of the table. "He'd straighten out
this snarl we're drifting into. Looks to me as if
there would be some powder burnt before this thing
is over. What do your people say about it?" and
he nodded at Oliver. He had served the turkey, and
was now sharpening the carver for the boiled ham,
trying the edge with his thumb, as Shylock did.

"I haven't been at home for some time, sir," replied Oliver, in a courteous tone—he intended to be
polite to the end—"and so I cannot say. My father's letters seem to be very anxious, but mother
doesn't think there'll be any trouble; at least she
said so in her last letter."

Silas looked up from under the tufts of cotton·

wool. Were the mothers running the politics of the South, he wondered?

"And there's another thing you folks might as well remember. We're not going to let you break up the Union, and we're not going to pay you for your slaves, either," and he plunged the fork into the ham that the spectacled waitress had laid before him and rose in his chair, the knife poised in his hand to carve it the better.

"Mr. Horn hasn't got any slaves to sell, father—didn't you hear him say so? His father freed his," laughed Margaret. Her father's positiveness never really worried her. She rather liked it at times. It was only because she had read in Oliver's face the impression her father was making upon him that she essayed to soften the force of his remarks.

"I heard him, Margaret, I heard him. Glad of it—but he's the only man from his parts that I ever heard who did. The others won't give 'em up so easy. They hung John Brown for trying to help the negroes free themselves, don't forget that." Oliver looked up and knitted his brows. Silas saw it. "I'm not meaning any offence to you, young man," he said quickly, waving the knife toward Oliver. "I'm taking this question on broad grounds. If I had my way I'd teach those slave-drivers—" and he buried the knife in the yielding ham, " that——"

"They did just right to hang him," interrupted

325

John. " Brown was a fanatic, and ought to have stayed at home. No one is stronger than the law. That's where old Ossawatomie Brown made a mistake." Everybody was entitled to express his or her opinion in this house except the dear old mother. Margaret's fearless independence of manner and thought had been nurtured in fertile soil.

Mrs. Grant had been vainly trying to get the drift of the conversation, her hand behind her ear.

" Parson Brown, did you say, John? He married us, sir," and she turned to Oliver. " He lived here over forty years. The church that you passed was where he preached."

John laughed, and so did Silas, at the old lady's mistake, but Oliver only became the more attentive to his hostess. He was profoundly grateful to the reverend gentleman for coming out of his grave at this opportune moment and diverting the talk into other channels. Why did they want to bother him with all this talk about slavery and the South, when he was so happy he could hardly stay in his skin? It set his teeth on edge—he wished that the dinner were over and everybody down at the bottom of the sea but Margaret; he had come to see his sweetheart —not to talk slavery.

" Yes, I saw the church," and for the rest of the dinner, Oliver was entertained with the details in the life of the Rev. Leonidas Brown, including his man-

326

ner of preaching; the crowds who would go to hear him; the number converted under the good man's ministrations; to all of which Oliver listened with a closeness of attention that would have surprised those who knew him unless they had discovered that his elbow had found Margaret's during the recital, and that the biography of every member of Brown's congregation might have been added to that of the beloved pastor without wearying him in the slightest degree.

When the nuts were served—Silas broke his with his fingers—his host made one more effort to draw Oliver into a discussion, but Margaret stopped it by exclaiming, suddenly:

"Where shall Mr. Horn smoke, mother?" She wanted Oliver to herself—the family had had him long enough.

"Why, does he want to *smoke?*" she answered, with some consternation.

"Yes, of course he does. All painters smoke."

"Well, I don't know; let me see." The old lady hesitated as if seeking the choice between two evils. "I suppose in the sitting-room. No—the library would be better."

"Oh, I won't smoke at all if your mother does not like it," Oliver protested, springing from his chair.

"Oh, yes, you will," interrupted John. "I never

327

smoke, and father don't, but I know how good a pipe tastes. Let's go into the library."

Margaret gave Oliver the big chair and sat beside him. It was a small room, the walls almost hidden with books; the windows filled with flowering plants. There was a long table piled up with magazines and pamphlets, and an open fireplace, the wall above the mantel covered with framed pictures of weeping-willows worked out with hair of dead relatives, and the mantel itself with faded daguerreotypes propped apart like half-opened clam-shells.

Mr. Grant on leaving the dining-room walked slowly to the window without looking to the right or left, dropped into a chair and gazed out through the leaves of a geranium. The meal was over. Now he wanted rest and quiet. When Mrs. Grant entered the library and saw the wavy lines of tobacco-smoke that were drifting lazily about the room she stopped, evidently annoyed and uneasy. No such sacrilege of her library had taken place for years; not since her Uncle Reuben had come home from China. The waves of smoke must have caught the expression on her face, for she had hardly reached Oliver's chair before they began stealing along the ceiling in long, slanting lines until they reached the doorway, when with a sudden swoop, as if frightened, and without once looking back, they escaped into the hall.

The dear lady laid her hand on Oliver's shoulder, bent over him in a tender, motherly way, and said:

"Do you think it does you any good?"

"I don't know that it does."

"Why should you do it, then?"

"But I won't if you'd rather I'd not." Oliver sprang to his feet, took his pipe from his mouth, and was about to cross the room to knock the ashes from it into the fireplace when Margaret laid her hand on his arm.

"No, don't stop. Mother is very foolish about some things—smoking is one of them."

"But I can't smoke, darling," he said, in an undertone, "if your mother objects." The mother law was paramount, to say nothing of the courtesy required of him. Then he added, with a meaning look in his eyes—"Can't we get away some place where we can talk?" Deaf mothers are a blessing sometimes.

Margaret pressed his hand—her fingers were still closed over the one holding the pipe.

"In a moment, Ollie," and she rose and went into the adjoining room.

Mrs. Grant went to her husband's side, and in her gentle mission of peace put her arm around his neck, patting his shoulder and talking to him in a low tone, her two yellow-white curls streaming

329

down over the collar of his coat. Silas slipped his hand over his wife's and for an instant caressed it tenderly with his cold, bony fingers. Then seeing Oliver's eyes turning his way he drew in his shoulders with a quick movement and looked askance at his guest. Any public show of affection was against Silas's creed and code. If people wanted to hug each other, better do it upstairs, he would say, not where everybody was looking on, certainly not this young man, who was enough of a mollycoddle already.

John, now that Margaret had gone, moved over from the lounge and took her seat, and the two young men launched out into a discussion of flies and worms and fish-bait, and whether frog's legs were better than minnows in fishing for pickerel, and what was the best-sized shot for woodcock and Jack-snipe. Oliver told of the ducking-blinds, of the Chesapeake, and of how the men sat in wooden boxes sunk to the water's edge, with the decoy ducks about them, and shot the flocks as they flew over. And John told of a hunting trip he had made with two East Branch guides, and how they went loaded for deer and came back with a bear and two cubs. And so congenial did they find each other's society that before Margaret returned to the room—she had gone into her studio to light the lamp under the tea-kettle—the two young fellows had discovered that they were both

very good fellows indeed, especially Oliver and especially John, and Oliver had half promised to come
up in the winter and go into camp with John, and
John met him more than half-way with a promise
to accept Oliver's invitation for a week's visit in Kennedy Square the next time he went home, if that
happy event ever took place, when they would both
go down to Carroll's Island for a crack at a canvas-
back.

This had gone on for ten minutes or more—ten
minutes is an absurdly long period of time under
certain circumstances—when Margaret's voice was
heard in the doorway:

" Come, John, you and Mr. Horn have talked long
enough; I want to show him my studio if you'll spare
him a moment."

John knew when to spare and when not to—oh,
a very intelligent brother was John! He did not
follow and talk for another hour of what a good time
he would have duck-shooting, and of what togs he
ought to carry—spoiling everything; nor did he send
his mother in to help Margaret entertain their guest.
None of these stupid things did John do. He said
he would go down to the post-office if Oliver didn't
mind, and would see him at supper, and Margaret
said that that was a very clever idea, as nobody had
gone for the mail that day, and there were sure to
be letters, and not to forget to ask for hers. Aw·

fully sensible brother was John. Why aren't there more like him?

Entering Margaret's studio was like going back to Moose Hillock. There were sketches of the interior of the school-house, and of the children, and of the teacher who had taught the year before. There was Mrs. Taft sitting on that very porch, peeling potatoes, with a tin pan in her lap—would they ever forget that porch and the moonlight and the song of the tree-toads, and the cry of the loon? There was Hank in corduroys, with an axe over his shoulder; and Hank in a broad straw hat and no shoes, with a fishing-pole in one hand; and Hank chopping wood, the chips littering the ground. There was Ezra Pollard sitting in his buckboard with a buffalo-robe tucked about him, and Samanthy by his side. And best of all, and in the most prominent place, too, there was the original drawing of the Milo—the one she was finishing when Oliver upset Judson, and which, strange to say, was the only Academy drawing which Margaret had framed—besides scores and scores of sketches of people and things and places that she had made in years gone by.

The room itself was part of an old portico which had been walled up. It had a fireplace at one end, holding a Franklin stove, and a skylight overhead, the light softened by green shades. Here she kept her own books ranged on shelves over the mantel;

and in the niches and corners and odd spaces a few rare prints and proofs—two Guido Renis and a Leonardo, both by Raphael Morghen. Against the wall was an old clothes-press with brass handles, its drawers filled with sketches, as well as a lounge covered with chintz and heaped up with cushions. The door between the studio and library had been taken off, and was now replaced by a heavy red curtain. Margaret had held it aside for Oliver to enter, and it had dropped back by its own weight, shutting them both safely in.

I don't know what happened when that heavy red curtain swung into place, and mother, father, sea, sky, sun, moon, stars, and the planets, with all that in them is, were shut out for a too brief moment.

And if I did know I would not tell.

We go through life, and we have all sorts of sensations. We hunger and are fed. We are thirsty, and reach an oasis. We are homeless, and find shelter. We are ill, and again walk the streets. We dig and delve and strain every nerve and tissue, and the triumph comes at last, and with it often riches and honor. All these things send shivers of delight through us, and for the moment we spread our wings and soar heavenward. But when we take in our arms the girl we love, and hold close her fresh, sweet face, with its trusting eyes, and feel her warm breath

333

on our cheeks, and the yielding figure next our heart, knowing all the time how mean and good-for-nothing and how entirely unworthy of even tying her shoe-strings we are, we experience a something compared with which all our former flights heavenward are but the flutterings of bats in a cave.

And the blessed John did not come back until black, dark night!—not until it was so dark that you couldn't see your hand before you or the girl beside you, which is nearer the truth; not until the stout woman in spectacles with the conversational habit, had brought in a lard-oil lamp with a big globe, which she set down on Margaret's table among her books and papers. And when John did come, and poked his twice-blessed head between the curtains, it was not to sit down inside and talk until supper-time, but to say that it was getting cold outside and that they ought to have a fire if they intended to sit in the studio after supper. (Oh, what a trump of a brother!) And if they didn't mind he'd send Hopeful right away with some chips to start it. All of which Miss Hopeful Prime accomplished, talking all the time to Margaret as she piled up the logs, and not forgetting a final word to Oliver as she left the room, to the effect that she " guessed it must be kind o' comfortin' to set by a fire "—such luxuries, of course, to her thinking, being unknown in his tropical land, where the blacks went naked and the children lay

334

about in the sun munching watermelons and bananas.

What an afternoon it had been! They had talked of the woods and their life under the trees; of the sketches they made and how they could improve them, and would; of the coming winter and the prospect of the school being opened and what it meant to them if it did, and how much more if it did not, and she be compelled to remain in Brookfield with Oliver away all winter in New York, and of a thousand and one other things that lay nearest their hearts and with which neither you nor I have anything to do.

It was good, Margaret thought, to talk to him in this way, and see the quick response in his eyes and feel how true and helpful he was.

She had dreaded his coming—dreaded the contrasts which she knew his presence among them would reveal. She knew how punctiliously polite he was, and how brusque and positive was her father. She realized, too, how outspoken and bluff was John, and how unaccustomed both he and her dear deaf mother were to the ways of the outside world. What would Oliver think of them? What effect would her home life have on their future? she kept saying to herself.

Not that she was ashamed of her people, certainly not of her father, who really occupied a higher position than any of his neighbors. He was not only a deacon in the church and chairman of the School Board, but he had been twice sent to the Legislature, and at one time had been widely discussed as a fitting candidate for Governor. Nobody in Brookfield thought the less of him because of his peculiarities —many of his neighbors liked him the better for his brusqueness; they believed in a man who had the courage of his convictions and who spoke out, no matter whose toes he trod on.

Nor could she be ashamed of her brother John— so kind to everybody; so brave and generous, and such a good brother. Only she wished that he had some of Oliver's courtesy, and that he would take off his hat when a lady spoke to him in the road, and keep it off till she bade him replace it, and observe a few of the other amenities; but even with all his defects of manner—all of which she had never before noticed—he was still her own dear brother John, and she loved him dearly.

And as for her mother—that most gentle and gracious of women—that one person in the house who was considerate of everybody's feelings and tolerant of everybody's impatience! What could Oliver find in her except what was adorable? As she thought of her mother, a triumphant smile crossed her face. "That's the one member of the Grant family," she said to herself, " whom my fine gentleman must admit is the equal of any one of his top-lofty kinsfolk in Kennedy Square or anywhere else." Which outburst the scribe must admit to himself was but another proof of the fact that no such thing as true democracy exists the world over.

None of these thoughts had ever crossed her mind up to the time she met Oliver on the bridge that first sunny morning. He had never discussed the subject of any difference between their two families, nor had he ever criticised the personality of anyone she knew. He had only *been himself*. The change in her views had come gradually and unconsciously to her as the happy weeks flew by. Before she knew it she had realized from his talk, from his gestures, even from the way he sat down or got up, or handled his knife and fork, or left the room or entered it, that some of her early teachings had led her astray, and that there might be something else in life worth having outside of the four cardinal virtues—economy, industry, pluck, and plain-speaking. And if there were—and she was quite certain of it now—would Oliver find them at Brookfield Farm? This was really the basis of her disquietude; the kernel of the nut which she was trying to crack.

If any of these shortcomings on the part of his entertainers had been apparent to Oliver, or if he had ever drawn any such deductions, or noted any such contrasts, judged by the Kennedy

337

Square code, no word of disappointment had passed his lips.

Some things, it is true, during his visit at the farm, had deeply impressed him, but they were not those that Margaret feared. He had thought of them that first night when going over the events of the day as they passed in review before him. One personality and one incident had made so profound an impression upon him that he could not get to sleep for an hour thinking about them. It was the stalwart figure of John Grant in his broad-brimmed straw hat and heavy boots striding up the garden-path with his scythe over his shoulder. This apparition, try as he might, would not down at his bidding.

"Think of that young fellow," he kept repeating to himself. "The eldest son and heir to the estate no doubt, a college-bred man and a most charming gentleman, working like a common laborer in his father's field. And proud of it, too—and would do it again and talk about it. And yet I was so ashamed of working with my hands that I had to run away from home for fear the boys would laugh at me."

Margaret heard the whole story from Oliver's lips the next morning with many adornments, and with any amount of good resolutions for the future. She listened quietly and held his hand the closer, her eyes dancing in triumph, the color mounting to her cheeks, but she made no reply.

338

SOME DAYS AT BROOKFIELD FARM

Neither did she return the confidence and tell Oliver how she wished her father could see some things in as clear a light, and be more gentle and less opinionated. She was too proud for that.

And so the days, crowded thick with emotions, sped on.

The evening of their first one came and passed, with its half-hours when neither spoke a word and when both trembled all over for the very joy of living; and the morning of the second arrived, bringing with it a happiness she had never known before, and then the morning of the third—and the last day.

They had kept their secret even from John. Oliver wanted to inform her father at once of his attachment, telling her it was not right for him to accept the hospitality of her parents unless they understood the whole situation, but she begged him to wait, and he had yielded to her wishes.

They had all discussed him at their pleasure.

"Nice chap that young Horn," John had said to her the night before. "We had three or four of 'em in my class, one from Georgia and two from Alabama. They'd fight in a minute, but they'd make up just as quick. This one's the best of the lot." He spoke as if they had all belonged to another race—denizens of Borneo or Madagascar or the islands of the Pacific.

"I have sent my love to his mother, my dear,"

Mrs. Grant had confided to her early that same morning. " I am sure he has a good mother. He is so kind and polite to me, he never lets me remember that I am deaf when I talk to him," and she looked about her in her simple, patient way.

" Yes—perhaps so," said Silas, sitting hunched up in his chair. " Seems sort of skippy-like to me. Something of a Dandy Jim, I should say. Good enough to make men painters of, I guess." Artists in those days had few friends North or South.

None of these criticisms affected Margaret. She didn't care what they thought of him. She knew his heart, and so would they in time.

When Oliver had said all his public good-byes to the rest of the family—the good-byes with which we have nothing to do had been given and taken in the studio with the curtains drawn—he joined Margaret at the gate.

They were standing in the road now, under the giant elm, waiting for the stage. She stood close beside him, touching his arm with her own, mournfully counting the minutes before the stage would come, her eyes up the road. All the light and loveliness of the summer, all the joy and gladness of life, would go out of her heart when the door of the lumbering vehicle closed on Oliver.

CHAPTER XVII

His good-byes said, one absorbing thought now filled Oliver's mind—to reach Kennedy Square on the wings of the wind and there to pour into the ears of his mother and Miss Lavinia, and of anyone else who would listen, the whys and wherefores of his love for Margaret, with such additional description of her personal charms, qualities, and talents as would bring about, in the shortest possible time, the most amicable of relations between Kennedy Square and Brookfield Farm. He was determined that his mother should know her at once. He knew how strong her prejudices were and what her traditions would cause her to think of a woman who led the life that Margaret did, but these things did not deter him. A new love now filled his heart—another and a different kind of love from the one he bore his mother. One that belonged to him; one that was his own and affected his life and soul and career. He was prepared to fight even harder for this desire of his soul than for his art.

There being no air-ships available for immediate

341

charter, nor big balloons waiting for passengers, with sand-bags ready for instant unloading, nor any underground pneumatic tubes into which he could be pumped and with a puff landed on his own doorstep in Kennedy Square, the impatient lover was obliged to content himself with the back seat of the country stage and a night ride in the train down the valley.

Then came a delay of a week in New York waiting for the return of Mr. Slade to the city—"whom you must by all means see before coming home," so his mother's letter ran. This delay was made bearable by Waller, Bowdoin, and old Professor Cummings who went into spasms of delight over the boys' sketches. Waller especially predicted a sure future for him if he would have the grit to throw overboard every other thing he was doing and "stick it out and starve it out" until he pulled through and became famous.

Mr. Slade, while welcoming him with both hands, was not so cheering. The financial and political situations were no better, he said. They had really become more alarming every day. The repudiation of Northern accounts by Southern merchants had ceased—at least some of Morton, Slade & Co.'s customers had redeemed their obligations and had forwarded them their overdue remittances, tiding them over for a time—but no one could say what was in store for any firm whose business lay largely in the

Southern States. He would, however, make his word good. Oliver's situation was still open, and he could again occupy his desk as soon as he returned from Kennedy Square. The length of his service depended entirely on whether the country would go to war or whether its difficulties could be satisfactorily settled in the next Congress.

But none of these things—none of the more depressing ones—dulled for an instant the purpose or chilled the enthusiasm of our young lover. Wars, pestilence, financial panics and even social tidal-waves might overwhelm the land and yet not one drop of the topmost edge of the flood could wet the tips of his high-stepping toes: Margaret was his: he trod an enchanted realm.

An enthusiasm of equal intensity, but of quite a different kind, had taken possession of the Horn mansion as the hour of Oliver's arrival approached, as anyone would have noticed who happened to be inside its hospitable walls. Something out of the common was about to happen. There was an unusual restlessness in Malachi totally at variance with his grave and dignified demeanor. His perturbation was so great that he even forgot the time-honored custom of wheeling his master's chair into position and the equally time-honored salutation of " yo' chair's all ready, Marse Richard." It was noticed, too, that he could not keep out of the hall. Richard had to speak to him twice and Mrs. Horn had lifted her head in astonishment when that hitherto attentive darky handed her Richard's spectacles instead of her own. Or he would start to enter the dining-room, his hands laden with plates, or the library, his arms filled with logs to replenish the fire, and then stop suddenly and listen with one foot raised, standing like an old dog locating a partridge. So nervous did he become as the twilight deepened, and he began to set the table for supper, that he dropped a cup, smashing it into atoms, a thing that had not happened to him before in twenty years—one of the blue and gilt—priceless heirlooms in the family, and only used when a distinguished guest was expected. At another time he would have dropped the whole tray with everything upon it, had not Aunt Hannah saved it in time. How she came to be in the pantry with her two eyes on the front door, when her place was in the kitchen with both of them on the pots and kettles, no one could tell. Everything seemed to be at sixes and sevens in the old house that night.

And the other members of the household inside the drawing-room seemed just as restless. Richard, who had raked the coals of his forge, closed the green door of his workshop, and had dressed himself an hour earlier than usual, much to Malachi's delight, became so restless that he got up from his easy-chair half a dozen times and roamed aimlessly about the room, stopping to pick up a book, reading a line and laying it down again. Mrs. Horn dropped so many stitches that she gave up in despair, and said she believed she would not knit.

Malachi heard him first.

"Dat's him—dat's Marse Ollie," he cried. "I know dat knock. Here he is, Mistis. Here he is!" He sprang forward, threw wide the door and had him by the hand before the others could reach him.

"Fo' Gawd, Marse Ollie, ain't ol' Malachi glad ter git his han's on yer once mo'!"

It was unseemly and absurd how the old man behaved!

And the others were not far behind.

"My boy," exclaimed Mrs. Horn, as she held him close to her breast. There are few words spoken in times like this.

Richard waited behind her until that imperceptible moment of silence had passed—the moment a mother gets her arms around the son she loves. Then when the sigh of restful relief that always follows had spent itself, and she had kissed him with his cheek held fast to hers, Oliver loosened his hold and threw his arms about his father's neck, patting him between his shoulder-blades as he kissed him.

"Dear old dad! Oh, but it's good to get home! And Aunt Hannah, you there?" and he extended his hand while his other arm was still around his father's neck.

"Yas, Marse Ollie, dat's me; dat's ol' Hannah," and she stepped closer and grasped his outstretched hand, smoothing it as she spoke. "Lord, Marse Ollie, but ain't you filled out? You is de probable son, sho', honey, come home to yo' people."

But Oliver was not through with Malachi. He must take both of his hands this time and look into his eyes. It was all he could do to keep from hugging him. It would not have been the first time.

"Been well, Mallie?"

Of course he had been; he saw it in his face. It was only to say something to which the old darky could reply to—to keep in touch with him—to know that he was speaking to this same old Malachi whom he had so dearly loved.

"Middlin' po'ly, yas—middlin' po'ly, suh."

Malachi had not the slightest idea what he was talking about. He had not been sick a minute since Oliver left. His heart was too near bursting with pride at his appearance and joy over his return for his mind to work intelligently.

"Dem Yankees ain't sp'iled ye; no, dey ain't. Gor-a-mighty, ain't Malachi glad." Tears were standing in his eyes now. There was no one but Richard he loved better than Oliver.

No fatted calf was spitted and roasted this night

on Aunt Hannah's swinging crane for this "probable son," but there was corn-pone in plenty and a chafing dish of terrapin—Malachi would not let Aunt Hannah touch it; he knew just how much Madeira to put in; Hannah always "drowned" it, he would say. And there was sally-lunn and Maryland biscuit; here, at last, Aunt Hannah was supreme— her elbows told the story. And last of all there was a great dish of escalloped oysters cooked in fossil scallop shells thousands of years old, that Malachi had himself dug out of the marl-banks at Yorktown when he was a boy, and which had been used in the Horn family almost as many times as they were years old. Oh, for a revival of this extinct conchological comfort! But no! It is just as well not to recall even the memories of this toothsome dish. There are no more fossils, neither at Yorktown nor anywhere else, and no substitute in china, tin, or copper will be of the slightest use in giving their flavor.

Supper served and over, with Oliver jumping up half a dozen times to kiss his mother and plumping himself down again to begin on another relay of pone or terrapin or oysters, much to Malachi's delight ("He do eat," he reported to Aunt Hannah. "I tell ye. He's bearin' very heavy on dem scallops. Dat's de third shell.")—the doors were opened with a flourish, and the three, preceded by Malachi, entered the drawing-room in time to welcome the neighbors.

Nathan, who was already inside sitting by the fire, his long, thin legs stretched out, his bunchy white hair, parted in the middle, falling to his collar's edge, sprang up and shook Oliver's hand heartily. He had charged Malachi, when he admitted him, to keep his presence secret. He wanted them to have Oliver all to themselves.

Miss Clendenning entered a moment later with both hands held out. She would not stop in the hall to unwind her nubia or take off her little fur boots, but motioned Oliver to her knees after she had kissed him joyously on both cheeks, and held out those two absurd little feet for his ministrations, while Mrs. Horn removed her nubia and cloak.

The rat-a-tat at the door was now constant. Judge Bowman and old Dr. Wallace and four or five of the young men, with the young girls, entered, all with expressions of delight at Oliver's return home, and later, with the air of a Lord High Mayor, Colonel John Clayton, of Pongateague, with Sue on his arm. Clayton was always a picture when he entered a room. He stood six feet and an inch, his gray hair brushed straight back, his goatee curling like a fish-hook at its end. "Handsome Jack Clayton" was still handsome at sixty.

After the Colonel had grasped Oliver's hand in

his warmest manner, Sue laid all of her ten fingers in his. It was as good as a play to watch the little witch's face as she stood for a moment and looked Oliver over. She had not written to him for months. She had had half a dozen beaus since his departure, but she claimed him all the same as part of her spoils. His slight mustache seemed to amuse her immensely.

"Are you glad to see me, Ollie?" she asked, looking archly at him from under her lashes.

"Why, Sue!"

Of course he was glad—for a minute—not much longer. How young she is, he thought, how provincial. As she rattled on he noticed the mass of ringlets about her face and the way her head was set on her shoulders. Her neck, he saw, was much shorter than Margaret's, and a little out of drawing. Nor was there anything of that fearless look or toss of the head like a surprised deer, which made Margaret so distinguished. Oliver had arrived at that stage in his affection when he compared all women to one.

All this time Sue was reading his mind. Trust a young girl for that when she is searching a former lover's eyes for what lies behind them. She was evidently nettled at what she found and had begun by saying "she supposed the Yankee girls had quite captured his heart," when the Colonel interrupted her by asking Oliver whether the Northern men

349

really thought they could coerce the South into giving up their most treasured possessions.

He had been nursing his wrath all day over a fresh attack made on the South by some Northern paper, and Oliver was just the person to vent it upon—not that he did not love the lad, but because he was fresh from the despised district.

"I don't think they want to, sir. They are opposed to slavery and so are a good many of us. You have a wrong idea of the life at the North, Colonel. You have never been North, I believe?"

"No, my dear Oliver, and I never intend to. If ever I go it will be with a musket. They have had it all their own way lately with their Harriet Stowes, William Lloyd Garrisons, and John Browns; it is our turn now."

"Who do you want to run through the body, Clayton?" asked Richard, joining the group and laying his hands affectionately on the Colonel's shoulders.

"Anybody and everybody, Richard, who says we are not free people to do as we please."

"And is anybody really saying so?"

"Yes; you see it every day in every Northern editorial—another to-day—a most villainous attack which you must read. These Puritans have been at it for years. This psalm-singing crew have always hated us. Now, while they are preaching meekness

350

and lowliness and the rights of our fellow-men—black ones they mean—they are getting ready to wad their guns with their hymn-books. It's all a piece of their infernal hypocrisy!"

"But why should they hate us, Clayton?" asked Richard in a half-humorous tone. He had no spirit of contention in him to-night, not with Oliver beside him.

"Because we Cavaliers are made of different stuff; that's why! All this talk about slavery is nonsense. These Nutmeg fellows approved of slavery as long as they could make a dollar out of the traffic, and then, as soon as they found out that they had given us a commercial club with which to beat out their brains, and that we were really dominating the nation, they raised this hue and cry about the down-trodden negro and American freedom and the Stars and Stripes and a lot of such tomfoolery. Do you know any gentleman who beats his negroes? Do you beat Malachi? Do I beat my Sam, whom I have brought up from a boy and who would lay down his life any day for me? I tell you, Richard, it is nothing but a fight for financial and political mastery. They're afraid of us; they've been so for years. They cried 'Wolf' when the fugitive slave law was passed and they've kept it up ever since."

"No, I don't believe it," exclaimed Richard, with a positive tone in his voice, "and neither do you,

351

Clayton. It's largely a question of sentiment. They don't believe one man should hold another in bondage."

" That's where you are wrong. They don't care a fippenny bit about the negro. If they ever succeed in their infernal purpose and abolish slavery, and set the negro adrift, mark my words, they won't live with him, and they won't let him come North and work alongside of their own people. They'll throw him back on us after they have made a beggar and a criminal of him. Only a Southerner understands the negro, and only a Southerner can care for him. See what we have done for them! Every slave that landed on our shores we have changed from a savage into a man. They forget this."

Judge Bowman joined in the discussion—so did Dr. Wallace. The Judge, in his usual ponderous way, laid down the law, both State and National— the Doctor, who always took the opposite side in any argument, asking him rather pointed questions as to the rights of the Government to control the several States as a unit.

Richard held his peace. He felt that this was not the night of all others to discuss politics, and he was at a loss to understand the Colonel's want of self-restraint. He could not agree with men like Clayton. He felt that the utterance of such inflammatory speeches only added fuel to the smouldering flame. If the ugly jets of threatening smoke that were creeping out everywhere because of the friction between the two sections were in danger of bursting into flame, the first duty of a patriot, according to his creed, was to stand by with pails of water, not with kegs of gunpowder. So, while Clayton's outspoken tirade still filled the room, he with his usual tact did all he could to soften the effect of his words. Then again, he did not want Oliver's feelings hurt.

Malachi's entrance with his tray, just as the subject was getting beyond control, put a stop to the discussion. The learned group of disputants with the other guests quickly separated into little coteries, the older men taking their seats about an opened card-table, on which Malachi had previously deposited several thin glasses and a pair of decanters, the ladies sitting together, and the younger people laughing away in a corner, where Oliver joined them.

Richard and Nathan, now that the danger was averted (they were both natural born peace-makers), stepped across the room to assist in entertaining Miss Clendenning. The little lady had not moved from the chair in which she sat when Oliver relieved her of her fur boots. She rarely did move when once she had chosen a place for herself in a drawing-room. She was the kind of woman who could sit in one place and still be surrounded—by half-moons of adorers if she sat against the wall, by full moons if she sat in the open. She had learned the art when a girl.

"If Clayton would go among these people, my dear Lavinia," said Richard, in a deprecating tone, drawing up a chair and seating himself beside her, "he would find them very different from what he thinks. Some of the most delightful men I have ever met have come from the States north of us. You know that to be so."

"That depends, Richard, on how far North you go," Miss Clendenning answered, spreading her fan as she spoke, looking in between the sticks as if searching for specimens. "In Philadelphia I find some very delightful houses, quite like our own. In New York—well, I rarely go to New York. The journey is a tiresome one and the hotels abominable. They are too busy there to be comfortable, and I do not like noisy, restless people. They give me a headache."

"Oliver has met some charming people, he tells me," said Richard. "Mr. Slade took him into his own home and treated him quite like a son."

"Of course he did; why not?" Miss Clendenning was erect now, her eyes snapping with roguish indignation. "Anybody would be glad to take Oliver into their home, especially when they have two marriageable daughters. Oliver's bow as he enters a room is a passport to any society in the world, my dear Richard. My Lord Chesterfield Clayton has no better manners nor any sweeter smile than our own Lorenzo. Watch Oliver now as he talks to those girls."

Richard had been watching him; he had hardly taken his eyes from him. Every time he looked at him his heart swelled the more with pride.

"And you think, Lavinia, Mr. Slade invited him because of his manners?" He was sure of it. He only wanted her to confirm it.

"Of course. What else?" and she cut her eye at him knowingly. "How many of the other clerks did he invite? Not one. I wanted to find out and I made Ollie write me. They are queer people, these Northerners. They affect to despise good blood and good breeding and good manners. That's all fol-de-rol—they love it. They are eternally talking of equality—equality; one man as good as another. When they say that one man is as *good* as another, Richard, they mean that *they* are as good, never the other poor fellow."

"Now, my dear Lavinia, stop a moment," laughed the inventor in protest. "You do not mean to say there are really no gentlemen north of us?"

"Plenty of gentlemen, Richard, but few thoroughbreds. There is a distinction, you know."

"Which do you value most?"

"Oh, the thoroughbred. A gentleman might some time offend you by telling you the truth about

355

yourself or your friends. The thoroughbred, never," and she lifted her hands in mock horror.

"And he could be a rogue and yet his manners would save him?"

"Quite true, dear Richard, quite true. The most charming man I ever met except your dear self "— and she smiled graciously and lowered her voice as if what she was about to tell was in the strictest confidence—"was a shrivelled-up old prince who once called on my father and myself in Vienna. He was as ugly as a crab, and walked with a limp. There had been some words over a card-table, he told me, and the other man fired first. I was a young girl then, but I have never forgotten him to this day. Indeed, my dear Nathan," and she turned to the old musician and laid her wee hand confidingly on his knee, "but for the fact that the princess was a most estimable woman and still alive, I might have been —well, I really forget what I might have been, for I do not remember his name, but it was something most fascinating in five or six syllables. Now all that man ever did to make that unaccountable impression upon me was just to pick up my handkerchief. Oh, Nathan, it really gives me a little quiver to this day! I never watch Oliver bow but I think of my prince. Now I have never found that kind of quality, grace, bearing, presence—whatever you may choose to call it—in the Puritan. He has not time to learn it. He despises such subtle courtesies,

They smack of the cavalier and the court to him. He is content with a nod of the head and a hurried handshake. So are his neighbors. They would grow suspicious of each other's honesty if they did more. Tut, tut, my dear Richard! My prince's grooms greeted each other in that way."

Richard and Nathan laughed heartily. "And you only find the manners of the ante-chamber and the throne-room South?" asked the inventor.

"Um—not always. It used to be so in my day and yours, but we are retrograding. It is unpardonable in our case because we have known better. But up there" (and she pointed in the direction of the North Star) "they never did know better; that's some excuse for them."

"Ah, you incorrigible woman, you must not talk so. You have not seen them all. Many of the men who do me the honor to come to my workroom are most delightful persons. Only last week there came one of the most interesting scientists that I have met for——"

"Of course, of course, I have not a doubt of it, my dear Richard, but I am talking of men, my friend, not dried mummies."

Again Richard laughed. One of his greatest pleasures was to draw Miss Clendenning out on topics of this class. He knew she did not believe onehalf that she said. It was the way she parried his thrusts that delighted him.

357

" Well, then, take Mr. Winthrop Pierce Lawrence. No more charming gentleman ever entered my house. You were in London at the time or you would certainly have dined with him here. Mr. Lawrence is not only distinguished as a statesman and a brilliant scholar, but his manners are perfect."

Miss Clendenning turned her head and looked at Richard under her eyelashes. " Where did you say he was from? "

" Boston."

" Boston? " A rippling, gurgling laugh floated through the room.

" Yes, Boston. Why do you laugh? "

" Bostonians, my dear Richard, have habits and customs, never manners. It is impossible that they should. They are seldom underbred, mind you, they are always overbred, and, strange to say, without the slightest sense of humor, for they are all brought up on serious isms and solemn fads. The excitement we have gone through over this outrageous book of this Mrs. Stowe's and all this woman movement is but a part of their training. How is it possible for people who believe in such dreadful persons as this Miss Susan Anthony and that Miss— something-or-other—I forget her name—to know what the word ' home ' really means and what graces should adorn it? They could never understand my ugly prince, and he?—well, he would be too polite to tell them what he thought of them. No, my dear

Richard, they don't know; they never will know, and they never will be any better."

Oliver had crossed the room and had reached her chair.

" Who will never be any better, you dear Midget? " he cried.

" You, you dear boy, because you could not. Come and sit by me where I can get my hand on you. If I had my way you would never be out of reach of my five fingers."

Oliver brought up a stool and sat at her feet.

" Your Aunt Lavinia, Ollie," said Richard, rising to his feet (this relationship was of the same character as that of Uncle Nathan Gill), " seems to think our manners are retrograding."

" Not yours? " protested Oliver, with a laugh, as he turned quickly toward Miss Clendenning.

" No, you sweetheart, nor yours," answered Miss Clendenning, with a sudden burst of affection. " Come, now, you have lived nearly two years among these dreadful Yankees—what do you think of them? "

" What could I think of people who have been so kind to me? Fred Stone has been like a brother, and so has everybody else."

Mrs. Horn had joined the group and sat listening.

" But their manners, my son," she asked. " Do you see no difference between them and—and—and your father's, for instance? " and she motioned toward Richard who was now moving across the room to speak to other guests.

"Dad is himself and you are yourself and I am myself," replied Oliver with some positiveness. "When people are kind I never stop to think how they do it."

"Lovely," Miss Clendenning whispered to Nathan. "Spoken like a thoroughbred. Yes, he is *better* than my ugly prince. He would always have remembered how they did it."

"And you see no difference either in the ladies?" continued Mrs. Horn, with increasing interest in her tones. "Are the young girls as sweet and engaging?" She had seen Margaret's name rather often in his letters and wondered what impression she had made upon him. Oliver's eyes flashed and the color mounted to his cheeks. Miss Clendenning saw it and bent forward a little closer to get his answer.

"Well, you see, mother, I do not know a great many, I am so shut up. Miss Grant, whom I wrote you about, is—well, you must see her. She is not the kind of girl that you can describe very well— she really is not the kind of girl that you can describe at all. We have been together all summer, and I stopped at her father's house for a few days when I came down from the mountains. They live in the most beautiful valley you ever saw."

Miss Clendenning was watching him closely. She caught a look that his mother had missed.

"Is she pretty, Ollie?" asked Miss Lavinia.

"She is better than pretty. You would not say the Milo was pretty, would you? There is too much in her for prettiness."

"And are the others like her?" The little lady was only feeling about, trying to put her finger on the pulse of his heart.

"No; there is nobody like her. Nobody I have ever met."

Miss Clendenning was sure now.

Malachi's second entrance—this time with the great china bowl held above his head—again interrupted the general talk.

Since the memory of man no such apple-toddy had ever been brewed!

Even Colonel Clayton, when he tasted it, looked over his glass and nodded approvingly at its creator —a recognition of genius which that happy darky acknowledged by a slight bend of his back, anything else being out of the question by reason of the size of the bowl he was carrying and the presence of his master and of his master's guests.

This deposited on a side table, another bowl filled with *Olio*—a most surprising and never-to-be-forgotten salad of chicken and celery and any number of other toothsome things—was placed beside it, together with a plate of moonshines and one of Maryland biscuits.

Then came some music, in which Oliver sang and

Miss Clendenning played his accompaniments—the old plantation melodies, not the new songs—and next the "wrappings up" in the hall, the host and hostess and the whole party moving out of the drawing-room in a body. Here Nathan, with great gallantry, insisted on getting down on his stiff marrow-bones to put on Miss Clendenning's boots, while the young men and Oliver tied on the girls' hoods, amid "good-byes" and "so glads" that he could come home if only for a day, and that he had not forgotten them, Oliver's last words being whispered in Miss Clendenning's ear informing her that he would come over in the morning and see her about a matter of the greatest importance. And so the door was shut on the last guest.

When the hall was empty Oliver kissed his father good-night, and, slipping his arm around his mother's waist, as he had always done when a boy, the two went slowly upstairs to his little room. He could not wait a minute longer. He must unburden his heart about Margaret. This was what he had come for. If his mother had only seen her it would be so much easier, he said to himself as he pushed open his bedroom door.

"You are greatly improved, my son," she said, with a tone of pride in her voice. "I see the change already." She had lighted the candle and the two were seated on the bed, his arm still around her.

"How, mother?"

" Oh, in everything. The boy is gone out of you. You are more reposeful; more self-reliant. I like your modesty too." She could tell him of his faults, she could also tell him of his virtues.

" And the summer has done you good," she continued. " I felt sure it would. Mr. Slade has been a steadfast friend of yours from the beginning. Tell me now about your new friends. This Miss Grant —is she not the same girl you wrote me about, some months ago—the one who drew with you at the art school? Do you like her people? " This thought was uppermost in her mind—had been in fact ever since she first saw Margaret's name in his letters.

" Her mother is lovely and she has got a brother —a Dartmouth man—who is a fine fellow. I liked him from the first moment I saw him; " Oliver answered simply, wondering how he would begin.

" Is her father living? "

" Yes."

" What kind of a man is he? "

" Well—of course, he is not like our people. He is a—well—he always says just what he thinks, you know. But he is a man of character and position." He was speaking for Margaret now. " They have more family portraits than we have." This was said in a tone that was meant to carry weight.

" And people of education? "

" Oh, I should certainly say so. It is nothing but books all over the house. Really, he has more books than Dad." This statement was to strengthen the one regarding the family ancestors—both telling arguments about Kennedy Square.

"And this girl—is she a lady?"

The question somehow put to flight all his mental manœuvres. "She is more than a lady, mother. She is the dearest—" He stopped, hesitated for an instant, and slipping his arm around his mother's neck drew her close to him. Then, in a torrent of words—his cheeks against hers—the whole story came out. He was a boy again now; that quality in him that would last all his life. She listened with her eyes on the floor, her heart torn with varying emotions. She was disturbed, but not alarmed. One phase of the situation stood out clearly in her practical mind—his poverty and the impossibility of any immediate marriage. Before that obstacle could be removed she felt sure his natural vacillation regarding women would save him. He would forget her as he had Sue.

"And you say her brother works in the fields and that her father and mother permitted this girl to leave home and sit night after night with you young men with no other protection than that of a common Irishwoman?" There was a tone of censure now in her voice that roused a slight antagonism in Oliver.

"Why not? What could harm her? There was no other place for her to go where she could learn anything."

Mrs. Horn kept still for a moment, looking on the floor. Oliver sat watching her face.

"And your family, my son," she protested with a certain patient disapproval in her tones. "Do they count for nothing? I, of course, would love anybody you would make your wife, but you have others about you. No man has a right to marry beneath him. Do not be in a hurry over this matter. Come home for your wife when you are ready to marry. Give yourself time to compare this girl, who seems to have fascinated you, with—Sue, for instance, or any of the others you have been brought up with."

Oliver shrugged his shoulders at the mention of Sue's name. He had compared her.

"You would not talk this way, dearie, if you could see her," he replied in a hopeless way as if the futility of making his mother understand was now becoming apparent to him. "She is different from anyone you ever met—she is so strong, so fine— such a woman in all that the word means. Not something you fondle and make love to, remember, but a woman more like a Madonna that you worship, or a Greek goddess that you might fear. As to the family part of it, I am getting tired of it all, mother. What good is Grandfather Horn or anybody else to me? I have got to dig my way out just as they did. Just as dear old Dad is doing. If he succeeds in his work who will help him but himself? There have

365

been times when I used to love to remember him sitting by his reading-lamp or with his violin tucked under his chin, and I was proud to think he was my father. Do you know what sets my blood on fire now? It is when I think of him standing over his forge and blowing his bellows, his hands black with coal. I understand many things, dearie, that I knew nothing about when I left home. You used to tell me yourself that everybody had to work, and you sent me away to do it. I looked upon it then as a degradation. I see it differently now. I have worked with all my might all summer, and I have brought back a whole lot of sketches that the boys like. Now I am going to work again with Mr. Slade. I do not like his work, and I do love mine, but I am going to stick to his all the same. I have got something to work for now," and his face brightened. "I am going to win!"

She did not interrupt him. It was better he should unburden his heart. She was satisfied with his record; if he went wrong she only was to blame. But he was not going wrong; nor was there anything to worry about—not even his art—not so long as he kept his place with Mr. Slade and only took it up as a relaxation from more weighty cares. It was only the girl that caused her a moment's thought.

She saw too, through all his outburst, a certain independence and a fearlessness and a certain fixedness of purpose that sent an exultant thrill through her even when her heart was burdened with the thought of this new danger that threatened him. She had sent him away for the fault of instability, and he had overcome it. Should she not now hold fast, as she had before, and save him the second time from this girl who was beneath him in station and who would drag him down to her level, and so perhaps ruin him?

"We will not talk any more about it to-night, my son," she said, in tender tones, leaning forward and kissing him on the cheek—it was through his affections that she controlled him. "You should be tired out with your day's journey and ought to rest. Take my advice—do not ask her to be your wife yet. Think about it a little and see some other women before you make up your mind."

A delicious tremor passed through Oliver. He *had* asked her, and she *had* promised! He remembered just the very day, the hour, the minute. That was the bliss of it all! But this he did not tell his mother. He would not hurt her any further now. Some other day he would tell her; when she could see Madge and judge for herself. No, not to-night, and so with the secret untold he kissed her and led her to her room.

And yet strange to say it was the one only thing in all his life that he had kept from her.

Ah! these mothers! who make lovers of their only sons, dominating their lives! How bitter must be the hours when they realize that another's arms are opening for them!

And these boys—what misgivings come; what doubts. How the old walls, impregnable from childhood, begin to crumble! How little now the dear mother knows—she so wise but a few moons since. How this new love steps in front of the old love and claims every part of the boy as its very own.

Faithful to her promise, Miss Clendenning waited the next morning for Oliver in her little boudoir that opened out of the library. A bright fire blazed and crackled, sending its beams dancing over the room and lighting up the red curtains that hung behind her writing-desk, its top covered with opened letters—her morning's mail: many bore foreign postmarks, and not a few were emblazoned with rampant crests sunk in little dabs of colored wax. She wore a morning gown of soft white flannel belted in at the waist. Covering her head and wound loosely about her throat was a fluff of transparent silk, half-concealing the two nests of little gray and brown knots impaled on hair-pins. These were the chrysalides of those gay butterfly side-curls which framed her sweet face at night and to which she never gave wing until after luncheon, no matter who called. The silk scarf that covered them this morning was in recognition of Oliver's sex.

She had finished her breakfast and was leaning forward in her rocking-chair, her elbows on her knees, her tiny feet resting on the fender. She was watching the fire-fairies at work building up their wonderful palaces of molten gold studded with opals and rubies. The little lady must have been in deep thought, for she did not know Oliver had entered until she felt his arm on her shoulder.

"Ah, you dear fellow. No, not there; sit right here on this cricket by my side. Stop, do not say a word. I have been studying it all out in these coals. I know all about it—it is about the mountain girl, this—what do you call her?"

"Miss Grant."

"Nonsense! What do *you* call her?"

"Madge."

"Ah, that's something like it. And you love her?"

"Yes." (Pianissimo.)

"And she loves you?"

"*Yes.*" (Forte.)

"And you have told her so?"

"YES!" (Fortissimo.)

"Whew!" Miss Clendenning caught her breath and gave a little gasp. "Well, upon my word! You don't seem to have lost any time, my young Romeo. What does her father say?"

"He doesn't know anything about it."

"Does anybody except you two babes in the wood?"

369

" Yes, her mother."

" And yours? You told her last night. I knew you would."

" Not everything; but she is all upset."

" Of course she is. So am I. Now tell me—is she a lady? "

" She is the dearest, sweetest girl you——"

" Come now, come now, answer me. They are all the dearest and sweetest things in the world. What I want to know is, is she a *lady?* "

" Yes."

" True now, Ollie—honest? "

" Yes, in every sense of the word. A woman you would love and be proud of the moment you saw her."

Miss Clendenning took his face in her hands and looked down into his eyes. " I believe you. Now what do you want me to do? "

" I want her to come down here so everybody can see her. If I had a sister she could invite her, and it would be all right, and maybe then her mother would let her come."

" And you want me to play the sister and have her come here? "

Oliver's fingers closed tight over Miss Clendenning's hand. " Oh, Midget, if you only would, that would fix everything. Mother would understand then why I love her, and Madge could go back and tell her people about us. Her father is very bitter against everybody at the South. They would feel differently if Madge could stay a week with us."

" Why won't her father bring her? "

" He never leaves home. He would not even take her to the mountains, fifteen miles away. She could never paint as she does if she had relied upon him. Mother and Mr. Grant are both alike in their hatred of art as a fitting profession for anybody, and I tell you that they are both wrong."

Miss Clendenning looked up in surprise. She had never seen the boy take a stand of this kind against one of his mother's opinions. Oliver saw the expression on the little lady's face and kept on, his cheeks flushed and a set look about his eyes.

" Yes, wrong. I have never believed mother could be wrong in anything before, and when she wanted me to give up painting I did so because I thought she knew best. But I know she's not right about Madge, and if she is wrong about her, how do I know she was not wrong about my working with Mr. Crocker? "

Margaret's words that day in the bark slant were now ringing in his ears. He had never forgotten them—" Your mother cannot coddle you up forever."

Miss Clendenning held her peace. She was not astonished at the revolt in the boy's mind. She had seen for months past in his letters that Oliver's individuality was asserting itself. It was the new **girl**

371

whom he was defending—the woman he loved. This had given him strength. She knew something of what he felt, and she knew what blind obedience had done for her. With a half-smothered sigh, she reached over Oliver's head, dipped a quill pen in her inkstand, and at Oliver's dictation, wrote Margaret's address.

"I will invite her at once," she said.

Long after Oliver had gone Miss Clendenning sat looking into the fire. The palaces of rose and amber that the busy fingers of the fire fairies had built up in the white heat of their enthusiasm were in ruins. The light had gone out. Only gray ashes remained, with here and there a dead cinder.

Miss Clendenning rose from her chair, stood a moment in deep thought, and said, aloud:

"If she loves him, she shall have him. There shall be no more desolate firesides if I can help it."

Early the next morning, she mailed by the first post a letter so dainty in form and so delicate in color that only a turtle-dove should have carried it to Brookfield Farm, and have dropped it into Margaret's hand. This billet-doux began by inviting Miss Margaret Grant of Brookfield Farm to pass a week with Miss Lavinia Clendenning, of Kennedy Square, she, Miss Lavinia, desiring to know the better one who had so charmed and delighted "our dear Oliver," and ended with "Please say to your good mother, that I am twice your age, and will take as much care of you as if you were my own daughter. I feel assured she will waive all ceremony when she thinks of how warm a greeting awaits you."

Margaret looked at the post-mark, and then at the little oval of violet wax bearing the crest of the Clendennings—granted in the time of Queen Elizabeth for distinguished services to the Throne—and after she had read it to her mother, and had shown the seal to her father, who had put on his glasses, scanned it closely, and tossed it back to her with a dry laugh, and after she had talked it all over with John, who said it was certainly very kind of the woman, and that Oliver's people were evidently " nobs," but, of course, Madge couldn't go, not knowing any of them, Margaret took a sheet of plain white paper from her desk, thanked Miss Clendenning for her kind thought of her, and declined the honor in a firm, round hand. This she closed with a red wafer, and then, with a little bridling of her head and a determined look in her face, she laid the letter on the gate-post, ready for the early stage in the morning.

This missive was duly received by Miss Clendenning, and read at once to Mrs. Horn, who raised her eyebrows and pursed her lips in deep thought. After some moments she looked over her glasses at Miss Lavinia and said:

" I must say, Lavinia, I am very greatly astonished. Won't come? She has done perfectly right. I think all the better of her for it. Really, there may be something in the girl after all. Let me look at her handwriting again—writes like a woman of some force. Won't come? What do you think, Lavinia?"

"Merely a question of grandmothers, my dear; she seems to have had one, too," answered the little old maid, with a quizzical smile in her eye, as she folded the letter and slipped it in her pocket.

CHAPTER XVIII

Margaret's decision saddened Oliver's last days at home, and he returned to New York with none of his former buoyancy. Here other troubles began to multiply. Before the autumn was gone, Morton, Slade & Co., unable longer to make headway against the financial difficulties that beset them, went to the wall, involving many of their fellow-merchants. Oliver lost his situation, in consequence, and was forced to support himself during the long dreary winter by making lithographic drawings for Bianchi, at prices that barely paid his board. His loneliness in the garret room became more intense, Fred being much away and the occupants of the other rooms being either strangers to him or so uncongenial that he would not make their acquaintance.

To his own troubles were added other anxieties. The political outlook had become even more gloomy than the financial. The roar of Sumter's guns had reverberated throughout the land, and men of all minds were holding their breath and listening, with ears to the ground, for the sound of the next shot. Even Margaret's letters were full of foreboding. " Father is more bitter against the South than ever," she wrote. "He says if he had ten sons each should shoulder a musket. We must wait, Ollie dear. I can only talk to mother about you. Father won't listen, and I never mention your name before him. Not because it is you, Ollie, but because you represent a class whom he hates. Dear John would listen, but he is still in Boston. Even his fellow-classmen want to fight, he says. I fear all this will hurt my work, and keep me from painting."

These letters of Margaret's, sad as they were, were his greatest and sometimes his only comfort. She knew his ups and downs and they must have no secrets from each other. From his mother, however, he kept all records of his privations during these troublous months. Neither his father nor his dear mother must deprive themselves for his benefit.

During these dreary days he often longed for Kennedy Square and for those whom he loved, but it was not until one warm spring day, when the grass was struggling into life, and the twigs on the scraggy trees in Union Square were growing pink and green with impatient buds and leaves that he had his wish. Then a startling telegram summoned him. It read as follows:

"Father ill. Come at once.

"MOTHER."

Instinctively Oliver felt in his pockets for his purse. There was just money enough to take him to Kennedy Square and back.

His mother met him at the door.

"It was only a fainting turn, my son," were her first words. "I am sorry I sent for you. Your father is himself again, so Dr. Wallace says. He has been working too hard lately—sometimes far into the night. I could have stopped you from coming; but, somehow, I wanted you—" and she held him close in her arms, and laid her cheek against his. "I get so lonely, my boy, and feel so helpless sometimes."

The weak and strong were changing places. She felt the man in him now.

Nathan was in the library. He and Malachi had been taking turns at Richard's bedside. Malachi had not closed his eyes all night. Nathan came out into the hall when he heard Oliver's voice, and put his hand on his shoulder.

"We had a great scare, Ollie," he said, "but he's all right again, thank God! He's asleep now—better not wake him." Then he put on his coat and went home.

Malachi shook his head. "Sumpin's de matter wid him, an' dis ain't de las' ob it. Drapped jes' like a shote when he's hit, Marse Oliver," he said, in a low whisper, as if afraid of disturbing his master on the floor above. "I was a-layin' out his clo'es an' he called quick like, 'Malachi! Malachi!' an' when I got dar, he was lyin' on de flo' wid his head on de mat. I ain't nebber seen Marse Richard do like dat befo'—" The old servant trembled as he spoke. He evidently did not share Nathan's hopeful views. Neither did Dr. Wallace, although he did not say so to anyone.

Their fears, however, were not realized. Richard not only revived, but by the end of the week he was in the drawing-room again, Malachi, in accordance with the time-honored custom, wheeling out his chair, puffing up the cushions, and, with a wave of the hand and a sweeping bow, saying:

"Yo' ch'ar's all ready, Marse Richard. Hope you'se feelin' fine dis evenin', sah!"

The following day he was in his "li'l' room," Oliver helping him. It was the lifting of the heavy plate of the motor that had hurt Richard, so Nathan told him; not the same motor which Oliver remembered; another, much larger and built on different lines. The inventor now used twenty-four cells instead of ten, and the magnets had been wrapped with finer wire.

These days in the shop were delightful to Oliver. His father no longer treated him as an inexperienced youth, but as his equal. "I hope you will agree with me, my son," he would say; or, "What do you think of the idea of using a 'cam' here instead of a lever?" or, "I wish you would find the last issue of the *Review*, and tell me what you think of that article of Latrobe's. He puts the case very clearly, it seems to me," etc. And Oliver would bend his head in attention and try to follow his father's lead, wishing all the

378

time that he could really be of use to the man he re-
vered beyond all others, and so lighten some of the
burdens that were weighing him down.

And none the less joyful were the hours spent with
his mother. All the old-time affection, the devotion
of a lover-son, were lavished upon her. And she was
so supremely happy in it all. Now that Richard had
recovered, there was no other cloud on her horizon,
not even that of the dreaded mortgage which owing
to some payments made Richard by a company using
one of his patents had been extended and its interest
paid for two years in advance in deference to her
urgent request. All anxiety as to the Northern girl
had happily passed out of her mind. If Oliver intended marrying Miss Grant he would have told her,
she knew. Then again, he was so much stronger and
wiser now—so much more thoughtful than he had
been—so much more able to keep his head in matters
of this kind.

As his position was different with his father in
the " li'l' room " and with his mother in the stillness
of her chamber—for often they talked there together
until far into the night—so were his relations altered
with his old friends and neighbors in the drawing-
room. While the young men and girls filled the
house as had always been their custom, the older men,
as well, now paid their respects to Richard Horn's
son.

" One of our own kind," Judge Bowman said to

Richard. "Does you credit, Horn—a son to be proud of."

Even Amos Cobb came to look him over, a courtesy which pleased Richard who greatly admired the Vermonter, and who had not hesitated to express his good opinion of him on more than one occasion before his own and Cobb's friends.

"A man of force, gentlemen," Richard had said, "of great kindness of heart and with a wide range of vision. One who has the clearest ideas of what makes for the good of his country; a man, too, not ashamed of his opinions and with ample courage to defend them. He deserves our unqualified respect, not our criticism."

When Cobb heard of Richard's outspoken defence of him he at once called on the inventor at his workshop—a thing he had not done for months, and asked to see the motor, and that same night astonished the circles about the club tables, by remarking, in a tone of voice loud enough for everybody to hear: "We have all been wrong about Horn. He has got hold of something that will one day knock steam higher than Gilderoy's kite." A friendship was thus established between the two which had become closer every day—the friendship of a clearer understanding; one which was unbroken during the rest of their lives.

It was quite natural, therefore, that Amos Cobb should be among Oliver's earliest callers. He must

have been pleased with his inspection, for he took occasion at the club to say to Colonel Clayton, in his
quick, crisp way:

" Dropped in at Horn's last night. His boy's over
from New York. Looks like a different man since
he quit fooling round here a couple of years ago.
Clean cut a young fellow as I've seen for many a day.
Got a look out of his eyes like his mother's. Level-
headed woman, his mother—no better anywhere. If
all the young bloods South had Oliver Horn's ideas
we might pull through this crisis."

To which my Lord Chesterfield of Kennedy Square
merely replied only with a nod of the head and a
drawing together of the eyebrows. He found it difficult to tolerate the Vermonter in these days with his
continued tirades against " The epidemic of insanity
sweeping over the South," as Cobb would invariably
put it.

The scribe now reaches a night in Oliver's career
fraught with such momentous consequences that he
would be glad to leave its story untold:

An unforgettable night indeed, both for those
who were assembled there, and for him who is the
chronicler. He would fain lay down his pen to recall again the charm and the sweetness and the old-
time flavor of that drawing-room: the soft lights of
the candles; the perfume of the lilacs coming in
through the half-open windows; the merry laugh

of the joyous girl running through the Square to be ushered by Malachi a moment later into the presence of her hostess, there to make her courtesied obeisance before she joined a group of young people around one of the red damask-covered sofas. And then Richard, dear Richard, with his white hair and his gracious speech, and Miss Clendenning with her manners of foreign courts, and the sweet-voiced hostess of the mansion moving about among her guests; her guests who were her neighbors and her friends; whose children were like her own, and whose joys and sorrows were hers—guests, neighbors, friends many of whom after this fatal night were to be as enemies never to assemble again with the old-time harmony and love.

Malachi had brewed the punch; the little squat glasses were set out beside the Canton china bowl, for it was the night of the weekly musical and an unusually brilliant company had assembled in honor of Oliver's arrival and of Richard's recovery.

The inventor was to play his own interpretations of Handel's Largo, a favorite selection of Ole Bull, and one which the inventor and the great virtuoso had played together some years before.

Miss Clendenning had taken her place at the piano, Nathan standing beside her to turn the leaves of the accompaniment.

Richard had picked up his violin, tucked it under his chin, poised the bow, and that peculiar hush which always precedes the sounding of the first notes on evenings of this kind had already fallen upon the room, when there came a loud rap at the front door that startled everyone and the next instant Colonel Clayton burst in, his cheeks flaming, his hat still on his head.

"Ten thousand Yankees will be here in the morning, Horn!" he gasped, out of breath with his run across the Square, holding one hand to his side as he spoke, and waving an open telegram in the other. "Stop! This is no time for fiddling. They're not going round by water; they're coming here by train. Read that," and he held out the bit of paper.

The Colonel's sudden entrance and the startling character of the news, had brought every man to his feet.

Richard laid down his violin, read the telegram quietly, and handed it back.

"Well, suppose they do come, Clayton?"

His voice was so sustained, and his manner so temperate, that a certain calming reassurance was felt.

"Suppose they *do* come! They'll burn the town, I tell you," shouted the infuriated man, suddenly remembering his hat and handing it to Malachi. That's what they're coming for. We want no troops in our streets, and the Government ought to know it. It's an outrage to send armed men here at this time!"

"You're all wrong, Clayton," answered Richard, without raising his voice. "You have always been wrong about this matter. There are two sides to this question. Virginia troops occupied Harper's Ferry yesterday. If the authorities consider that more troops are needed to protect Washington, that's their affair, not yours nor mine."

"We'll *make* it our affair. What right has this damnable Government to march their troops through a free and sovereign State without its permission? Whom do they think this town belongs to, I want to know, that this Northern scum should foul it. Not a man shall set foot here if I can help it. I would rather——"

Richard turned to stay the torrent of invectives in which such words as "renegades," "traitors," "mud-sills," were heard, but the Colonel, completely unmanned by the rage he was in, and seemingly unconscious of the presence of the ladies, waved him aside with his hand, and faced the row of frightened, expectant faces.

"Gentlemen, when you are through with this tomfoolery, I shall be glad if you will come to the club; any of you who have got guns had better look them up; they'll be wanted before this is over. We'll meet these dirty skinflints with cold lead and plenty of it."

Oliver's face flushed at the Colonel's words, and he was about to speak, when his mother laid her hand on his arm. Visions of the kindly face of Professor Cummings, and the strong well-knit figure of Fred

Stone, John Grant, Hank, Jonathan Gordon, and the others whom he loved came before his eyes.

Richard raised his hand in protest:

"You are mad, Clayton; you don't know what you are doing. Stop these troops and our streets will run blood. I beg and beseech you to keep cool. Because South Carolina has lost her head, that is no reason why we should. This is not our fight! If my State called me to defend her against foreign invasion, old as I am I would be ready, and so should you. But the Government is part of ourselves, and should not be looked upon as an enemy. You are wrong, I tell you, Clayton."

"Wrong or right, they'll have to walk over my dead body if they attempt to cross the streets of this town. That's my right as a citizen, and that I shall maintain. Gentlemen, I have called a meeting at the club at ten o'clock to-night. All of you able to carry a gun will do me the kindness to be present. I'd rather die right here in my tracks than let a lot of low-lived mud-sills who never entered a gentleman's house in their lives come down here at the beck and call of this rail-splitter they've put in the White House and walk over us rough-shod! And you, Horn, a Virginian, defend it! By God, sir, it's enough to make a man's blood boil!"

The inventor's eyes flashed. They blazed now as brightly as those of Clayton. Not even a life-long friend had the right to use such language in his presence, or in that of his guests. Richard's figure grew tense with indignation. Confronting the now reckless man, he raised his hand and was about to order him out of the house when Oliver stepped quickly in front of his father.

"You are unjust, Colonel Clayton." The words came slowly between the boy's partly closed teeth. "You know nothing of these people. I have lived among them long enough not only to know but to love them. There are as many gentlemen North as South. If you would go among them as I have done, you would be man enough to admit it."

The Colonel turned upon him with a snarl:

"And so you have become a dirty renegade, have you, and gone back on your blood and your State? That's what comes of sending boys like you away from home!"

The guests stood amazed. The spectacle of the most courteous man of his time acting like a blackguard was more astounding than the news he had brought. Even Malachi, at the open door, trembled with fear.

As the words fell from his lips Mrs. Horn's firm, clear voice, crying "Shame! Shame!" rang through the room. She had risen from her seat and was walking rapidly to where the Colonel was standing.

"Shame, I say, John Clayton! How dare you speak so? What has our young son ever done to you,

The Colonel turned upon him with a snarl.

that you should insult him in his father's house?
What madness has come over you?"

The horrified guests looked from one to the other.
Every eye was fixed on the Colonel, shaking with
rage.

For a brief instant he faced his hostess, started to
speak, checked himself as if some better judgment
prevailed, and with upraised hands flung himself
from the room, shouting, as he went:

"Ten o'clock, gentlemen! Chesapeake Club!
Every man with a gun!"

Richard, astounded at Clayton's action and now
thoroughly convinced of the danger of the situation
and determined to do what he could to thwart the
efforts of such men as the Colonel and his following,
laid his violin in its case, turned to his frightened
guests and with a few calming words and a promise
to send each one of them word if any immediate
danger existed, called Oliver and Nathan to him,
and taking his cloak and hat from Malachi's outstretched trembling hands started for the club.
Once outside it was easy to see that a feeling of
intense and ominous excitement was in the air.
Even on the sidewalk and on the street corners, men
stood silent, huddled together, their eyes on the
ground, the situation being too grave for spoken
words.

On arriving they found its halls already filled
with angry and excited men discussing the threat-

ened invasion, many of whom met the young man with scowling looks, the Colonel having evidently informed them of Oliver's protest.

A few of the members had brought their sporting guns. These had been handed to the gouty old porter, who, half-frightened out of his wits, had stacked them in a row against the wall of the outer hall. Billy Talbot arrived a few moments later carrying a heavy fowling-piece loaded for swan. He had been dining out when summoned and had hurriedly left the table, excusing himself on the ground that he had been " called to arms." He had taken time, however, to stop at his own house, slip out of his English dress-suit and into a brown ducking outfit.

" We'll shoot 'em on the run, damn 'em—like rabbits, sir," he said to Cobb as he entered, the Vermonter being the only man likely to communicate with the invaders and so make known the warlike intentions of at least one citizen, and the utter hopelessness of any prolonged resistance. Waggles, who had followed close on his master's heels, was too excited to sit down, but stood on three legs, his eye turned toward Talbot, as if wanting to pick up any game which Billy's trusty fowling-piece might bring down.

A quiet, repressed smile passed over Oliver's face as he watched Waggles and his master, but he spoke no word to the Nimrod. He could not help thinking how Hank Pollard would handle the fashion-plate if he ever closed his great bony hands upon him.

Judge Bowman now joined the group, bowing to Richard rather coldly and planting himself squarely in front of Oliver.

"There's only one side to this question, young man, for you," he said. "Don't be fooled by those fellows up in New York. I know them—known them for years. Look up there"—and he pointed to the portrait of Oliver's ancestor above the mantel. "What do you think he would do if he were alive to-day? Stick to your own, my boy—stick to your own!"

General Mactavish now hurried in, drawing off his white gloves as he entered the room, followed by Tom Gunning, Carter Thom, and Mowbray, an up-country man. The four had been dining together and had also left the table on receipt of the Colonel's message. They evidently appreciated the gravity of the situation, for they stood just outside the excited group that filled the centre of the large room, listening eagerly to Richard's clear tones pleading for moderation—"in a crisis which," he urged, "required the greatest public restraint and self-control," and which would surely "plunge the State into the most horrible of wars" if those about him listened to the counsels of such men as Clayton and Judge Bowman.

During the whole discussion Amos Cobb stood

silent, leaning against the mantel-piece, his cold gray eyes fixed on the excited throng, his thin lips curling now and then. When the Defence Committee, in spite of Richard's protest, had at last been formed, and its members formally instructed to meet the enemy outside the city and protest, first by voice and then, if necessary, by arms, against the unwarrantable invasion of the soil of their State, the Vermonter buttoned up his coat slowly, one button after another, fastened each one with a determined gesture, drew on his gloves, set his lips tight, singled out Oliver and Richard, shook their hands with the greatest warmth, and walked straight out of the club-house. Some time during the night he drove in a hack to Mr. Stiger's house; roused the old cashier from his sleep; took him and the big walled-town-key down to the bank; unlocked the vault and dragged from it two wooden boxes filled with gold coin, his own property, and which the month before he had deposited there for safe-keeping. These, with Stiger's assistance, he carried to the hack. Within the hour, the two boxes with their contents were locked up in a bureau-drawer in his own house awaiting their immediate shipment to New York.

The next morning Malachi's wizened face was thrust inside Oliver's bedroom door. He was shaking with terror, his eyes almost starting from his head.

THE LAST HOURS OF A CIVILIZATION

" Marse Ollie, Marse Ollie, git up quick as you kin! De Yankees is come; de town is black wid 'em! "

Oliver sprang from his bed and stood half-dazed looking into Malachi's eyes.

" How do you know? Who told you?"

" I done seen 'em. Been up since daylight. Dey got guns wid 'em. Fo' Gawd dis is tur-ble! " The old man's voice trembled—he could hardly articulate.

Oliver hurried into his clothes; stepped noiselessly downstairs so as not to wake his father and mother, and, closing the front door softly behind him, stood for a moment on the top step. Should he forget the insults of the night before and go straight to Colonel Clayton, and try to dissuade him from his purpose, or should he find the regiment and warn them of their danger?

A vague sense of personal responsibility for whatever the day might bring forth took possession of him —as though the turning-point in his life had come, without his altogether realizing it. These men from the North were coming to his own town, where he had been born and brought up, and where they should be hospitably received. If Clayton had his way they would be met with clenched hands and perhaps with blows. That these invaders were armed, and that each man carried forty rounds of ammunition and was perfectly able to take care of himself, did not impress him. He only remembered that they were

391

of the same blood as the men who had befriended him, and that they were in great personal danger.

The angry shouts of a crowd of men and boys approaching the Square from a side street, now attracted his attention. They rushed past Oliver without noticing him, and, hurrying on through the gate, crossed the park, in the direction of the railroad station and the docks. One of the mob, lacking a club, stopped long enough to wrench a paling from the rickety fence enclosing the Square, trampling the pretty crocuses and the yellow tulips under foot. Each new arrival, seeing the gap, followed the first man's example, throwing the branches and tendrils to the ground as they worked, until the whole panel was wrecked and the vines were torn from their roots. As they swept by the Clayton house, half a dozen men, led by the Colonel, ran down the steps and joined the throng.

Oliver, seeing now that all his efforts for peace would be hopeless, ran through the Square close behind the shouting mob, dashed down a side street parallel to that through which the cars carrying the troops were to pass on their way to Washington, turned into an alley, and found himself on the water-front, opposite one of the dock slips.

These slips were crowded with vessels, their bow-sprits, like huge bayonets, thrust out over the car-tracks, as if to protect the cellars of the opposite warehouses, used by the ship-chandlers for the storage of coarse merchandise, and always left open during the day. The narrow strip of dock-front, between the car-tracks and the water-line—an unpaved strip of foot-trodden earth and rotting planks, on which lay enormous ship-anchors, anchor-chains in coils, piles of squared timber, and other maritime properties, stored here for years—was now a seething mass of people completely hiding the things on which they stood.

Oliver mounted a pile of barrels in front of one of these ship-chandler cellars, and, holding to an awning-post, looked off over the heads of the surging crowd and in the direction of the railroad station at the end of the long street. From his position on the top barrel he could see the white steam of the locomotives rising above the buildings and the line of cars. He could see, too, a yard engine backing and puffing, as if making up a train.

Suddenly, without apparent cause, there rose above the murmurs of the street an ominous sound, like that of a fierce wind soughing through a forest of pines. All eyes were directed down the long street upon a line of cars that had been shunted on the street-track; about these moved a group of men in blue uniforms, the sun flashing on their bayonets and the brass shields of their belts.

Oliver, stirred by the sound, climbed to the top of the awning-post for a better view and clung to the cross-piece. Every man who could gain an inch of

393

vantage, roused to an extra effort by the distinct roar, took equal advantage of his fellows. Sailors sprang farther into the rigging or crawled out to the end of the bowsprits; the windows of the warehouses were thrown up, the clerks and employees standing on the sills, balancing themselves by the shutters; even the skylights were burst open, men and boys crawling out edging their way along the ridge-poles of the roofs or holding to the chimneys. Every inch of standing-room was black with spectators.

The distant roar died away in fitful gusts as suddenly as it had arisen, and a silence even more terrifying fell upon the throng as a body of police poured out of a side street and marched in a compact body toward the cars.

Then came long strings of horses, eight or ten in tandem. These were backed down and hooked to the cars.

The flash of bayonets was now cut off as the troops crowded into the cars; the body of police wheeled and took their places ahead of the horses; the tandems straightened out and the leaders lunged forward under the lash. The advance through the town had begun.

All this time the mob about Oliver stood with hands clenched, jaws tight shut, great lumps in their throats. Their eyes were the eyes of hungry beasts watching an approaching prey.

As the distant rumbling of the cars, drawn by

teams of straining horses, sounded the nearer, a bare-headed man, with white hair and mustache and black garments that distinguished him from the mob about him, and whom Oliver instantly recognized as Colonel Clayton, mounted a mass of squared timber lining the track, ran the length of the pile, climbed to the topmost stick, and shouted, in a voice which reverberated throughout the street:

" Block the tracks! "

A torrent of oaths broke loose as the words left his lips, and a rush was made for the pile of timber. Men struggled and fought like demons for the end of the great sticks, carrying them by main strength, crossing them over the rails, heaping them one on the other like a pile of huge jack-straws, a dozen men to a length, the mobs on the house-tops and in the windows cheering like mad. The ends of the heavy chains resting on the strip of dirt were now caught up and hauled along the cobbles to be intertwined with the squared timber; anchors weighing tons were pried up and dragged across the tracks by lines of men urged on by gray-haired old merchants in Quaker-cut dress coats, many of them bare-headed, who had yielded to the sudden unaccountable delirium that had seized upon everyone. Colonel Clayton, Carter Thom, and Mowbray could be seen working side by side with stevedores from the docks and the rabble from the shipyards. John Camblin, a millionnaire and nearly eighty years of age, head of

395

the largest East India house on the wharves, his hat
and wig gone, his coat split from the collar to the
tails, was tugging at an anchor ten men could not have
moved. Staid citizens, men who had not used an oath
for years, stood on the sidewalks swearing like street-
toughs; others looked out from their office-windows,
the tears streaming down their cheeks. A woman
with a coarse shawl about her shoulders, her hair
hanging loose, a broom in one hand, was haranguing
the mob from the top of a tobacco hogshead, her
curses filling the air.

Oliver held to his seat on the cross-piece of the
awning, his teeth set, his eye fixed on the rapidly
advancing cars, his mind wavering between two
opinions—loyalty to his home, now invaded by troops
whose bayonets might be turned upon his own people,
and loyalty to the friends he loved—and to the
woman who loved him!

The shouting now became a continuous roar. The
front line of policemen, as they neared the obstruc-
tions, swung their clubs right and left, beating back
the crowd. Then the rumbling cars, drawn by the
horses, came to a halt. The barricades must be
reckoned with.

Again there came the flashing of steel and the in-
termingling of blue and white uniforms. The troops
were leaving the cars and were forming in line to
pass the barricades; the officers marching in front,
the compact mass following elbow to elbow, their eyes

straight before them, their muskets flat against their shoulders.

The approaching column now deployed sharply, wheeled to the right of the obstruction, and became once more a solid mass, leaving the barricades behind them, the Chief of Police at the head of the line forcing the mob back to the curbstone, laying about him with his club, thumping heads and cracking wrists as he cleared the way.

The colonel of the regiment, his fatigue cap pulled over his eyes, sword in hand, shoulders erect, cape thrown back, was now abreast of the awning to which Oliver clung. Now and then he would glance furtively at the house-tops, as if expecting a missile.

The mob looked on sullenly, awed into submission by the gleaming bayonets. But for the shouts of the police, beating back the crowd, and the muttered curses, one would have thought a parade was in progress.

The first company had now passed—pale, haggard-looking men, their lips twitching, showing little flecks of dried saliva caked in the corners of their mouths, their hands tight about the butts of their muskets.

Oliver looked on with beating heart. The dull, monotonous tramp of their feet strangely affected him.

As the second line of bayonets came abreast of the awning-post, a blacksmith in a red shirt and leather

397

apron, his arms bared to the elbow, sprang from the packed sidewalk into the open space between the troops and the gutter, lifted a paving stone high above his head and hurled it, with all his might, straight against the soldier nearest him. The man reeled, clutched at the comrade next him, and sank to the ground. Then, quick as an echo, a puff of white smoke burst out down the line of troops, and a sharp, ringing report split the air. The first shot of defence had been fired.

The whole column swayed as if breasting a gale.

Another and an answering shot now rang through the street. This came from a window filled with men gesticulating wildly. Instantly the troops wheeled, raised their muskets, and a line of fire and smoke belched forth.

A terrible fear, that paled men's faces, followed by a moment of ominous silence, seized upon the mob, and then a wild roar burst out from thousands of human throats. The rectangular body of soldiers and the ragged-edged mob merged into a common mass. Men wrenched the guns from the soldiers and beat them down with the butt ends of the muskets. Frenzied policemen hurled themselves into the midst of the disorganized militia, knocking up the ends of their muskets, begging the men to hold their fire. The air was thick with missiles; bricks from the house-tops; sticks of wood and coal from the fire-places of the offices; iron bolts, castings, anything the crazed mob could find with which to kill their fellow-men. The roar was deafening, drowning the orders of the officers.

Oliver clung to his post, not knowing whether to drop into the seething mass or to run the risk of being shot where he was. Suddenly his eye singled out a soldier who stood at bay below him, swinging his musket, widening the circle about him with every blow. The soldier's movements were hampered by his heavy overcoat and army blanket slung across his shoulder. His face and neck were covered with blood and dirt, disfiguring him beyond recognition.

At the same instant Oliver became conscious that a man in blue overalls was creeping up on the soldier's rear to brain him with a cart-rung that he held in his hand.

A mist swam before the boy's eyes, and a great lump rose in his throat. The cowardice of the attack incensed him; some of the hot blood of the old ancestor that had crossed the flood at Trenton flamed up in his face. With the quickness of a cat he dropped to the sidewalk, darted forward, struck the coward full in the face with his clenched fist, tumbling him to the ground, wrenched the rung from his hands, and, jumping in front of the now almost overpowered soldier, swung the heavy stick about him like a flail, clearing the space before him.

The assaulting crowd wavered, fell back, and then, maddened at Oliver's defence of the invader, with a wild yell of triumph, swept the two young men off their feet, throwing them bodily down the steps of a ship-chandler's shop, the soldier knocked senseless by a blow from a brick which had struck him full in the chest.

Oliver lay still for a moment, raised his head cautiously and, putting forth all his strength, twisted his arms around the stricken man and rolled with him into the cellar. Then, springing to his feet, he slammed the door behind them and slipped in the bolt, before the mob could guess his meaning.

Listening at the crack of the door for a moment, and finding they were not pursued, he stooped over the limp body, lifted it in his arms, laid it on a pile of sails, and ran to the rear of the cellar for a bucket standing under a grimy window, scarcely visible in the gloom, now that the door was shut.

Under the touch of the cold water, the soldier slowly opened his eyes, straining them toward Oliver, as if in pain.

The two men looked intently at each other, the soldier passing his hand across his forehead as if trying to clear his brain. Then lifting himself up on his elbow he gasped:

"Horn! Horn! My God!"

Oliver's heart stopped beating.

"Who are you?"

"John Grant."

Oliver saw only Margaret's face!

THE LAST HOURS OF A CIVILIZATION

As though he were working for the woman he loved—doing what she would have done—he knelt beside the wounded man, wiped the blood and grime from his cheeks with his own handkerchief, loosening his coat, rubbing his hands, murmuring " Old fellow," " Dear John ": there was no time for other interchange of speech.

When at last Grant was on his feet the two men barricaded the doors more strongly, rolling heavy barrels against them, the sounds from the street seeming to indicate that an attack might be made upon them. But the mob had swept on and forgotten them, as mobs often do, while the fugitives waited, hardly daring to speak except in detached whispers, lest some one of the inmates of the warehouse overhead might hear them.

Toward noon a low tap was heard at the window, which was level with an alley in the rear, and a man's hand was thrust through a broken pane. Oliver pressed Grant's arm, laid his finger on his lips, caught up a heavy hammer lying on an oil-barrel, crept noiselessly along the wall toward the sound, and stopped to listen. Then he heard his name called in a hoarse whisper.

" Marse Ollie! Marse Ollie! Is you in here? "

" Who is it? " Oliver called back, crouching beneath the window, his fingers tight around the handle of the hammer.

" It's me, Marse Ollie."

"You! Malachi!"

"Yassir, I'se been a-followin' ye all de mawnin'; I see 'em tryin' to kill ye an' I tried to git to ye. I kin git through—yer needn't help me," and he squeezed himself under the raised sash. "Malachi like de snake—crawl through anywheres. An' ye ain't hurted?" he asked when he was inside. "De bressed Lord, ain't dat good! I been a-waitin' outside; I was feared dey'd see me if I tried de door."

"Where are the soldiers?"

"Gone. Ain't nobody outside at all. Mos' to de railroad by dis time, dey tells me. An' dere ain't nary soul 'bout dis place—all run away. Come 'long wid me, son—I ain't gwine ter leabe ye a minute. Marse Richard'll be waitin'. Come 'long home, son. I been a-followin' ye all de mawnin'." The tears were in his eyes now. "An' ye ain't hurted," and he felt him all over with trembling hands.

John raised himself above the oil-barrels. He had heard the strange talk and was anxiously watching the approaching figures.

"It's all right, Grant—it's our Malachi," Oliver called out in his natural voice, now that there was no danger of being overheard.

The old man stopped and lifted both hands above his head.

"Gor'-a-mighty! an' he ain't dead?" His eyes had now become accustomed to the gloom.

" No; and just think, Mally, he is my own friend. Grant, this is our Malachi whom I told you about."

Grant stepped over the barrel and held out his hand to the old negro. There are no class distinctions where life and death are concerned.

" Glad to see you. Pretty close shave, but I guess I'm all right. They'd have done for me but for your master."

A council of war was now held. The uniform would be fatal if Grant were seen in it on the street. Malachi must crawl into the alley again, go over to Oliver's house, and return at dusk with one of Oliver's suits of clothes; the uniform and the blood-stained shirt could then be hidden in the cellar, and at dark, should the street still be deserted, the three would put on a bold front and walk out of the front door of the main warehouse over their heads. Once safe in the Horn house, they could perfect plans for Grant's rejoining his regiment.

Their immediate safety provided for, and Malachi gone, Oliver could wait no longer to ask about Margaret. He had been turning over in his mind how he had best broach the subject, when her brother solved the difficulty by saying:

" Father was the first man in Brookfield to indorse the President's call for troops. He'd have come himself, old as he is, if I had not joined the regiment. He didn't like you, Horn; I always told him he was wrong. He'll never forgive himself now when he hears what you have done for me," and he laid his hand affectionately on Oliver's shoulder as he spoke. " I liked you as soon as I saw you, and so did mother, and so does Madge, but father was always wrong about you. We told him so, again and again, and Madge said that father would see some day that you got your politeness from the Cavaliers and we got our plain speaking from the Puritans. The old gentleman was pretty mad about her saying so, I tell you, but she stuck to it. Madge is a dear girl, Horn. A fellow always knows just where to find Madge; no nonsense about her. She's grown handsome, too—handsomer than ever. There's a new look in her face, somehow, lately. I tell her she's met somebody in New York she likes, but she won't acknowledge it."

Oliver drank in every word, drawing out the brother with skilful questions and little exclamatory remarks that filled Grant with enthusiasm and induced him to talk on. They were young men again now—brothers once more, as they had been that first afternoon in the library at Brookfield. In the joy of hearing from her he entirely forgot his surroundings, and the dangers that still beset them both; a joy intensified because it was the first and only time he had heard someone who knew her talk to him of the woman he loved. This went on until night fell and Malachi again crawled in through the

404

same low window and helped John into Oliver's clothes.

When all was ready the main door of the warehouse above was opened carefully and the three men walked out—Malachi ahead, John and Oliver following. The moonlit street was deserted; only the barricades of timber and the litter of stones and bricks marked the events of the morning. Dodging into a side alley and keeping on its shadow side they made their way toward Oliver's home.

When the three reached the Square, the white light of the moon lay full on the bleached columns of the Clayton house. Outside on the porch, resting against the wall, stood a row of long-barrelled guns glinting in the moon's rays. Through the open doorway could be seen the glow of the hall lantern, the hall itself crowded with men. The Horn house was dark, except for a light in Mrs. Horn's bedroom. The old servant's visit had calmed their fears, and they had only to wait now until Oliver's return.

Malachi stationed Oliver and John Grant in the shadow of the big sycamore that overhung the house, mounted the marble steps and knocked twice. Aunt Hannah opened the door. She seemed to be expecting someone, for the knock was instantly followed by the turning of the knob.

Malachi spoke a few words in an undertone to Hannah, and stepped back to where the two young men were standing.

405

"You go in, Marse Oliver. Leabe de gemman here wid me under de tree. Everybody's got dere eye wide open now—can't fool Malachi—I knows de signs."

Oliver walked leisurely to the door, closed it softly behind him, and ran upstairs into his mother's arms.

Malachi whispered to Grant, and the two disappeared in the shadows. At the same moment a bolt shot back in a gate in the rear of the yard—a gate rarely unbolted. Old Hannah stood behind it shading a candle with her hand. Malachi led the way across the yard, through the green door of Richard's shop, mounted the work-bench, felt carefully along the edge of a trap-door in the ceiling, unhooked a latch, pushed it up with his two hands, the dust sifting down in showers on his head, and disclosed a large, empty loft, once used by the slaves as a sleeping-room, and which had not been opened for years.

Assisted by the negro's arms, Grant climbed to the floor above, where a dim skylight gave him light and air. A cup of hot coffee was then handed up and the door of the trap carefully fastened, Malachi rumpling the shavings on the work-bench to conceal the dust, No trace of the hiding-place of the fugitive was visible.

When Malachi again reached the front hall, it was in response to someone who was hammering at the door as if to break it down. The old man peered cautiously out through the small panes of glass. The sidewalk was crowded with men led by Colonel Clayton, most of them carrying guns. They had marched over from Clayton's house. Among them was a *posse* of detectives from the Police Department.

In answer to their summons Richard had thrown up the window of his bedroom and was talking to Clayton, whose voice Malachi recognized above the murmurs and threats of the small mob.

"Come down, Horn. Oliver has proved traitor, just as I knew he would. He's been hiding one of these damned Yankees all day. We want that man, I tell you, dead or alive, and we are going to have him."

When the door was flung wide Clayton confronted, not Richard, but Oliver.

"Where's that Yankee?" cried Clayton. He had not expected to see Oliver. "We are in no mood for nonsense—where have you hidden him?"

Malachi stepped forward before Oliver could answer.

"Marse Oliver ain't hid him. If you want him go hunt him!"

"You speak like that to me, you black scoundrel," burst out the Colonel, and he raised his arm as if to strike him.

"Yes—me! Ain't nobody gwine ter tech Marse Oliver while I lib. I's as free as you is, Marse Clayton. Ain't no man can lay a han' on me!"

The Colonel wheeled angrily and gave an order to
407

one of the detectives in a low voice. Oliver stood irresolute. He knew nothing of Grant's whereabouts.

The detective moved from the Colonel's side and pushed his way closer to where Oliver stood.

"There's no use your denying it, young feller; we've heard the whole story from one of our men who saw you jump in front of him. You bring him out or we'll go through the place from cellar to garret."

Oliver gazed straight at the speaker and still held his peace. He was wondering where Grant had hidden himself and what John's chances were if the crowd searched the house. Malachi's outburst had left him in the dark.

Mrs. Horn and Richard, who had followed Oliver and were standing half way down the stairs, looked on in astonishment. Would Clayton dare to break all the rules of good manners, and search the house, she whispered to Richard.

Another of the detectives now stepped forward— a dark, ugly-looking man, with the face of a bull-dog.

"Look here! I'll settle this. You and two men crossed the Square ten minutes ago. This nigger is one of 'em; where's the other?"

Malachi turned and smiled significantly at Oliver —a smile he knew. It was the smile which the old man's face always wore whenever some tortuous lie of the darky's own concoction had helped his young master out of one of his scrapes.

"I am not here to answer your questions," Oliver replied quietly, a feeling of relief in his heart.

The officer turned quickly and said with an oath to one of the detectives, "Send one man to the alley in the rear, and place another at this door. I'll search the yard and the house. Let no one of the family leave this hall. If that nigger moves put the irons on him."

The men outside made a circle about the house, some of them moving up the alley to watch the rear. Clayton leaned against the jamb of the door. He addressed no word to Richard or Mrs. Horn, nor did he look their way. Oliver stood with folded arms under the eight-sided hall-lantern which an officer had lighted. Now and then he spoke in restrained tones to his mother, who had taken her seat on the stairs, Richard standing beside her. It was not the fate of the soldier that interested her—it was the horror of the search. Richard had not spoken except to direct Malachi to obey the officer's orders. The horror of the search did not affect the inventor—that only violated the sanctity of the home: it was the brute force behind it which appalled him—that might annihilate the Republic.

"It is the beginning of the end," he said to himself.

409

The tread of heavy feet was again heard coming through the hall. Malachi turned quickly and a subdued smile lighted his wrinkled face.

The two detectives were alone!

" He is not there, Colonel Clayton," said the man with the bull-dog face, slipping his pistol into his hip pocket. " We went through the yard and the outhouses like a fine tooth-comb and made a clean sweep of the cellar. He may have gotten over the wall, but I don't think it. There's a lot of broken bottles on top. I'll try the bedrooms now."

As the words fell from his lips Mrs. Horn rose from her seat on the stairs, straight as a soldier on guard. The light from the lantern illumined her gray hair and threw into strong relief her upraised hand—the first of millions raised in protest against the invasion of the homes of the South. The detective saw the movement and a grim smile came into his face.

" Unless they'll bring him out," he added, slowly. " This young feller knows where he is. Make him tell."

Colonel Clayton turned to Oliver. " Is he upstairs, Oliver? "

" No."

" You give me your word of honor, Oliver, that he is not upstairs? "

" I do."

" Of course he'd say that. Here, I'll know pretty
410

d—— quick," muttered the detective moving toward
the stairway.

The Colonel stepped forward and barred his way
with his arm.

" Stay where you are! You don't know these people. If Oliver says he is not upstairs I believe him.
These Horns don't know how to lie. Your information is wrong. The man never entered the house.
You must look for the Yankee somewhere else."
Waiting until the detectives had left the hall, he
raised his hat, and with some show of feeling said:

" I am sorry, Sallie, that we had to upset you so.
When you and Richard see this matter in its true
light you'll think as I do. If these scoundrels are to
be permitted to come here and burn our homes we
want to know which side our friends are on."

" You are the judge of your own conduct, John
Clayton," she answered, calmly. " This night's work
will follow you all your life. Malachi, show Colonel
Clayton to the door and close it behind him."

Three nights later Malachi admitted a man he had
never seen before. He was short and thick-set and
had a grim, firmly set jaw. Under the lapel of his
coat was a gold shield. He asked for Mr. Horn, who
had lately been living in New York. He would not
come inside the drawing-room, but sat in the hall cn
the hair-cloth sofa, his knees apart, his cap in his
hand.

411

" I'm the Chief of Police," he said to Oliver, without rising from his seat, " and I come because Mr.
Cobb sent me. That's between ourselves, remember.
You'll have to get out of here at once. They've got
a yarn started that you're a government detective
sent down here to spot rebel sympathizers and they'll
make it warm for you. I've looked into it and I know
it ain't so, but this town's in no shape to listen to
anything. Besides, a while ago one of my men found
your friend's uniform in the cellar where you hid it
behind the barrels and the handkerchief all blood,
with your name on it; and they've got you dead to
rights. That'll all be out in the morning papers and
make it worse for you. You needn't worry about
him. He's all right. Mr. Cobb found him at daylight
this morning just where your nigger left him and
drove him over to the junction. He's with his regiment by this time. Get your things together quick
as you can. I'll wait for you and see you safe aboard
the owl train."

Within the hour Oliver had turned his back on his
home and all that he loved.

CHAPTER XIX

THE SETTLING OF THE SHADOW

The bruised crocuses never again lifted their heads in Kennedy Square.

With the settling of the shadow—a shadow black with hate—men forgot the perfume of flowers, the rest and cool of shady nooks, the kindling touch of warm hands, and stood apart with eyes askance; women shuddered and grew pale, and sad-faced children peered out through closed blinds.

Within the Square itself, along paths that had once echoed to the tread of slippered feet, armed sentries paced, their sharp challenges breaking the stillness of the night. Outside its wrecked fences strange men in stranger uniforms strode in and out of the joyless houses; tired pickets stacked their arms on the unswept piazzas, and panting horses nibbled the bark from the withered trees; rank weeds choked the gardens; dishevelled vines clung to the porches, and doors that had always swung wide to the gentle tap of loving fingers were opened timidly to the blow of the sword-hilt.

Kennedy Square became a tradition.

Some civilizations die slowly. This one was shattered in a day by a paving-stone in the hands of a thug.

413

CHAPTER XX

Frederick Stone, N.A., member of the Stone Mugs, late war correspondent and special artist on the spot, paused before the cheerful blaze of his studio fire, shaking the wet snow from his feet. He had tramped across Washington Square in drifts that were over his shoe-tops, mounted the three flights of steps to his cosey rooms, and was at the moment expressing his views on the weather, in terms more forcible than polite, to our very old friend, Jack Bedford, the famous marine-painter. Bedford, on hearing the sound of Fred's footsteps, had strolled in from his own studio, in the same building, and had thrown himself into a big arm-chair, where he was sitting hunched up, his knees almost touching his chin, his round head covered by a skull-cap that showed above the chair-back.

" Nice weather for ducks, Jack, isn't it? Can't see how anybody can get here to-night," cried Fred, striking the mantel with his wet cap, and scattering the rain-drops over the hearth. " Just passed a Broadway stage stuck in a hole as I came by the New York Hotel. Been there an hour, they told me."

" Shouldn't wonder. Whose night is it, Fred?"

asked Jack, stretching out one leg in the direction of the cheery blaze.

" Horn's."

" What's he going to do ? "

" Give it up. Ask me an easy one. Said he wanted a thirty by forty. There it is on the easel," and Fred moved a chair out of his way, hung his wet coat and hat on a peg behind the door, and started to clear up a tangle of artillery harness that littered the floor.

" Thirty by forty, eh," grunted Jack, from the depths of his chair. " Thunder and Mars! Is the beggar going to paint a panorama? Thought that canvas was for a new cavalry charge of yours! " He had lowered the other leg now, making a double-barrelled gun of the pair.

" No; it's Horn's. He's going to paint one of the fellows to-night."

" In costume ? " Jack's head was now so low in the chair that his eyes could draw a bead along his legs to the fire.

" Yes, as an old Burgomaster, or something with a ruff," and he kicked an army blanket into a corner as he spoke. " There's the ruff hanging on that pair of foils, Waller sent it over." Then his merry eyes fell on Jack's sprawled-out figure, his feet almost in the grate—a favorite attitude of his neighbor's when tired out with the day's work, comfortable perhaps, but especially objectionable at the moment.

" Here—get up, you old stick-in-the-mud. Don't

sit there, doubled up like a government mule," he laughed. (The army lingo still showed itself once in a while in Fred's speech.) " Help me get this room ready or I'll whale you with this," and he waved one end of a trace over his head. " If the fellows are coming they'll be here in half an hour. Shove back that easel and bring in that beer—it's outside the door in a box. I'll get out the tobacco and pipes."

Jack stretched both arms above his head, emitted a yawn that could be heard in his room below, and sprang to his feet.

Fred, by this time, had taken down from a closet a tin box of crackers, unwrapped a yellow cheese, and was trimming its raw edges with a palette knife. Then they both moved out a big table from the inner room to the larger one, and, while Jack placed the eatables on its bare top, Fred mounted a chair, and began lighting a circle of gas-jets that hung from the ceiling of the skylight. The war-painter was host to-night, and the task of arranging the rooms for the comfort of his fellow-members consequently devolved upon him.

The refreshments having been made ready, Fred roamed about the rooms straightening the pictures on the walls—an old fad of his when guests of any kind were expected—punching the cushions and Turkish saddle-bags into plumpness, that he had picked up in a flying trip abroad the year the war was over, and stringing them along the divan ready for the backs and legs of the club-members. Next he stripped the piano of a collection of camp sketches that had littered it up for a week, dumped the pile into a closet, and, with a sudden wrench of his arms, whirled the instrument itself close against the wall. Then some fire-arms, saddles, and artillery trappings were hidden away in dark corners, and a lay figure, clothed in fatigue cap and blue overcoat, and which had done duty as "a picket" during the day, was wheeled around with its face to the wall, where it stood guard over Fred's famous picture of "The Last Gun at Appomattox." His final touches were bestowed on the grate-fire and the coal-scuttle, both of which were replenished from a big pine box in the hall.

Jack Bedford, meanwhile, had busied himself rolling another table—a long one—under the circle of gas-jets so that the men could see to work the better, and loading it with palettes, china tiles, canvases, etc., to be used by the members of the club in their work of the evening. Last of all and not by any means the least important, Jack, by the aid of a chair, gathered together, on the top shelf of the closet, the unique collection of stone beer-mugs from which the club took its name. These he handed down one by one to Fred, who arranged them in a row on one end of the long table. The mugs were to hold the contents of sundry bottles of beer, now safely stowed away in the lidless, pigeon-holed box, standing in the hall, which Fred unloaded later, placing the bottles on the window-sill outside to cool.

Before they had ended their preparations, the stamping of feet on the stair was heard, the door was thrown back, and the several members of the club began to arrive.

The great Waller came first, brushing the snow from his shaggy coat, looking like a great bear, growling as he rolled in, as was his wont. Close behind him, puffing with the run upstairs, and half-hidden behind Waller's broad shoulders, trotted Simmons, the musician.

Not the tousled, ill-clad Waller, the "Walrus" of former days—no one dared to call the painter by any such names since his picture took the Médaille d'Honneur at Paris—and not the slender, smooth-faced Simmons, who in the old days was content to take his chances of filling a vacancy at Wallack's or the Winter Garden, when some one of the regular orchestra was under the weather; but a sleek, prosperous, rotund Waller, with a bit of red in his button-hole, a wide expanse of shirt-front, and a waxed mustache; and a thoughtful, slightly bald, and well-dressed Simmons, with gold eyeglasses, and his hair worn long in his neck as befitted the leader of an orchestra whose concerts crowded the Academy to the doors.

These two arrivals nodded to Jack and Fred, Waller cursing the weather as he hung up his coat on a peg behind the door (unnecessary formalities of every kind, including the shaking of hands and asking after each other's health, were dispensed with by men who saw each other several times a day at their different haunts), and Simmons, without stopping to take off his wet coat, flung his hat on the divan, crossed the room, and seated himself at the piano.

"Went this way, Waller, didn't it?" said Simmons striking the keys, continuing the conversation the two had evidently had on the stairs. "Never heard Parepa in better voice. She filled every corner of the house. Crug told me he was up in Africa in the back row and never missed a note. Do you remember this?" and the musician's fingers again slipped over the keys, and one of the great singer's trills rippled through the room, to which Waller nodded approvingly, mopping his wet face with his handkerchief as he listened.

The opening and shutting of the door, the stamping of feet, the general imprecations hurled at the climate, and the scattering of wet snow and rain-drops about the entrance became constant. Crug bustled in—a short, thick-set, rosy-cheeked young fellow in a black mackintosh and a white silk muffler—a 'cellist of repute, who had spent two years at the conservatoire, and who had once played for Eugénie at one of her musicales at the Tuileries, a fact he never let you forget. And close behind him came Watson, the landscape-painter, who had had two pictures accepted by the Royal Academy—one of them hung on the line, a great honor for an American; and after them blue-eyed, round-faced Munson, a pupil of Kaulbach, and late from Munich; as well as Harry Stedman, Post, the art-critic, and one or two others.

Each man as he entered divested himself of his wet garments, warmed his hands at the blazing grate-fire, and, reaching over the long table, picked up a clay or corn-cob pipe, stuffing the bowl full of tobacco from a cracked Japanese pot that stood on the mantel. Then striking a match he settled himself into the nearest chair, joining in the general talk or smoking quietly, listening to what was being said about him. Now and then one would walk to the window, raise the sash, uncork a bottle of beer where Fred had placed it, empty its contents into one of the mugs, and resume his seat—mug in one hand, pipe in the other.

Up to this time no work had been done, the courtesies of the club permitting none to begin until the member whose night it was had arrived.

As the half-hour slipped away the men began to grow restless.

"If it's Horn's night why the devil doesn't he come, Fred?" asked Waller, in a querulous tone. Although the great sheep-painter had lost his sobriquet since the old days, he had never parted with his right to growl.

"He'll be here," cried Simmons from his seat by the piano. His fingers were still rippling gently over the keys, although he had stopped once just long enough to strip off his wet overcoat. "I met him at Margaret Grant's this afternoon. She had a little tea."

"There every afternoon, isn't he, Simmons?" asked Munson, who was smoking quietly.

"Shouldn't wonder," came the response between the trills.

"How's that affair coming on?" came a voice out of the tobacco-smoke.

"Same old way," answered someone at the lower end of the table—"still waiting for the spondulix."

"Seen her last picture?" remarked Watson, knocking the ashes from his pipe. "The one she scooped the medal with?"

"Yes. Rouser, isn't it?" called out Waller. "Best thing she has done yet. She's a great woman. Hello! there he is! This is a pretty time for him to put in an appearance!"

The door opened and Oliver walked in, a wet umbrella in one hand, his coat-collar turned up, his mustache beaded with melted snow-drops.

"What's it doing outside, Ollie, raining cats and dogs?" Jack called out.

"No, going to clear up. It's stopped snowing and getting colder. Oh, what a night! I love a storm like this, it sets my blood tingling. Sorry to keep you waiting, gentlemen, but I couldn't help it. It won't make any difference; I can't begin, anyway. Bianchi

won't be here for an hour. Just met him on the street
—he's going to bring a guest, he says."

" Who's he going to bring?" shouted Simmons,
who had risen from his seat at the piano, and was now
sorting out some sheets of music that Fred had just
laid on its top.

" He won't tell; says it's a surprise," answered
Oliver, slipping off his coat.

" A surprise, is it?" grumbled Waller. " I'll bet
it's some greasy foreigner." He had left Simmons's
side and was now standing by the mantel, filling a pipe
from the bowl. " Bianchi has always got a lot of
cranks about him."

Oliver hung his wet coat among the row of garments lining the wall—he had come twice as far as
the others—crowded his dripping umbrella into a
broken Chinese jar that did duty as a rack, and, catching sight of the canvas, walked toward the easel holding the thirty by forty.

" Where did you get it, Freddie?" he said, putting
his arms around the shoulders of his old chum and
dragging him toward the easel for a closer inspection
of the grain of the canvas.

" Snedecor's."

" Just right, old man. Much obliged," and he felt
the grain of the cloth with his thumb. " Got a ruff?"
and he glanced about him. " Oh, yes; I see.
Thanks."

The men, now that Oliver had arrived, drew up

around the long table. Some began setting their palettes; others picked out, from the common stock before them, the panels, canvases, china plates, or sheets of paper, which, under their deft touches, were so soon to be covered with dainty bits of color.

It was in many ways a remarkable club. Most of its members had already achieved the highest rank in their several professions and outside the walls of this eyrie were known as earnest, thoughtful men, envied and sought after by those who respected their aims and successes.

Inside these cosey rooms all restraint was laid aside and each man's personality and temperament expressed itself without reserve. Harry Stedman, who, perhaps, had been teaching a class of students all the morning in the new building of the National Academy of Design, each one of whom hung upon his words as if he had been inspired, could be found here a few hours later joining in a chorus with a voice loud enough to rattle every mug on the table.

Waller, who doubtless that same night, had been the bright particular star at some smart dinner uptown, and whose red ribbon had added such *éclat* to the occasion, and whose low voice and quiet manners and correct, conventional speeches had so charmed and captivated the lady on his right, would, when once in this room, sit astride some chair, a pipe in one hand, a mug of beer in the other. Here he would discuss with Simmons or Jack or Oliver his

preference of Chopin over Beethoven, or the difference between Parepa-Rosa and Jenny Lind, or any
topic which had risen out of the common talk, and all
too with a grotesqueness of speech and manner that
would have frozen his hostess of the dinner-table
dumb with astonishment could she have seen him.

And so with the others. Each man was frankly
himself and in undress uniform when under Fred's
skylight, or when the club was enjoying any one of
its various festivals and functions.

Oliver's election into the organization had, therefore, been to him one of the greatest honors he had
received since his skill as a painter had been recognized by his fellows—an honor not conferred upon
him because he had been one of the earlier members
of the old Union Square organization, many of whom
had been left out, but entirely because he was not
only the best of fellows, but among the best of painters as well. An honor too, which brought with it
the possibility of a certain satisfying of his tastes.
Only once before had he found an atmosphere so congenial and that was when the big hemlocks that he
loved stood firm and silent about him—companions
in a wilderness that rested him.

The coming together of such a body of men representing, as they did, the choicest the city afforded
in art, literature and music, had been as natural
and unavoidable as the concentration of a mass of
iron filings toward a magnet. That insatiable

424

hunger of the Bohemian, that craving of the craftsman for men of his kind, had at last overpowered them, and the meetings in Fred's studio were the inevitable result.

Many of these devotees of the arts had landed on the barren shores of America—barren of even the slightest trace of that life they had learned to love so well in the *Quartier Latin* in Paris and in the Rathskellers of Munich and Dusseldorf—and had wandered about in the uncongenial atmosphere of the commonplace until this retreat had been opened to them. Some, like Fred Stone and Jack Bedford, who had struggled on through the war, too much occupied in the whirl of their life to miss at the time the associations of men of similar tastes, had eagerly grasped the opportunity when it came, and others, like Oliver, who had had all they could do to get their three meals during the day and a shelter for the night, had hardly been conscious of what they wanted until the club had extended to them its congenial surroundings.

On the trio of painters we knew best in the old days these privations and the uncertainties and disappointments of the war had left their indelible mark. You became aware of this when you saw them among their fellow-workers. About Fred's temples many tell-tale gray hairs were mingled with the brown, and about his mouth and eyes were deeper lines than those which hard work alone would have cut. He

425

carried a hole, too, in his right arm—or did until the
army surgeon sewed it up—you could see it as a blue
scar every time he rolled up his sleeve—a slight sou·
venir of the Battle of Five Forks. It was bored out
by a bullet from the hands of a man in gray when
Fred, dropping his sketch-book, had bent to drag a
wounded soldier from under an overturned caisson.
He carried no scar, however, in his heart. That
organ beat with as keen a sympathy and as warm a
spirit of *camaraderie* as it did when it first opened
itself to Oliver's miseries in Union Square.

Jack Bedford, gaunt and strong of limb, looking
a foot taller, had more than once been compelled to
lay down his painter's palette and take up the sign-
painter's brush, and the tell-tale wrinkles about his
eyes and the set look about his mouth testified but
too plainly to the keenness of his sufferings.

And Oliver—

Ah! what of Oliver, and of the changes in him
since that fatal night in Kennedy Square when he had
been driven away from his home and made an out-
cast because he had been brave enough to defend a
helpless man?

You can see at a glance, as you watch him standing
by the big easel, his coat off, to give his arm freer play,
squeezing the tubes of color on his palette, that he is
not the boy you knew some years ago. He is, you
will admit, as strong and alert-looking as he was that
morning when he cleared the space in front of Mar·

garet's brother with a cart-rung. You will concede, too, that the muscles about his chest and throat are as firmly packed, the eyes as keen, and the smile as winning, but you will acknowledge that the boy in him ends there. As you look the closer you will note that the line of the jaw is more cleanly cut than in his younger days; that the ears are set closer to the finely modelled head; that the nose is more aquiline, the eyes deeper, and that the overhanging brow is wrinkled with one or more tight knots that care has tied, and which only loosen when his face breaks into one of his old-time smiles. The mustache is still there —the one which Sue once laughed at; but it has lost its silky curl and stands straight out now from the corners of his mouth, its points reaching almost to the line of his ears. There is, too, beneath it a small imperial, giving to his face the debonair look of a cavalier, and which accentuates more than any other one thing his Southern birth and training. As you follow the subtle outlines of his body you find too, that he is better proportioned than he was in his early manhood; thinner around the waist, broader across the shoulders; pressed into a closer mold; more compact, more determined-looking. But for the gleam that now and then flashes out of his laughing eyes and the winning smile that plays about his mouth, you would, perhaps, think that the years of hardship through which he has passed have hardened his nature. But you would be wrong about the hardening process, although you would have been entirely right about the hardship.

They had, indeed, been years of intense suffering, full of privations, self-denial, and disappointments, not only in his New York home but in Kennedy Square, whenever at long intervals he had gone back to the old house to cheer its inmates in their loneliness—a loneliness relieved only by the loyalty of old Malachi and Hannah and the affection and sympathy of their immediate relatives and of such close friends as Amos Cobb, who had never left his post, Miss Clendenning, Dr. Wallace, Nathan and some others. But this sympathy had not always been extended to Oliver—not by his old schoolmates and chums at least. Even Sue had passed him in the street with a cold stare and not a few of the other girls—girls he had romped with many a night through the cool paths of Kennedy Square, had drawn their skirts aside as he passed lest he should foul them with his touch.

But his courage had not wavered nor had his strength failed him. The same qualities that had made Richard stick to the motor were in his own blood. His delicately modelled slender fingers, white as ivory, and as sure as a pair of callipers —so like his father's—and which as we watch him work so deftly arranging the colors on his palette, adjusting the oil-cup, trying the points of the brushes on his thumb-nail, gathering them in a sheaf in his left hand as they answer his purpose. had served him in more ways than one since he took that midnight ride back from his old home in Kennedy Square. . These same hands that look so white and well-kept as he stands by his easel in the full glare of the gas-jets, had been his sole reliance during these days of toil and suffering. They had provided all the bread that had gone into his mouth, and every stitch of clothes that had covered his back. And they had not been over-particular as to how they had accomplished it nor at what hours or places. They had cleaned lithographic stones, the finger-nails stained for weeks with colored inks; they had packed hardware; they had driven a pen far into the night on space work for the daily papers; they had carried a dinner-pail to and from his lodgings to the factory two miles away where he had worked—very little in this pail some of the time; they had posted ledgers, made office-fires, swept out stores—anything and everything that his will compelled, and his necessities made imperative. And they had done it all forcefully and willingly, with the persistence and sureness of machines accomplishing a certain output in so many hours. Joyfully too, sustained and encouraged by the woman he loved and whose heart through all his and her vicissitudes was still his own.

All this had strengthened him; had taught him that any kind of work, no matter how menial, was worthy of a gentleman, so long as his object was obtained—

in this case his independence and his livelihood. It had been a bitter experience at first, especially for a Southerner brought up as he had been; but he had mastered it at last. His early training had helped him, especially that part which he owed to his mother, who had made him carry the market-basket as a boy, to humble a foolish and hurtful pride. He was proud enough of it now.

But never through all these privations had these same white hands and this tired body and brain been so occupied that they could not find time during some one of the hours of the day and night to wield the brush, no matter how urgent had been the call for the week's board—wielding it, too, so lovingly and knowingly, and with such persistency, that to-night although still poor—he stood recognized as a rising man by the men in the front rank of the painters of his time.

And with his mother's consent, too. Not that he had asked it in so many words and stood hesitating, fearing to take the divergent path until he could take her willing blessing with him. He had made his decision firmly and against her wishes. She had kept silent at first, and had watched his progress as she had watched his baby steps, tearfully—prayerfully at times—standing ready to catch him if he fell. But that was over now. The bigness of her vision covering margins wide enough for new impressions, impressions which her broad mind, great enough and

430

honest enough to confess its mistakes, always welcomed and understood, had long since made clear
to her what in her early anxiety she had ignored:
—that if her son had inherited the creative and
imaginative gifts of his father (those gifts which
she so little understood), he had also inherited
from her a certain spirit of determination, together with that practical turn of mind which had
given the men of her own family their eminence. In
proof of this she could not but see that the instability
which she had so dreaded in his earlier years had
given way to a certain fixedness of purpose and firm
self-reliance. The thought of this thrilled her as
nothing else in his whole career had ever done. All
these things helped reconcile her to his choice of a
profession.

Oliver, now thoroughly warm and dry, busied himself getting his brushes and paints together and
scraping off one of Fred's palettes. Bianchi's bald
head and fat, red, smooth-shaven face with its double
chin—time had not dealt leniently with the distinguished lithographer—had inspired our hero to attempt a " Franz Hals smear," as Waller called it, and
the Pole, when he arrived, was to sit for him in
the costume of an old Dutch burgomaster, the
big white ruff furnishing the high lights in the
canvas.

By the time Oliver had arranged his palette the
club had settled itself for work, the smoke from the

pipes floating in long lines toward the ceiling, befogging the big white albatross that hung from a wire in the skylight. Munson, who had rubbed in a background of bitumen over a square tile, sat next to Fred, who was picking out, with the end of a wooden match, the outlines of an army-wagon sketched on a plate smeared with color. Simmons was looking over a portfolio that Watson, a new member, had brought with him, filled with a lot of his summer sketches made on the Normandy coast.

One view of the fish-market at Dieppe caught Oliver's eye. The slant of light burnishing the roof of the church to silver and flooding the pavement of the open square, crowded with black figures, the white caps of the fish-women indicated by crisp pats of the brush, pleased our painter immensely.

"Charming, old man," said Oliver, turning to Watson. "How long did it take you?"

"About four hours."

"Looks like it," growled Waller, reaching over Oliver's shoulder and drawing the sketch toward him. "That's the gospel of ' smear,' Horn," and he tossed it back. "Not a figure in the group has got any drawing in it."

Waller had set his face against the new out-door school, and never lost a chance to ridicule it.

"That's not what Watson is after," exclaimed Oliver. "The figures are mere accessories. The dominating light is the thing; he's got that "—and he held

432

the sketch close to the overhead gas-jets so that the members could see it the better.

"Dominating light be hanged! What's the use of slobbering puddles of paint over a canvas and calling it *plein air*, or impressionism, or out-of-doors, or some such rot? Get down to business and *draw*. When you have done that you can talk. It can't be done in four hours, and if some of you fellows keep on the way you're going, you'll never do it in four years."

"A four hours' sketch handled as Watson has this," said Oliver, thoughtfully, "is better than four years' work on one of your Hudson Rivery things. The sun doesn't stand still long enough for a man to get more than an expression of what he sees—that is if he's after truth. The angle of shadow changes too quickly, and so do the reflected lights."

"What's the matter with the next day?" burst out Waller. "Can't you take up your sketch where you left off? You talk as if every great picture had to be painted before luncheon."

"But there is no 'next day,'" interrupted Watson. "I entirely agree with Horn." He had been listening to the discussion with silent interest. "No next day like the one on which you began your canvas. The sky is different—gray, blue, or full of fleecy, sunny clouds. Your shadows are more purple, or blue or gray, depending on your sky overhead, and so are your reflections. If you go on and try to piece out your sketch, you make an almanac of it—

433

not a portrait of what you saw. I can pick out the Mondays, Tuesdays, and Wednesdays on that kind of a sketch as soon as I see it. Nature is like a bird—if you want to surprise her, you must let go both barrels when she rises; if you miss her at your first shot you will never have another chance—not at that particular bird."

"Well, but suppose you *do* happen to have two days alike," insisted Waller. "I have seen thirty days on a stretch in Venice without a cloud. What then?" The bird simile had evidently not appealed to the great critic.

"Then ten chances to one you are not the same man you were the day before," replied Watson, calmly, laying down his pipe. "You have had bad news from home or your liver is out of order, or worse still, you have seen some new subject which has taken hold of you and your first enthusiasm has oozed away. If you persist in going on you will either undo what you did yesterday or you will trust to your memory of what you *think* yesterday was, to finish your sketch by. The first fills it full of lies and the second full of yourself; neither have anything to do with nature. Four hours, Waller, not a minute more. You'll come to it before you die."

"That depends on what you have got to paint with," snapped out Jack Bedford, who was trying to clean a dingy-looking palette with a knife. "Whose dirt-dump is this, anyhow?" and he held it up to view. " Might as well try to get sunlight out of powdered brick. Look at that pile of mud,⌐ and he pointed to some dry color near the thumb-hole.

" Which palette? " came a voice.

Jack held it up for the inspection of the room.

" Oh, that's Parker Ridgway's," answered Fred. " He was here the other day and made a half-hour's sketch of a model I had."

The announcement of Ridgway's name was greeted with shouts of laughter. He was a society painter of the day, pupil of Winterha er and Meyer von Bremen, and had carried off m re portraits and at higher prices than all the other en put together.

" Keep on! keep on! Laugh av iy," grumbled Waller squeezing a tube of Prussian blue on his palette. " When any one of you fellows can get $4,000 for a season's work you can talk; until you do, you can keep your mouths shut as tight as Long Island clams."

" Who got it? "

" The Honorable Parker Ridgway, R.A., P.Q., and I don't know but X.Y.Z.," roared Waller.

" I'd like to know how? " asked Watson, reaching over Fred's arm for the bottle of turpentine.

" That's what he did," snapped out Waller.

" Did what? "

" Knew how."

" But he doesn't know how," cried Munson from across the table. " I sat alongside of that fellow at the

Ecole for two years. He can't draw, and never could. His flesh was beastly, his modelling worse, and his technique—a botch. You can see what color he uses," and he pointed to the palette Jack was trying to clean.

"Granted, my boy," said Waller. "I didn't say he could *paint;* I said he knew how to earn $4,000 in three months painting portraits."

"He never painted a portrait worth four cents. Why, I knew——"

"Dry up, Munson!" interrupted Jack. "Go on, Waller, tell us how he did it."

"By using some horse-sense and a little tact; getting in with the procession and holding his end up," retorted Waller, in a solemn tone.

"Give him room! Give him room!" cried Oliver, with a laugh, pouring a little dryer into his oil-cup. He loved to hear Waller talk. "He flings his words about as if they were chunks of coal," he would always say.

The great man wheeled his chair around and faced the room. Oliver's words had sounded like a challenge.

"Keep it up!—pound away," he cried, his face reddening. "I've watched Ridgway ever since he arrived here last spring, and I will give you his recipe for success. He didn't fall overboard into a second-rate club as soon as he got here and rub his brushes on his coat-sleeve to look artistic. Not much!

436

He had his name put up at the Union; got Croney to cut his clothes, and Leary to make his hats, played croquèt with the girls he knew, drove tandem—his brother-in-law's—and dined out every night in the week. Every day or two he would haul out one of his six-foot canvases, and give it a coat of bitumen. Always did this when some club swell was around who would tell about it."

"Did it with a sponge," muttered Munson. " Old trick of his! "

" Next thing he did," continued Waller, ignoring Munson's aside, " was to refuse a thousand-dollar commission offered by a vulgar real-estate man to paint a two-hundred-pound pink-silk sofa-cushion of a wife in a tight-fitting waist. This spread like the measles. It was the talk of the club, of dinner-tables and piazzas, and before sundown Ridgway's exclusiveness in taste and artistic instincts were established. Then he hunted up a pretty young married woman occupying the dead-centre of the sanctified social circle, went into spasms over her beauty—so classic, such an exquisite outline; grew confidential with the husband at the club, and begged permission to make just a sketch only the size of his hand—wanted it for his head of Sappho, Berlin Exhibition. Next he rented a suite of rooms, crowded in a lot of borrowed tapestries, brass, Venetian chests, lamps and hangings; gave a tea—servants this time in livery—exhibited his Sappho; refused a big price for it from the

437

husband; got orders instead for two half-lengths, $1,500 each, finished them in two weeks, declined more commissions on account of extreme fatigue; disappeared with the first frost and the best cottage people; booked three more full-lengths in New York —two to be painted in Paris and the other on his return in the spring; was followed to the steamer by a bevy of beauties, half-smothered in flowers, and disappeared in a halo of artistic glory just $4,000 in."

Fred broke out into a roar, in which the whole room joined.

"And you call that art, do you?" cried Munson, laying down his palette. His face was flushed, his eyes snapping with indignation.

"I do, my babbling infant," retorted Waller. "I call it the art of making the most of your opportunities and putting your best foot foremost. That's a thing you fellows never seem to understand. You want to shuffle around in carpet-slippers, live in a garret, and wait until some money-bags climbs up your crazy staircases to discover you. Ridgway puts his foot in a patent-leather pump and silk stocking, and never steps on a carpet that isn't two inches thick. Merchants, engineers, manufacturers, and even scientists, when they have anything to sell, go where there is somebody to buy; why shouldn't an artist?"

"Just like a fakir peddling cheap jewelry," said Stedman, in a low voice, sending a cloud of smoke to the ceiling.

" Or a bunco-man trading watches with a farmer," remarked Jack Bedford. " What do you say, My Lord Tom-Noddy "—and he slapped Oliver on the back. The sobriquet was one of Jack's pet names for Oliver—all the Kennedy Square people were more or less aristocrats to Jack Bedford, the sign-painter— all except Oliver.

" I think Waller's about half-right, Jack. As far as Ridgway's work goes, you know and I know that there isn't one man or woman out of a hundred among his brother-in-law's friends who knows whether it's good or bad—that's the pity of it. If it's bad and they buy it, that's their fault for not knowing any better, not Ridgway's fault for doing the best he knows how. By silk stockings and pumps I suppose Waller means that Ridgway dressed him- self like a gentleman, had his hair cut, and paid some attention to his finger-nails. That's why they were glad to see him. The day has gone by when a painter must affect a bob-tailed velveteen jacket, long hair, and a slouch hat to help him paint, just as the day has gone by when an artist is not an honored guest in any gentleman's house in town."

" Bravo, Tom-Noddy! " shouted Jack and Fred in a breath. " Drink, you dear old pressed brick. Put your nose into this! " and Fred held a mug of beer to Oliver's lips.

Oliver laid down his sheaf of brushes—buried his nose in the cool rim of the stone mug, the only beverage the club permitted, and was about to continue his talk, when his eye rested on Bianchi, who was standing in the open door, his hand upraised so as to bespeak silence.

"Here—you beautiful, bald-headed old burgo-master!" shouted Oliver. "Get into your ruff right away. Been waiting half an hour for you and——"

Bianchi put his fingers to his lips with a whispered hush, knit his brow, and pointed significantly behind him. Every eye turned, and a breathless silence fell upon the group, followed by a scraping of chairs on the floor as each man sprang to his feet.

Bianchi's surprise had arrived!

CHAPTER XXI

" THE WOMAN IN BLACK "

In the doorway, immediately behind Bianchi and looking over the little man's head, stood a woman of perhaps forty years of age in full evening toilet. About her head was wound a black lace scarf, and hanging from her beautiful shoulders, half-concealing a figure of marvellous symmetry, was a long black cloak, open at the throat, trimmed with fur, and lined with watermelon pink silk. Tucked in her hair was a red japonica. She was courtesying to the room with all the poise and graciousness of a prima donna saluting an audience.

Oliver sprang for his coat and was about to cram his arms into the sleeves, when she cried:

"Oh, please don't! I wish I could wear a coat myself, so that I could take it off and paint. Oh! the smell of the lovely pipes! It's heavenly, and it's so like home. Really," and she looked about her, "this is the only place I have seen in America that I can breathe in. I've heard of you all winter and I so wanted to come. I would not give dear Bianchi any rest till he brought me. Oh! I'm so glad to be here."

441

Oliver and the others were still standing, looking in amazement at the new-comer. One of the unwritten laws of the club was that no woman should ever enter its doors, a law that until this moment had never been broken.

While she was speaking Bianchi stepped back, and took the tips of the woman's fingers within his own. When she had finished he thrust out one foot and, with the bow of an impresario introducing a new songstress, said:

"Gentlemen of the Stone Mugs, I have the honor of presenting you to the Countess Kovalski."

Again the woman courtesied, sweeping the floor with her black velvet skirt, broke out into a laugh, handed her cloak and scarf to Bianchi, who threw them over the shoulders of the lay figure, and moved toward the table, Fred, as host, drawing out a chair for her.

"Oh!—what lovely beginnings—" she continued, examining the sketches with her lorgnette, after the members had made their salutations, "Let me make one. I studied two years with Achenbach. You did not know that Bianchi, did you? There are so many things you do not know, you lovely man." She was as much at home as if she had been there every evening of her life.

Still, with the same joyous self-contained air she settled herself in Fred's proffered chair, picked up one of Jack's brushes, reached over his shoulder, and

with a " please-hold-still, thank you," scooped up a
little yellow ochre from his palette, and unloaded it
on a corner of a tile. Then, stripping off her bracelets,
she piled them in a heap before her, selected a Greek
coin dangling from the end of one of them, propped
it up on the table and began to paint; the men,
all of whom were too astonished to resume their
work, crowding about her, watching the play of
her brush; a brush so masterful in its technique
that before the picture was finished the room broke
out in unrestrained applause.

During all this time she was talking in German to
Crug, or in French to Waller, only stopping to light
a fresh cigarette which she took from a jewelled
case and laid beside her. She could, no doubt, have
as easily lapsed into Russian, Choctaw, or Chinese
had there been any such strange people about.

When the men had resumed their customary seats
and the room had once more settled to work—it had
only been a question of sex that had destroyed the
equilibrium, a question no longer of value now that
the fair intruder could really *paint*—Oliver bent
over her and said in his most gallant manner:

" If the Countess Kovalski will be gracious enough
to excuse Bianchi (he had never left her elbow) I
will try and make a burgomaster of him. Perhaps
you will help me tie this around his neck," and he held
out the white ruff. He had put on his coat despite
her protest.

"What, dear Bianchi in a ruff! Oh! how perfectly charming! That's really just what he looks like. I've always told him that Rembrandt ought to have seen him. Come, you sweet man, hold up your beautiful Dutch face."

As she spoke she caught the ruff from Oliver's hand and stretched out her bare arms toward Bianchi.

"No, I'm not going to pose now," protested the Pole, pushing back her hands. "You can get me any time. Take the Countess, Horn. She'd make a stunner."

"Yes! Yes! Please do," she laughed, springing from her seat and clapping her hands with all the gayety and joyousness of a child over some expected pleasure.

Oliver hesitated for an instant, as he looked down into her eyes, wondering whether his brush could do justice to their depth. Then he glanced at her supple figure and white skin in contrast to the black velvet, its edge softened by the fall of lace, the dominant, insistent note of the red japonica in her blue-black hair, the flesh tones brilliant under the gas-jets. The color scheme was exactly what he had been looking for all winter—black, white, and a touch of red.

"I have never been so honored, Madame. Nothing could give me greater pleasure," he answered, with a dry smile. "May I escort your ladyship to the platform?" And he held out his hand and conducted her to the stand facing the big easel.

Then there followed a scene such as many of the
Stone Mugs had not shared in since they left the
Latin Quarter.

The Countess stood erect on the raised platform,
with head up and slightly turned, the full glare of
the gas-jets falling upon her neck and throat, made
all the more brilliant by reason of the dark green
walls of Fred's studio, which formed the background
behind her. One arm was partly raised, a lighted
cigarette between her fingers; the other was lost in
the folds of the velvet gown. She posed as naturally
and as easily as if she had done nothing else all her
life, and with a certain bravado and swing that enchanted everybody in the room.

One talent demanded of the artist members of the
club when they sought admission, and insisted upon
by the Committee, was the ability, possessed in a
marked degree by Oliver, of making a rapid, telling
sketch from life, and at night. So expert had most
of the members become that many of their pictures
made under the gas-light were as correct in their
color-values as those done in the day-time. In this
Oliver was past-master. Most of his own work had
to be done under artificial light during the long
years of his struggle.

The men—they were again on their feet—crowded
closer, forming a circle about the easel. They saw
that the subject appealed to Oliver, and they knew
how much better he could paint when his heart was in

his work. His picture of Margaret Grant in the Tam-o'-Shanter cap, the best portrait at the last exhibition, had proved that.

Oliver saw the interest shown in his work and put himself on his mettle. He felt that not only his own reputation, but the honor of the Stone Mugs, was at stake. He felt, too, a certain pride and confidence in the sureness of his touch—a touch that the woman he loved believed in—one she had really taught him herself. He began by blocking in with a bit of charcoal the salient points of the composition. Fred stood on his left hand holding a cigar-box filled with tubes of color, ready to unscrew their tops and pass them to Oliver as he needed them.

As the dark background of greenish black, under the vigorous strokes of his brush, began to relieve the flesh tones, and the coloring of the lips and the japonica in the hair took their places in the color-scheme, a murmur of applause ran through the room. No such piece of night-work had ever been painted since the club had come together, and certainly not before.

" A Fortuny, by thunder! " burst out Waller. He had been the first man to recognize Oliver's talent in the old days and had always felt proud of his foresight.

For two hours Oliver stood before his canvas, the Countess resting now and then, floating over to the piano, as Simmons had done, running her fingers over

446

For two hours Oliver stood before his canvas

its keys, or breaking out into Polish, Hungarian, or French songs at the pleasure of the room. During these rests Oliver turned the picture to the wall. He did not wish her to see it until it was finished. He was trying some brush tricks that Madge loved, some that she had learned in Couture's atelier, and whose full effect could only be recognized in the finished work.

When the last touches of Oliver's brush had been laid on the canvas, and the modest signature, O. H., as was the custom, had been affixed to its lower left-hand corner, he made a low salaam to the model and whirled the easel in front of her.

The cry of delight that escaped her lips was not only an expression of her pleasure, but it convinced every man in the club that the Countess's technical knowledge of what constituted a work of art equalled her many other accomplishments. She sat looking at it with thoughtful, grave face, and her whole manner changed. She was no longer the woman who had so charmed the room. She was the connoisseur, the expert, the jury of last resort. Oliver watched her with absorbing interest as he sat wiping his forehead with his handkerchief.

"Monsieur Horn," she said, slowly, as if weighing each word, "if you come to my country they will cover you all over with medals. I had no idea anyone in this new land could paint as you do. You are a master. Permit me, Monsieur, to make you my obeisance—" and she dipped back on one foot and swept the floor with her skirts.

Oliver laughed, returned the bow with a mock flourish, and began rolling down his shirt-cuffs; a thrill quivering through him—that thrill only felt by a painter when he is conscious that some work of his brush has reached the high-water mark of his abilities. For only the artist in him had been at work. What stirred him was not the personality of the Countess—not her charm nor beauty but the harmony of the colors playing about her figure: the reflected lights in the blue-black of her hair; the soft tones of the velvet lost in the shadows of the floor, and melting into the walls behind her; the high lights on the bare shoulder and arms divided by the severe band of black; the subdued grays in the fall of lace uniting the flesh tones and the bodice; and, more than all, the ringing note of red sung by the japonica tucked in her hair and which found its only echo in the red of her lips—red as a slashed pomegranate with the white seed-teeth showing through. The other side of her beautiful self—the side that lay hidden under her soft lashes and velvet touch, the side that could blaze and scorch and burn to cinders—that side Oliver had never once seen nor thought of.

This may have been because, while his fingers worked on, his thoughts were somewhere else, and that he saw another face as he mixed his colors, and

448

not that of the siren before him. Or it may have been that, as he looked into the eyes of the Countess, he saw too deeply into the whirlpool of passion and pain which made up the undercurrent in this beautiful woman's strange life.

Not so the others. Many of whom were the most serious-minded of men where women were concerned. Crug—who, to quote Waller, had drifted into a state of mind bordering on lunacy—was so completely taken off his feet that he again led her ladyship by her finger-tips to the piano, and, with his hand on his heart, and his eyes upraised, begged her to sing for him some of the songs of her native land and in the tongue of her own people; the Countess complying so graciously and singing with such consummate taste and skill, throwing her soul into every line, that the men soon broke out in rounds of applause, crowding about her with the eagerness of bees around a hive—all except Waller and Oliver, who sat apart, quietly watching her out of the corners of their eyes.

The portrait was forgotten now; so were the sketches and tiles, and the work of the evening. So was everything else but the woman who dominated the room. She kept her seat on the piano-stool, the centre of the group, as a queen of the ballet sits on a painted throne, flashing her eyes from one to the other, wheeling about to dash off an air from some unknown opera—unknown to those who listened—

449

laying her lighted cigarette on the music-rack as she played, and whirling back again to tell some anecdote of the composer who wrote it, or some incident connected with its production in Vienna or Warsaw or St. Petersburg—the club echoing her every whim.

It is not to be wondered at, therefore, that the staid and sober-minded Stone Mugs, under these conditions, completely lost their heads, and that when Oliver picked up an empty beer-mug, the symbol of the club used in all ceremonies, and began filling it with the names of the members which he had written on slips of paper, preparatory to the drawing of the lottery for the picture which he had just finished—every meeting-night a lottery was drawn, the lucky winner possessing the picture of the evening—Crug and Munson should have simultaneously sprung to their feet, and, waving their hands over their heads, have proposed, in one and the same breath, that " Our distinguished visitor " should have the privilege of adding her own name to those in Oliver's mug—the picture to be her own individual property should her patronymic be the first to be drawn from its open mouth.

Waller started to his feet to object, and the words of protest were half out of his mouth when Oliver stopped him. A woman was always a woman to Oliver, no matter what her past or present station in life might be. It was her sex that kept him loyal when any discourtesy was involved.

"THE WOMAN IN BLACK"

"Keep still, old man," he whispered. "They've gone crazy, but we can't help it. Get on your feet and vote."

When the sound of the " ayes " adopting Crug and Munson's motion had died away, Oliver inscribed her initials upon a small piece of paper, dropped it in the mug, held it high above the lady's head, and asked her to reach up her dainty fingers and pick out the name of the lucky possessor of " The Woman in Black," as the picture had now been christened. The white arm went up, the jewelled fingers felt about nervously among the little ballots, and then the Countess held up a twisted bit of paper.

A burst of applause filled the room. The scrap of paper bore the initials of the Countess! " The Woman in Black " was her property.

But the most extraordinary part by far of the evening's performance was still to come.

When the hour of midnight had arrived—the hour of dispersal, a rule rarely broken—the Countess called to Bianchi and directed him to go out into the hall and bring in her long black stockings and stout shoes, which she had taken off outside Fred's door, and which she had left hanging on a nail.

I can see her now—for I, too, was leaning over the same table, Oliver beside me, watching this most extraordinary woman of another world, a woman who had been the idol of almost every capital in Europe, and whom I knew (although Oliver did not) had been

451

quietly conducted out of some of them between dark and daylight—I can see her now, I say, sitting on the piano-stool, facing the group, the long, black silk stockings that Bianchi had brought her in her hands. I remember just the way in which, after loosening her dainty, red-heeled slippers, she swept aside her skirts, unfastened her garters, and, with the same unconsciousness and ease with which she would have slipped a pair of rubbers over a pair of shoes, drew the long black stockings over her flesh-colored ones, refastening the garters again, talking all the time, first to one and then the other; pausing only to accentuate some sentence with a wave of her shoe or stocking or cigarette, as the action suited the words.

That the group about her was composed solely of men made not the slightest difference. She was only trying to save those precious, flesh-colored silk stockings that concealed her white skin from the slush and snow of the streets. As to turning her back to her hosts during this little change of toilet—that was the last thing that entered her head. She would as soon have stepped into a closet to put on her gloves.

And then again, why should she be ashamed of her ankles and her well-turned instep and dainty toes, as compact in their silk covering as peas in a pod! She might have been, perhaps, in some one of the satin lined drawing-rooms around Madison Square or Irving Place, but not here, breathing the blue smoke of a dozen pipes and among her own kind—the kind she had known and loved and charmed all her life.

After all it was but a question of economy. Broadway was a slough of mud and slush, and neither she nor Bianchi had the price of a carriage to spare.

Oliver watched her until the whole comedy was complete; then, picking up his wet sketch and handing it with the greatest care to Bianchi, who was to conduct her ladyship to her lodgings, he placed the long black cloak with the fur-trimming and watermelon-colored silk lining about her beautiful, bare shoulders, and, with the whole club following and waving their hands good-night, our young gentleman bowed her out and downstairs with all the deference and respect he would have shown the highest lady in the land.

CHAPTER XXII

"MARGARET GRANT—TOP FLOOR"

One spring morning, some time after the visit of the Countess to the club and the painting of her portrait by Oliver—the incident had become the talk of the studios before the week was out—Oliver sat in his own rooms on the top floor, drinking his coffee— the coffee he had boiled himself. The janitor had just slipped two letters through a slit in the door. Both lay on the floor within reach of his hand. One was from his mother, bearing the postmark of his native city; the other was from a prominent picture-dealer on Broadway, with a gallery and big window looking out on the street.

Oliver broke the seal of his mother's letter, and moved his chair so that the light from the overhead skylight would fall on its pages.

It read as follows:

"MY DARLING BOY: Your father goes to you to-morrow. Mr. Cobb was here last night with a letter from some gentleman of means with whom he has been corresponding. They want to see the motor, so your father and Nathan leave on the early train.

"This man's continued kindness is a constant sur-

prise to me. I have always thought it was he who prevented the mortgage from being foreclosed, but I
never knew until yesterday that he had written his
name under my own the second time the note was to
be renewed, and that he has kept it there ever since.
I cannot speak of this to him, nor must you, if you see
him, for poor old Mr. Steiger told me in confidence.
I am the more glad now that we have always paid
the interest on the note. The next payment, which
you have just sent me, due on the first of the month,
is now in my bureau-drawer ready for the bank, but
I will not have to use it now.

" Whether the mortgage can ever be paid off I do
not know, for the farm is ruined, I fear. Mr. Mowbray's cousin, who drove over last week to see what
was left of the plantations in that section, writes me
that there is nothing remaining of your grandfather's
place but the bare ground and the house. All the
fences have been burned and many of the beautiful
trees cut down for firewood. The Government still
occupies the house and one of the outbuildings, although most of the hospital stores have been moved
away. The last half-year's rent which was held back,
owing to some new ruling from Washington, came, I
am thankful to say, two days ago in a check from the
paymaster here, owing to Mr. Cobb's intercession.
He never loses an opportunity to praise you for what
you did for that poor young soldier, and Mr. Steiger
told me that when those in authority heard from Mr.

Cobb which Mrs. Horn it was, they ordered the rent paid at once. He is always doing just such kindnesses for us. But for this rental I don't know how we would have been able to live and take care of those dependent upon us. We little knew, my son, when we both strove so hard to save the farm that it would really be our only support. This rent, however, will soon cease and I tremble for the future. I can only pray my Heavenly Father that something will come out of this visit to New York. It is our only hope now.

"Don't lose sight of your father for a moment, my son. He is not well and gets easily fatigued, and although he is greatly elated over his promised success, as we all are—and he certainly deserves to be—I think you will see a great change in him these last few months. I would not have consented to his going had not Nathan gone with him. Nathan insists upon paying the expenses of the trip; he says it is only fair that he should, as your father has given him an interest in the motor. I earnestly hope for some results, for I shall have no peace until the whole amount of the mortgage is paid back to the bank and you and Mr. Cobb are released from the burden, so heavy on you, my boy.

"There is no other news to tell you. Sue Clayton brought her boy in to-day. He is a sweet little fellow and has Sue's eyes. She has named him John Clayton, after her father. They have made another attempt to find the Colonel's body on the battle-field, but without success. I am afraid it will never be recovered.

"Lavinia sends her love. She has been much better lately. Her army hospital work has weighed upon her, I think. Three years was too long.

"I have the last newspaper notices of your academy picture pinned on my cushion, and I show them to everybody who comes in. They always delight me. You have had a hard fight, my son, but you are winning now. No one rejoices more than I do in your success. As you said in your last letter, the times have really changed. They certainly have for me. Sorrow and suffering have made me see many things in a different light these last few years.

"Malachi and Hannah are well, but the old man seems quite feeble at times.

"Your loving mother,

"Sallie T. Horn."

Dear lady, with your soft white hair and deep brown eyes that have so often looked into mine! How dreary were those long days of hate and misery! How wise and helpful you were to every living soul who sought your aid, friend and foe alike. Your great heart sheltered and comforted them all.

Oliver read the letter through and put his lips to the signature. In all his life he had never failed to kiss his mother's name at the bottom of her letters.

457

The only difference was that now he kissed them with an added reverence. The fact of his having proved himself right and her wrong in the choice of his profession made loyalty with him the more tender.

"Dear, dear mother!" he said to himself. "You have had so much trouble lately, and you have been so plucky through it all." He stopped, looked dreamily across the room, and added with a sigh: "But she has not said one word about Madge; not one single word. She doesn't answer that part of my letter; she doesn't intend to."

Then he opened the other communication which read:

"DEAR MR. HORN: Please call here in the morning. I have some good news for you.
                    "JOHN SNEDECOR."

Oliver turned the picture-dealer's letter over, peered into the envelope as if he expected to find some trace of the good news tucked away in its corners, lifted the tray holding his frugal breakfast, and laid it on the floor outside his door ready for the janitor's morning round. Then, picking up his hat, he locked his door, hung an "out card" on the knob, and, strolling downstairs, stepped into the fresh morning air. He knew the dealer well. He had placed two of old Mr. Crocker's pictures with him—one of which had been sold.

When he reached Snedecor's gallery he found the big window surrounded with a crowd gazing intently at an upright portrait in a glittering gold frame, to which was affixed an imposing-looking name-plate bearing the inscription:

"THE WOMAN IN BLACK,
BY OLIVER HORN"

So this was Snedecor's good news!

Oliver made his way through the crowd and into the open door of the shop—the shop was in front, the gallery in the rear—and found the proprietor leaning over a case filled with artists' supplies.

" Has she had it *framed*, Snedecor? " asked Oliver, with a light laugh.

" Not to any alarming extent! I made that frame for Mr. Peter Fish. She sent it here for sale, and Fish bought it. He's wild about it. Says it's the best thing since Sully. He wants you to paint his daughter; that's what I wanted to see you about. Great card for you, Mr. Horn. I congratulate you! "

Oliver gave a low whistle. His own good fortune was for the moment forgotten in his surprise at the woman's audacity. Selling a sketch painted by one of the club! one which had virtually been *given* to her. " Poor Bianchi! He does pick up the queerest people. I wonder if she was out of stockings," he said half-aloud.

459

"Oh, you needn't worry about the Madame; she won't suffer for clothes as long as she's got that pair of eyes in her head. You just ought to have seen her handle old Fish. It was beautiful. But, see here now, you don't want to make old Peter a present of this portrait of his daughter. He's good for a thousand, I tell you. She got a cracking price for that one," and he pointed to the picture.

Again Oliver laughed.

"A cracking price? She must have needed the money bad." The more he thought of it the funnier it seemed.

Snedecor looked surprised. He was thinking of Fish's order and the amount of his commission. Most of Oliver's remarks were unintelligible to him—especially his reference to the stockings.

' "What shall I say to him?" Snedecor asked at last.

"Oh, nothing in particular. Just send him to my studio. I'll be in all to-morrow morning."

"Well, but don't you think you'd better go and see him yourself now? He's too big a bug to run after people. That kind of thing don't come every day, you know; you might lose it. Why, he lives right near you in that swell house across the Square."

"Oh, I know him very well," said Oliver, nodding his head. "No, let him come to-morrow to me; it won't hurt him to walk up three flights of stairs. I'm busy to-day. Now I think of it, there's one thing, though, you *can* tell him, and please be particular about it—there will be no advance over my regular price. I don't care to compete with her ladyship."

Without waiting to hear the dealer's protest he stepped outside the shop and joined the crowd about the window, elbowing each other for a better view of the portrait. No one recognized him. He was too obscure for that. They might after this, he thought with an exultant throb, and a flush of pride crossed his face.

As he walked down Broadway a sense of the humor of the whole situation came over him. Here for years he had been working day and night; running the gauntlet of successive juries and hanging committees, with his best things rejected or skied until his Tam-o'-Shanter girl made a hit; worrying, hoping against hope, racking his brain as to how and when and where he would find the path which would lead him to commercial success—a difficult task for one too proud to beg for favors and too independent to seek another's aid—and here, out of the clear sky, had come this audacious Bohemienne, the pet of foyer and studio—a woman who presented the greatest number of contrasts to the things he held most dear in womankind—and with a single stroke had cleared the way to success for him. And this, too, not from any love of him, nor his work, nor his future, but simply to settle a board-bill or pay for a bonnet.

Again Oliver laughed, this time so loudly that the man in front turned and looked at him.

"A cracking price," he kept repeating to himself, "a cracking price, eh? and out of old Peter Fish! Went fishing for minnows and hooked a whale, and another little fish for me! I wonder what she baited her hook with. That woman's a genius."

Suddenly he caught sight of the sign of a Long Island florist set up in an apothecary's window between the big green and red glass globes that lined its sides.

Turning on his heel he entered the door.

"Pick me out a dozen red japonicas," he said to the boy behind the counter.

Oliver waited until each short-stemmed blossom was carefully selected, laid on its bed of raw cotton, blanketed with the same covering, and packed in a paper box. Then, taking a card from his pocket, he wrote upon its back: "Most grateful thanks for my share of the catch," slipped it into an envelope, addressed it to "The fair Fisher, The Countess Kovalski," and, with a grim smile on his face, kept on down Broadway toward the dingy hotel, the resort of all the Southerners of the time, to arrange for rooms for his father and Nathan Gill.

Having, with his card and his japonicas, dismissed the Countess from his mind, and to a certain extent his obligations, the full importance of this new order of Peter Fish's began to take possession of him. The color rose in his cheeks and an old-time spring and lightness came into his steps. He knew that such a

commission, and from such a man, would at once gain
for him a recognition from art patrons and a standing
among the dealers. Lasting success was now assured
him in the line he had chosen for his life's work. It
only remained for him to do the best that was in him.
Better than all, it had come to him unasked and without any compromising effort on his own part.

He knew the connoisseur's collection. It filled the
large gallery adjoining his extensive home on Washington Square and was not only the best in the city,
containing as it did examples of Sir Thomas Lawrence, Sir Joshua Reynolds, Chrome, Sully, and
many of the modern French school—among them
two fine Courbets and a Rousseau—but it had lately
been enriched by one or more important American
landscapes, notably Sanford Gifford's "Catskill
Gorge" and Church's "Tropics"—two canvases
which had attracted more than usual attention at
the Spring Exhibition of the Academy. An order,
therefore, for a family portrait from so distinguished
a patron not only gave weight and dignity to the work
of any painter he might select, but it would unquestionably influence his many friends and acquaintances
to go and do likewise.

As Oliver, his eyes aglow, his whole heart filled
with joy, stepped quickly down the street the beauty
of the day made him throw back his shoulders
and drink in long deep breaths, as if he would fill his
very pores with its vitality. These early spring days

in New York—the most beautiful the world over; not even in Italy can one find better skies—always affected him in this way. There was a strength-giving quality in the ozone, a brilliancy in the sunshine, and a tempered coolness in the air to be found nowhere else. There was, too, a certain picturesqueness in the sky-line of the houses—a sky-line fringed with jets of white steam from the escape-pipes of numerous fires below, which appealed to his artistic sense. These curling plumes that waved so triumphantly in the sparkling morning light, or stirred by the wind, flapped like milk-white signal flags, breaking at last into tatters and shreds, blurring the edges of chimney and cornice, were a constant source of delight to the young painter. He would often stop to watch their movements, and as often determine to paint them at the first opportunity. They seemed to express to him something of the happy freedom of one released from pent-up toil; a freedom longed for in his own heart, and which had rarely been his since those blessed days under Moose Hillock, when he and Margaret roamed the woods together.

Still a third cause of rejoicing—and this sent a flutter around his heart—was the near prospect of meeting his dear old father, whom he had not seen for months; not since his last visit home, and whose long years of struggle and waiting seemed now to be so nearly ended.

With these last joyous thoughts filling his mind, he

stepped quickly through the corridor of the hotel,
approached the desk, and had just given the names
of his father and Nathan to the clerk, when a man
behind the counter interrupted him with:

" Just arrived. Got in this morning. There they
are by the window."

Two quaint-looking old gentlemen were gazing out
upon the rush of Broadway—two old gentlemen
so unusual that even the *habitues* of the place, those
who sat tilted back all day chipping the arms of their
chairs with their pen-knives, or sipping countless
toddies and juleps, were still staring at them in undisguised astonishment. One—it was Nathan—wore
a queer hat, bushy, white hair, and long, pen-wiper
cloak: it was the same cloak, or another just like it;
the same, no doubt; few new clothes had been bought
during the war. And the other—and this was his
own dear father—wore a buff waistcoat, high white
silk scarf, and brown frock coat, with velvet collar.
Neither of them were every-day sights around the
corridors of the New York Hotel: even among a
collection of human oddities representing every State
in the South.

" We thought it best to take the night train, my
son," said Richard, starting up at Oliver's caressing
touch—he had put both hands on his father's shoulders. " You got your dear mother's letter of course.
Oh, I'm so glad to see you! Sit down here alongside
of us. How well you are looking, my son," and he

patted him lovingly on the arm. " What a whirl it all is! Nathan and I have been here for hours; we arrived at six o'clock. Did you ever see anything like it? The people never seem to stop coming. Ah! this is the place for you, my boy. Everything is so alive, so full of purpose, so intense, so delightful and inspiring to me. And such a change in the years since I was here."

He had brought the motor with him. It lay at the moment in a square box inside the office-railing. Not the big one which he had just perfected—that one was at home under the window in the old shop, in the back yard in Kennedy Square—but a smaller working model made of pine wood, with glass-tumblers for jars and imitation magnets wrapped round with thread instead of wire—the whole unintelligible to the layman, but perfectly clear to the scientist. He had with him, too, packed in a small carpet-bag, which lay within reach of his hand, all the patents which had been granted him as the work progressed—besides a huge bundle of papers, such as legal documents, notices from the scientific journals, and other data connected with the great Horn Galvanic Motor, which was soon to revolutionize the motive power of the world. Tucked away in his inside pocket, ready for instant use, was Amos Cobb's letter, introducing " the distinguished inventor, Mr. Richard Horn, of Kennedy Square," etc., etc., to the group of capitalists who were impatiently waiting his arrival, and who

were to furnish the unlimited sums of money necessary in its development—unlimited sums being ready
for any scheme, no matter how chimerical, in the
flush times through which the country was then
passing.

"I have succeeded at last, my boy, as I wrote you,"
continued Richard, with glowing eyes. "Even that
small motor at home—the one you know—that one
has a lifting power of a hundred pounds. All that is
necessary now is to increase the size of the batteries
and the final result is assured. Let me show you
this "—and, oblivious of the many eyes fastened on
him, he drew toward him the black carpet-bag and
took out a sheet of paper covered with red and blue
lines. "You see where the differences are. And you
see here "—and he pointed out the details with his
thin white finger—"what I have done since I explained to you the new additions. This drawing,
when carried out, will result in a motor with a lifting
capacity of ten tons. Ah, Oliver, I cannot tell you
what a great relief has come to me now that I know
my life's work is crowned with success."

Nathan was quite as happy. Richard was his sun
god. When the light of hope and success flashed in
the inventor's quiet, thoughtful face, Nathan basked
in its warmth and was radiant in its glow. He needed
all the warmth he could get, poor old man. The cold
chill of the days of fear and pain and sorrow had well-
nigh shrivelled him up; he showed it in every line

of his body. His shoulders were much more bent; his timid, pipe-stem legs the more shaky; the furrows about his face deeper; the thin nose more transparent. All during the war he had literally lived in Richard. The cry of the " extras " and the dull tramp of march-ing troops, and the rumbling of cars laden with army supplies had jarred on his sensitive ear as would discordant notes in a quartette. Days at a time he would hide himself away in Richard's workshop, helping him with his bellows or glue-pot, or piling the coals on the fire of his forge. The war, while it lasted, paralyzed some men to inaction—Nathan was one of them.

" At last, Oliver, at last! " Nathan whispered to Oliver when Richard's head was turned for a moment. " Nothing now but plain sailing. Ah! it's a great day for dear Richard! I couldn't sleep last night on the train for thinking of him."

As Oliver looked down into Nathan's eyes, glisten-ing with hope and happiness, he wondered whether, after all these long years of waiting, his father's genius was really to be rewarded? Was it the same old story of success—one so often ending in defeat and gloom, he thought, or had the problem really been solved? He knew that the machine had stood its initial test and had developed a certain lifting power; his father's word assured him of that; but would it continue to develop in proportion to its size?

He turned again toward Richard. The dear face

was a-light with a new certainty; the eyes brilliant,
the smiles about the lips coming and going like summer clouds across the sun. Such enthusiasm was not
to be resisted. A fresh hope rose in the son's heart.
Could this now almost assured success of his father's
help him with Madge? Would their long waiting
come any nearer to being ended? Would the sum of
money realized be large enough to pay off the dreaded
mortgage, and there still be enough for the dear home
and its inmates?

He knew how large this hoped-for sum must be,
and how closely his own and his mother's honor were
involved in its cancellation. Her letter had indeed
stated the facts—this motor was now their only hope
outside the work of his own brush.

Perhaps, after all, his lucky day had come. The
first gleam of light had been this order of Peter Fish's
to paint his daughter, and now here, sitting beside
him, was his father with a letter in his pocket addressed to Amos Cobb from one of the richest men
in New York, who stood ready to pay a small fortune
for the motor. Then he thought of his mother.
What a delight it would be when she could be freed
from the millstone that had hung around her neck
for years.

He must go and tell Margaret and take his father
and Nathan with him. Yes, his lucky day *had* come.

Soon the two delighted and astonished old gentlemen, under Oliver's guidance, were making their way

up Broadway ostensibly to see his picture at Snedecor's, but really to call upon the distinguished painter,
Margaret Grant, whom everyone was talking about,
both in New York and in Kennedy Square, for one
of her pictures graced Miss Clendenning's boudoir at
that very moment. Our young Romeo had waited
too many months for someone from Kennedy Square
to see the woman he loved, and now that the arms of
his father and Nathan were linked in his own, and
their legs subject to his orders, he did not intend to
let many precious minutes pass before he rang Margaret's studio bell.

When Snedecor's window was reached Richard
stopped short in amazement.

"Yours, Oliver! Marvellous! Marvellous!"
Richard exclaimed, when the three had wedged their
way into the crowd to see the better. "A fine strong
picture, and a most superb looking woman. Why, I
had no idea! Really! Really"—and his voice trembled. He was deeply touched. The strength of the
coloring, the masterly drawing, the admiring crowd
about the window, greatly surprised him. While he
had been closeted with his invention, thinking only
of its success and bending every energy for its completion, this boy of his had become a master.

"I didn't do my full duty to you, my son," he
said, with a tone of sadness in his voice, when they
had resumed their walk up Broadway. "You lost
much time in finding your life's work. I should

470

have insisted years ago that you follow the trend
of your genius. Your dear mother was not willing and I let it go, but it was wrong. From something she said to me the other night I feel sure she
sees her mistake now, but I never mention it to her,
and do you never let her know I told you. Yes! You
started too late in life, my boy."

" No, dear old daddy; I started just in the nick of
time and in the right way."

How could he have thought anything else on this
lovely spring morning, with the brightest of skies
overhead, his first important order within his grasp,
his dear old father and Nathan beside him, and the
loveliest girl in the world or on the planets beyond
waiting for him at the top of her studio stairs!

" It's most kind of you to say so," continued Richard, dodging the people as he talked, " but couldn't
you have learned to work by following your own
tastes ? "

" No dad. I was too confounded lazy and too fond
of fun. And then the dear mother wanted me to go
to work, and that was always enough for me."

" Oh, my son, it does me good to hear you say so "
—and a light shone on the old gentleman's face.
" Yes! you *always* considered your mother. You
can't think how she has suffered during these terrible
years. But for the good offices of Mr. Cobb whose
kindness I shall never forget, I do not see how she
could have gone through them as she has. Isn't it

471

THE FORTUNES OF OLIVER HORN

fine, my son, to think it is all over? She will never have to worry again—never—never. The motor will end all her troubles. She did not believe in it once, but she does now.

They continued on up Broadway, Oliver in the middle, Richard's arm in his; he hurrying them both along; steering them across the streets; avoiding the trucks and dragging them past the windows they wanted to look into, with promises of plenty of time for that to-morrow or next week. Only once did he allow them to catch their breath, and that was when they passed the big bronze statue overlooking Union Square, and then only long enough for the two to take in its outlines and from its pedestal to fix their eyes on the little windows of Miss Teetum's boarding-house, where he had spent so many happy and un-happy days.

Soon the two breathless old gentlemen and equally breathless young guide—the first condition due to the state of the two old gentlemen's lungs and the second due entirely to the state of this particular young gentleman's heart—stood in a doorway just off Madison Square, before a small bell-pull bearing above it a tiny sign reading: " Margaret Grant. Top Floor."

" Miss Grant has been at home only a few months," Oliver burst out as he rang the bell and climbed the stairs. " Since her father's death she has been in Paris with her mother, her cousin, Higbee Shaw the

sculptor, and her brother John. A shell injured the
drum of John's ear, and while she painted he was
under the care of a French specialist. He is still
there with his mother. If you think I can paint just
wait until you see Miss Grant's work. Think, dad!
she has taken two medals in Munich, and last year
had honorable mention at the Salon. You remember her brother, of course, don't you, Uncle Nat, the
one Malachi hid over father's shop? "

Uncle Nat nodded his head as he toiled up the
steps. He remembered every hour of the hideous
nightmare. He had been the one other man besides
Richard and the Chief of Police to shake Oliver's
hand that fatal night when he was exiled from Kennedy Square.

Mrs. Mulligan, in white apron, a French cap on
her head, and looking as fresh and clean as a trained
nurse, opened the door. Margaret had looked her
up the very day she landed, and had placed her in
charge of her apartment as cook, housekeeper, and
lady's maid, with full control of the front door and of
her studio. The old woman was not hard to trace; she
had followed the schools of the academy from their
old quarters to the new marble building on Twenty-
third Street, and was again posing for the draped-life
class and occasionally lending a hand to the new janitor. Margaret's life abroad had taught her the
secret of living alone, a problem easily solved when
there are Mrs. Mulligans to be had for the asking.

"Yes, Mr. Oliver, she's insoide. Oh! it's fri'nds ye hev wid ye!" and she started back.

"Only my father and Mr. Gill," and he brushed past Mrs. Mulligan, parted the heavy portières that divided Madge's working studio from the narrow hall, thrust in his head and called out, in his cheeriest voice:

"Madge, who do you think is outside? Guess! Father and Uncle Nat. Just arrived this morning."

Before Margaret could turn her head the two stood before her: Richard with his hat in his hand, his brown overcoat with the velvet collar over his arm— he had slipped it off outside—and Nathan close behind, still in the long, pen-wiper cloak.

"And is it really the distinguished young lady of whom I have heard so much?" exclaimed Richard with his most courtly bow, taking the girl's outstretched hand in both of his. "I am so glad to see you, my dear, both on your own account and on account of your brother, whom we once sheltered. And how is he now? and your dear mother?"

To all of which Margaret answered in low gentle tones, her eyes never leaving Richard's, her hand still fast in his; until he had turned to introduce Nathan so that he might pay his respects.

Nathan, in his timid halting way, stepped from behind Richard, and taking her welcoming hand, told her how much he had wanted to know her, since he had seen the picture she had painted, then hanging in Miss Lavinia's home; both because it was the work of a woman and because too—and he looked straight into her eyes when he said it and meant every word—she was the sister of the poor fellow who had been so shamefully treated in his own city. And Margaret, her voice breaking, answered that, but for the aid of such kind friends as himself and Oliver, John might never have come back, adding, how grateful she and her whole family had been for the kindness shown her brother.

While they were talking, Richard, with a slight bow as if to ask her permission, began making the tour of the room, his glasses held to his eyes, examining each thing about him with the air of a connoisseur suddenly ushered into a new collection of curios.

"Tell me who this sketch is by," he asked, stopping before Margaret, and pointing to a small Lambinet, glowing like an opal on the dull-green wall of the studio. "I so seldom see good pictures that a gem like this is a delight. By a Frenchman! Ah! Yes, I see the subtlety of coloring. Marvellous people, these Frenchmen. And this little jewel you have here? This bit of mezzo in color. With this I am more familiar, for we have a good many collections of old prints at home. It is, I think—yes—I thought I could not be mistaken—it is a Morland," and he examined it closely, his nose almost touching the glass.

The next instant he had crossed the room to the

window looking out over the city, the smoke and steam of a thousand fires floating over its wide expanse.

" Come here, my son," he called to Oliver. " Look over that stretch of energy and brains. Is it not inspiring? And that band of silver, moving so quietly and resistlessly out to sea. What a power for good it all is, and what a story it will tell before the century is out."

Margaret was by his side as he spoke. She had hardly taken her eyes from him since he entered the room—not even when she was listening to Nathan. All her old-time prejudices and preconceived estimates of Richard were slipping away. Was this the man whom she used to think of as a dreamer of dreams, and a shiftless Southerner? This charming old gentleman with the air of an aristocrat and the keen discernment of an expert? She could hardly believe her eyes.

As for Oliver, his very heart was bursting with pride. It had all happened exactly as he had wanted it—his father and Margaret had liked each other from the very first moment. And then she had been so beautiful, too, even in her long painting-apron and her hair twisted up in a coil on her head. And the little blush of surprise and sweetness which had overspread her face when they entered, and which his father must have seen, and the inimitable grace with which she slipped from her high stool,

and with a half courtesy held out her hand to welcome her visitors, and all with the *savoir faire* and
charm of a woman of the world! How it all went
straight to his heart.

If, however, he had ever thought her pretty in this
working-costume, he thought her all the more captivating a few minutes later in the little French jacket
—all pockets and buttons—which she had put on as
soon as the greetings were over and the tour of the
room had been made in answer to Richard's delighted
questions.

But it was in serving the luncheon, which Mrs.
Mulligan had brought in, that his sweetheart was
most enchanting. Her full-rounded figure moved so
gracefully when she bent across to hand someone a
cup, and the pose of the head was so delicious, and it
was all so bewitching, and so precisely satisfied his
artistic sense. And he so loved to hear her talk
when she was the centre of a group like this, as much
really to see the movement of her lips and the light
in her eyes and the gracious way in which she moved
her head as to hear what she said.

He was indeed so overflowing with happiness over
it all, and she was so enchanting in his eyes as she
sat there dispensing the comforts of the silver tray,
that he must needs pop out of the room with some
impromptu excuse and disappear into the little den
which held her desk, that he might dash off a note
which he tucked under her writing-pad—one of their

hiding-places—and which bore the lines: " You. were never so much my queen as you are to-day, dearest," and which she found later and covered with kisses before he was half way down the block on his way back to the hotel with the two old gentlemen.

She was indeed beautiful. The brow was wider and whiter, perhaps, than it had been in the old days under the bark slant, and the look out of the eyes a trifle softer, and with a certain tenderness in them— not quite so defiant and fearless; but there had been no other changes. Certainly none in the gold-brown hair that Oliver so loved. That was still her glory, and was still heaped up in magnificent masses, and with the same look about it of being ready to burst its bonds and flood everything with a river of gold.

" Lots of good news to-day, Madge," Oliver exclaimed, after they had all taken their seats, his father on Margaret's right, with Nathan next.

" Yes, and I have got lots of good news too; bushels of it," laughed Margaret.

" You tell me first," cried Oliver bending toward her, his face beaming; each day they exchanged the minutest occurrences of their lives.

" No—Ollie—Let me hear yours. What's it about? Mine's about a picture."

" So's mine," exclaimed Oliver, his eyes brimming with fun and the joy of the surprise he had in store for her.

" But it's about one of your *own* pictures, Ollie."

"So's mine," he cried again, his voice rising in merriment.

"Oh, Ollie, tell me first," pleaded Margaret with a tone in her voice of such coaxing sweetness that only Richard's and Nathan's presence restrained him from catching her up in his arms and kissing her then and there.

"No, not until you have told me yours," he answered with mock firmness. "Mine came in a letter."

"So did mine," cried Margaret clapping her hands. "I don't believe yours is half as good as mine and I'm not going to wait to hear it. Now listen—" and she opened an envelope that lay on the table within reach of her hand. "This is from my brother John—" and she turned toward Richard and Nathan. "He and Couture, in whose atelier I studied, are great friends. Now please pay attention Mr. Autocrat—" and she looked at Oliver over the edge of the letter and began to read—

"Couture came in to-day on his way home and I showed him the photograph Ollie sent me of his portrait of you—his 'Tam-o'-Shanter Girl' he calls it. Couture was so enthusiastic about it that he wants it sent to Paris at once so that he can exhibit it in his own studio to some of the painters there. Then he is going to send it to the Salon. So you can tell that 'Johnnie Reb' to pass it along to me by the first steamer; and you can tell him, too, that his last letter is a month old, and I am getting hungry for another."

479

"There now! what do you think of that? **Mr.** Honorable Mention."

Oliver opened his eyes in astonishment.

"That's just like John, bless his heart!" he answered slowly, as his glance sought the floor. This last drop had filled his cup of happiness to the brim— Some of it was glistening on his lashes.

"Now tell me your good news—" she continued, her eyes still dancing. She had seen the look but misunderstood the cause.

Oliver raised his eyes—

"Oh, it's not nearly as good as yours, Madge, in one way and yet in another it's a heap better. What do you think? Old Peter Fish wants me to paint his daughter's portrait."

Margaret laid her hand on his.

"Oh, Oliver! Not Peter Fish! That's the best thing that has happened yet," and her face instantly assumed a more serious expression. "I know the girl —she will be an easy subject; she's exactly your type. How do you know?"

"Just saw John Snedecor in answer to a letter he wrote me. Fish has bought the 'Woman in Black.' He's delighted with it."

"Why, I thought it belonged to the Countess."

"So it did. She sold it."

"Sold it!"

"Yes. Does it surprise you?"

"No; I can't say that it does. I am glad, though,

that it will stay in the country. It's by far the best thing you or anybody else has done this season. I was afraid she would take it back with her. Poor woman! she has had a hard life, and it doesn't seem to get any better, from what I hear."

"You know the original, then, my dear?" asked Richard, holding out his second cup of tea for an-other lump of sugar, which Margaret in her excite-ment had forgotten. He and Nathan had listened with the keenest interest to the reading of John Grant's letter and to the discussion that had fol-lowed.

"I know *of* her," answered Margaret as she dropped it in; "and she knows me, but I've never met her. She's a Pole, and something of a painter, too. She studied in the same atelier where I was, but that was before I went to Paris. Her husband became mixed up in some political conspiracy and was sent to Siberia, and she was put across the frontier that same night. She is very popular in Paris; they all like her, especially the painters. There is nothing against her except her poverty." There could be no-thing against any woman in Margaret's eyes. "But for her jewels she would have had as hard a time to get on as the rest of us. Now and then she parts with one of her pearls, and between times she teaches music. You must see the picture Oliver painted of her—it will delight you."

"Oh, but I have!" exclaimed Richard, laying

down his cup. "We looked at it as we came up. It is really a great picture. He tells me it is the work of two hours and under gas-light."

"No, not altogether, father. I had a few hours on it the next day," interrupted Oliver.

"Strong, isn't it?" continued Margaret, without noticing Oliver's explanation. "It is really better in many ways than the girl in the Tam-o'-Shanter cap—the one he painted of me. That had some of Lely's qualities about it, especially in the flesh tones. He always tells me the inspiration to paint it came from an old picture belonging to his uncle. You know that of course?" and she laid a thin sandwich on Nathan's plate.

"You mean Tilghman's Lely—the one in his house in Kennedy Square? Oh," said Richard, lifting his fingers in appreciation, "I know every line of it. It is one of the best Lely's I ever saw, and to me the gem of Tilghman's collection."

"Yes; so Ollie tells me," continued Margaret. "Now this picture of the Countess is to me very much more in Velasquez's method than in Lely's. Broader and stronger and with a surer touch. I have always told Ollie he was right to give up landscapes. These two pictures show it. There is really, Mr. Horn, no one on this side of the water who is doing exactly what Oliver is." She spoke as if she was discussing Page, Huntington or Elliott or any other painter of the day, not as if it was her lover. "Did you notice how the lace was brushed in and all that work about the throat—especially the shadow tones? "

She treated Richard precisely as if he was one of the guild. His criticisms of her own work—for he had insisted on seeing her latest picture and had even been more enthusiastic over it than he had been over Oliver's—and his instant appreciation of the Lambinet, convinced her, even before he had finished the tour of the room, that the quaint old gentleman was as much at home in her atmosphere as he was in that of his shop at home discussing scientific problems with some *savant*.

" I did, my dear. It is quite as you say," answered Richard, with great earnestness. " This ' Woman in Black,' as he calls it, is painted not only with sureness and with an intimate knowledge of the textures, but it seems to me he has the faculty of expressing with each stroke of his brush, as an engraver does with his burin, the rounds and hollows of his surfaces. And to think, too, my dear," he continued, " that most of it was done at night. The color tones, you know "—and his manner changed, and a more thoughtful expression came into his face—the scientist was speaking now—" are most difficult to manage at night. The colors of the spectrum undergo some very curious changes under artificial light, especially from a gas consuming as much carbon as our common carburetted hydrogen. The greens, owing to the absorption of the yellow rays, become the brighter,

483

and the orange and red tones, from the same reason, the more intense, while the paler violets and, in fact, all the tertiaries, of a bluish cast lose——"

He stopped, as he caught a puzzled expression on her face. " Oh, what a dreadful person I am," he exclaimed, rising from his seat. " It is quite inexcusable in me. Please forgive me, my dear—I was really thinking aloud. Such ponderous learned words should be kept out of this delightful abode of the Muses, and then, I assure you, I really know so little about it, and you know so much." And he laughed softly, and made a little bow as a further apology.

" No. I don't know one thing about it, nor does any other painter I know," she laughed, blowing out the alcohol lamp, " not quite in the same way. And if I did I should want you to come every day and bring Mr. Gill with you to tell me about it." Whereupon Nathan, replying that nothing would give him more pleasure (he had been silent most of the time— somehow no one expected him to talk much when Richard was present), struggled to his feet at an almost imperceptible sign from the inventor, who suddenly remembered that his capitalists were waiting for him, pulled his old cloak about his shoulders and, with Richard leading the way, they all four moved out into the hall and stood in the open doorway.

When they reached the top stair outside the studio·

door Richard stopped, took both of Margaret's hands in his, and said, in his kindest voice and in his gravest and most thoughtful manner, as he looked down into her face:

"My dear Miss Grant, may I tell you that I have to-day found in you the realization of one of my day-dreams? And will you forgive an old man when he says how proud it makes him to know a woman who is brave enough to live the life you do? You are the forerunner of a great movement, my dear—the mother of a new guild. It is a grand and noble thing for a woman to sustain herself with work that she loves"—and the dear old gentleman, lifting his hat with the air of a courtier, betook himself down-stairs, followed by Nathan, bowing as he went.

No wonder he rejoiced! Most of the dreams of his younger days were coming true. And now this wom-an—the beginning of a new era—the opening out of a new civilization. And ahead of it a National Art that the world would one day recognize!

He tried to express his delight to Oliver, and turned to find him, but Oliver was not beside him nor did he join his father for five minutes at least. That young gentleman—just as Richard and Nathan had reached the *bottom* of the second flight of stairs—had suddenly remembered something of the utmost importance which he had left in the *inner* room, and which he could not possibly find until Madge, waiting by the banister, had gone back to help him look for

485

it, and not then, until Mrs. Mulligan had left them both and shut the kitchen-door behind her. Yes, it was quite five minutes, or more, before Oliver clattered down-stairs after his guests, stopping but once to look up through the banisters into Margaret's eyes—she was leaning over for the purpose—his open hand held up toward her as a sign that it was always at her command.

CHAPTER XXIII

MR. MUNSON'S LOST FOIL

For a quiet, orderly, well behaved and most dig-nified street, Tenth Street, at seven o'clock one April night was disgracing itself in a way that must have shocked its inhabitants. Cabs driving like mad were rattling over the cobbles, making their way toward the old Studio Building. Policemen were shouting to the drivers to keep in line. Small boys were dart-ing in and out, peering into the cab windows and calling out to their fellows: " Ki Jimmy! see de Ingin wid de fedder-duster on his head "—or, " Look at de pill in de yaller shirt! My eye, ain't he a honey-cooler! "

At the entrance of the building, just inside the door where the crowd was thickest, stood two men in armor with visors down—stood so still, that the boys and bystanders thought they had been borrowed from some bric-a-brac shop until, in an unguarded moment, one plumed knight rested his tired leg with a rattling noise that sounded like a tin-peddler shifting his pack or the adjustment of a length of stovepipe. Behind the speechless sentinels, leading into the narrow cor-ridor, stretched a red carpet bordered by rows of

palms and evergreens and hung about with Chinese
lanterns.

At the end of this carpet opened a door that
looked into a banquet hall as rich in color and as
sumptuous in its interior fittings as an audience-
chamber of the Doges at a time when Venice ruled
the world. The walls were draped with Venetian silks
and Spanish velvets, against which were placed
Moorish plaques, Dutch brass sconces holding clusters of candles, barbaric spears, bits of armor, pairs
of fencing foils, old cabinets, and low, luxurious divans. Thrust up into the skylight, its gaff festooned
with trawl-nets, drooped a huge sloop's sail, its graceful folds breaking the square lines of the ceiling; and
all about, suspended on long filigree chains, swung
old church-lamps of brass or silver, burning ruby
tapers.

In the centre of this glow of color stood a round
table, its top covered with a white cloth, and laid with
covers for fifty guests. On this were placed, in orderly confusion, great masses of flowers heaped up
in rare porcelain vases; silver candelabra bearing
lighted candles; old Antwerp brass holding bon-bons
and sweets; Venetian flagons filled with rare wines;
Chinese and Japanese curios doing service as ash-
receivers and match-safes; Delft platters for choice
dishes; besides Flemish mugs, Bavarian glasses,
George III. silver, and the like.

At the head of this sumptuous board was placed a

chair of state, upholstered in red velvet, studded with brass rosettes, the corners of its high back surmounted by two upright gilt ornaments. This was to hold the Master of the Feast, the presiding officer who was to govern the merry spirits during the hours of the revel. In front of this royal chair was a huge stone mug crowned with laurel. This was guarded by two ebony figures, armed with drawn scimitars, which stood at each side of the throne-seat. From these guards of honor radiated two half-circles of lesser chairs, one for each guest—of all patterns and periods: old Spanish altar-seats in velvet, Dutch chairs in leather, Italian chairs in mother-of-pearl and ivory—all armless and quite low, so low that the costumed slaves, who were to wait on the royal assembly, could serve the courses without having to reach over the backs of the guests.

Moving about the room, rearranging the curios on the cabinets, adding a bit of porcelain to the collection on the table, shifting the lights for better effect, lounging on the wide divans, or massed about the doorway welcoming the new arrivals as they entered, were Italian nobles of the sixteenth and seventeenth centuries, costumed with every detail correct, even to the jewelled daggers that hung at their sides, all genuine and of the period; cardinals in red hats and wonderful church robes, the candle-grease of the altar still clinging to their skirts; Spanish grandees in velvet and brocade; Indian rajahs in baggy silk trousers and embroidered waistcoats, with Kohinoors flashing from their turbans—not genuine this time but brilliant all the same; Shakespeares, Dantes (one of each), besides courtiers, nobles, gallants, and gentry of various climes and periods.

All this splendor of appointment, all these shaded candles, hanging-lamps, Venetian glass, antique furniture, rich costumes, Japanese curios, and assorted bric-a-brac, were gathered together and arranged thus sumptuously to add charm and lustre to a banquet given by the Stone Mugs to those of their friends most distinguished in their several professions of art, literature, and music.

Indeed any banquet the Club gave was sure to be as unique as it was artistic.

Sometimes it would be held in the hold of an abandoned vessel left high and dry on a lonely beach, which, under the deft touches of the artists of the Club, would be transformed in a night to the cabin of a buccaneer filled with the loot of a treasure ship. Sometimes a canal boat, which the week before had been loaded with lime or potatoes, would be scoured out with a fire-hose, its deck roofed with awnings and hung with lanterns, its hatches lined with palms, and in the hold below a table spread of such surprising beauty, and in an interior so gorgeous in its appointments that each guest, as he descended the carpeted staircase leading from the deck above to the carpeted keelson below, would rub his eyes wondering

490

whether he had not been asleep, and had suddenly awakened aboard Cleopatra's barge.

Again the club would hold a Roman feast in one of Solari's upstairs rooms—the successor to Riley's of the old days—each man speaking ancient Latin with Tenth Street terminals, the servants dressed in tunics and sandals, and the members in togas. Or they would make a descent at midnight on Fulton Market and have their tomcods scooped from the fish-boxes alive and broiled to their liking while they waited; or they would take possession of Brown's or Farrish's for mugs of ale and English chops. But it was always one so different from any other function of its class that it formed the topic of the studios for weeks thereafter.

To-night it was the humor of the club to reproduce as closely as possible, with the limited means at their disposal—for none of the Stone Mugs were rolling in wealth, nor did these functions require it—some one of the great banquets of former times, not to be historically or chronologically correct, but to express the artistic atmosphere of such an occasion.

That there were certain unavoidable and easily detected shams under all this glamour of color and form did not lessen the charm of the present function.

Everybody, of course, knew before the evening was over, or could have found out had he tried, that the two knights in armor who guarded the side-walk entrance to this royal chamber, and who had been the target of the street-rats until they took their places at the inside door, were respectively Mr. Patrick McGinnis, who tended the furnace in the basement of the Tenth Street Studio Building, stripped for the occasion down to his red flannels, and Signore Luigi Bennelli, his Italian assistant.

A closer inspection of the two ebony blackamoors, with drawn scimitars, who guarded the royal chair at the head of the table, would have revealed the fact that they were not made of ebony at all, but of veritable flesh and blood—the blackamoor on the right being none other than Black Sam, the bootblack who shined shoes on the corner of the avenue, and his bloodthirsty pal on the left the kinky-haired porter who served the grocer next door; the only " honest " thing about either of them, to quote Waller, being the artistic clothes that they stood in.

Further investigation would have shown that every one of the wonderful things that made glad and glorious the big square room on the ground floor of the building, from the brass sconces on the walls to the hanging church lamps, with everything that their lights fell upon, had been gathered up that same morning from the several homes and studios of the members by old black Jerry, the official carman of the Academy, and had been dumped in an indiscriminate heap on the floor of the banquet hall, where they had been disentangled and arranged by half a dozen painters of the club; that the table and table-cloth had been borrowed from Solari's; that the very rare and fragrant old Chianti, the club's private stock, was from Solari's own cellars *via* Duncan's, the grocer; and that the dinner itself was cooked and served by that distinguished boniface himself, assisted by half a dozen of his own waiters, each one wearing an original Malay costume selected from Stedman's collection and used by him in his great picture of the Sepoy mutiny.

Moreover there was not the slightest doubt that the " Ingin," who was now bowing so gravely to the master of ceremonies, was no other than the distinguished Mr. Thomas Brandon Waller, himself; " N.A., Knight of the Legion of Honor, Pupil of Piloty, etc., etc.; " that the high-class mandarin in the sacred yellow robe and peacock feather who accompanied him, was Crug the 'cellist; that the bald-headed gentleman with the pointed beard, who looked the exact presentment of the divine William, was Munson; and that the gay young gallant in the Spanish costume was none other than our Oliver. The other nobles, cavaliers, and hidalgos were the less known members of the club, who, in their desire to make the occasion a success, had fitted themselves to their costumes instead of attempting to fit the costumes to themselves, with the difference that each man not only looked the character he assumed but assumed the character he looked.

But no one, even the most knowing; no student

of costumes, no reader of faces, no discerner of character, no acute observer of manners and times—in glancing over the motley company would have thought for one instant that, in all this atmosphere of real unrealism, the two old gentlemen who had just entered leaning on Oliver's arm—one in a brown coat with high velvet collar and fluffy silk scarf, and the other in a long pen-wiper cloak which, at the moment was slipping from his shoulders—were genuine specimens of the period of to-day without a touch of make-up about them; that their old-time manners, even to the quaint bows they both gave the master of ceremonies, as they entered the royal chamber, were their very own, part of their daily equipment, and that nothing in the gorgeous banquet hall, from the jewelled rapier belted to Oliver's side, and which had once graced the collection of a prince, down to the priceless bit of satsuma set out on the table and now stuffed full of cigarettes (the bit could be traced back to the Ming dynasty), were any more *veritable* or genuine, or any more representative of the best their periods afforded than these two quaint old gentlemen from Kennedy Square.

Had there been any doubt in the minds of any such wiseacre, either regarding their authenticity or their quality, he had only to listen to Oliver's presentation of his father and friend and to hear Richard say, in his most courteous manner and in his most winning voice:

"I have never been more honored, sir. It was more than kind of you to wish me to come. My only regret is that I am not your age, or I would certainly have appeared in a costume more befitting the occasion. I have never dreamed of so beautiful a place."

Or to see him lift his hand in astonishment as he swept his eye over the room, his arm still resting on the velvet sleeve of Oliver's doublet, and hear him add, in a half whisper:

"Wonderful! Wonderful! Such harmony of color; such an exquisite light. I am amazed at the splendor of it all. What Aladdin among you, my son, held the lamp that evoked all this beauty?"

Or still more convincing would it have been had he watched him moving about the room, shaking every man's hand in turn, Oliver mentioning their real names and their several qualifications, and afterward the characters they assumed, and Richard commenting on each profession in a way quite his own.

"A musician, sir," he would have heard him exclaim as he grasped Simmons's hand, over which hung a fall of antique lace; "I have loved music all my days. It is an additional bond between us, sir. And the costume is quite in keeping with your art. How delightful it would be, my dear sir, if we could discard forever the sombre clothes of our day and go back to the velvets and silks of the past."

"Mr. Stedman, did you say, my son?" and he turned to Oliver. "You have certainly mentioned
495

this gentleman's name to me before. If I do not mistake, he is one of your very old friends. There is no need of your telling me that you are *Lorenzo.* I can quite understand now why *Jessica* lost her heart."

Or to see him turn to Jack Bedford with: " You don't tell me so! Mr. John Bedford, did you say, Oliver? Ah, but we should not be strangers, sir. If I am right, you are a fellow-townsman of ours, and have already distinguished yourself in your profession. Your costume is especially becoming to you, sir. What discernment you have shown. Permit me to say, that with you the old adage must be reversed —this time the man makes the clothes."

The same adage could really have been applied to this old gentleman's own dress, had he but only known it. He had not altered it in twenty years, even after it had become a matter of comment among his neighbors in Kennedy Square.

" I always associate one's clothes with one's manners," he would say, with a smile. " If they are good, and suited to the occasion, best not change them." Nathan was of the same mind. The wide hat, long, evenly parted hair, and pen-wiper cloak could be traced to these same old-fashioned ideas. These idiosyncrasies excited no comment so far as Nathan was concerned. He was always looked upon as belonging to some antediluvian period, but with a progressive man like Richard the case, his neighbors thought, might have been different.

MR. MUNSON'S LOST FOIL

As Richard moved about the room, saluting each one in turn, the men in and out of costume—the guests were in evening dress—looked at each other and smiled at the old gentleman's quaint ways, but the old gentleman, with the same ease of manner and speech, continued on quite around the table, followed closely by Nathan, who limited his salutations to a timid shake of the fingers and the leaving of some word of praise or quaint greeting, which many of them remember even to this day.

These introductions over—Oliver had arrived on the minute—the ceremony of seating the guests was at once begun. This ceremony was one of great dignity, the two men-at-arms escorting the Master of the Feast, the Most High Pan-Jam, Frederico Stono, N.A., to his Royal Chair, guarded by the immovable blackamoors, the members and guests standing until His Royal Highness had taken his seat, and then dropping into their own. When everyone was in his place Richard found himself, to his delight, on the right of Fred and next to Nathan and Oliver—an honor accorded to him because of his age and relationship to one of the most popular members of the club, and not because of his genius and attainments —these latter attributes being as yet unknown quantities in that atmosphere. The two thus seated together under the especial care of Oliver—a fact which relieved the master of ceremonies of any further anxiety on their account—were to a certain

extent left to themselves, the table being too large for general conversation except with one's neighbors.

The seat in which he had been placed exactly suited Richard's frame of mind. With an occasional word to Fred, he sat quite still, talking now and then in low tones to Nathan, his eyes taking in every detail of the strange scene.

While Nathan saw only the color and beauty of it all, Richard's keener mind was analyzing the causes that had led up to such a gathering, and the skill and taste with which the banquet had been carried out. He felt assured that the men who could idle so luxuriously, and whose technical knowledge had perfected the artistic effects about him, could also work at their several professions with equal results. He was glad that Oliver had been found worthy enough to be admitted to such a circle. He loved, too, to hear his son's voice and watch the impression his words made on the room. As the evening wore on, and he listened to his banter, or caught the point of the jests that Oliver parried and heard his merry laugh, he would slip his hand under the table and pat his boy's knee with loving taps of admiration, prouder of him than ever. His own pleasures so absorbed him that he continued to sit almost silent, except for a word now and then to Nathan or a monosyllable to Fred.

The guests who were near enough to observe the visitors closely soon began to look upon Richard and

Nathan as a couple of quaint, harmless, exceedingly well-bred old gentlemen, rather provincial in appearance and a little stilted in their manners, who, before the evening was over, would, perhaps, become tired of the gayety, ask to be excused, and betake themselves to bed. All of which would be an eminently proper proceeding in view of their extreme age and general infirmities, old gentlemen of three score years and over appearing more or less decrepit to athletes of twenty and five.

Waller was the only man who really seemed to take either of them seriously. After a critical examination of Richard's head in clear relief under the soft light of the candles, he leaned over to Stedman and said, in a half whisper, nodding toward Richard:

"Stedman, old man, take that in for a minute. Strong, isn't it? Wouldn't you like to paint him as a blessed old Cardinal in a red gown? See how fine the nose is, and the forehead. Best head I've seen anywhere. Something in that old fellow."

The dinner went on. The Malays in scarlet and yellow served the dishes and poured the wine with noiseless regularity. The men at arms at each side of the door rested their legs. The two blackamoors, guarding the High Pan-Jam's chair, and who had been promised double pay if they kept still during the entire evening, had not so far winked an eyelid. Now and then a burst of laughter would start from one end of the table, leap from chair to chair, and end in a deafening roar in which the whole room joined. Each man was at his best. Fred, with entire gravity, and with his sternest and most High Pan-Jam expression, told, just after the fish was served, a story of a negro cook at a camp so true to life and in so perfect a dialect that the right-hand blackamoor doubled himself up like a jack-knife, much to the astonishment of those on the far side of the big round table, who up to that moment had firmly believed them to be studio properties with ebony heads screwed on bodies of iron wire, the whole stuffed with curled hair. Bianchi, who had come in late, clothed in a Burgomaster's costume and the identical ruff that Oliver had expected to paint him in the night when the Countess took his place, was called to account for piecing out his dress with a pair of breeches a century behind his coat and hat, and had his voice drowned in a roar of protests before he could explain.

Batterson, the big baritone of the club, Batterson with the resonant voice, surpassed all his former efforts by singing, when the cheese and salads were served, a Bedouin love-song, with such power and pathos and to the accompaniment of a native instrument so skilfully handled that the room rose to its feet, waving napkins, and the great Carvalho, the famous tenor—a guest of Crug's, each member could invite one guest—who was singing that week at the

MR. MUNSON'S LOST FOIL

Academy of Music, left his seat and, circling the table, threw his arms about the singer in undisguised admiration.

When the cigars and *liqueurs* had been passed around—these last were poured from bubble-blown decanters and drunk from the little cups flecked with gold that Munson had found in an old shop in Ravenna—the chairs were wheeled about or pushed back, and the members and guests rose from the table and drifted to the divans lining the walls, or threw themselves into the easy-chairs that were being brought from the corners by the waiters. The piano, with the assistance of the two now crestfallen and disappointed blackamoors, who, Eurydice like, had listened and lost, was pushed from its place against the wall; Crug's 'cello was stripped of its green baize bag and Simmons's violin-case opened and his Stradivarius placed beside it. The big table, bearing the wreck of the feast, more captivating even in its delightful disorder than it had been in its orderly confusion, was then, with the combined help of all the Malays, moved gently back against the wall, so as to widen the space around the piano, its *débris* left undisturbed by special orders from the Royal Chair, the rattling of dishes while their fun was in progress being one of the things which the club would not tolerate.

While all this rearranging of the banquet-hall was going on, Simmons was busying himself putting a new bridge under the strings of his violin, tightening its bow, and testing the condition of his instrument by that see-saw, harum-scarum flourish so common to all virtuosos;—no function of the club was ever complete without music—the men meanwhile settled themselves comfortably in their seats; some occupying their old chairs, others taking possession of the divans, the gay costumes of the members, and the black coats and white shirt-fronts of the guests in high relief against the wrecked dinner-table presenting a picture as rich in color as it was strong in contrast.

What is so significant, by the way, or so picturesque, as a dinner-table wrecked by good cheer and hospitality? The stranded, crumpled napkins, the bunching together of half and wholly emptied glasses, each one marking a period of content—the low candles, with half dried tears still streaming down their cheeks (tears of laughter, of course); the charming disorder of cups on plates and the piling up of dishes one on the other—all such a protest against the formality of the beginning! and all so suggestive of the lavish kindness of the host. A wonderful object-lesson is a wrecked dinner-table, if one cares to study it.

Silence now fell upon the room, the slightest noise when Simmons played being an unpardonable sin. The waiters were ordered either to become part of the wall decoration or to betake themselves to the outside hall, or the infernal regions, a suggestion of Waller's when one of them rattled some glasses he was carrying on a tray.

Simmons tucked a handkerchief in the band of his collar, balanced his bow for an instant, looked around the room, and asked, in a modest, obliging way:

" What shall it be, fellows? "

" Better give us Bach. The aria on the G strings," answered Waller.

" No, Chopin," cried Fred.

" No, you wooden-head, Bach's aria," whispered Waller. " Don't you know that is the best thing he does? "

" Bach it is then," answered Simmons, tucking his instrument under his chin.

As the music filled the room, Richard settled himself on one of the large divans between Nathan and Oliver, his head lying back on the cushions, his eyes half closed. If the table with its circle of thoughtful and merry faces, had set his brain to work, the tones of Simmons's violin had now stirred his very soul. Music was the one thing in the world he could not resist.

He had never heard the aria better played. He had no idea that anyone since Ole Bull's time could play it so well. Really, the surprises of this wonderful city were becoming greater to him every hour. Nathan, too, had caught the infection as he sat with his body bent forward, his head on one side listening intently.

When the last note of Simmons's violin had ceased vibrating, Richard sprang to his feet with all the buoyancy of a boy and grasped the musician by the hand.

"My dear sir, you really astound me! Your tone is most exquisite, and I must also thank you for the rendering. It is one quite new to me. Ole Bull played it, you remember—excuse me," and he picked up Simmons's violin where he had laid it on the piano, tucked it under his chin, and there vibrated through the room, half a dozen quivering notes, so clear and sweet that all eyes were instantly directed toward the quaint old gentleman, who still stood with uplifted bow, the violin in his hand.

"Where the devil did he learn to play like that?" said one member to another. "Why I thought he was an inventor."

"Keep your toes in your pumps, gentlemen," said Waller under his breath to some men beside him, as he sat hunched up in the depths of an old Spanish armchair. He had not taken his eyes from Richard while the music went on. "We're not half through with this old fellow. One thing I've found out, any how—that's where this beggar Horn got his voice."

Simmons was not so astounded; if he were he did not show it. He had recognized the touch of a musician in the very first note that came from the strings, just as the painters of the club had recognized the artist in the first line of the Countess's brush.

MR. MUNSON'S LOST FOIL

"Yes, you're right, Mr. Horn," said Simmons, as Richard returned him the instrument. "Now I come to think of it, I do remember having heard Ole Bull phrase it in that way you have. Stop a moment; take my violin again and play the air. There's another instrument here which I can use. I brought it for one of my orchestra, but he has not turned up yet," and he opened a cabinet behind him and took out a violin and bow.

Richard laughed as he again picked up Simmons's instrument from the piano where he had laid it.

"What an extraordinary place this is," he said as he adjusted the maestro's violin to his chin. "It fills me with wonder. Everything you want seems to be within reach of your hand. You take a bare room and transform it into a dream of beauty; you touch a spring in a sixteenth century cabinet, and out comes a violin. Marvellous! Marvellous!" and he sounded the strings with his bow. "And a wonderful instrument too," he continued, as he tightened one of its strings, his acute ear having detected a slight inaccuracy of pitch.

"I'm all ready, Mr. Simmons; now, if you please."

If the club and its guests had forgotten the old gentleman an hour before, the old gentleman had now quite forgotten them.

He played simply and easily, Simmons joining in, picking out the accompaniment, entirely unaware that anybody was listening, as unaware as he would
505

have been had only the white-haired mistress been present, and perhaps Malachi stepping noiselessly in and out. When he ceased, and the audience had broken out into exclamations of delight, he looked about him as if surprised, and then, suddenly remembering the cause of it all, said, in a low, gentle voice, and with a pleasant smile: " I don't wonder you're delighted, gentlemen. It is to me the most divine of all his creations. There is only one Bach." That his hand had held the bow and that the merit of its expression lay with him, never seemed to have entered his head.

When the applause had died out, and Oliver with the others had crowded around his father to congratulate him, the young fellow's eyes fell upon Nathan, who was still sitting on the long divan, his head resting against the wall, his trembling legs crossed one over the other, the thin hands in his lap—Richard's skill was a never-ending delight to Nathan, and he had not lost a note that his bow had called out. The flute-player had kept so quiet since the music had begun, and had become so much a part of the decorations—like one of the old chairs with its arms held out, or a white-faced bust staring from out a dark corner, or some portrait that looked down from the tapestries and held its peace—that almost everyone had forgotten his presence.

The attitude of the old man—always a pathetic one, brought back to Oliver's mind some memory from out his boyhood days. Suddenly a forgotten strain from Nathan's flute floated through his brain, some strain that had vibrated through the old rooms in Kennedy Square. Springing to his feet and tip-toeing to the door, he passed between the two men in armor—rather tired knights by this time, but still on duty—ran down the carpeted hall between the lines of palms and up one flight of stairs. Then came a series of low knocks. A few minutes later he bounded in again, his rapier in his hand to give his legs freer play.

"I rapped up Mitchell, who's sick in his studio upstairs, and got his flute," he whispered to Waller. "If you think my father can play you should hear Uncle Nat Gill," and he walked toward Nathan, the flute held out toward him.

The old gentleman woke to consciousness at the sight of the instrument, and a slight flush overspread his face.

"Oh, Oliver! Really, gentlemen—I—of course, I love the instrument, but here among you all—" and he looked up in a helpless way.

"No, no, Uncle Nat," cried Oliver, pressing the flute into Nathan's hand. "We won't take any excuse. There is no one in my town, gentlemen," and he faced the others, "who can play as he does. Please, Uncle Nat—just for me; it's so long since I heard you play," and he caught hold of Nathan's arm to lift him to his feet.

"You are quite right, my son," cried Richard, " and I will play his accompaniment."

Oliver's announcement and Richard's endorsement caused a stir as great as Richard's own performance. A certain curiosity took possession of the room, quite distinct from the spirit of merriment which had characterized it before. Many of the men now left their seats and began crowding about the piano—red cardinals, cavaliers, nobles, and black-coated guests looking over each other's shoulders. Everybody was getting more and more mystified.

"Really, Fred," whispered Waller, who still sat quietly watching the two visitors—he had not taken his eyes from them since Richard in his enthusiasm sprang forward to grasp Simmons's hand—"this is the most ridiculous thing I ever saw in my life. First comes this fossil thoroughbred who outplays Simmons, and now comes this old nut-cracker with his white tow-hair sticking out in two straight mops, who is going to play the flute! What in thunder is coming next? Pretty soon one of them will be pulling rabbits out of somebody's ears, or rubbing gold watches into canary birds."

Nathan took the flute from Oliver's outstretched hand, bowed in a timid way like a school-boy about to speak a piece, turned it over carefully, tried the silver keys to see that they responded easily to the pressure of his fingers, and raised it to his lips. Rich-

508

ard picked up the violin and whispered to Munson, with whom he had been talking—the one member who could play the piano as well as he could paint or fence—who nodded his head in assent.

Then, with Richard leading, the four—one of the guests a 'cellist of distinction took Max Unger's place—began Max's arrangement of the overture to " Fidelio "; the one Richard and Nathan had played so often together in the old parlor in Kennedy Square, with Miss Clendenning and Unger: an arrangement which had now become known to most musical amateurs.

There is not a man yet alive who has forgotten the tones of Nathan's flute as they soared that night through the clouds of tobacco-smoke that filled the great banquet-hall. Every shade and gradation of tone was a delight. Now soft as the cooing of doves, now low as the music of a brook rippling over the shallows and again swelling into song like a chorus of birds rejoicing in the coming of spring.

Not until the voice in the slender instrument had become silent and the last note of Richard's bow had ceased reverberating—not, in fact, until both men had laid down their instruments, and had turned from the piano—did the room seem to recover from the spell that had bound it. Even then there was no applause; no clapping of hands nor stamping of feet. There followed, from members and guests alike, only a deep, pent-up sigh and a long breath of relief, as if from a strain unbearable. Simmons, who had sat with his head buried in his hands, gave no other sign of his approval than by rising from his chair, taking Nathan's thin hand in his own and grasping it tightly, without a word. Stedman blurted out, in a low voice to himself: "My God! Who ever heard anything like that?" and remained fixed to his seat. As for Richard and Nathan, they resumed their places on the divan as men who had read a message not their own to willing ears.

Another, and quite a different mood now took possession of the room. Somehow the mellow tones of Nathan's flute had silenced the spirit of the rollicking buffoonery which had pervaded the evening.

The black-coated guests, with superlative praise of the good time they had had, and with renewed thanks for the privilege, began to bid Fred, the Master of Ceremonies, good-night. Soon only the costumed members, with Richard and Nathan, were left. So far from being tired out with the night's diversion, these two old gentlemen seemed to have just wakened up.

Those remaining drew their chairs together, lighted fresh cigars, and sat down to talk over the events of the evening. Richard related an anecdote of Macready when playing the part of *Hamlet;* Stedman told of the graceful manner in which Booth, a few months before, in the same part, had handed the flageolet to the musicians, and the way the words fell from his lips, "You would play upon me"; Oliver, addressing his words rather to his father than to the room—acting the scene as he talked, and in his tight-fitting doublet, looking not unlike the tragedian himself, cut in with a description of the great tragedian's first night at the Winter Garden after his seclusion—a night when the whole house rose to greet their favorite and cheered and roared and pounded everything within reach of their hands and feet for twenty minutes, while Booth stood with trembling knees, the tears rolling down his cheeks. Munson remarked with some feeling—he was an intimate friend of the actor—that he remembered the night perfectly, having sat behind Oliver, and that Booth was not only the most accomplished actor but the best swordsman ever seen on the American or any other stage. Munson was an expert fencer himself, as was evidenced by the scar on his left cheek, received when he was a student at Heidelberg, and so thought himself competent to judge.

While Munson was speaking the great Waller had risen from his seat for the first time, gathered his gorgeous raiment closer about him, crossed the room, and now stood filling a thin glass from a Venetian flagon that graced the demoralized table.

"Booth's a swordsman, is he?" he said, pushing back his turban from his forehead, and walking toward Munson, glass in hand, his baggy trousers and tunic making him look twice his regular size. "You

511

know as much about fencing, Munson, as you do about the lost tribes of Israel. Booth handles his foil as a policeman does a rattan cane in the pit of the Bowery. Forrest is the only man in this country who can handle a blade."

"I do, do I?" cried Munson, springing to his feet and unhooking a pair of foils decorating the wall. "Stop where you are, you caricature of Nana Sahib, or I'll run you through the body and pin you to the wall like a beetle, where you can kick to your heart's content. Here, catch this," and he tossed one of the foils to Waller.

"A ring! A ring!" cried the men, with one of those sudden inspirations that often swept over them, jumping from their seats and pushing back the chairs and music-racks to give the contestants room.

Waller laid down his wine-glass, slipped off his turban and gold embroidered tunic with great deliberation, threw them over to Oliver, who caught them in his arms, tightened his sash, grasped the foil in his fat hand, and with great gravity made a savage lunge at the counterfeit presentment of William Shakespeare, who parried his blow without moving from where he stood. Thereupon the lithe, well-built young fellow teetered his foil in the air, and with great nicety pinked his fat antagonist in the stomach, selecting a gilt band just above his sash as the point of contact.

A mock battle now ensued, Munson chasing Wal-

ler about the room, the members roaring with laugh·
ter, Richard, with Oliver's assistance, having mounted the divan to see the better, clapping his hands like
any boy and shouting, "Bravo! Bravo! Now the
uppercut, now the thrust! Ah, well done. Capital!
Capital!"

Oliver listened in wonder to the strange expres·
sions that dropped from his father's lips. Up to that
moment he had never known that the old gentleman
had ever touched a foil in his life.

The next instant Richard was on the floor again,
commiserating with Waller, who was out of Munson's
reach and out of breath with laughter, and congratulating Munson on his skill as a swordsman.

"I only noticed one flaw, my dear Mr. Munson,
in your handling," he cried, with a graceful wave of
the hand, "and that may be due to your more modern
way of fencing. Pardon me"—and he picked up
Waller's foil where he had dropped it, and the fine
wrist with the nimble fingers, that had served him so
well all his days, closed over the handle of the foil.
"The thrust in the old days was made *so*. You,
I think, made it *so*"—and two flashes at different
angles gleamed in the candle-light.

Munson, as if to humor the old gentleman, threw
up his foil, made a pass or two, and, to his intense astonishment, received the button of Richard's foil on
his black velvet jacket and within an inch of his heart.

Everybody on the floor at once circled about the

contestants. The spectacle of an old gentleman in a snuff-colored coat and high collar, having a bout with a short gentleman in shorter velvet trunks, silk hose, and steel buckles, was one too droll and too exhilarating to lose—anachronistic it was, yet quite in keeping with the surroundings. More exhilarating still was the extreme punctiliousness with which the old gentleman raised the handle of his foil to his chin after he had made his point, and saluted his antagonist as if he had been some knight of King Arthur's table.

Still more fascinating was the way in which the younger man settled down to work, his brow knit, his lips tightly closed, the members widening out to give them room, Oliver and Nathan cheering the loudest of them all as Richard's foil flashed in the air, parrying, receiving, now up, now down, his right foot edging closer, his dear old head bent low, his deep eyes fixed on his young antagonist, until, with a quick thrust of his arm and a sudden upward twist of his hand, he wrenched Munson's foil from his grasp and sent it flying across the room.

Best of all was the joyful yet apologetic way with which Richard sprang forward and held out his hand to Munson, crying out:

"A fluke, my dear Mr. Munson; quite a fluke, I assure you. Pray forgive me. A mere lucky accident. My old fencing master, Martini, taught me that trick. I thought I had quite forgotten it. Just think! it is forty years since I have had a foil in my hands," and, laughing like a boy he crossed the room, picked up the foil, and, bowing low, handed it to the crestfallen man with the air of a gallant.

Half the club, costumed as they were—it was now after midnight, and there were but few people in the streets—escorted the two old men back to their hotel. Munson walked beside Richard; Waller, his flowing skirts tucked up inside his overcoat, stepped on the right of Nathan; Oliver, Fred, and the others followed behind, the hubbub of their talk filling the night: even when they reached the side door of the hotel and rang up the night porter, they must still stand on the sidewalk listening to Richard's account of the way the young gallants were brought up in his day; of the bouts with the foils; and of the duels which were fought before they were willing to take their leave.

When the last good-byes had been given, and Oliver had waved his rapier from the doorstep as a final farewell to his fellow-members before he saw his father upstairs to bed, and the delighted escort had turned on their heels to retrace their steps up Broadway, Waller slipped his arm into Munson's, and said, in his most thoughtful tone, one entirely free from cynicism or badinage:

"What a lovely pair of old duffers. We talk about Bohemia, Munson, and think we've got it, but we haven't. Our kind is a cheap veneer glued to commonplace pine. Their kind is old mahogany, solid all the way through—fine grain, high polish and no knots. I only wish they lived here."

CHAPTER XXIV

Each day Margaret's heart warmed more and more to Richard. He not only called out in her a tenderness and veneration for his age and attainments which her own father had never permitted her to express, but his personality realized for her an ideal which, until she knew him, she had despaired of ever finding. While his courtesy, his old-time manners, his quaintness of speech and dress captivated her imagination, his perfect and unfailing sympathy and constant kindness completely won her heart. There was, too, now and then, a peculiar tone in his voice which would bring the tears to her eyes without her knowing why, until her mind would recall some blunt, outspoken speech of her dead father's in answer to the very sentiments she was then expressing to Richard, who received them as a matter of course—a remembrance which always caused a tightening about her heart.

Sometimes the inventor would sit for her while she sketched his head in different lights, he watching her work, interested in every stroke, every bit of composition. She loved to have him beside her easel criticising her work. No one, she told Oliver, **had ever** been so interested before with the little niceties

517

of her technique—in the amount of oil used, in the way the paints were mixed; in the value of a palette knife as a brush or of an old cotton rag as a blender, nor had any one of her sitters ever been so enthusiastic over her results.

There was one half-hour sketch which more than all the others astonished and delighted him—one in which Margaret in her finishing touches had eschewed brushes, palette-knife and rag, and with one dash of her dainty thumb had brought into instant relief the subtle curves about his finely modelled nose. This filled him with wonder and admiration. His own fingers had always obeyed him, and he loved to find the same skill in another.

To Richard these hours of intercourse with Margaret were among the happiest of his life. It was Margaret, indeed, who really helped him bear with patience the tedious delays attendant upon the completion of his financial operations. Even when the final sum was agreed upon—and it was a generous one, that filled Oliver's heart with joy and set Nathan's imagination on fire—the best part of two weeks had been consumed before the firm of lawyers who were to pass upon Richard's patents were willing to certify to the purchasers of the stock of the Horn Magnetic Motor Company, as to the priority of Richard's invention based on the patent granted on August 13, 1856, and which covered the principle of the levers working in connection with the magnets.

During these tedious delays, in which his heart had vibrated between hope and fear, he had found his way every afternoon to Margaret's studio, Nathan having gone home to Kennedy Square with his head in the clouds when the negotiations became a certainty. In these weeks of waiting the Northern girl had not only stolen his heart, taking the place of a daughter he had never known—a void never filled in any man's soul—but she had satisfied a craving no less intense, the hunger for the companionship of one who really understood his aims and purposes. Nathan had in a measure met this need as far as unselfish love and unswerving loyalty could go; and so had his dear wife, especially in these later years, when her mind had begun to grasp the meaning of the social and financial changes that the war had brought, and what place her husband's inventions might hold in the new régime. But no one of these, not even Nathan, had ever understood him as clearly as had this young girl.

When it grew too dark to paint, he would make her sit on a stool at his feet, while he would talk to her of his life work and of the future as he saw it—often of things which he had kept shut away in his heart even from Nathan. He would tell her of the long years of anxiety; of the sleepless nights; of his utter loneliness, without a friend to guide him, while he was trying to solve the problems that had blocked his path; of the poverty of these late years, all the more pitiful because of his inability at times to buy even the bare materials and instruments needed for his work; and, again, of his many disappointments in his search for the hoped-for link that was needed to make his motor a success.

Once, in lowered tones and with that eager, restless expression which so often came into his face when standing over his work-bench in his little shop, baffled by some unsolved problem, he told her of his many anxieties lest some other brain groping along the same paths should reach the goal before him; how the *Scientific Review*, the one chronicle of the discoveries of the time, would often lie on his table for hours before he had the courage to open it and read the list of patents granted during the preceding months, adding, with a voice full of gentleness, " I was ashamed of it all, afterward, my dear, but Mrs. Horn became so anxious over our daily expenses, and so much depended on my success."

This brave pioneer did not realize, nor did she, that they were both valiant soldiers fighting the good fight of science and art against tradition and provincialism—part of that great army of progress which was steadily conquering the world!

As she listened in the darkening shadows, her hand in his, her fingers tight about his own, he, reading the sympathy of her touch, and fearing to have distressed her by his talk, had started up, and in his cheery, buoyant voice cried out:

"But it is all over now, my child. All past and gone. The work of my life is finished. There's plenty now for all of us. For my dear wife who has borne up so bravely and has never complained, and for you and Oliver. Your waiting need not be long, my dear. This last happiness which has come to me"—and he smoothed her hair gently with his thin hand and drew her closer to him—"seems the greatest of them all."

The two were seated in this way one afternoon, Margaret resting after a day's work, when Oliver opened the door. She had made a sketch of Richard's head that very morning as he lay back in a big chair, a strong, vigorous piece of work which she afterward finished.

Richard looked up and his face broke into a joyous smile.

"Bring a chair, my son," he cried, "and sit by me. I have something to say to you." When, a few moments later, Margaret had left the room to give some directions to Mrs. Mulligan, he added: "I have been telling Margaret that you both do wrong in putting off your marriage. These delays fret young people's lives away. She tells me it is your wish. What are you waiting for?"

"Only for money enough to take care of her, father. Madge has been accustomed to more comforts than I can give her. She would, I know, cheerfully give up half of her income, small as it is, to me if I would let her, but that is not the way I want to make her happy. Don't worry, dear old dad, the Fish portrait will pull us out "—and he leaned down and put his arms about his father's neck as he used to do when he was a boy. "I shall get there before long."

Oliver did not tell his father what a grief it had been to him to keep Madge waiting, nor how he had tried to make it up to her in every way while he had made his fight alone. Nor did he tell Richard of the principal cause of his waiting—that the mortgage to which his mother had pledged her name and to which he had morally pledged his own was still unpaid.

Richard listened to Oliver's outburst without interrupting him.

"I only wanted to do the best I could for you my son," he answered, laying his fingers on Oliver's hand. "I was thinking of nothing but your happiness. During the last few days, since I have become assured that this negotiation would go through, I have decided to carry out a plan which has long been in my mind and which, now that I know about Margaret, makes it all the more necessary. I am going to make provision for you immediately. This, I hope, will be to-morrow or the next day at farthest. The contracts are all ready for our signatures, and only await the return of one of the attorneys who is out of town. The cash sum they pay for the control of the patents is, as you know, a considerable one; then I get nearly half of the capital stock of the new company. I am going to give you, at once, one-third of the money and one-third of the stock."

Oliver raised his hand in protest, but Richard kept on.

" It is but just, my son. There are but three of us —your mother, yourself, and I. It is only your share. I won't have you and Margaret waiting until I am gone "—and he looked up with a smile on his face.

Oliver stood for a moment dazed at the joyous news, his father's hand in his, the tears dimming his eyes. While he was thanking him, telling him how glad he was that the struggle was over and how proud he was of his genius, Margaret stole up behind him and put her hands over his eyes, bidding him guess who it was—as if there could be another woman in the whole world who would take the liberty. Oliver caught her in his arms and kissed her, whispering in her ears the joyous news with her cheek close to his; and Margaret looked from one to the other, and then put her arms around Richard and kissed him without a word—the first time she had ever dared so much.

Oh, but there were joyous times that followed!

Mrs. Mulligan, at a whispered word from her mistress, ran down-stairs as fast as her old legs could carry her and came back with her arms full of bundles, which she dumped upon her small kitchen-table.

And Margaret put on a clean white apron, white as snow, and rolled up her sleeves, showing her beautiful arms above her elbows—Oliver always vowed that she had picked them up where the Milo had dropped them—and began emptying the contents of a bowl of oysters, one of Mrs. Mulligan's packages, into a chafing-dish. And Oliver wheeled out the table and brought out the cloth, and dear old Richard, his face full of smiles, placed the napkins with great precision beside each plate, puckering them up into little sheaves, "just as Malachi would have done," he said; and then Margaret whispered to Oliver if he didn't think "it would be just the very thing," they were "so anxious to see him"—and Oliver thought it would—he was cutting bread at the moment, and getting it ready for Mrs. Mulligan to toast on her cracker-box of a range; and Margaret, with her arms and her cheeks scarlet, ran out in the hall and down the corridor, and came back, out of breath, with two other girls—one in a calico frock belted in at her slender waist, and the other in a black bombazine and a linen collar. And Richard looked into their faces, and took them both by the hand and told them how glad he was to be permitted to share in their merrymakings; and then, when Oliver had drawn out the chairs—one was a stool, by the way—the whole party sat down, Oliver at the foot and Richard on Margaret's right, the old gentleman remarking, as he opened his napkin, that but one thing was wanting to complete his happiness, and that was Oliver's mother, who of all women in the world would enjoy the occasion the most.

But the happiest time of all was over the soup, or rather over the tureen, or rather what was inside of it—or worse still, what was not. This wonderful soup had been ordered at the restaurant across the way, and was to be brought in smoking hot at the appointed time by a boy. The boy arrived on the minute, and so did the tureen—a gayly flowered affair with a cover, the whole safely ensconced in a basket. When the lid was lifted and Margaret and the two girls looked in, a merry shout went up. Not a drop of soup was in the tureen! The boy craned his head in amazement, and Mrs. Mulligan, who stood by with the plates, and who had broken out into violent gestures at the sight was about to upbraid the boy for his stupidity, when Margaret's quick eye discovered a trail of grease running down the table-cloth, along the floor and out of the door. Whereupon everybody got up, including Richard, and with roars of laughter followed the devious trail out into the hall and so on down the staircase as far as they could see. Only when Mrs. Mulligan on their return to the room held up the tureen and pointed to a leak in its bottom, was the mystery explained.

And so the merry dinner went on.

Ah, dear old man, if these happy days could only have gone on till the end.

On the afternoon of the day following this joyous night—the day the contracts were to be signed, a culmination which would make everybody happy—Margaret hurried up the stairs of her building, and pushed open the door. She knew she should find the inventor waiting for her, and she wanted to be the first to get the glad news from his lips. It was varnishing day at the Academy, and she had gone down to put the last touches on her big portrait—the one of " Madame X." that she had begun in Paris the year before.

Richard did not move when she entered. He was leaning back in the chair she had placed for him, his head on his hand, his attitude one of thoughtful repose, the light of the fast-fading twilight making a silhouette of his figure. She thought he was dozing, and so crept up behind him to make sure.

" Ah, my dear, is that you? " he asked. The voice did not sound like Richard's.

" Yes—I thought you were asleep."

" No, my child—I'm only greatly troubled. I'm glad you have come "—and he took her hand and smoothed it with his own. " Bring your stool; I have something to say to you."

Without taking off her bonnet and cloak, she took her place at his feet. The tones of his voice chilled her. A great fear rose in her heart. Why she could not tell.

" Has anything happened to Oliver? " she asked, eagerly.

" No, nothing so terrible as that. It is about the motor. The bankers have refused the loan, and the attorneys have withdrawn the papers."

" Withdrawn the papers! Oh, no it can't be! " She had leaned forward now, her anxious, startled eyes looking into his.

" Yes, my dear; a Mr. Gorton from Maine has per-fected a machine which not only accomplishes what I claim for my own, but is much better in every way. The attorneys have been looking into this new motor for a week past, so I learn now. Here is their letter " —and he put his hand in his pocket and took out a white envelope. " They will, perhaps, take up Mr. Gorton's machine instead of mine. I made a hasty examination of this new motor this morning with my old friend Professor Morse, and we both agree that the invention is all Mr. Gorton claims for it. It is only a beginning, of course, along the lines of gal-vanic energy, but it is a better beginning than mine, and I feel sure it is all the inventor claims for it. I have so informed them, and I have also written a let-ter to Mr. Gorton congratulating him on his suc-cess." The calmness and gentleness of his voice thrilled her.

" I suppose I ought to have telegraphed the news to Mrs. Horn, as I promised," he continued, slowly, as if each word gave him pain, " but I really had not the heart, so I came up here. I've been here all the afternoon hoping you would come in. The room felt a little cold, my dear, and your good woman made a fire for me, as you see. You don't mind, do you?"

Margaret bowed her head on his hands and kissed the thin fingers that lay in her own. Her heart was full to bursting. The pathos of the bent figure, the despairing sound of his voice—so unlike his buoyant tones; the ghostly light that permeated the room, so restful always before, so grewsome and forbidding now, appealed to her in a way she had never known. She was not thinking of herself, nor of Oliver, nor of the wife waiting for the news at home; she was only thinking of this dear old man who sat with bowed head, his courage gone, all the joyousness out of his life. What hurt her most was her own utter helplessness. In most things she could be of service: now she was powerless. She knew it when she spoke.

"Is it ended?" she asked at last, her practical mind wanting to know the worst.

"Yes, my child, ended. I wish I could give you some hope, but there is none. I shall go home to-morrow and begin again;—on what I do not know—something—I cannot tell."

Oliver's footsteps sounded in the outer hall. She rose quickly and met him on the outside, half closing the door, so that she could tell him the dreadful news without being overheard.

"Broken their promises to father! Impossible! Why? What for? Another invention? Oh, it cannot be!"

He walked quickly toward him. "But father, what about your patents? They can't rob you of them. Suppose this man's motor is better."

Richard did not move. He seemed unwilling to look his son in the face.

"Let me take hold of this thing." Oliver was bending over him now, his arms about his neck. "I'll see Mr. Slade at once. I met him this morning and told him you were here, and he is coming to call on you. He has always stood by me and will now. These people who have disappointed you are not the only ones who have got money. Mr. Slade, you know, is now a banker himself. I will begin to-morrow to fight this new man who——"

"No, no, my son, you must do nothing of the kind," said Richard leaning his cheek wearily against Oliver's hand, as if for warmth and protection, but still looking into the fire. "It would not be right to take from him what he has honestly earned. The lifting power of his machine is four times my own, and the adjustment of the levers much simpler. He has only accomplished what I failed to do. I am not quite sure but I think he uses the same arrangement of levers that I do, but everything else is his. Such a man is to be helped, not worried with lawsuits. No, my son, I must bear it as best I may. Your poor mother!" He stopped suddenly and passed his hand over his eyes, and in a broken, halting voice, added: "I've tried so hard to make her old age happier. I fear for the result when the news reaches her. And you and this poor girl!"—and he reached out his hand to Margaret—"this is the part that is hardest to bear."

Oliver disengaged his arm from his father's neck and walked up and down the room, Madge watching him. His mind was searching about for some way to stem the tide of disaster. Every movement of his body expressing his determination. He was not thinking of himself. He saw only Madge and his mother. Then he turned again and faced his father.

"Will you let me try?" he urged in a firm voice.

"No, Oliver! Positively no."

As he spoke he straightened himself in his chair and turned toward Oliver. His voice had regained something of its old-time ring and force. "To rob a man of the work of his brain is worse than to take his purse. You will agree with me, I know, when you think it over. Mr. Gorton had never heard of my invention when he perfected his, nor had I ever heard of his when I perfected mine. He is taking nothing from me; how can I take anything from him? Give me your hand my son; I am not feeling very well." His voice fell again as if the effort had been too much for him. "I think I will go back to the hotel. A night's rest will do me good."

He rose slowly from his chair, steadied himself by holding to Oliver's strong arm, stood for an instant looking into Margaret's eyes, and said, with infinite tenderness:

"Come closer, my daughter, and kiss me."

She put her arms about him, cuddling her head against his soft cheek, smoothing his gray hair with her palm.

"My child," he said, "you have been a delight and joy to me. A woman like you is beyond price. I thank you from the bottom of my heart for loving my son."

With something of his old manner he again straightened himself up, threw his shoulders back as if strengthened by some new determination, walked firmly across the room, and picked up his cloak. As he stood waiting for Oliver to place it about his shoulders, he put his hand to his side, with a quick movement, as if smitten by some sudden pain, staggered backward, his head upon his breast, and would have sunk to the floor but for Oliver's hand. Margaret sprang forward and caught his other arm.

"It's nothing, my son," he said, between his gasps for breath, holding on to Oliver. "A sudden giddiness. I'm often subject to it. I, perhaps, got up too quickly. It will pass over. Let me sit down for a moment."

Half supporting him, Oliver put his arm about his father and laid him on the lounge.

As Richard's head touched the cushion that Margaret had made ready, he gave a quick gasp, half rose as if to breathe the better, and fell back unconscious.

When the doctor arrived Richard was lying on Margaret's bed, where Oliver had carried him. He had rallied a little, and had then sunk into a deep sleep. Margaret sat beside him, watching every breath he drew, the scalding tears streaming down her face.

The physician bent closer and pressed his ear to the sleeping man's breast.

"Has he been subject to these attacks?" he said, in a grave tone.

"I know of only one some years ago, the year the war broke out, but he recovered then very quickly," answered Oliver.

"Is your mother living?"

"Yes."

"Better send her word at once."

CHAPTER XXV

The night wind sighed through the old sycamores of Kennedy Square. A soft haze, the harbinger of the coming spring, filled the air. The cold moon, hanging low, bleached the deserted steps of the silent houses to a ghostly white.

In the Horn mansion a dim light burned in Richard's room and another in the lower hall. Everywhere else the house was dark.

Across the Square, in Miss Clendenning's boudoir, a small wood fire, tempering the chill of the April night, slumbered in its bed of ashes, or awakened with fitful starts, its restless blaze illumining the troubled face of Margaret Grant. The girl's eyes were fixed on the dying coals, her chin in her hand, the brown-gold of her wonderful hair gold-red in the firelight. Now and then she would lift her head as if listening for some approaching footstep. Miss Clendenning sat beside her, leaning over the hearth in her favorite attitude, her tiny feet resting on the fender.

The years had touched the little lady but lightly since that night when she sat in this same spot

533

and Oliver had poured out his heart to her. She was the same dainty, precise, lovable old maid that she had been in the old days of Kennedy Square, when the crocuses bloomed in the flower-beds and its drawing-rooms were filled with the wit and fashion of the day. Since that fatal night when Richard had laid away his violin and brother had been divided against brother, and Kennedy Square had become the stamping ground of armed men, she had watched by the bedsides of a thousand wounded soldiers, regardless of which flag they had battled under. The service had not withered her. Time had simply stood still, forgetting the sum of its years, while it marked her with perennial sweetness.

"I'm afraid he's worse," Margaret said, breaking the silence of the room, as she turned to Miss Clendenning, "or Ollie would have been here before this. Dr. Wallace was to go to the house at eleven, and now it is nearly twelve."

"The doctor may have been detained," Miss Clen'denning answered. "There is much sickness in town."

For a time neither spoke. Only the low muttering of the fire could be heard, or the turning of some restless coal.

"Margaret," Miss Clendenning said at last—it had always been "Margaret" with the little lady ever since the day she had promised Oliver to love the woman whom he loved; and it was still "Mar-

garet" when the women met for the first time in
the gray dawn at the station and Miss Clendenning
herself helped lead Richard out of the train—
"There is a bright side to every trouble. But for
this illness you would never have known Oliver's
mother as she really is. All her prejudices melted
away as soon as she looked into your face. She loves
you better every day, and she is learning to depend
on you just as Richard and Oliver have done."

"I hope she will," the young woman answered,
without moving. "It breaks my heart to see her
suffer as she does. I see my own mother in her so
often. She is different in many ways, but she is
the same underneath—so gentle and so kind, and
she is so big and broad-minded too. I am ashamed
to think of all the bitter feelings I used to have in
my heart toward her."

She stopped abruptly, her hands tightly folded in
her lap, her shoulders straightened. Margaret's confessions were always made in this determined way,
head thrown back like a soldier's, as though a new
resolve had been born even while an old sin was
being confessed.

"Go on," said Miss Clendenning. "I understand. You mean that you did not know her."

"No; but I thought her narrow and proud, and
that she disliked me for influencing Oliver in his
art, and that she wanted to keep him from me and
from my ideals. Oh, I've been very, very wicked!"

"Not wicked, my dear—only human. You are not the first woman who did not want to divide a love with a mother."

"But it wasn't exactly that, dear Cousin Lavinia. I had never met anyone who obeyed his mother as Ollie did, and—and—I almost hated her for being his guide and counsel when—oh, not because she did not love him too, just as I did—but because I thought that I could really help him most—because I believed in his talent and she did not, and because I knew all the time that she was ruining him, keeping him back, spoiling his career, and——"

Again she stopped and straightened herself, her beautiful head held higher. Those who knew Margaret well would have known that the worst part of her confession was yet to come.

"I suppose I was hurt too," she said, slowly accentuating each pause with a slight movement of the head. "That I was *little* enough and *mean* enough and *horrid* enough for that. But he was always talking of his mother as though she never did anything but sit still in that white shawl of hers, listening to music, while everybody waited on her and came to her for advice. And I always thought that she couldn't understand me nor any other woman who wanted to work. When Ollie talked of you all, and of what you did at home, I couldn't help feeling she must think that I and all my people belonged to some different race and that when she saw me she would judge me by some petty thing that displeased her, the cut of my skirt, or the way I carried my hands, or something else equally trivial, and that she would use that kind of thing against me and, perhaps, tell Ollie, too. Father judged Oliver in that way. He thought that Ollie's joyousness and his courtesy, even his way of taking off his hat, and holding it in his two hands for a moment—you've seen him do it a hundred times—was only a proof of his Southern shiftlessness—caring more for manners than for work. Mother didn't; she understood Ollie better, and so did John, but father never could. That's why I wouldn't come when you asked me. You wouldn't have judged me, I know, but I thought that she would. And now—oh, I'm so sorry I could cry."

"It was only another of the mistakes and misunderstandings that divided us all at that time, my dear," Miss Clendenning answered. "This dreadful war could have been averted, if people had only come together and understood each other. I did not think so then, but I do now."

"And you don't think me wicked, Cousin Lavinia?" Margaret asked with a sudden relaxation of her figure and something infinitely childlike and appealing in her tone. "You really don't think me wicked, do you?"

"Not wicked, dear; only human, as I said a moment ago. Yet you have been stronger than I. You have held on and won; I let go and lost."

Margaret bent forward and laid her finger on Miss Clendenning's knee.

" Lost what, Cousin Lavinia? " she asked, in surprise.

" My lover."

" When? "

" When I was just your age."

" Did he die? " asked Margaret in awed tones, overcome all at once with the solemnity of the hour and a strange new note in Miss Lavinia's voice.

" No, he married someone else."

" He never—never loved you, then." There was a positiveness now in her intonations.

" Yes, he did, with all his heart. His mother came between us."

Again silence fell on the room. Margaret would not look at Miss Clendenning. The little old maid had suddenly opened the windows of her heart, but whether to let a long-caged sorrow out or some friendly sympathy in, she could not tell.

" May I know about it? " There was a softer cadence now in the girl's voice.

" It would only make you unhappy, dear. It was all over forty years or more ago. Sallie, when she saw you, put her arms about you. You had only to come together. The oftener she sees you, the more she will love you. My lover's mother shut the door in my face."

" In your face? Why? "

538

Margaret moved closer to Miss Clendenning, stirred by a sudden impulse, as if she could even now protect her from one who had hurt her.

Miss Lavinia bent forward and picked up the brass tongs that lay on the fender at her feet. She saw Margaret's gesture, but she did not turn her head. Her eyes were still watching the smouldering embers.

"For no reason, dear, that you or any other Northern woman could understand. An old family quarrel that began before I was born."

Margaret's cheeks flushed and a determined look came into her face.

"The coward! I would not have cared what his mother or anybody else did, or how they quarrelled. If I loved you I would have married you in spite of everything."

"And so would he." She was balancing the tongs in her hand now, her eyes still on the fire. She had not looked at Margaret once.

"What happened then?"

Miss Clendenning leaned forward, spread the tongs in her little hands, lifted an ember and tucked it closer to its neighbor. The charred mass crumbled at the touch and fell into a heap of broken coals.

"I am a Clendenning, my dear; that is all," she answered, slowly.

Margaret stared at her with wide-open eyes. That a life should be wrecked for a mere question of family pride was something her mind could not fathom.

"Have you regretted it since, Cousin Lavinia?" she asked, calmly. She wanted to follow it out now to the end.

Miss Clendenning heaped the broken coals closer together, laid the tongs back in their place on the fender, and, turning to Margaret, said, with a sigh:

"Don't ask me, my dear. I never dare ask myself, but do you keep your hand close in Oliver's. Remember, dear, close—close! Then you will never know the bitterness of a lonely life."

She rose from her seat, bent down, and, taking Margaret's cheeks between her palms, kissed her on the forehead.

Margaret put her arms about the little lady, and was about to draw her nearer, when the front door opened and a step was heard in the hall. Miss Lavinia raised herself erect, listening to the sound.

"Hark!" she cried, "there's the dear fellow, now"—and she advanced to meet him, her gentle countenance once more serene.

Oliver's face as he entered the room told the story.

"Not worse?" Margaret exclaimed, starting from her chair.

"Yes—much worse. I have just sent word to Uncle Nat"—and he kissed them both. "Put on your things at once. The doctor is anxious."

Miss Lavinia caught up her cloak, handed Mar-

garet her shawl, and the three hurried out the front-
door and along the Square, passing the Pancoast
house, now turned into offices, its doors and windows covered with signs, and the Clayton Mansion,
surmounted by a flag-pole and still used by the Government. Entering the park, they crossed the site
of the once lovely flower-beds, now trampled flat—
as was everything else in the grounds—and so on
to the marble steps of the Horn Mansion.

Mrs. Horn met them at the top of the stairs. She
put her arms silently about Margaret, kissed her
tenderly, and led her into Richard's room. Oliver
and Miss Clendenning stood at the door.

The master lay under the canopy of the four-post
bedstead, his eyes closed, the soft white hair lost in
the pillows, the pale face tinged with the glow of
the night lamp. Dr. Wallace was standing by the
bed watching the labored breathing of the prostrate
man. Old Hannah sat on the floor at Richard's feet.
She was rocking to and fro, making no sign, crooning inaudibly to herself, listening to every sound.

Margaret sank to her knees and laid her cheek
on the coverlet. She wanted to touch something
that was close to him.

The head of the sick man turned uneasily. The
doctor bent noiselessly down, put his ears close to
the patient's breast, touched his pulse with his
fingers, and laid his hand on his forehead.

"Better send for some hot water," he whispered

to Mrs. Horn when he had regained her side. Margaret overheard, and started to rise from her knees, but Mrs. Horn waved her back. " Hannah will get it," she said, and stooped close to the old woman to give the order. There was a restrained calmness in her manner that sent a shiver through Margaret. She remembered just such an expression on her mother's face when her own father lay dying.

The old servant lifted herself slowly, and with bent head and crouching body crept out of the room without turning her face toward her master. The superstition of the negroes about the eyes of a dying man kept hers close to the floor—she did not want Richard to look at her.

Dr. Wallace detected the movement—he knew its cause—and passed out of the sick chamber to where Oliver stood with Miss Clendenning.

" Better go down, Oliver, and see that the hot water is sent up right away," he said. " Poor old Hannah seems to have lost her head."

" Has there been any further change, Doctor? " Oliver asked, as he started for the stairs.

" No, not since you went. He is holding his own. His hands feel cold, that is all." To Miss Lavinia he said: " It is only a question of hours," and went back into the room.

Oliver hurried after Hannah. He intended to send Malachi up with the hot water and then persuade the old woman to go to bed. When he reached the lower hall it was empty; so were the parlors and the dining-room. At the kitchen-door he met Hannah. She had filled the pitcher and had turned to carry it upstairs. Oliver stopped her.

"Where is Malachi, aunty?"

Hannah pointed through the open door to Richard's little shop in the back yard and hurried on. Oliver walked quickly through the damp, brick-paved yard, now filled with the sombre shadows of the night, and pushed open the green door. The place was dark except for a slant of moonlight which had struggled through the window-pane and was illumining the motor where it rested in its customary place under the sash.

"Malachi, are you here?"

A sob was the only answer.

Oliver stepped inside. The old man was on his knees, his head and arms lying flat on Richard's work-bench. Oliver bent down and laid his hand on the old servant's head.

"Mally!"

"I hear ye, Marse Ollie, an' I hearn Hannah. I tell you same as I tol' her—ain't no use fetchin' no water; ain't no use no mo' for no doctor, ain't no use, ain't no use. I ain't never goin' to say no mo' to him, 'Chairs all ready, Marse Richard.' I ain't never goin' to wait on him no mo'. Come close to me, Marse Ollie; get down an' let me tell ye, son."

He had lifted his head now, and was looking up

into Oliver's eyes, the tears streaming down his face.

"He freed me; he gimme a home. He ain't neber done nothin' but love me an' take care o' me. When I bin sick he come in an' he set by me. 'You got a fever, I think, Malachi,' he say. 'Go to bed dis minute. Cold, is you? Git dat blanket out'n my room an' put it on yo' bed. Don't let me hab to tell ye dat agin, Malachi.' 'Marse Richard,' I'd say to him, 'I ain't got no coat fit to wear.' Dat was in de ol' days, when you warn't nuffin but a chile, Marse Ollie. 'Who says so, Malachi,' he say. 'I say so, Marse Richard.' 'Lemme see,' he'd say. 'Dat's so, dat ain't fit fer nobody to wear. Go upstairs to my closet, Malachi, an' git dat coat I was a-wearin' yisterday. I reckon I kin git on widout it.'"

Malachi had his head in his hands now, his body swaying from side to side. Oliver stood silent.

"When he come home de udder day an' I lif' him in de bed, he say, 'Don't you strain yo'se'f, Malachi. 'Member, you ain't spry as you was.' Oh, Gawd! Oh, Gawd! What's Malachi gwine to do?"

Oliver sat down beside him. There was nothing to say. The old servant's grief was only his own.

"Ebery night, Marse Ollie, sence he bin sick, I git so lonesome dat I wait till de house git still an' den I git out'n de bed and crope down-stairs an' listen at de bedroom door. Den I hear de mistis say: 'In pain, dear?' and he say, 'No, Sallie.' An' den

I crope up agin an' go to bed kind o' comforted. I was down agin las' night—mos' mawnin'—a-listenin', an' de mistis say: 'Kin I do sumpin' to ease de pain, dear?' an' he don't answer, only groan, and den I hear de bed creak, an' dat *short bref come.* Dat's the sign! I knows it. In de mawnin' he'll be gone. Can't fool Malachi; I knows de signs."

A gentle tap at the front door on the street sounded through the stillness. Oliver had left all the intervening doors between the dining-room and the shop open in his search for Malachi.

The old servant, with the lifelong habit upon him, started up to answer the summons.

"No, Mally, stay here," said Oliver. "I'll go. Some neighbor, perhaps, wanting to know how father is."

Oliver walked rapidly through the yard, tiptoed through the hall, and carefully turned the knob.

Amos Cobb stepped in.

"I saw the light, Oliver," he said, in a low tone, "and I knew you were up. I have an important telegram from New York in answer to one I sent this morning from my office here. Would it be possible for me to see your father? I know it is very late, but the matter is most urgent."

"I'm afraid not, Mr. Cobb. He is very low."

"Not serious?" Amos exclaimed, in alarm.

"Doctor Wallace thinks it is."

"You don't tell me so! I had no idea he was so ill!"

"Nor did we, sir; a change for the worse set in this evening."

Amos leaned back against the wall, his hat in his hand. The light from the eight-sided hall lamp fell on his thick-set shoulders and square, determined, honest face. The keen-eyed, blunt Vermonter's distress at the news was sincere and heartfelt.

"Could I attend to it, Mr. Cobb?" asked Oliver.

"Perhaps so. I've got those fellows now where the hair is short, and I'm going to make 'em pay for it."

"What is it about?"

Amos Cobb took a double telegram from his pocket. It was closely written and contained a long message.

"It's about your father's patents. This telegram is from the attorneys of the Gorton——"

Oliver laid his fingers on the open telegram in Cobb's hand, and said, in a positive tone:

"He will not rob this man of his rights, Mr. Cobb."

"It's not that! It is the other way. The attorneys of the Gorton Company refuse to rob your father of *his* rights. Further, the bankers will not endorse the Gorton stock until your father's patent —I think it is No. 18,131 "—and he examined the telegram closely—" yes, August 13, 1856, 18,131— is out of the way. They are prepared to pay a large price for it at once, and have asked me to see your father and arrange it on the best terms I can. The offer is most liberal. I don't feel like risking an hour's delay; that's why I'm here so late. What had I better do?"

Oliver caught Mr. Cobb's hand in his and a flash of exultant joy passed over his face as he thought of his father's triumph and all it meant to him. Then Margaret's eyes looked into his and next his mother's; he knew what it meant to them all. Then the wasted figure of his father rose in his mind, and his tears blinded him.

Amos stood watching him, trying to read his thoughts. He saw the tears glistening on Oliver's lashes, but he misunderstood the cause. Only the practical side of the situation appealed to the Vermonter at the moment. These New York men had cast discredit on his endorsement of Richard's priority in the invention and had tried to ignore them both. Now he held them tight in his grasp. Horn was a rich man.

"I'll be very quiet, Oliver," he continued, in a half-pleading tone, "and will make it as short as I can. Just let me go up. It can't hurt him"—and he laid his hand on Oliver's shoulder with a tenderness that surprised him. "I would never forgive myself if he should pass away without learning of his success. He's worked so hard."

Before Oliver could reply another low tap was heard at the door. Cobb turned the knob gently and Nathan stepped inside the hall. The old man had gone home and to bed, tired out with his ceaseless watching by Richard's bedside, and was only half dressed.

"Still with us?" he asked in trembling tones, his eyes searching Oliver's face. "Oh, thank God! Thank God! I'll go up at once"—and he passed on toward the stairway. Amos and Oliver followed.

As Nathan's foot touched the first step Doctor Wallace's voice sounded over the bannisters.

"Oliver! Malachi! Both of you—quick!"

The three bounded noiselessly up-stairs and entered the room. Richard lay high up on the pillows, the face in shadow, his eyes closed. Margaret was still on her knees, her head on the coverlet. Mrs. Horn stood on the other side of the bed, the same calm, fixed expression on her face, as if she was trying to read the unknowable. Dr. Wallace sat on a chair beside his patient, his fingers on Richard's pulse.

"Is he gone?" asked Oliver, stepping quickly to his father's side, his voice choking.

Dr. Wallace shook his head.

Amos Cobb drew near, and whispered in the doctor's ear. The old physician listened quietly, and nodded in assent. Then he leaned over his patient.

"Mr. Cobb has some good news for you, Richard," he said, calmly. "The bankers have recognized your patents, and are ready to pay the money——"

SMOULDERING COALS

The dying man's eyes opened slowly.

Amos stepped in front of the doctor, and bent down close to the bed.

"It's all right, Horn—all right! They can't get along without your first patent. Here's the telegram." He spoke with an encouraging cheeriness in his voice, as one would in helping a child across a dangerous place.

The brow of the dying man suddenly cleared; the eyes burned with their old steadiness, then the lips parted.

"Read it," he muttered. The words were barely audible.

Cobb held the paper so the dim light should fall upon it and read the contents slowly, emphasizing each word.

"Raise me up."

The voice seemed to come from his throat, as if his lungs were closed. Oliver started forward, but Cobb, being nearer, slipped his arm under the wasted figure, and with the tenderness of a woman, lifted him carefully, tucking the pillows in behind the thin shoulders for better support. Oliver sank softly to his knees beside Margaret.

Again the thin lips parted.

"Read it once more." The voice came stronger now.

Amos held the paper to the light, and the words of the telegram, like the low tick of a clock, again sounded through the hushed room.

For a brief instant the inventor's eyes sought each face in turn. As his gaze rested on Margaret and Oliver, he moved his thin white hand slowly along the coverlet, and laid it first on Oliver's and next on Margaret's head. Then, with a triumphant look lighting his face, he lifted his arms toward his wife.

" Sallie! " he called, and fell back on his pillow, lifeless.

CHAPTER XXVI

The crocuses are a-bloom once more. The lilac buds are bursting with the joy of the new spring. A veil of silver-gray floats over Moose Hillock. The idle brook, like a truant boy, dances in the sunshine, singing to itself as it leaps from ledge to pool.

All the doors and windows of the big studio on the side looking down the valley are open to the morning air. Through one of these Margaret has just entered, her arms full of apple blossoms. One spray she places in a slender blue jar, the delicate blush of the buds and the pale green of the leaves harmonizing with the gold-brown of her marvellous hair as she buries her face among them. All about the spacious room are big easels, half-finished portraits, rich draperies, wide divans, old brass, and rare porcelain.

In an easy chair, close to the window, with the fragrance of the blossoms around her, sits a white-haired old lady with a gossamer shawl about her shoulders. She is watching Margaret as she moves about the room, her eyes brimming with tenderness and pride. Now and then she looks toward a door

551

leading into the bedroom beyond, as if expecting someone.

Oliver stands before his easel, his palette and brushes in his hand. He is studying the effect of a pat of color he has just laid on the portrait of a young girl in a rich gown—the fourth full-length he has painted this year—the most important being the one of his father ordered by the Historical Society of Kennedy Square, and painted from Margaret's sketches.

Malachi—the old man is very feeble—moves slowly around a square table covered with a snow-white cloth, with seats set for four—one a high chair with little arms. In his hands are a heap of cups and saucers—the same Spode cups and saucers he looked after so carefully in the old house at home. These he places near the smoking coffee-urn.

Suddenly a merry, roguish laugh is heard, and a little fellow with gold-brown hair and big blue eyes peers in through the slowly opening door.

The old servant stops, and his withered face breaks into a smile.

"Is dat you, honey?" he cries, with a laugh. "Come along, son. Yo' cha'r's all ready, Marse Richard."

THE END

www.ingramcontent.com/pod-product-compliance
Lightning Source LLC
Chambersburg PA
CBHW032254020726
47495CB00001B/102